Praise for Song for the Missing

"This second novel confirms the young author's story-telling capabilities."
Le Monde

"Pierre Jarawan has written a luminous, intimate, staggering novel. His prose is powerful, impactful, poetic. A great read that won't leave you unmoved."
La grande parade

"*Song for the Missing* is another success, a fantastic second novel. What a joy to reencounter Pierre Jarawan's beautiful writing pen, and his talent for storytelling!"
Tu vas t'abîmer les yeux Blog

"We discovered the author last year with *The Storyteller*. A book that was a big success among our readers. I'm at a loss for words to describe the power of Pierre Jarawan's pen and prose in his latest novel, *Song for the Missing*."
Autour D'un Livre Bookshop

"A love letter to Lebanon and its people—a deft, sensitive book that steers clear of 'oriental' clichés, with a poetic narrative voice."
DANIEL SPECK, screenwriter

"It's a family story, and it's also a story of identity. It is a story of the entanglements of the Middle East and the Europeans and it is also—I think—a coming-of-age story."
Bayern 2's *Diwan: Das Büchermagazin*

T0054684

"A story that gets under your skin and shows that our lives are always the sum of everything that happened to the previous generations."
Münchner Merkur

"A highly poetic book in an equally poetic language."
Deutschlandfunk Kultur's *Lesart* podcast

"Pierre Jarawan once again proves to be a magician of language. He writes in a clear, poetic language that is deeply moving and impresses with enchanting and atmospheric images of Lebanon's cities. In a virtuoso way, Jarawan links the events of the Middle East, the civil war, and the Arab Spring with the life of the narrator—a story of Lebanon you won't forget."
Freie Presse

"Despite the lightness of the novel—which can also be read as a coming-of-age, love, friendship, and family story—it is a critical examination of Lebanon. Jarawan's narration retains the lightness he displayed in his debut, which has been translated into many languages."
Süddeutsche Zeitung

"Pierre Jarawan speaks confidently and warmly of the wounds of the war, repressed trauma, and the attitude towards life of a generation with limited hope. A wonderfully poetic—but also political—novel about Lebanon. Absolutely recommended."
Abendzeitung München

"A new Jarawan as we love him: sensitive, exciting, and tightly linked to the eventful history of the Middle East."
Rheinischer Spiegel Online

"Pierre Jarawan lets Lebanon come alive over decades in a sensual and factual manner, but also the friends Amin and Jafar, their thoughts and feelings, their strength, their abysses."
Welt am Sonntag

"Jarawan manages to maintain the high level of his first book. With his typical passion for telling stories, the fun of wonderfully poetic linguistic images that manage to bring smells and tastes to life, and a gripping and touching story, he again manages to bring Lebanon closer to us historically, politically, and emotionally."
Galore Literatur

"A gripping story that touches the central trauma of today's Lebanon."
Der Standard

"Jarawan, who adorns without overloading, succeeds in creating an impressive picture of Beirut, the former 'Paris of the Middle East,' before, during, and after the 15-year civil war. And the novel has become sadly topical due to current events, the explosion on August 4, 2020, in the city's port."
Göttinger Tagblatt

"This moving novel is dedicated to 17,000 people who disappeared without a trace during 15 years of civil war. But Jarawan also portrays the beauty and poetry of the country and recalls the great tradition of the hakawati, the Arab storytellers."
Madame

"In his novel, Pierre Jarawan artfully combines the most varied narrative strands into a larger whole."
Kaffeehaussitzer.de

"Humorous and sophisticated reading."
Acher- und Bühler Bote

"*Song for the Missing* is perhaps best compared to a colorful mosaic. Stone by stone the result is an unforgettable picture, a story with characters that stay in the heart."
Masuko13.com

"In *Song for the Missing*, Pierre Jarawan describes a moving fate."
Ostthüringer Zeitung

"The reader strolls and wanders through strange worlds of fragrant, intense street scenes full of sweet melancholy, biting fear, and teasing irony, where the imagination and grit of the shrewd Beirut youth are as at home as the memories of the countless people who turned into 'the missing,' when they disappeared forever."
Stadtkind

"The new novel by Pierre Jarawan: sensitive, exciting, and virtuoso, and linked to the dramatic history of the Middle East."
Erlesen

●

"This is a book everyone should read, everyone in the world. It's an important book, a beautiful book, a book that changes the way you look at the world. This book really opens your eyes and your heart to Lebanon and the people who are living there. It's a book you must read."
MANDA HEDDEMA, De Koperen Tuin, Netherlands

"Deserves to be huge."
Ignoring Life Blog

"Expansive and engaging."
David's Book World

"*The Storyteller* by Pierre Jarawan is one of those rare books that takes you on both the internal and external journeys of a character. We not only see how far Samir travels emotionally, but follow him on the geographic journey required for him to grow up and accept himself. A brilliant work for our times."
Qantara.de

"A literary debut of astounding maturity, refinement, and narrative power."
Literatur Abendzeitung

"Jarawan's narrative is captivating, fast-paced, and true to life—a fascinating exploration of the question of what it means to be influenced by several cultures at the same time."
Frankfurter Neue Presse

"His masterful debut successfully interweaves historical events with a suspense-filled investigation of one family's fate in a novel that deeply moves its readers."
New Books in German

"In a sweeping style reminiscent of oriental storytelling, Jarawan tells of escape, migration, and a family torn between two cultures. His debut succeeds in bringing foreign culture into focus and awakens in the reader a fascination with the Land of the Cedars."
Kulturtipp

"The story of an escape, of a family, and of the Middle East: how the fate of one family is inevitably linked with Lebanon's history. An enthralling novel which couldn't be more timely."
Rhein-Zeitung

"Pierre Jarawan has worked Lebanon's complicated history brilliantly into his debut novel."
TAZ

"This book is a masterwork—a debut of great class."
Booklover & Dreamcatcher

"There are many good reasons to read this book immediately. Above all, it's a wonderful, terrifically narrated, and timeless story that will enchant you!"
MIKE LITT, WDR 1 Live's *Klubbing*

"This new literary voice is particularly melodious and memorable. *The Storyteller* is an elegantly and unobtrusively narrated novel that shows us what is behind and beyond the narrow stuffy rooms that we call 'our world,' our Europe, our West. With this novel, the doors open to a thousand other beautiful, incomprehensible worlds."
ALEXANDER SOLLOCH, NDR Kultur, *Neue Bücher*

"A moving and wonderfully constructed story, full of beautiful images—Jarawan teaches us about both history and the future, without ever becoming didactic."
Tzum

"An exciting family mystery, focusing on both historical and current political situations; a testimony to the way migrants are torn between their old homeland and their new."
Ruhr Nachrichten

"A wonderful and authentic way of storytelling."
Boekenkrant

"A beautiful book full of fascinating storytelling and poetic language, that you devour without stopping for breath. If you start reading this book, you'll want to keep reading it, rereading it. A masterful and particularly fascinating debut for such a young writer—one we can hopefully expect a lot more from."
Leeskost

"Jarawan has produced a fairy tale that could be straight out of *One Thousand and One Nights*. From the very beginning, you float away on the story as if on a flying carpet."
NRC Handelsblad

"An engaging novel."
Mappa Libri

"A story worth telling."
De Volkskrant

"Pierre wanted to use the mystery of the plot to make sure the book was read, while capturing all the different nuances of Lebanese politics and society from the start of the civil war. And he succeeded."
Veja (Brazil)

"Moving, poignant, and passionate: Pierre Jarawan's novel is a magnificent declaration of love, but also a fabulous voyage that takes us far, very far, into exile, uprooting and plunging us into the heart of the terrible rifts that shook—and still shake—the country of cedars. The author unrolls the thread of Lebanese history, unties the knots of the political skein, and through Samir's journey, his familial quest, we witness the whole tragedy of this country, of which it was said that milk and honey flowed with the war. Throughout, this beautiful journey flirts with a very oriental poetry, which makes for a work that is both intense and superb, like a sunrise over the Chouf Mountains."
FABIENNE BOIDOT-FORGET, Librairie Gibier, Pithiviers

"It's been a while since I've read a book like this. It's well written, passionate, and dreamy. I am going to make it one of my favorites; I find this book sensational!"
ANNE PLOQUIN, FNAC Part-Dieu, Lyon

"I adored *The Storyteller*, I still have chills! A real lesson in the history of Lebanon, and a breathtaking family story! The characters are very engaging and well embodied. It's a novel of great realism, ultra-touching, we're dying to help Samir in his quest! Big thanks for this beautiful discovery!"
LYSE MENANTEAU, Le Matoulu, Melle

"Do not miss this exceptional novel! The moving story of a country. Destinies jostled by history. An overwhelming tale with a hypnotizing secret running through it. The desperate search for a father. An unforgettable book. It's a novel that managed to make me forget my vacation and the wonderful place where I was!"
GÉRARD COLLARD, La Griffe Noire, St Maur des Fossés

"There is a proverb that says: 'If you think you understand Lebanon, it's because no one has explained it to you properly.' A beautiful and rich novel by Pierre Jarawan that dives into the political and personal history of Lebanon, and prominently features the imagination of oriental tales."
SANDRINE BABU, L'Instant, Paris

"It's the story of a father who has mysteriously disappeared. It's also the story of a country ravaged by war. But above all, it's the story of a personal quest for salvation, fed by family tales and an idolized father. Dive into this luminous, moving debut novel, of which we can only salute the mastery."
DELPHINE CHARTIER, Librairie Jeux de Pages, St Jean d'Angély

"A very beautiful text on exile. How to become yourself when you have lived in the shadow of a missing father and that of a country narrated, imagined, idealized? The story of the civil war in Lebanon is embellished, in small touches, as if to whet our appetites. With its beautiful characters, a real humanist air emerges from this novel."
VIRGINIE, Librairie de Paris, St Etienne

"Pierre Jarawan, a young German author of Lebanese origin, displays with this debut novel a rich, romantic work of bluffing mastery, pulling the strings of his story one after another, taking us where we least expect, entertaining doubt until the last pages, and sprinkling his novel with characters of a strong presence."
Booksmoodsandmore.com

"Samir, of Lebanese origin, is born in Germany, where his family has settled. His father is a true storyteller, held in high esteem by his community. But one day, he disappears. To move on with his life, Samir follows in his father's footsteps to Lebanon. A beautiful moment! Magnificent."
MYRIAM, Librairie M Lire Anjou, Château Gontier

"Pierre Jarawan is a true storyteller whose vivid writing is able to evoke urgency and empathy where factual reporting cannot. He opens our eyes to the plight of refugees, torn between the love for their homeland and the lack of prospects in their own country."
JULIANE ZISKOVEN, Mayersche Buchhandlung, Dortmund

"I am most affected by the incredibly vivid language, and the subtle urgency. This is an important book at the right time."
MARTINA KRAUS, Ravensbuch, Friedrichshafen

"A miraculous book. Despite it being the last nice weekend of the fall, I didn't get out of my chair because I had to know how the story ends. I hope the book will meet with many enthusiastic readers."
JENNIFER MERTENS, Kurt Heymann, Hamburg

"A magnificent writer. Extremely personal, emotional, stirring, and outstandingly well written. A wonderful story of home, family, and the search for one's own roots."
HANS GRÜNTHALER, Buchhandlung Schmid, Schwabmünchen

"A wonderful book, an enchanting family story, and a perfect novel. The reader is continuously reminded of the great Rafik Schami."
WALTER REIMANN, Buchhandlung Hirslanden, Zürich

"Jarawan builds an incredible tension; seduces the reader into wildly speculating about a lost father's fate, and, in the end, surprises completely. The author creates a wonderful balance between a sensual tale and factual story—he both moved and mesmerized me."
JACQUELINE MASUCK, Dussman Das Kulturkaufhaus, Germany

"Pierre Jarawan's sentences are beautifully and quietly poetic, and incredibly powerful at the same time."
GISELA BLOCK, Hugendubel, München

"What a pleasure and delight it was to read this novel! The reader is fully immersed in the story, completely captivated, enchanted, and mesmerized. Jarawan is an exceptionally gifted storyteller."
CHRISTIAN NIEDERMEIER, Thalia Buchhandlung, Erlangen

"What a debut! With this book, Jarawan joins the ranks of the best contemporary authors in Germany."
VOLKER KEIDEL, Hugendubel, München

"*The Storyteller* thrilled me! I joined Samir on an exciting and touching journey, and spent the entire duration of the book in Lebanon."
MICHAELA MACZEJKA, Buchhandlung Zweymüller, Baden

"Extremely absorbing! *The Storyteller* is a captivating journey revealing the human condition and its contradictions. Wonderful!"
LILIAN DIONYSIA, Saraiva, Brazil

"In *The Storyteller*, German-Lebanese author Pierre Jarawan has created a work of art that explores the importance of family and nationality in the creation of an identity. Jarawan fills the book with stories of the Lebanese civil war, teaching the history of the country and the event without making it feel like you are learning anything or reading a history book. Samir, the main character, is incredibly relatable in his search for understanding of himself even though his circumstances are not something even close to anything I have experienced. Jarawan creates a cast of characters in which I cared about each and every one of them, despite their faults. A definite must-read."
PORTIA TURNER, The Book Cellar, USA

"*The Storyteller* is truly a work of art, one of those masterful books that from the moment you start reading it you begin to live two lives, moving back and forth between your own reality and Samir's story. And then, somewhere around the middle of the book, you become so invested in Samir you decide to transcend the triviality of your own life events to be a part of Samir's journey, a journey so poignant that it then becomes a part of you. It was an absolute honor to read an early review copy. I loved every page of this book."
SHONEE MIRCHANDANI, Bookazine, Hong Kong

"Reading those descriptive words, I felt myself in Lebanon. Jarawan has the ability to paint you a picture with his

expressive words and take you where you've never been. A true depiction of culture and identity. A story about history, family and the secrets that bind them. *The Storyteller* is a beautifully written novel that you do not want to miss."
TAMAR KASSABIAN, Virgin Megastore, Egypt

"A lovely—and perfectly titled—book, the storytelling is WONDERFUL! *The Storyteller* follows a son in search of his father and explores cultural identity and displacement, but is ultimately a story about family secrets, love, and friendship. Only 100 pages in but I love it!"
Drake The Bookshop, UK

"*The Storyteller* seamlessly integrates history and human reality into a beautiful fictional narrative. It accounts for what it feels like for humans living in diaspora to search for love and belonging in both their country of residence and country of origin. Above all, it illustrates a relationship bond that is rarely accounted for—a strong and loving relationship between a father and a son."
KHADIJA LAWAL, Virgin Megastore MENA, United Arab Emirates

"A great personal story intertwined with the 1982 Lebanon war. It's story of love, religion, race, and politics. A surprising ending after Samir's fast-paced investigation into his roots."
FRANK, Bluefountain, China

"As if in a fairy tale, you are visiting a foreign country, smelling the cedar trees and learning about Lebanon's history in this deeply touching story. You will be in the world of Samir from beginning to end. You will be unable to leave Samir and the other colorful characters, as you travel to the land in which the cedars whisper of a different, better world."

AYŞEN BOYLU, Homer Books, Turkey

"Jarawan's adeptness in the storytelling genre mixed with his knowledge of the Lebanese civil war creates a work that is both intensely lyrical and a powerful reflection on an important piece of recent history. This book has everything you could want: love, loss, mystery, history, and the wisdom gained from an insightful dive into a very complex political and religious history."

HANNAH, Malaprop's Bookstore, USA

"*The Storyteller* is one of those rare novels that elegantly interweaves history, culture, religion, identity, and family together in a heartbreaking and fascinating story of a young man's search for his father in Lebanon. But also Samir's search for his own identity, being torn between his Lebanese roots and the Germany that welcomed him and his family, when the war broke out in Lebanon.
A relevant story so many people can relate to. I love the fables Pierre Jarawan uses to tell the story, but also the suspense he builds up through the novel. Pierre Jarawan is a true storyteller!"

KRISTINA HAUBERG, *Politiken*, Denmark

"*The Storyteller* thrilled me! I joined Samir on an exciting and touching journey, and spent the entire duration of the book in Lebanon."

MICHAELA MACZEJKA, Buchhandlung Zweymüller, Germany

Song for the Missing

Pierre Jarawan

Song for the Missing

Translated from the German
by Elisabeth Lauffer

WORLD EDITIONS
New York, London, Amsterdam

Published in the USA in 2022 by World Editions LLC, New York
Published in the UK in 2022 by World Editions Ltd., London

World Editions
New York / London / Amsterdam

Printed by Lake Book, USA

World Editions is committed to a sustainable future. Papers used by
World Editions meet the FSC standards of certification.

This book is a work of fiction. Any resemblance to actual persons, living
or dead, or actual events is purely coincidental.

Library of Congress Cataloging in Publication Data is available

ISBN 978-1-64286-107-5

First published as *Ein Lied für die Vermissten* in Germany in 2020 by
Piper Verlag GmbH

The translation of this work was supported by a grant from the
Goethe-Institut.

GOETHE
INSTITUT

Twitter: @WorldEdBooks
Facebook: @WorldEditionsInternationalPublishing
Instagram: @WorldEdBooks
YouTube: World Editions
www.worldeditions.org

Book Club Discussion Guides are available on our website.

What remains now are fragments.
And you, buried deep within me
like a slideshow telling
of those days we disappeared into
city maps, only to reemerge
from the sea.

Hasune el-Choly

enjoy on the rocky coastline. Shadows on the azure sea, Middle East Airlines flights descending, carrying a steady stream of tourists to the Paris of the Middle East. The light of dawn over the mountains flooding the city with color—that was the old Beirut. Or the dim glow of jazz clubs and bars at night, where the spotlights glinted off Jemela Omar's jewelry as she sang and belly danced. Not a stone's throw down the boardwalk was the venerable Saint George Hotel, where heavy carpets dampened the sound of rumors, its pile full of secrets whispered between spies at the bar, shady figures on the chessboard of the city. Beirut was stray dogs roving the streets; and sometimes Maurice, the young waiter at Mar Elias, would feed them marinated chicken livers he had sneaked from the kitchen. Because Beirut meant abundance, it meant brotherly love and consideration, when half the city funneled into the mosques for Friday prayers and later reemerged to the sound of church bells from the east summoning Christians to evening services. Beirut before the war meant sound. City of song and melody! People sang on the street, muezzins sang from minarets, nuns sang with the congregation in church. The din of money changers clamoring in Place des Martyrs, lovers laughing on the Corniche, vendors haggling at the souk around the Place de l'Étoile clock tower, and Achmed Aziz, the shoe shiner outside the Moonlight Hotel, murmuring *Have a nice day* to Marlon Brando and Brigitte Bardot. In this shimmering city of contradictions, the Armenian jeweler played checkers with the Maronite tailor and Shiite fruit seller, while in a café outside the bazaar you'd share a hookah and inquire after the health of the family, but never mention religion. Because holidays were celebrated together, and a city home to many religions celebrates many holidays. Beirut was Dikran Najarian, the lutenist who sang his songs beneath the lancet windows on Rue Monot, ballads that made women blush in their rooms. And Beirut was Hussein Badir, the souvenir salesman on Rue Hamra, always grumbling about declining worry-bead sales, worried that people weren't sufficiently worried.

There's storytelling and then there's silence. And the questions in between. What about the mistrust? The fears, the doubts? How could what came later have happened, and why? You're met with silence in the very places you should find answers. Sand and desert. Geography books teach us that Lebanon is the only Arab country without a desert, but that isn't true. The desert is everywhere, and within it, there's no language for remembrance. No language for memory. The silence you're asking about is more profound than stillness, because stillness never really consumes everything. A clock's ticking or refrigerator's hum remains, even in the smallest space. Add to that the muted rumble of everyday life outside the window. Quiet, hush, stillness—there are plenty of wrong words you could choose.

Silence is different. It engulfs the horizon and devours all it touches, and whatever sense of certainty you had hoped to discover steals away like a gloved cat burglar.

Even in the olden days, storytellers in the cafés and public squares in Isfahan, Cairo, Damascus, and Beirut knew there was more to the desert than mere emptiness. Beneath the sand were entire cities, civilizations that at some point had sunk.

"A single grain of sand," one of the old masters told

First Verse

How often do we recall those moments we later see as turning points?

A House with Many Rooms

Any story will appear in a different light, depending on where its telling begins. This one, for instance, could open with the pair of coffins—no more than crude wooden boxes, really—excavated from a construction site before the eyes of the public. Or with ash falling from the sky, just before the first buildings started to burn, when it was reasonable to fear that everything would repeat itself. It could also open with an image of Grandmother and me standing by a wall overgrown with weeds, and her saying, *Here. Right here is where it happened.* Or with another image, that of a drawing a man who would later become famous gave me when I was thirteen. The story could also start with my tracing the girl's course as she first crossed the flea market, then later left the ghost train at the amusement park before disappearing from my life. Or with the sight of a hand reaching for a coat in a beautiful old theater. Or, and this strikes me as most appropriate, at a spot exactly in the middle, on a day five years ago. Because everything is connected. And as far as I can say, that was a day that projected into both past and future.

2006

A thousand bombs had fallen on Beirut, and I had finally arrived. You could hear it all the way out here, in the seclusion of the house I'd retreated to: distant jets racing across the sky, then a delay and the diminished growl of detonations. Soundwaves traveled up from the city to the mountains within seconds. They rose from the valley and rolled over the lonely hillsides and the stone walls of my house. A tremor in the air. Tall cypresses swayed outside the windows. Birds issued from the branches. Had it not been a bright summer day with barely a cloud overhead, I'd have thought it was thunder. A summer storm.

I stood at the kitchen window and watched the birds swarm across the sky. They leaned into the wind, moving in dense formation like a woven swath, then scattered over the hilltops and disappeared from sight. I set aside my tools and went outside. It was August, the air full of warmth and moisture. The smell of wood, resin, and foliage cloaked the garden. The house sat in a hollow flanked by two hills, and a narrow driveway, the entrance to which was easy to miss, led a few hundred yards from the edge of the property straight to the road. I crossed the garden, walked down the driveway in my slippers, and checked the mailbox. I had painted it blue, so it stood out among the trees concealing the house. The mailbox was empty. There was another detonation. Faint and far away.

I went back inside, put coffee on to brew, and returned to the garden, where I sat down on a rickety chair long battered by wind and weather that creaked ominously under my weight. A lizard darted out from under a stone and paused in a sunny spot two arm's lengths away.

"Don't worry," I said. "We're safe here."

The news updates that reached me from Beirut were like atmospheric ghost lights, brief anecdotes I caught twice a week when I ventured off the property. There was a sizable intersection about fifteen minutes' walk from my driveway. From the bed of his pickup, a man by the name of Walid sold bread, rice, vegetables, and medication the locals had ordered from him. The houses up here were so scattered that making deliveries to each would have taken him hours, and at some point before my time, folks had agreed that this spot was as close to central as you could get.

Those days at the intersection were the only time I ever really saw my neighbors. Many of them had been born here. They said hello and we chatted. On more than one occasion, they invited me over. Dinner, a refreshing drink in the summer heat, polite conversation. I think they were wary of me. No one else under thirty lived up here in these houses built at the turn of the century, almost two hours by car from Beirut. Whoever had bought that place in the hills must be some kind of misfit, then. That house on the overgrown plot.

Walid left the radio on as he distributed his wares, so the news in recent weeks had worked its way into conversation. Air raid on Qana. In Beirut, Hezbollah-held neighborhoods were under fire, with militants hunkering down in civilian homes. The power station in Jiyeh had sustained damage during clashes and was now spilling thousands of tons of oil into the sea.

"The water is black off the coast of Byblos," Walid added, hoisting two sacks of potatoes from the bed of his truck into a woman's wheelbarrow. "A thick black coating, and whatever the fishermen manage to snag is already dead."

I stood there and tried to recall the rippling banners, the cheering and dancing. That was barely a year ago. People had openly wept with joy when the Syrian Army withdrew. After thirty years of military occupation. Following weeks of protest and public pressure, the last remaining tanks had rolled over the border, back to where they came from. I had walked around Beirut that day, the city enveloped in the fading light, dark blue, almost night, buildings throwing long shadows, and within those shadows, great swarms of people and a sensation of static crackling. I saw people embrace, heard them cry: *Finally! Our country is finally ours to lead!* It was like a song, happy and hopeful, and I remember thinking: *Maybe, just maybe, this is the start of something good, even for me.*

"'We will annihilate Hezbollah and set Lebanon back by twenty years,'" Walid now quoted an Israeli general. "That's what they said. Twenty years. They've destroyed the airport, the major highways, and the bridges. They've even cordoned off the sea." Walid rose, his figure framed by the sky behind him. He gazed down upon us from the bed of his truck, our messenger from the capital.

In the brief time I'd been living up here, my anxiety had subsided. More and more often, I was surprised by moments of brilliant optimism, sparked by the most unlikely things: sunlight wandering across the living room wall, and at twelve noon exactly, illuminating the picture I'd hung there. Or the silent spectacle of a lavishly empty landscape extending over hills, valley folds, and mountain ranges beneath bright blue skies. Or when a forgotten song unexpectedly came to mind, complete with lyrics and melody. I rarely woke up during the night anymore. Most mornings, I even felt rested, and I had a hard time remembering what it was like to fear that, at any moment, the ground beneath my feet could give way and drag me down into never-ending free fall.

This was in part because of all the stuff demanding my attention around the house. I spent my days sanding wooden shutters that had once been painted blue, checking the roof tiles in certain spots, retightening screws in doorways and shelves, and wiping dust from every sloped surface, crooked windowsill, and piece of furniture, until I collapsed into bed at night. The house was changing me as it had changed itself. The plot had once been sprawling and well tended, but over time nature had encroached, weeds and thick grass claiming sovereignty over the driveway and path to the road, ivy enveloping the old stone walls and windowsills, hedges and trees running riot.

There were some evenings when, as I sat outside the house and the cypresses swayed in the twilight like shadow dancers, I had the liberating feeling that nothing—not mosquitos, not the distant sounds of war—could ever disturb the seclusion I had found out here.

Sitting out in the garden that August day in 2006, I was just waiting for noon to roll around. Walid was usually pretty punctual in reaching the intersection, and this time, I'd ordered a few things too. Given the Israeli assault on the country—retaliation, so they said, for the abduction of two soldiers—Walid had asked that we start ordering in bulk, as there was no telling whether the route would remain passable in the coming weeks.

As I emerged from my reverie, I was startled by a dark stain on the flagstone beside me, swarmed with flies. How long had I been thinking about Walid and his bleak updates? Barely a moment ago, that lizard had been sunning itself there. Now it was gone. The stain and flies seemed to indicate something had happened, though I could see no sign of struggle, nothing that might explain the lizard's absence. Just that empty space.

Then I noticed the bird, because it blinded me. It was perched on the uppermost branch of the apple tree, its plumage reflecting the sunlight. A shikra. How beautiful! And how big! There was a certain pride about the animal. A bearing that made it appear at once disconnected and dignified, like an aged king. Perched there on the branch, its pale feathered cloak quivered in the wind passing through the leaves. Sharp talons, powerful gray beak, and eyes the color of black pearls that contained something distant and radiant. The tranquility in its gaze was unsettling, because I knew those eyes caught everything, saw everything: the dancing spots of light on rooftops hundreds of yards away, the twitch of a mouse among the rocks, Walid's black truck, still miles away and taking a different route today than usual. And me. Of course it saw me. The bird observed me with an indifference that hurt my feelings, I was annoyed to realize. The indifference contained a haughtiness that made me feel small and meaningless, whereas the animal was untouchable. I'm certain it sensed my unease as I looked at it and came to realize it had been here, in my garden, and pilfered something without my noticing. Its imposing presence stood in harsh contrast to the silence of its earlier action. I hadn't even seen its shadow.

The predator must have sensed the gust of wind before it arose. A change in weather in the blink of an eye. In one fluid motion, it spread its wings, carved a line through the air, and disappeared in the distance.

Then I felt it too, the wind coming in over the hills.

When I was younger, after we moved back from Germany, my grandmother and I lived in a small apartment in a neighborhood in East Beirut. Back then, I loved moments like these—the dreamy transience of the quiet before a storm. Everything appeared to stand still, with an electric charge in the air, loose sheets of newspaper eddying on the sidewalks, wilted apple blossom petals dancing in the gutters, mothers' hands closing around children's fingers, pulling them in front doors, and Jafar, who lived nearby, running down the street, stopping under my window, and crying out, "Amin, we have to find the cartoonist before the world ends!"

Summoned by the refreshing breeze, clouds gathered overhead, closing in on the blue. Memories I had suppressed and thought were forgotten now arose: Jafar and me crouched by a crumbling mud wall at the flea market, counting the money we had duped people into paying us. Jafar, who was blind in one eye but a natural-born detective. He could find those who didn't want to be found. And Grandmother. The way she closed the window, climbed into bed, and pulled the blankets over her head when a storm came sweeping down the street and through her consciousness.

They arrived a little later. I had grown so accustomed to the silence, I jumped at the sound of the engine. As I stepped out into the rain, Walid's black truck pulled up to the driveway. My first thought was that he must have decided to make home deliveries today, because of the weather, but then the passenger door opened and a woman climbed out. She was wearing a black robe under her coat, and the hem brushed the ground as she ran, hunched, through the rain. She was carrying a bag. I recognized her. She'd gotten old.

"Hello, Amin," Umm Jamil said.

As she hung her dripping coat on a hook by the door and sat down in the living room, I brought the things I'd ordered from Walid into the kitchen, put the tea-kettle on to boil, and rummaged around for cookies, nuts, or anything else I could offer her to eat. The rain pattered on the windows.

Sitting across from me later, after she'd delivered the news of my grandmother's death, Umm Jamil studied my face over the steaming tea. Perhaps I appeared consternated or preoccupied, because she asked gently, "Do you understand what I just told you?"

"Yes."

"It came as a total surprise," Umm Jamil said. "No one saw it coming."

"Was she in the hospital? Was she ... sick?"

"No. She died peacefully in her sleep. She was at home. Yara and I had made breakfast plans, so I was the one who found her."

Yara. I had never called her by her first name. To me, she had always been *Teta*, Grandmother.

I could feel Umm Jamil searching my face for a reaction. For any identifiable emotion behind the severity I was presumably exuding.

"How are you, Amin? Is there anything I can do for you?"

"No, thanks," I said quietly. "I'm fine." I paused, then added, "Thank you, all of you, for always being there for her."

She regarded me in silence, perhaps even reproaching me wordlessly: *unlike you*. But then she said, "What happened, happened. I didn't come here to pass judgment on the matter. You had your reasons to turn your back on her." She gave this statement some space, as if silence could lend it greater credibility, then leaned forward, had a sip of tea, and added, "But I want you to know that your teta always protected you. Her entire life. She was convinced that the approach she took was the right one."

I can still remember the perfume Umm Jamil was wearing. Musk with a hint of jasmine. That smell was enough to unleash thousands of memories. Seeing her sitting here was disorienting. As if my house were the lobby of a theater and she—years older now, her makeup removed—had emerged from the dressing room following a performance.

"Abbas says hello," she said. "As do the others. Abu Amar, Nadya, Fida. They all send their condolences."

At the sound of those names in this room, which to me had always felt like a warm den, my arms broke out in goosebumps. Umm Jamil noticed. She leaned over the table and touched my hand. Blue veins beneath wrinkled skin. Liver spots on the back of her hand. I didn't dare look her in the eyes.

The sounds of the waning storm swept past the house. Umm Jamil's hand rested on mine, and I was determined to leave mine where it was, not to draw back, not to tremble.

"Are you sure this house is where you should be?" she asked after a while.

When I finally looked at her, she smiled. There was pain in the smile, empathy and pity at once. The way an older person smiles at someone in the process of making the same mistakes she once did. Not condescending, but tender.

"It's the only place I possibly could be," I said.

That night, long after Umm Jamil had left and driven back to the city with Walid, I stood in the doorway to my bedroom and gazed at the untouched bed. There was no calming down. I could barely imagine closing my eyes for more than a minute. I don't know if it was my dreams I feared or the prospect of lying awake, tossing and turning. The inner turmoil was simply too great. I can still see myself standing there. Then I recall the days Grandmother would come pick me up from school, taking cover from the rain under the linden trees outside the schoolyard gate. *Care to join me?* she'd ask, and I now realize that those must have been the moments in which she was revealing to me her fear.

We hadn't spoken in more than a year. In some mysterious way, though, she remained part of my daily life, despite my silence, which she respected. Even without direct contact, I encountered her regularly in dreams and heard her continuing to speak to me. Whatever she said in these dreams and memories, though, my life was governed by the things my teta *hadn't* said, the things she *hadn't* told me.

Umm Jamil had stayed for about an hour. She and the others would take care of everything, she said; the funeral was in three days, and if I wanted, they'd let me know the details. It may have been the first time I fully grasped that Grandmother's small band of friends were more than chance acquaintances. They'd been like family to one another.

Then Umm Jamil and I said goodbye. Barely ten seconds later, though, there was another knock on my door.

"You don't have a phone up here, do you?"

"Yes, of course I do. Why?"

"Here's why," she said, rummaging through her purse. "Here. I almost ran off with it." She produced a slip of paper. There was a number written on it. No name.

"While I was at Yara's, a woman from Canada called. You should call back. She said it was urgent."

I worried the slip of paper, first putting it on the cabinet in the living room, then moving it beside the telephone, all without dialing the number. If it was evening here, what time was it in Canada? Early morning? I had long hoped to receive a call from there. But now, in the dull silence of my house, where raptors and spirits of the past had so suddenly appeared, I couldn't bring myself to call back. I feared more bad news. After a while, I turned away from the phone, went downstairs, and left the house.

The storm had cleared the air. Starry night. A few remaining clouds, gray and misshapen like dust bunnies, rolled past the moon. Raindrops clung to blades of grass. Even the stain on the flagstone where I'd seen the lizard had disappeared. I crossed the garden and just kept walking. The hems of my pants soon darkened, and the wet soaked through my shoes and socks. I continued on for some time, my gaze trained straight ahead, as I tried to cast off whatever it was I was feeling. Grief or shame or both. Eventually I reached a hilltop and looked back over the valley. Moonlight fell on the cypresses and stone exterior of the house. Twelve years earlier, I had stood in this spot with Grandmother. We had driven into the mountains for the fruit harvest, and, compelled by a mood I can no longer comprehend, she had shown me the old house. The garden was magical, even then, and the blue shutters gleamed in the late summer sun.

"If the house belongs to you, why don't we live there?" I asked her.

She took me by the hand and squeezed a little too hard.

"Because I sold it, Amin. It doesn't belong to me anymore. We need the money for the café, for your school, and for our new life in the city."

The finality in her voice and the force of her grip shut me up.

Back in Beirut later that evening, and still sorting through my impressions of the day, I stood looking out the window at the city—at the silhouettes of tower cranes and high-rises emerging in the distance.

"Who do you think will live up there, once all those skyscrapers are finished?" I asked.

Unwittingly, perhaps, she revealed more about herself in her answer to this one question than in any other response she ever gave, though there was no way for me to know it at the time. I can't say for certain whether it was bitterness I heard in her tone, or mockery. Coming from her, either would have fit.

"Our country is a house with many rooms, Amin." That's what she said to me. "Those who don't want to remember live in some of the rooms. Those who can't forget dwell in the others. And the murderers always live upstairs."

Camera Obscura

The man had planted himself menacingly in front of Jafar. Veins bulged on his forehead. Sweat ran down his neck and disappeared into his upturned collar. His hand rested on the shoulder of a boy—clearly his son—who spat on the ground and looked primed to light into Jafar. Had they not drawn such a crowd, it seemed likely those two would have lost control by now. Between his clenched fists and jutting head, the kid appeared a near-perfect copy of his dad. The man scowled at the flimsy booklet in his son's hand, then at Jafar, who stood with his back against the wall, with no escape in sight.

Though he'd already said what needed saying, the man was still venting. He took a deep breath and repeated, "You ripped me off. You insulted both my son and me. You'll pay for that!"

I stood frozen in place several yards off, a bucket of popcorn under each arm.

Jafar spotted me there. Almost imperceptibly, he shook his head to warn me not to come any closer.

*

There was a circus in town around then, and Jafar and I could often be found ranging about the area, visiting the flea market held every weekend on the lot outside the tents. We climbed the gnarled poplars that edged the premises and tried to sneak a peek at the caravans, which were clustered behind the tent like a pack of dozing animals. The world they contained was unknown to us and inspired a yearning for faraway lands. Not because the circus came from France, but because of the extraordinary beings we glimpsed behind the privacy fencing from our elevated hideaway. When the applause erupted from the tent between acts, we saw them assembled in the closed-off area behind the entrance: fairylike winged women and tattooed midgets deep in conversation or focused on their stretches. Wiry escape artists buttoned up their vests and circled their wrists to loosen up, and there were hulking, red-bearded fire breathers who used torches to scratch their backs. There was a dancer, too. She leapt onto the slack rope that had been rigged among the caravans and ran through her routine, her arms spread. They were like forgotten figures from the pages of a fantastical tale the writer never finished, as if he'd stood up from his desk and never returned, leaving them to pass the time unattended. Several caravans were bolted with heavy locks. Jafar and I suspected beasts of prey behind their doors.

Far beyond the big top, the boxy towers of Beirut filled the sky. Cranes protruded from urban ravines like dinosaur necks, and along the thin line between buildings and horizon, the summer air shimmered.

The world around the tent we observed from our hiding spot seemed removed from all that, an entire universe of its very own.

We sat up in the poplar, peering over the fence and eating dried apricots we had swiped from a street vendor in the neighborhood. We dangled our legs and day-dreamed about sitting ringside in the darkened tent at least once before this magnificent, alien world vanished. All we needed was a little cash.

"It'll cost at least ten dollars," Jafar said.

"For seats up front or in the back?"

"We get to choose. It's open seating. We'll need fifteen if we want to get popcorn to share."

"We definitely need popcorn, but I'd rather have my own."

"Okay, then more like eighteen or twenty." Jafar lifted the comic book he was holding to his good eye and studied the cover again.

It was hot that afternoon in July. The flea market was directly in the sun. The second-to-last performance of the day was underway inside the circus tent, and a cheery melody floated over the grounds.

Jafar had fished the comic book out of a box half an hour earlier at the flea market. He'd bought it for ten cents, shrugged his shoulders, and said "It's worth a shot."

Then we had climbed the tree.

To keep his balance, he braced himself with one hand on the branch and handed the comic over.

"We can totally pull it off," he said. "We should be able to get twenty dollars for this. What do you think?"

The cover seemed cluttered at first glance, but there was something about it—I couldn't quite look away. The red lettering of the title flashed:

GIANT-SIZE X-MEN

with smaller script in the lower left-hand corner proclaiming:

A scrum of intriguing characters populated the space between the lettering: A man with iron claws. An African goddess with a black-and-gold cape. This enormous guy made of metal and a monster with a hairy blue face. The superheroes appeared to be spilling out of the book, out of a hole torn in the paper cover, charging straight at the viewer. Hidden behind them, I noticed upon closer inspection, were more characters. Their bearing was different. Their eyes were wide with fear, and they shielded themselves with their hands, as if they'd been ambushed.

"It's from 1975," Jafar said as he checked the date. "And there's a *one* beside it. Do you think that means first edition?"

"No clue," I said. "It might also stand for January. But we could say it's a first edition."

"So how much would that be worth?"

"I don't know. Are first editions usually worth something?"

"It sounds good, anyway. Gives us something to work with."

"How many other comics were in that box?"

"Looked like over a hundred."

"Meaning it's barely worth the ten cents we paid for it."

"Not yet, anyway," Jafar responded.

The comic book was in decent shape, aside from a few creases. Seemed to me it had sat in the sun for a while, because the cover was faded along the top. The colors popped, though, as I paged through it.

"What we need is a really good story." Jafar rolled up the napkin in his lap and put the last apricot in his mouth. "One that'll even hook someone who doesn't give a crap about comics." He swallowed without chewing properly, licked his fingertips, and recalled our golden rule: "It's not about the comic book itself. There's got to be something else we can say makes it valuable. Like we did with that ugly picture frame. Or the porcelain pug figurine that lady bought off us."

"Or that broken mirror."

"Or the bedside lamp."

"Or the typewriter."

"Or that heinous vase."

"You're right," I said. "Those were good stories."

It was the best day we'd ever had, this one day two weeks earlier. Six sales in just four hours. Eighty dollars, forty each. The circus hadn't arrived yet, although posters heralded its approach. We took a taxi back into the city, rolled the windows down and felt like kings. "Oh coachman, turn up the music," Jafar called to the driver, and we laughed a little too hysterically. We got out at Luna Park to ride the Ferris wheel; we bought cigarettes, chocolate-covered bananas, and raffle tickets, ate way too much ice cream, and made our way home late that night with empty pockets and upset stomachs. I don't remember who first hatched the plan, but it usually went like this: Jafar would buy something at the flea market for cheap, and we'd cook up some story to lend it the value we had decided for it. I then receded into the background while Jafar set out to *bring the goods to the people*, as we liked to say.

We had spent three dollars on the ugly picture frame and sold it for thirty. Jafar wasn't exactly a math whiz— he was often stumped by simple subtraction. When it came to calculating monetary appreciation, however, he could do it in his sleep: "Nine hundred percent," he proclaimed, his eyes aglow, as we stuffed the money in our pockets.

The frame had hung in the banquet hall on the top floor of the Holiday Inn Beirut, we told people. When the Battle of the Hotels broke out during the civil war, it had been moved to the basement with other works of art for safekeeping. At the time, so our story went, it had framed *The Secret of the Juniper Tree*, one of the first examples of still life in Oriental painting. Later, when the hotel was captured, the piece was discovered and stolen, the overture to an astonishing odyssey through the underbelly of Beirut: the painting was traded for the release of a hostage, then hung on the wall behind an officer's desk for a year, before vanishing once again during a bombing, only to resurface months later in Marseille. There it passed through the hands of countless shifty characters—nighttime rendezvous in underground parking garages and under bridges, briefcases stuffed with cash, furtive handshakes—before finally going missing in the shadows of the black market, while the frame itself remained in Beirut, where it was recognized years later by an art expert, who spotted it in a secondhand bookshop and bought it for $200. "That expert was my uncle," Jafar then said, "and now he wants us to sell it, me and my dad, who's unfortunately a little under the weather today. Oh, my uncle? He emigrated to Canada just before the war ended. Any of his stuff valued at less than $1,000, he asked us to sell, because it wouldn't be worth shipping. We had other frames for sale too, but this one here is unfortunately the last." Without batting an eye, Jafar asked a hundred dollars for it. We walked away with thirty, proof enough that the more outrageous the lie, the more likely someone would believe it.

What did these early experiences with storytelling trigger in me? When I think back on those moments— Jafar and me racking our brains to decide on figures and phrasing, moving scenes back and forth like puzzle pieces, till they clicked into place—I feel a hint of warmth and fleeting happiness. I'm convinced that those stories were more than boyish pranks, even then. They gave us a sense of our own significance.

We were earnest in planning our scams. For stories like the one about the picture frame, we went so far as to conduct research. We watched bootleg copies of gangster films and combed market stalls, digging through boxes for art books. Or we interviewed weary stallkeepers, who were almost impossible to escape once they started pontificating.

There are some paintings by Jan Vermeer that display such differentiated use of light and shadow that they resemble modern photography, but do not correspond to what would have been visible to the naked eye of the painter. We learned that one day from a seller; it sounded like a warning. He told us Vermeer had used a camera obscura for help, as had many of his contemporaries, so he wasn't even a genius, as far as that was concerned. Truth in art was by nature illusory, but every deception eventually came to light, he continued. He spoke in an undertone, his gaze trained on us, as if we were to blame for this fact. Jafar and I had never heard of Vermeer, but we liked the idea of a darkroom that captured an image of the world and flipped it upside down. We adopted the term into our vocabulary as though it were code. Sitting in the evening shadows of a mud wall, counting our haul for the day, we would look at each other and say the words in turn: *camera obscura.*

For inspiration, we sometimes paged through the city maps and history books I bought myself, tattered volumes about historical figures, stacks lugged home from the flea market and jumbled bookshops. I collected postcards of famous sites as well as maps of Beirut that I found in a book from 1977, renderings on a scale of 1:5000 of an intact city center with the names of streets that had long since disappeared. I had a folder of black-and-white photos from the fifties and sixties—the souk with its stone arcades, the harbor, an unscathed Place des Martyrs. In the evenings I spread them out on my bedroom floor, an assemblage of houses, streets, and squares that had all been lost.

In a way, this was an attempt to create a life in which I might feel safe. I think the books provided a sense of security about a place where I had, after all, lived for only a few months. Although I had roots here, I'd spent my whole life in Germany. Upon our return to Lebanon, I was intrigued by the many unfamiliar streets and neighborhoods, but I must admit I occasionally found them spooky, too. It was a period of empty spaces. Entire buildings and factories stood there unused, sparsely illuminated by vagrants, looters, or secret lovers; vacant lots materialized unexpectedly behind apartment buildings, and sometimes, when Jafar and I were walking home from the flea market, we passed through neighborhoods that seemed dead, cross-hatchings of darkened streets and alleys full of rubble, where we'd spot only a handful of people—mostly children—who sat in dark corners and refused to speak.

Jafar was familiar with many of the ruins and knew how to get inside. One night, he took me to a building by the overgrown railroad tracks, which he said used to run all the way to Damascus but had been shut down since the war. We clambered in through a window. Jafar led me down a corridor past former offices, where indentations in the carpet revealed where filing cabinets had once stood. In one hall, he showed me old operating consoles, rusty levers, and workbenches, then we climbed inside empty diesel tanks that echoed the sound of our steps. I'm not sure how he decided which buildings to take me to, but even then I felt certain there were nights he poked around these spots by himself. At the end of the hall was a room with a glass front that overlooked the entire facility. A map hung on the wall, depicting the rail network. Pinheads protruded from junctions. Below the glass front was a control panel. We pushed buttons and pulled levers, but no lights turned on, and the room remained as dark as the dots on the wall marking faraway places the trains had once traveled.

Later on, we sat on the tracks in the moonlight, gazing east toward Syria.

"You're woken by the sound of birdsong in the morning, and the inner courtyards are full of blossoming bitter orange trees." Jafar said it as quietly as if I weren't there. "I read that in a letter."

"What letter was that?"

He fished out a crumpled piece of paper and handed it to me.

Dear Samira, dear children, the first line read.

"Just some letter," he said.

Other nights, we would enter buildings families had fled during the war. We crept through living rooms, bedrooms, and kitchens, up to the top floors, where we gazed out at the city—gray water tanks atop thousands of roofs and thousands upon thousands of lights. I usually stood at the window, spellbound, whereas Jafar wandered around. He opened cupboards, dressers, and drawers, looking for letters left behind.

Were anyone to ask what comes to mind when reflecting on my youth, it would be the nighttime hours spent in those buildings my first summer in Beirut. I loved those outings, the secret spots and sounds— creaking floorboards, pigeons fluttering aloft, broken glass crunching underfoot. If the building was really tall, full of twists and turns, these sounds were often the only thing you could hear.

I still remember how, on some of these expeditions, Jafar would change. There were things between us that remained unspoken. I've probably hung on to that image of the city from above, the sight of distant windows, some dark, others lit, because there were moments with Jafar that similarly alternated between light and shadow. It was as if the rooms in those buildings made him aware of the line between us; he sensed there were everyday things each of us had experienced that the other hadn't, and which divided us.

He disappeared once, and I eventually found him sitting cross-legged by a big hole in the wall, his back to me. It was a long way down. He heard me approaching.

"Come here, Amin. I wanna show you something."

I sat down beside him on the floor.

"Here."

He'd placed a heavy object in my hand. The grenade was an iridescent grayish blue. Its surface gleamed like marble.

"Where'd you get this?"

"It was up here by the couch. I picked it up."

Silence.

"Why would anyone leave something like this lying around?"

He studied my face, as if astounded I could ask such a thing.

"These places are full of them. The yards outside, too. There are warheads in the ruins that smashed through roofs but never exploded. Same goes for grenades. Or they were left on purpose. Sometimes militias had to retreat in a hurry, so they would mine the buildings they'd lost. Other times they just forgot their ammo."

"How do you know all that?"

He didn't respond.

Up to that point, our outings had always seemed more magical to me than unsafe. Jafar was born just a few months before me, but I still remember how much older and more experienced he suddenly appeared. The flickering lights of the city illuminated his face from the side. It looked like he was on fire.

"It's heavy," I said. "Heavier than I would've thought."

Jafar had frozen in place, as if he knew he'd return to the shadows if he leaned back. He didn't say anything.

"What are you going to do with it?"

"Why?"

"Because it's dangerous."

"Do you like it?"

"Yeah ... I guess so."

"It looks like a boob, don't you think?"

I nodded uncertainly.

"It's a present."

At first I didn't respond, then worked up the courage to say, "I don't want it." I handed the grenade back to him.

Jafar's fingers traced the curves of the grenade and slowly glided over the pin.

"Too bad."

He leaned back. Then he pressed the button above the lever.

"'Cause it's a really good lighter," he added, looking at the flame now rising from it and illuminating his face from below.

This other time, I found a radio in a room with a pile of charred logs in the middle. Soot had blackened the wallpaper, and the smell of smoke hung in the air. I turned on the radio, and we listened to a song by Majida El Roumi. I stared out the window, enjoying the view. The song cut out at some point, interrupted by a different melody signaling the news. The host delivered the day's headlines: *The Palestinian Liberation Organization, or PLO, has relocated headquarters from Tunisia to Gaza ... Anti-whaling activist Paul Watson's boat was rammed by a Norwegian Coast Guard cutter ... Snipers in the besieged city of Sarajevo have ...* I hadn't realized Jafar was no longer beside me until I heard the sound of crunching glass. He sat in the far corner of the room, grimacing, his eyes closed and hands over his ears. I'd never seen him like that before. He didn't calm down until I turned off the radio. I would later learn that the theme music for the news hadn't changed since the war, meaning anyone who heard it flashed back to announcements of impending bombardments or warnings to avoid certain streets. Jafar didn't mention any of that to me. He didn't relax until I'd steered him outside, and when I cautiously broached the subject later on, all he said was "Don't worry, man. It was just the camera obscura" to help me understand whatever was hidden inside him: a dark room in which part of the world was flipped upside down.

There are many such moments, cast in unsteady

light, that come back to me today for reasons I can't name. Much of what happened later that summer was more formative, left a deeper imprint, and played a far greater role in defining the course my life would take than those fragments of moonlit nights.

As reconstruction continued, with more and more ruins and dilapidated buildings disappearing, I began taking notes and created a list of hiding spots threatened by demolition. I recorded their locations along with certain architectural features: slanted roof, green door, twenty-two balconies. Or that the hole left by a missile entering the northern facade looked like Greenland, whereas the exit hole on the southern side resembled Alaska. Nothing around me seemed permanent, and perhaps because I felt my world had grown more fragile—the way walls and people were fragile, and the way buildings and city squares disappeared over time, just as people had disappeared during the war—I must have thought I could save things from being forgotten by preserving them in lists and stories.

Up in the poplar, Jafar suddenly said, "I have an idea."

He set the comic book in his lap and produced a can of coke from the backpack he'd nestled between two branches. "It's warm now, anyway."

He held the can against my forehead, like he had to prove it. Then he opened it and picked up the comic. He turned back the cover and emptied the can onto the title page, like an artist dousing a canvas in paint.

The next show started in two hours. I wanted to see the tightrope walkers; Jafar wanted to see the big cats. We worked out the details of our story while we waited for the page to dry. Then we left our viewing perch in the tree.

*

Holding the buckets of popcorn, I tried to make sense of what had gone wrong. The hostility in the air was palpable and seemed to have carried over to bystanders, mostly young and older men. They had formed a semicircle that was tightening like a noose around the action. Peering through the crowd, I could see father and son, both seething with anger. Between his popped collar, rolled-up sleeves, and smug expression, the boy looked like a classic bully from some American teen movie who locks his classmates in the storage closet or shoves them down the stairs, just because he can.

Jafar was clearly struggling to calm down both father and son. To others, he may have appeared unfazed, but I could tell he was nervous. There was one unmistakable sign: the upper lid of his glass eye began to twitch.

I ran through our story again in my mind. It was no worse than others we'd pulled off in the past, and this one, too, had worked at first. The minute the comic sold, Jafar had given me some cash, and I'd run for popcorn while he bought our circus tickets. I even asked how it went, and he gave me a thumbs-up and said "Piece of cake."

Though my imagination was more active, Jafar was the better storyteller by far. I would share my ideas, but he brought the stories to life, embellishing them, adding mood and description. There was no question that this time, too, he'd created a whole universe in which the comic book—as we discussed—once belonged to a young waiter at the fabled Saint George Hotel, who'd bought it out of boredom at the bus station, then taken it to work, where that evening, as he tended the bar, he found himself face to face with Peter O'Toole, the star of *Lawrence of Arabia*. We had watched the movie a few days earlier. I imagined Jafar describing that legend of the silver screen—the look of suffering around his mouth, the ash-blond hair, the fine network of lines around his eyes (those famous eyes of O'Toole's), which I presumed Jafar effusively compared to the blue of hyacinths in bloom—till the man began to take shape, sitting there at the bar at the Saint George Hotel, all alone and three sheets to the wind.

"Hey, you. Get me another gin."

"Are you sure you'd like another, sir?"

"Sure I'm sure, kid."

"We also have very good water," Jafar imitated the server, who was concerned about the well-being of his famous guest. O'Toole bristled at first, but then launched into an anecdote Jafar had invented as a little flourish. I could picture him slipping into the role of the drunk superstar, slurring his words as he told the bartender his story: "I was in Dublin once. There was a little pub, and I went in for a nightcap. At some point, the barman said to me, 'Sir, I think you've had enough!' To which I said, 'No. No! I still want much, much more to drink,' but he was going to kick me out. So I bought the bar." The young waiter, we had decided, then gave his guest the gin he'd ordered, so he wouldn't buy the Saint George Hotel, and once O'Toole was even drunker, the waiter asked for his autograph. The movie star signed the cover of the comic book, but with a final swipe of his hand accidentally knocked over his tumbler of gin, immediately blurring the ink. Nevertheless, the waiter took the comic home and saved it for many years, because it now held double meaning: for a fraction of a second, it had borne the autograph of a living legend, and the gin that had wiped out that very autograph, leaving no more than a stain, served as a lifelong reminder of the dangers of alcohol and the transience of fame. Jafar must have concluded the story as usual: "And that young waiter just happens to have been my uncle. He emigrated to Canada right before the war ended. He left behind lots more stuff, but me and my dad—who's sick today—have already sold most of it for him."

So what had gone wrong? I tried to move in closer.

"Thirty dollars!" the father now hissed. "You scammed thirty dollars out of me with your ridiculous story! I didn't believe a word you said, and if my son hadn't wanted that damn comic book so bad, I'd've said to hell with you from the get-go." He paused to pat his offspring on the shoulder. "Fortunately for us, and unfortunately for you, we passed by the stall with the comic books. You pulled a fast one on us."

"Yeah, you little cheat." The son spat toward Jafar again. "Sucks for you!"

Murmuring rose around me.

Too close. Jafar had stayed too close to the stall where we'd bought the comic. Had he moved to the other end of the flea market to hawk it, we'd be in the clear.

Jafar was still trying to salvage the situation. He said something I couldn't hear.

"What?" the man roared. "What's that supposed to mean?"

I elbowed my way through the crowd, popcorn buckets jostling hips and ribcages.

"Yeah, well ..." Jafar lifted his hands in a calming gesture, managed a smile, and took a cautious step forward. "Everyone here knows that stall. The comics there are okay—in decent condition and everything—

and cost significantly less. There are millions of comic books kicking around, but like I already said, none are as valuable as the one I sold you. As I explained ..."

Our eyes met. I nodded at him. Jafar went on, maintaining the veracity of our tale and explaining why the stain the international superstar had left on the page—which quite possibly contained traces of his saliva, no less—was easily worth thirty dollars. I barely heard him, though, because I had just spotted that girl again. She also saw me. We'd noticed each other in line for popcorn earlier, or rather, she had been rooted to the spot some distance away, squinting at the popcorn stand through the steady flow of people, as if there were something secret to be discovered there, and so what caught my eye was actually less her than her stillness. When I looked back moments later, after paying for the two buckets, she was gone. Now here she was again. Upon getting a closer look, I found I couldn't take my eyes off her. She stood amid the agitated crowd, about ten yards away from me, and watched the fight with restrained curiosity—she appeared almost shy, her arms folded, as if she wasn't used to being surrounded by people and the thought of bumping into unknown bodies frightened her. She kept peeking at me, too. I could only guess at her build under her black robe. Her hair was concealed by a black hijab. I couldn't even have said what it was I found so captivating about her. There was something there, though, that gave me butterflies, and the scrutiny in her gaze made me nervous. Where was she from? Was she alone? As if to answer my question, the girl cast a sidelong glance at the furious pair confronting Jafar—her father and brother.

The man had initially listened to Jafar's counter-argument with a disdainful, almost amused expression, but he was growing impatient. When Jafar finished, the man looked down at him and took another step closer.

The people around me began to debate. Some thought thirty was a reasonable price for the comic, provided the story was true. Others called for the little cheat to be turned in to the police.

"He's lying!" the boy erupted. "This comic isn't worth anything. It's dirty and ugly. The ones over there are better." He came up so close to Jafar, their foreheads touched. "Take your damn comic back, or else ..." He feigned a headbutt. Jafar dodged the movement, tripped, and fell. The boy laughed cruelly.

The father lowered his hand, expecting it to land on his daughter's shoulder, but the girl had shrunk back. At the sight of his hand hovering in the air, she took a step forward to reestablish the contact she was expected to provide. He leaned over and whispered something in her ear. With stooped shoulders, she disappeared among the bystanders, who cleared a path for her. She soon returned with the comic-book vendor.

My heart skipped a beat, then began to pound so violently I feared everyone could hear.

How often do we recall those moments we later see as turning points? How often do we use those moments to construct the foundation for a house of memories, whose rooms we pace, saying: Is this where joy turned to suffering or suffering turned to joy? Is this how we discover the truth about how we became who we are?

I remember how scared I was we'd be thrown in jail or beaten up. I also remember thinking back, in that moment, to what had happened that time in the apartment, when the radio was playing and the door to

Jafar's dark room had opened a crack, and I felt certain this would become my own darkest hour: a door to a room where the world was turned upside down.

When I saw the man who'd sold us the comic approaching, I knew we were done for. I've replayed this scene so many times, I can pause it like a film and study the individual stills:

The girl's father has the vendor swear to those assembled that Jafar purchased the comic from him, and that the ominous stain was not there just a few hours ago. "He sneaks around here all the time," the seller says, and the crowd around me edges forward hungrily. I feel caught between the bodies. My view of Jafar is blocked, but I picture him shrinking further, his back coming up against the wall. I can see the girl. She's bowing her head with her eyes closed, as if wishing she were invisible. There's something unsettling about her stance, but I don't realize until later, after everything's over, that in that moment she knows exactly what's going to happen. She has experienced it herself. Then someone steps aside, and I have a view of the action. Jafar cowers on the ground while the girl's brother kicks around him with the tip of his shoe, spraying sand into Jafar's face, insulting and humiliating him like a street dog. The father stands to the side with his arms folded, watching his son become a man. He laughs. No one yells "Stop!" A frenzied hooting and shrieking instead, the sound of raptors. I don't notice it happen, but I must have dropped the popcorn, because when I topple forward, my hands are empty. I lean over Jafar's body and get dirt and gravel to the face too, and I close my eyes, just waiting for the inevitable blow to my back, tensing every muscle. But nothing happens. For what feels like an eternity, nothing happens. When I open my eyes and turn my head, both boy and man have disappeared. A figure has edged in between us and them.

"Please stop," the man said. "You don't realize what you're doing."

I got to my feet, knocked the dust from my clothes, and looked around. My heart was still racing. The crowd had fallen silent. All eyes were on the young man who seemed to have materialized out of nowhere. I expected the father and son to shove him aside and lay into us, but they appeared too perplexed and did nothing of the sort.

The sun was already low in the sky. Trees poured their shadows onto the pavement like water, between them islands of light and the mute crowd. The young man bent down to pick up the comic book lying in the dirt. He ran a finger over the cover, carefully, as though it were a fine leatherbound volume.

"You truly don't realize what you're doing," he said again softly.

The girl's father pushed up his sleeves a little more. Then he stretched his arms out and cracked his knuckles.

"Mind your own business," he said brusquely. "These kids conned me and insulted my son. They took us for fools. I know exactly what I'm doing."

Jafar stood up behind me and came to my side. Out of the corner of my eye, I saw him check himself for injuries and wipe something from his cheek, either tears or dust.

The young man didn't look at us.

"I'm not talking about the boys," he said, handing the father the comic book. "It seems you have no idea what you're holding there."

"What's going on here? Are you with them? Peter

O'Toole, the Saint George Hotel—was that something you cooked up?" The father took another step forward, but the young man didn't move an inch. "This comic book can't be worth more than ten cents. And the boys damaged it, so they should be begging my son for forgiveness. They owe me the thirty dollars I paid for it, plus another hundred for injuring my honor."

Jafar edged in closer to me. The reference to the man's honor swung at us like a wrecking ball.

The young man shook his head.

"I don't know these two. Whatever they did is of no concern to me. But you should know that the comic book you purchased is extremely sought after," he said, letting his words ring in the pause that followed. "Which is interesting, considering it was something of a trial balloon. Ever heard of Stan Lee and Jack Kirby? The Incredible Hulk, Iron Man, or Thor? All creations of theirs." He uttered the superheroes' names as if they were friends. As if they were real and out there, somewhere. "They first conceived the X-Men series in 1963. The idea behind it was novel at the time. Until that point, you know, superheroes were just unusual individuals who put on costumes or gained their superpowers from external sources."

He did not seem to be addressing anyone in particular, and wasn't even speaking very loudly, which made bystanders step in closer to hear. Either he failed to notice the attention, or it didn't bother him. His composure struck me as unique.

"The X-Men were the first to be *born* with such powers. In other words, from birth onward they were always different and therefore feared and spurned by society, unlike the other superheroes." He briefly turned his head toward Jafar and me standing there covered in dust, then he turned back to the father. "The series was popular among illustrators and authors, but didn't enjoy much commercial success. Six years later it was discontinued."

"So this comic book is a forgery?" the father asked, tapping on the year printed in the upper left-hand corner. "This says 1975. That doesn't line up with what you just said."

The young man smiled. Not disrespectfully, though. More like he'd expected the question.

"What you're holding is one of the most legendary comic books of all time," he said.

I sensed Jafar jerking his head around to face me, but I couldn't tear my eyes away from the scene. I tried to get a closer look at our rescuer, but the sun was already low in the sky, and all I could discern was his backlit silhouette.

"In 1975, Len Wein revived the concept and produced this issue as a test. *Giant-Size X-Men* #1. He made a significant change, though. Just take a look at the figures on the cover." He pointed to direct the father's attention to the image. "The old X-Men were replaced by a group that was, for the first time ever, multinational, multiethnic, and thus multiconfessional."

By now everyone was listening, and I had to wonder if he'd intentionally placed *multiconfessional* at the end of his list, to give it extra weight. Who was this man, and how did he know these things? A hush had settled over the lot. Everyone who had hoped for things to escalate now stared awkwardly at the ground, hands in their pockets.

"The message behind this series was always political." The young man looked at the ground now, too, as if he'd find the right words there. "It was a story about people who were rejected from society, despised, and persecuted, simply because they were different, but who refused to give up hope for the peaceful coexistence of all peoples. You see?"

No one spoke. The girl's brother chewed his lip. Her father weighed the comic book in his hand, as if he could determine its value that way. "So," he finally said, "how much?"

"Tough to say. May I?" Our protector reached for the comic. He carefully turned it over and seemed to choose his words deliberately. "Creases are relatively unimportant, and besides, we see very few here. Yellowing is the bigger concern," he said, paging through the comic. "In our case, those spots are limited to the front cover. We also don't appear to be missing any pages." He paused to think, then said, "If this comic book were sealed in mint condition, it could easily fetch a couple thousand dollars."

I heard Jafar gasp and felt him grope for my wrist.

"The issue here is the stain," the young man continued. "Coffee, tea, or soda stains diminish the value substantially."

"It was gin," Jafar croaked.

"Same difference," he said, without turning around. He handed the comic back to the girl's father. "The stain is only on the cover, though. The other pages are undamaged. If you found an eager buyer or really fervent fan, I'd say you could get up to two hundred for it. It might also be worth hanging on to for a few years."

Someone whistled through their teeth.

"Two hundred dollars," Jafar whispered.

Sitting under the big top later, where green and red spotlights raced across the circus ring and up into the stands, my mind kept wandering. Tightrope walkers balanced high above our heads and the sound of drumming rattled our seats, but I couldn't stop thinking about that girl. The crowd had dispersed soon after the young man stopped talking. The comic-book seller laid a hand on his upper arm and offered him fifty dollars to appraise his entire inventory. The girl's father was swarmed by men, who clapped him on the shoulder, congratulating him on his purchase, while others gathered around her brother, smiling and feigning punches, as though in praise of his performance.

"Are you hurt?" she asked in that brief moment we escaped observation.

"No," I said, staring at my dirty clothes in embarrassment.

I was slightly ashamed, but also felt that any second not spent looking at her amounted to time irretrievably lost. Her hijab had slipped back a bit, revealing her black hairline. Standing close for the first time, I could finally get a better look. She was pretty and radiated something rare, a shimmering alertness, honest interest. I noticed several beauty marks among the tiny hairs on her neck, and on her cheeks, too—her pale skin was strewn with them. As if whoever had created her face didn't know what to do with the leftover black paint on his paintbrush, but was then struck by a brilliant idea. She fascinated me in a way I couldn't put into words.

When I looked back into her eyes, I saw a flicker that touched some buried part of me I hadn't even known existed.

"Where were all the big cats?" Jafar griped as we exited the tent. It had gotten dark. The city lights twinkled in the distance.

"Hang on a sec," I said, grabbing his arm.

We were already some distance from the tent when I spotted our rescuer sitting under a tree. He noticed us, appeared to think twice, then waved us over. Jafar and I exchanged a look. He was maybe twenty—seven or eight years older than us. Guys his age usually chased us off whenever they caught us on a shady bench or poking around back courtyards, so we tended to steer clear if we could help it.

He was sitting on a folding chair behind an easel with a big sheet clipped in place. From where he sat, he could see the entire flea market with the circus tent at the far end.

"How was the show?" he asked when we reached him.

"Good," I said.

"It was all right," Jafar said.

He had drawn the big top. It was impressively detailed and almost three-dimensional, with dark cross-hatching where the fabric threw shadows. The red and white stripes that met at a spire in the middle were so accurately reproduced in black and white, it was like he'd traced a photograph. All he had changed was the area where the flea market stood. The scene was transformed into a fantastical bazaar: fairylike creatures fluttered over the stalls, in front of which a clutch of tattooed dwarves was haggling; an escape artist standing atop a dais doffed his straitjacket, a fire-breather produced a glowing flame, and tightrope walkers balanced on electrical lines in the background.

"Too bad all this'll disappear soon," he said. "The circus is moving on in a few days."

We didn't know how to respond.

I had never seen such a vivid, obsessively detailed drawing style. From the moment I saw the piece, I knew

I had to have it. I wanted to add it to my collection of lost places.

"Is this drawing for sale?" I blurted out.

Jafar eyed me. He knew as well as I did that we didn't have a cent between us.

"No," the young man replied. "I hadn't intended to sell it."

"Because it's a first edition?"

He laughed out loud, but it sounded forced.

"No. 'Cause it's not worth much." He stared blankly for a moment, pressing his lips together, then smiled and said, "I'll give it to you. In remembrance of the circus and your little prank."

We looked at the ground in shame.

The streets were filling with rush-hour traffic, and the sounds of the city rolled in from the distance.

"Would you sign it, too?" I asked.

"Yes, please," Jafar interjected. "That way, if you become famous someday, it'll be worth more."

I elbowed him in the side.

I've given away or misplaced many of the books and photographs I collected back then, but I still have that drawing. It's matted and framed, and you need to take it out to see the inscription:

For the storytellers,

he wrote,

by Younes Abboud.

Storms

She later said it was the twilight. The twilight in the city. That it was unique here in Beirut. She loved the word—the *twilight* between buildings, the *twilight* over the sea as the fishing boats returned, the *twilight* on tiles and furniture in our rooms. She would often pause then, say *twilight* in German—*Dämmerlicht*—and try to translate it into Arabic for whomever she was talking to, by describing the nuances of this light. She also liked to say *Sehnsucht*—yearning. A beautiful word, because it could express both joy and grief.

Gedankenwelt. Fernweh. Habseligkeiten. The world of one's thoughts. Pining for distant places. One's few, portable possessions.

Basically all she had brought back from Germany was a selection of beautiful words. In the thirteen or so years we had lived there, she had made barely any effort to learn the language properly. Whatever she needed for shopping or appointments with authorities, she would learn by heart or pluck from a slim dictionary she had. Other times she'd take me or a neighbor along to translate at parent-teacher conferences or immigration.

The flaming eye of day breaks apart
In sweet death, and its colors fade,
While in fair twilight, boldly blossoms start
To open, in the hated glow its embers laid.

"What was that word?" she asked after I read the Schiller poem aloud in the living room. I had to memorize it for school.

"Which one do you mean?"

"Could you reread the whole thing? There, that one—please say that again."

"*Dämmerlicht.*"

I still remember her diffident laughter when I tried to teach her certain words. Words I thought would be good for her to know. And I recall the time she grabbed my sleeve in sudden, almost childlike surprise at her unexpectedly perfect pronunciation of the word *Katze* —cat. She then stuck out and prodded her tongue in wonderment, as if it were an alien instrument she had just learned to play.

The appeal certain words held for her emerged first from their sound. Sometimes she would love the sound of a word, but if its meaning failed to intrigue, she'd forget all about it. That was usually the case. Sometimes, though, it was the word's meaning that stuck with her. I remember the time she was prescribed an ointment to treat a rash, and I heard her laughing in the bathroom. She couldn't stop laughing, and when I cautiously opened the door, I found her standing at the mirror. "*Hautfarben,*" she said—skin-colored—pointing at her arm and the smear of cream, which she had assumed would be transparent, but was instead several shades lighter than her skin or mine.

The German words she hung on to after our return to Lebanon and kept using, her Arabic discreetly peppered with foreign terms, allowed me to understand her better in hindsight. As if they constituted a lexicon of her soul. Depending on the words—and when and how she used them—it was possible to gain insight into her emotional life.

Frühlingserwachen, Herzenswunsch, Tausendschön, or *Sommerfrische*—spring awakening, heart's desire, daisy, summer holiday—those were words for good days.

Mutterseelenallein, hasenherzig, Tautropfen, and *Vergissmeinnicht*—all alone, lily-livered, dewdrop, forget-me-nots—those were used on the other days.

Ana ashar hasenherzig alyom—I feel lily-livered today. She once said that when I got home from school at lunchtime. She was still in her nightgown, hadn't brushed her hair, and sat with the curtains drawn and her legs pulled up onto the chair, as if something were lurking on the floor or behind the cupboards.

A word we both liked: *Antlitz*. Visage.

I remember how the skin on her face felt. Rough like parchment, and the many deep creases inscribed in her features told a visible story that required no words. She didn't talk much, but brooded. Sometimes these thoughts were like tidal waves that pressed against the inside of her forehead, where they appeared as wrinkles. The roughness of her skin was never unpleasant, though, and when she tucked me in, I always hoped our cheeks would touch for longer than her whisper of *Good night*.

There was a certain distance about her. Not that she was ever cold or tactless—she was extremely caring and attentive, but it always seemed as though moments of intimacy and tenderness required extra effort of her.

People who didn't know Grandmother often misinterpreted her distinctive high cheekbones as a sign of arrogance. They were just a little too pronounced, especially in photos. What went unseen, meanwhile, was the fragility that would consume her out of nowhere, like the times I heard her pacing around the apartment late at night, or the mornings when, overwhelmed by the very thought of the tasks ahead, however minor, she simply decided to stay in bed, and I went to school without breakfast. Depending on the situation, the most unlikely things could throw her off-kilter.

Sometimes I spied on her and tried to imagine what she had been like as a young woman. Long before I was born, before my mother was born. She never talked about it. To her, there was nothing beautiful about words like *earlier, back then,* or *once.*

We had a neighbor who often stopped by for coffee. His name was Abbas, and he told me he was from southern Lebanon. He had been a silkworm farmer before the war and sold his silk to carpet makers across the Middle East. I liked him because he was chatty and gestured a lot when he spoke, as if our living room were a stage. Grandmother must have known him from before we moved to Germany—they seemed comfortable around each other and mentioned names of people and distant places that I gathered were mutual acquaintances or points at which their paths had crossed. For instance, they talked once about a theater production they'd attended on the same evening. They recalled such names as Nidal al-Achkar, Antoine Courbage, and Raymound Gebara—famous actors, the silkworm farmer explained—and alluded to places that had a nice ring to them, like Le Grand Théâtre de Beirut, and as Abbas spoke, Grandmother nodded her head knowingly. Their reunion in a foreign land, thousands of miles away from those places, seemed to retroactively establish a more solid basis for their fleeting acquaintance, a basis that justified the silkworm farmer's regular appearances in our household. Several times a week, he would knock on our door and be ushered inside. I was seven or eight and tried to draw more information out of him about how, exactly, they knew each other.

One autumn weekend, while Grandmother stirred a pot of stew in the kitchen, Abbas waited in the living room, his hands folded. He had intended to leave much earlier, but it was a blustery day and raining heavily, so she'd invited him to stay for dinner. We sat on the sofa, and he told me about an exhibition of my grandmother's drawings he had seen once in Beirut. It was the first I'd ever heard about her being an artist. Abbas still remembered where the show was held—the Joseph Matar Gallery—and could recall some of the guests and even the names of individual pieces. As he spoke, I observed her standing at the range on the other side of the room. She was listening to him, and at a certain point stopped what she was doing, absorbed in his words, her left hand holding the spoon in the air, till the stew burned.

My entire childhood, I was surrounded by exiles who romanticized our homeland so readily that I couldn't help but believe that *our sea* was the most beautiful, *our sunlight* the softest, *our mountains* the most imposing, and *our culture* the richest. What they couldn't explain, though, was why none of them wanted to go back.

In 1981, just weeks after my parents' death, Grandmother had left for Germany with me. Through nighttime silence in a taxi to Damascus, and from there to Istanbul, Athens, and finally Munich. That's what she told me; kids at school were asking. There was a whole bulletin board in our classroom dedicated to the topic of *Our Roots*, and my teacher had invited me to add to it. So I grilled my grandmother. At school I told anyone who cared to listen about our adventurous journey, and in my enthusiasm may have added an eye-popping detail or two, as it was pretty much the only story I knew about myself at such a young age. It was a story, not a memory. I was nine months old when we left Lebanon, which meant none of my memories of home could be real, let alone reliable. Living in public housing on the outskirts of Munich had always felt temporary. We owned minimal kitchenware, and over the twelve years we were there, our other furnishings remained spartan, too.

In the spring of 1994, Grandmother withdrew me from school. Neighbors came for what little furniture we had, and at some point we went to the mall to buy me a suitcase.

"What'll it be like?" I asked her when our departure date was finally set. The suitcase was splayed in the middle of my room, and I had started making piles of clothes and other belongings to the left and right, depending on whether the stuff was coming with me or staying behind. "I can't even picture it. What's going to happen to us?"

"It'll all work out," she said. "We'll settle down in no time, Amin."

Even then I could tell—more in her voice than in the words she chose, and in the way she half turned away as she spoke—that she wasn't so sure herself.

Twelve years after fleeing Beirut, now we were going back. In my backpack was a postcard my classmates had all signed with goodbye messages. I caught my first glimpse of the country from the airplane. I didn't feel anything at the sight and couldn't have said whether the sea down below was more beautiful than any other; in the setting sun, however, it appeared rimmed in red. Like a closed wound, I thought. A country the color of newly healed skin.

*

Three large coffee grinders ground the beans into a filter, and various cakes were displayed on baking sheets in the illuminated glass case. The ceiling lights shone down on a sea of golden cutlery, dessert plates, and floor lamps positioned in corners. The room was flooded with a shimmering warmth that cloaked fixtures and guests alike. The café was on the ground floor of a building dating back to the French Mandate, and between its coziness, modest size, and furnishings— ornate oak tables and chairs, enamel vases of fresh flowers—it felt like 1920s Paris or Berlin. A few days had passed since the incident at the flea market. Not many people had shown up by the time I arrived. There was a strained silence in the room—sighs and enunciated exhales, like a classroom full of students taking a test—and I saw mostly older women and men gathered before the framed pictures Grandmother had hung on the walls. She, meanwhile, stood off to the side, behind the counter, watching their reactions. She seemed excited. It was her first exhibition in such a long time.

The café had been Grandmother's dream, one I'm sure she had nurtured for some time, plans for its realization taking shape in private. She signed the rental agreement a few weeks after our return and opened Café Yara on a bustling side street full of boutiques, galleries, and folks in need of refreshment. The new work seemed to transform my grandmother into what might have been an earlier version of herself. She was seized by a sense of purpose I had until now never witnessed in her. Late into the night, she sat in the pool of light cast by her desk lamp in the living room, sorting delivery slips and invoices; she sketched floor plans, arranging furniture she had yet to buy, and made calls to distributors. She got up early to comb neighborhood junk shops for furniture and fittings. Out of nowhere, Grandmother started doing things she'd never done before: She hummed songs. She kissed me on the forehead when I left the apartment. And I noticed dust collecting on the little bottle labeled *amitriptyline* that she'd brought from Germany and kept in the bathroom cabinet.

The familiar light, the familiar smells and sounds of the city clearly helped. In any case, she changed, and though I should have been encouraged by these changes, I experienced the very opposite. I didn't feel swept up in her wake—I felt left behind. Lost in a tangle of unknown alleyways, blindsided by the otherness of these new impressions. We had never really followed the news in Germany. Grandmother had been careful to turn off the TV or radio as soon as coverage shifted to international headlines. Whenever we did happen upon images, whether on the front pages or in television specials we weren't expecting when we tuned in, the scenes from Beirut seemed so foreign and far away that they were easy for me to block out.

Now, though, surrounded by ruins and rubble, evidence of past violence and the forces behind it, I was gripped with uncertainty. At night, when the foreignness of this new backdrop threatened to overwhelm me, I forced myself asleep by thinking of Germany, and in particular its smells: water heavy with chlorine at the public pool, as we lay on the flagstones to dry off; ripe fruit in wind-tousled meadows in late fall; damp pine forests in November. Or I looked at the clock and imagined what my former classmates were doing that very moment—gym class, horsing around in the schoolyard, playing near the woods, all those things. I did that a lot, until I started at my new school and met Jafar, who banished my fear of the ruins by leading me into their bowels.

I was at my most sensitive then, desperate for explanations that never came. I didn't dare ask Grandmother about her earlier life in Beirut, for fear her cheery new self might crack.

Then there was the sense I got that the people in this country felt conquered by peace. They couldn't find the words for what was happening around them.

"Beirut is still divided ... in here," a taxi driver said once, tapping his forehead. We were driving along the former Green Line, the thoroughfare that had divided the city into East and West during the war. I can still recall how surreal yet scarily beautiful it was to see greenery growing from the asphalt on a major street, weeds sprouting from sidewalks. As if we'd stumbled into a Jacek Yerka painting, in which the man-made yields to nature. Green creepers wound their way through torched cars and bullet-pocked facades. The city appeared either submerged or recently rediscovered. "There are a hundred Beiruts," the taxi driver said.

Grandmother gazed silently out the window at the passing ruins.

Beirut was like a repair shop. The sound of construction downtown floated through the city day and night:

cement mixers and generators, hydraulic breakers and buzz saws, hammer drills and welding equipment. Their relentless activity was carried down the streets on the wind. The workers' shouting above the noise was like the lyrics of a song heralding the return of normalcy. Or at least suggesting it. Sometimes, access routes downtown were temporarily closed, and convoys of trucks would thunder through our neighborhood toward the coastal highway, to dump rubble into the sea. I often watched the vehicles pass, their beds loaded so high with twisted steel beams that they nearly snagged lower balconies, where women stood, cursing the noise.

I was deeply vexed by the contradictions in this city. There were glitzy displays in newly opened clothing and jewelry shops, expensive boutiques, and posters on the sides of shell structures depicting the apartments to come. One of these read *Beirut—Ancient City of the Future*. Below, in smaller type, a promise that the world would be a better place in the new millennium: *Projected completion by late 1999*. Another poster proclaimed *Dreams really do come true—luxury living + vibrant nightlife*. Banners advertising plastic surgeons hung from bridges. It seemed the residents of the city felt compelled to keep up; buildings and bodies alike were being restored. People got facelifts, then stepped out onto newly paved streets. Evidence of these attempts to regain lost youthfulness was everywhere you looked, as if it were warranted to eradicate the traces of that violent past—or really, any past—by whatever means necessary.

During those first few weeks, it was almost impossible to ignore what I saw going on around the city. For the most part, waves of yearning for Germany surged within me.

I like to believe that Grandmother perceived my distress at some point. That she wasn't oblivious to it, and that she therefore recognized the need to grant me access to her world. She began to open up. For the first time, I started learning more about her earlier life. We took the car to Tripoli. She was born there in 1934. On a side street she pointed out a crooked building that looked like an old shoe.

"That's where my father had his dyeworks," she told me. "Early in the morning men from the tannery would deliver the leather, which his workers then hauled out back to the vats. All day long they stood out there, stomping on the hides to work the red dye deep into the pores. My father ... when he came inside at night, he smelled like the wet hides of animals slaughtered earlier that day."

There was nothing about the place that suggested its past existence as a dyeworks. I liked standing there with Grandmother, though, and to my surprise, the city streets seemed to prompt her to continue: "The nights in the Old City of Tripoli were quiet," she said as we left the building behind and strolled down serpentine paths to the sea. "Around eight thirty, activity on the streets abruptly quieted, and life moved indoors. From my room, all I would hear outside was the night watchman whistling to himself or maybe, very occasionally, the blast of a ship horn from the roadstead. Hardly anyone dared to go outside after nightfall, because the streets of the Old City were dark and scary. They seemed dangerous to us kids, not least because of the many fairy tales about the night that were intended to keep us from sneaking out the window. They said nighttime in the Old City was like nights a hundred years ago. There was a lamplighter, who lit the gas streetlights around the city. And a night watchman, who wandered around with a baton, guarding the streets and marketplaces, checking the locks on store-fronts, and carrying out ancient rituals passed down to him by his predecessors."

"Are they still around today?"

"No. That was a long time ago. Here we are, look. Here's where the New Town began. This area was colonized by the French after the First World War."

The cityscape really did change. The narrow lanes gave way to broad boulevards lined with cypresses and poplars.

"Life was different here."

"What do you mean?"

"The night," she said. "New Town nights were different. We called them *Mandate Nights*." She started telling me about rollicking soldiers, dancing couples, and white neon lights that grew rapidly in number over the years and illuminated shop windows after dark. Their sparkle reached all the way to the Old City, a lure for many residents, who stole out of their homes to experience the magic of Mandate Nights for themselves. "Even the night watchman took a turn around this neighborhood. We were tickled by the sight, because he just ambled along like the rest of us, as if he'd forgotten his job."

When we finally reached the shore, Grandmother unexpectedly said, "And here's where I started to paint."

The wind sweeping over the water tugged at her hair and blouse.

"Your first picture?"

She smiled. "Yes. My first picture."

"What did you paint?"

She pointed into the distance. "A few ships."

"Do you still have it?"

"No."

"Why not?"

"Because I wasn't *allowed* to paint."

"I don't get it."

"It was considered indecent, Amin. I would sit right here, where we're standing, and paint ships or people in restaurants. But I had to do it in secret. There were morality police around every corner, or even worse, gossiping neighbors, and what I was doing—simply sitting out in the open with paint and paintbrush—was deemed improper. I couldn't risk my father finding out about it."

"Wow," I said, and was immediately struck by how lame I'd sounded, but it was the one word that expressed how I felt. "So what did you do with the paintings?"

"As soon as I finished one, I'd throw it away somewhere in the Old City."

"Really? And your father never found out?"

"No, no, he did." She paused. "Eventually. But that's another story."

Whenever I think back to Grandmother's account, it seems like a parable, a clumsy attempt of hers to pass along a bit of advice.

The sum of these fragmentary memories changed her into someone I could place in time, like the historical figures in the books I collected—a date of birth, a city, a vague image of her as a young woman surreptitiously breaking the rules. I was surprised by her sharing this, because the fact that she tended to limit these recollections to her childhood was not lost on me. There were chapters in her life that she guarded like a night watchman. Alleys and pathways of memory never touched by the light. She would pause a lot while speaking, as if continually gauging how much she wanted to reveal. Yet it helped me. Her description of nighttime in Tripoli's Old City left an indelible mark on me, and I anticipated that the new town poised to emerge in Beirut would do so with glittery evenings comparable to those in the New Town that had illuminated Grandmother's childhood after dark in that coastal city. All it would take for that to happen, I believed, were patience and optimism.

*

Only two people came to visit after we first moved into the small apartment in East Beirut. One was Umm Jamil, who surprised me with a big hug and a kiss on both cheeks, as if we'd known each other for years, though we had just met. The other was Abbas, the silkworm farmer from Sidon. I was stunned to see him here. Grandmother hadn't mentioned that he had returned to Lebanon as well. He shook my hand in greeting. Without a word to explain his appearance, he headed for the living room. He sank into the armchair with a sigh, as if months hadn't passed since he saw us off at Munich Airport.

As I eyed him from the doorway, speechless with surprise, he folded his hands across his belly and studied the picture on the opposite wall. It was an oil painting Grandmother had always owned. Framed, it was about two by three feet. Part of an exterior house wall was visible along the edge of the canvas, and in the middle was an apple tree in a meadow, a young woman sitting with her back leaned against the trunk. I knew that my mother had painted it. In France. Many years earlier. That's what Grandmother always told me; I would just nod and keep my questions to myself. The picture had hung opposite the couch in Germany too—it was the only sizable object she had brought back with us, and perhaps Abbas was recalling that as he waited for her to carry in the coffee tray.

"You good, Amin?"

"Yeah, I'm good."

"How's school?"

"It's Easter break."

"Really? Back in my day, we didn't get any vacation. School went all year round." He laughed, his belly shaking.

Countless visits would follow, but this was one of the only times he asked about my life or how I was. In Germany he had always launched into one tale or another, but now, after this brief exchange, he seemed at a loss. He got up after a minute and approached the picture, as if he had just noticed something. Then he mumbled an excuse and disappeared into the kitchen to join Grandmother.

Unlike Umm Jamil, who usually stayed late into the night, who helped me with homework or quizzed me in French vocab, and whose soft voice I could sometimes hear from my room as I was going to bed, the silkworm farmer—who started knocking at our door two or three times a week—was restless in a way that I didn't recognize from our time together in Germany. Sitting in our armchair, he would tap his foot, as if in time to a melody only he could hear. He couldn't keep his hands still and would slide his glass or fork around on the tabletop as he spoke. He pulled a handkerchief from his pocket and dabbed the sweat from his brow repeatedly, even when the ceiling fan was on high. He was always running his fingers through his beard, and his eyes wandered so much I got the feeling he wanted to commit every last corner and piece of furniture in the apartment to memory.

Since Abbas always stopped by unannounced, there were several occasions when Grandmother wasn't around and I had to sit there alone with him until she returned from shopping or whatever else she was doing.

"Why does he come here all the time?" I asked one day after he'd left.

She was putting away groceries in the kitchen and shrugged.

"That's how it is in Lebanon," was all she said. "Guests have a way of turning up for coffee when you're right in the middle of doing a thousand things."

Once when I was alone with Abbas, his gaze lingered on three bedsheets draped over a number of square objects on the floor and leaning against the wall.

"What's all that?"

I shrugged my shoulders. "Those are Teta's pictures."

"Pictures? Does that mean Yara's painting again?"

I nodded. She had indeed started painting again and installed herself in one corner of the living room. A week or two earlier she had come grunting through the door, an easel under one arm, and we set it up together by the living room window—the one window in the apartment that got enough light, even in late afternoon. I hadn't seen the pictures, since Grandmother covered them with sheets at night, and when I asked, she sternly reminded me that I would have a chance to see them at the exhibition she was planning.

Abbas furrowed his brow.

"That's interesting," he said. Then he leaned back in

the armchair, exhaled completely, and closed his eyes as if he'd forgotten I was in the room.

When school started up again, I told Jafar about the silkworm farmer and his weird behavior. I mentioned how rarely he stayed for dinner and that his visits were usually brief. I also thought it was weird how often he asked Grandmother how things were going at the café, though maybe he was just curious or trying to break the ice. One moment in particular had stuck with me: Abbas mentioned "business contacts" to her, then shot a glance at me. I was sitting on the couch with a book and pretended I hadn't heard.

In class a few days later, Jafar slipped me a note listing all the possible explanations:

Your grandma is a retired spy, SF is an Israeli agent hired to reactivate her
SF went insane the moment he returned to Lebanon
"Business contacts" = code for Neapolitan silkworm smugglers (armed & dangerous)
SF is a cocaine dealer. Stuffs his silkworms with drugs before shipping to regions south of the Nile
Your grandma's café is a drug hub
SF doesn't have any friends
SF is in love with your grandma
SF is your real father

Life gradually gained structure over the course of the spring. The more time passed, the busier things got. After school I often helped out in the café, where I was getting to know the regulars who came in to say hi to Grandmother or to sit and chat with her in the corner. Sometimes, people I had first seen at Café Yara would turn up at our apartment a few days later. They came unexpectedly and at unusual times of day. Each time I opened the door, the new arrivals would nod warmly or hug me, hang up their coats in the hall, and disappear into the living room, where the others, who'd been waiting, greeted them. Working at the café was like stumbling into a play where someone's sitting at the bar or a table in the corner, and you can't tell at first if they're just a customer or part of the cast. I came to assume that every person who crossed the threshold of the café would eventually appear on our doorstep, so I started paying closer attention to faces, just to be safe.

There were about twelve people who regularly stopped by that first spring. Men and women who introduced themselves as friends of Grandmother's, but whom she hadn't mentioned to me before, like Nadia, whose last name I never learned. She had supposedly been head costume designer at the Grand Théâtre before the war, an allegation she reinforced with anecdotes. Like the time she had tailored a coat for one of Nidal al-Achkar's roles, and the actress loved it so much she offered Nadia $2,000 for it. One evening, after polishing off a glass of arrack, her red lipstick lining the rim, Nadia told us a story about Grandmother as a young woman: she had once marched past the chain-smoking stagehands and through the catacombs of the Grand Théâtre and knocked on Dalida's dressing room door to thank the singer for her performance; Dalida had just brought the sold-out hall to its feet. Nadia told us how shocked Grandmother was, how she'd had to reach for a chair, when the famed diva set aside her hand mirror and stood to ask, "You're *the* Yara el-Maalouf? I own one of your paintings!"

I was in the corner paging through TV listings when Nadia told us this story, but I noticed the way Grandmother looked over at me, and I made a mental note to remember this particular anecdote.

Then there was a guy called Abu Amar, who introduced himself as an artist and told me he gathered toys, clothing, and other stuff the tide washed up on shore, and built sculptures or decorated trees with them. Abu Amar hobbled like a battered tin figurine, and one time, while the others were busy discussing something else, he leaned in and whispered, as if it were a secret, "My work explores the past, you know? I use things that went missing, then reappeared, returned by the sea. There's no escaping the past. It always catches up with us." He nodded warmly as he spoke, and I pretended to understand what he was trying to tell me.

Who were these people? Had Grandmother met them in years past, when she was still painting? It seemed unlikely in some cases; there were certain visitors to those evening gatherings who appeared to be meeting Grandmother and her guests for the first time. A woman from West Beirut, for instance, who—perhaps to avoid an awkward silence—quietly told us she hadn't been here in the eastern part of the city in nineteen years. I can still see Grandmother leaning over the table, reaching for her hand. The woman later left the apartment with Umm Jamil on her arm.

Recounting scenes from the café and our apartment can feel like reliving my own theater of the absurd, one in which widows, costume designers, and silkworm farmers grace the stage, and where a man called Abu Amar materializes and recites cryptic lines about the past. Although someone was missing: Abbas was never there in the evening. He tended to come around lunchtime and leave before the others arrived.

I usually sat quietly in the corner while the adults discussed everything imaginable, though things rarely grew heated. Reconstruction was a regular topic at these gatherings. Abu Amar was especially critical of rehabilitation projects in the destroyed city center.

"What about memory or historical legacy?" he asked one evening. "Everything about this building boom is wrong," he grumbled. "The city is 6,000 years old. Fragments from the Bronze Age are buried beneath its streets. Beirut has survived seven earthquakes and many wars, but today it's run by investors and construction managers. They drive their excavators through our neighborhoods and tear down anything found standing on valuable property. Take the fifties, for example, or the sixties. Back then, we liked hanging out in that part of the city. All of us."

Even the women from West Beirut nodded at this point.

Abu Abbas continued, "But now? Now it's all Armani, Rolex, Dior. They call that a modern reinterpretation of the old markets? It's nothing but a two-bit fantasy of the Orient aimed at tourists. None of us can afford to shop there ever again, let alone live there. I'm telling you, in no time the whole area will look like a corpse in makeup."

Murmurs of agreement.

"Everyone knows why *they're* anxious to tear the old buildings down."

To my surprise, it was Grandmother who said that.

No one responded, as if everyone really did know. Everyone, that is, except me.

They were all gathered in the living room that evening when I returned from our nerve-racking experience at the flea market, Younes Abboud's sketch under one arm. I peeked through a crack in the door, then slid the drawing under my bed, washed my face and hands, and took a seat in the corner, a little off to the side of the group.

They were discussing Samir Geagea, a figure whose background interested me. His story dominated headlines at the time. He was evidently a high-ranking militia commander during the war. He'd been arrested a few months earlier and charged with ordering an attack on a church, and now, while he stood trial, Geagea was stuck in a jail cell three floors underground at the Ministry of Defense.

"He'll get off," Nadia, the costume designer, said. "So many crimes were committed during the war, yet none of the perpetrators has ever had a thing to fear."

"Believe me, as long as the Syrians are here, those who don't side with them will have hell to pay." Abu Amar set down his drink and eyed the others over the top of his glasses. "You've all read about the arrests, haven't you? Geagea is now on trial, which I think is good, because whether he was involved in the church attack or not—he was, as you say, Nadia, one of countless criminals—he killed and opened new fronts along with the rest of them. It's bad news for his wartime followers, though. I heard that dozens have already been detained, most without the slightest pretext. The Syrians are shaping our country as they see fit. Welcome to the new Lebanon!" Abu Amar raised his glass, but no one followed suit.

Unfortunately, those evenings—which afforded me fleeting insight into these strangers' lives and opinions—came to an abrupt end for me. The very next day, Grandmother announced she no longer needed me at the café. She had spoken to a man looking for help with a special job and arranged that, for a few hours every night, I would be the one to provide that help. She assured me that the work would be fun and even earn me a little money. It was decided, despite my protestations, that I would no longer spend my evenings at home; instead, I would be working at the National Museum, where I met Saber Mounir, who I now believe was not entirely blameless for the series of events that would follow.

As I mentioned, many of the books I bought and collected back then have gone missing over the years. The old city maps are gone now, too, but I still have my notebooks. The notebook Grandmother gave me in Germany was the first of many, the start of a lifelong habit of writing everything down—everything for which I sought answers, everything that kept me up at night. The handwriting is hard to decipher on some pages, where I scribbled down single words and hasty sketches, the connection between the two difficult to deduce. I can no longer follow all of my earlier thoughts.

Several pages contain descriptions of the neighborhood, some so perfunctory they conjure few images. Others are so detailed I can see the spots clearly: the sandlots between ruins where we'd play soccer after school. The narrow alleys, lifelines that wound their way through the neighborhood, where the buildings were so close together you always knew who was watching TV and what channel, who was cooking or using the toilet, who was getting dressed up for dinner or fighting or making love. Other entries included the openings to stories I never finished or poems I never showed anyone. There are notes about my work at the

National Museum and Saber Mounir, whose favorite line was *I see wondrous things!* and whom I'll be coming back to. There are descriptions of life with Grandmother, like the day in Tripoli and other anecdotes or quirks I noticed and deemed significant.

I jotted down my thoughts about the girl at the flea market, things I wondered about her. I even attempted a pencil sketch of her face. Many pages are filled with notes about Jafar, too. About our experiences together, the nights in abandoned buildings, or descriptions of sun-drenched afternoons on the rocks along the coast. There are also pages dedicated to my parents: long letters outlining my day and commenting on the weather, like those written to people who are still alive.

I wrote in those little notebooks throughout my youth and later still, in 2006, when I moved into the house with the overgrown garden in the mountains, to escape the unremitting chaos in Beirut and other demons. My notes are my anchor now, as I recount those bygone years. Few are dated, so memories get mixed up. The chronology blurs and connections emerge that never existed. Some entries, however, *are* dated. One in particular I kept coming back to.

July 14, 1994 is printed at the top, as if to start a new journal entry, but it's just a note, circled and underlined several times.

Ask Jafar: who or what is L84/91?

Marcel Duchamp was adamant that his final piece, *Étant donnés*, be viewed exclusively through two peepholes in a door set in the gallery wall. This level of immersion was intended to awaken a childlike curiosity. At the moment of discovery, the artwork became a shared secret.

Paging through the notebooks blanketing the floor of my study is like peering through a hole in the door, only instead of an artwork behind it, there's the sense of a fairy tale, a sense that always seems to emerge when we look back on our childhood years later and reinterpret what we see. We all know the formula. Someone returns home from a faraway land to save the day. Seemingly peripheral characters appear without warning and disappear as suddenly, their significance not revealed until years later. There's someone hiding a secret and someone else trying to expose it. Ruthless overlords govern the land, and a touch of magic is in the air.

In the circus performance Jafar and I saw that day, I remember the magician summoning an audience member into the ring. He had the woman climb into a box that he had shown us was indestructible—no trapdoor in the bottom, no hidden mirrors. When he opened the box moments later, the woman was gone. On our way home, I started planning how to describe it to Grandmother. When I got there, though, our living room was full of people. What might she have said about my circus experience? She might have arched an eyebrow and asked me—after the guests had left—where I'd gotten the money for a ticket. Or instead she might have pulled me aside—in front of her guests—and patiently explained that there were far greater mysteries in this world, where the actual illusion wasn't the disappearance of the person; it was the belief that they would return. A magician, she would continue—and here too, I can't pin down her mood or tone of voice—a magician leads us to believe that a simple word or flourish can fix something that's been broken. Realistically, though, we always know it's a trick. Because in reality, the world remains broken, and the real magic is how people and things can vanish into thin air.

As I was saying, the moment I stepped into the café, I was immediately struck by a sense of focus in the room. I knew many of the people who had come to the opening. Abu Amar was there. Nadia, the costume designer. Several of the widows from West Beirut. Umm Jamil was also among the guests. She saw me, raised her hand to hip level, and waved discreetly. I mirrored the gesture. Even Abbas was there, standing in the cluster of people by the wall of pictures. His head was tilted, as if a heavy weight were attached to one ear.

I carefully squeezed past the bodies till I reached the front, feeling Grandmother's gaze behind me. I was truly surprised. Hadn't she told me her early paintings were of ships? Ships and chance observations of everyday life? These pictures didn't depict anything concrete. There was something chaotic, even violent, about them. What Grandmother had painted looked like a confluence of storms, myriad splashes of color flung at the canvas in a fury. Most surprising, though, were the names written on little cards thumbtacked to the wall. The paintings were named after countries: *Argentina. Cypress. Chad. Chile. Guatemala. El Salvador. Nepal.* They were arranged around one piece that seemed to define the center, like a fixed star, around which the others orbited.

It was a painting of nothing. Nothing but a white void.

The card below read: *L84/91.*

Hakawati

For much of the war, the crossing point outside the National Museum was the only way to get from one sector of the divided city to the other. Grandmother told me that. She described it as a heavily guarded zone controlled on either side by enemy militias who could quicken the city's pulse or bring it to a standstill with the wave of a gun barrel. Aid was smuggled through here after air raids, and Grandmother said that banks with branches in both parts of the city would even send employees to the crossing point at designated times to exchange in-house mail. Here, in the heart of Beirut, drivers were routinely forced out of their cars and interrogated. There were attacks and gun battles. The National Museum, one of the Mediterranean region's most hallowed institutions before the war, was located in the eye of the storm and sustained extensive damage over the years.

Stepping into the welcoming darkness of the museum, out of the summer evening sun, felt like entering a cave: earthy smells and muted light, echoes and hidden treasure. There were signs of destruction everywhere you looked, as if the war had ended just days earlier. Parts of the ceiling in the main hall had collapsed, forming towering heaps of rubble. Dripping pipes jutted out of walls, and the doors to the underground vaults were sealed off with stone blocks, like ancient tombs. Shortly after the war began, museum administration had many important artifacts moved underground or encased in reinforced concrete where they stood, to guard against theft or destruction.

By the time I started there, the corridors were alive with activity. Amid the ceaseless rumble of wheeled carts, men in security vests hurried this way and that; pickaxes struck concrete and orders were bellowed over the crunch of detritus, while workers armed with paintbrushes carefully uncovered mosaics or cleaned bronze busts with compressed air.

Contrary to what Grandmother had said, there didn't seem to be any obvious job for me, or even a contact person. I didn't know the guy she had supposedly made this arrangement with. My name was just on a list of volunteers, and whoever the shift leader was assigned me a new task each time. The first evening, Grandmother walked me to the bus stop near our house. She handed me a bag with two sandwiches and told me where to get off. A short time later, I was standing on a ladder in the main hall, broom in hand, clearing dirt off the pillars that supported the second story.

Suddenly I was making money. Not much, but it was the first time I had ever earned my own money without having to invent a story first. *Financially independent*, Jafar called it. He said it a lot: *Now you're financially independent.*

At the end of my first week, he and I went to Luna Park and I bought us a ton of candy. Then we rode the Ferris wheel and listened to the sound of the waves in the dark. We felt rich and happy. The museum was a new world to me, as if I had stepped through an enchanted mirror—like someone in a Jean Cocteau film —and into an unfamiliar room. Every day, I would feel my way forward, discover something new, and hang on tight. And although my tasks were rarely physically strenuous, I would collapse into bed late at night, after a quick wash, and the day's impressions would distill into wild dreams in which I did things of tremendous importance.

One evening, the shift leader unlocked a set of creaky double doors. There in front of me, illuminated by the moon alone, was a vast library. Upwards of seventeen thousand books had burned here after a grenade explosion. The fire raged for nine hours. The metal shelving melted into grotesque sculptures, soot particles sketched shadowy figures on the walls, and every last surface, it seemed, was coated in ash. The space appeared distorted, somehow thrown off-kilter. I will never forget that sight. At some point while sweeping up the charred remains of books, I noticed a man on the other side of the room, half-concealed in darkness. Bony frame. Silvery hair. The hint of a haggard face. I saw his hands, the fabric of his coat. He was on his knees, trailing his fingers through the ash and letting it fall from his loose fist, as if trying to grasp the remains of a lost treasure. I stared into the darkness. Took a few steps closer. He didn't appear to notice me. I heard him murmuring something. A prayer, or a story.

"That's Saber Mounir," the shift leader told me later when I asked about the man. "He ran the library till the museum was forced to close."

During breaks, the workers would sometimes discuss the hostages we kept hearing about on the radio. People who had been abducted during the war were turning up again. They'd been held captive in buildings like the ones Jafar and I explored at night. I saw them appear before journalists on TV and in newspapers, exhausted and blinded by the flash of cameras. Thousands of people from all walks of life had been seized, and just like the statues being freed from the caved-in vaults, some of those kidnapped during the war were catching their first glimpse of daylight after years of darkness.

When I had a few minutes, until someone needed help and called for me again, I often wandered around the building, unnoticed by busy workers, among the countless sculptures. Stony strangers with missing limbs gazing down on me. If no one was looking, I would stretch out a finger and touch them. And if there wasn't a plaque, I'd name them after the rescued people on the news.

The evenings in the museum provided me with a new kind of freedom: I could drift through the rooms as if walking a timeline through the centuries. It was how I first came to realize that this country, too, had a history. As a city, Beirut had always seemed uninterested in its past. A metropolis in which nothing mattered but the future. Cranes, houses clad in scaffolding, and advertising posters drove that message home. Despite its visual traces, history was like a mute beggar woman standing on the side of the road, whom you see but ignore in shame. In the charged atmosphere inside the National Museum, however, history was a queen ascending her throne. There was a holiness to each moment another piece of her former realm was liberated from its subterranean confines and brought back into the light.

Over time I discovered that many of the men could read a bucket of rubble as one might a mysterious, encrypted text. In what I saw as dirt and old scraps, they saw bygone lives. *Thermoluminescence dating, potassium-argon dating, dendrochronology*—the words they used at work were like magic spells that enabled them to deduce social processes from a copper hairpin or reconstruct burial rituals and cult worship sites from an arrangement of boulders. Witnessing these objects come to life as the men talked about them amazed me to no end. As I watched the men bent over shards and fragments, jotting down theories about buried cities and cultures, dates and names, the rooms of the museum came to feel like chambers of a brain whose sole function was remembrance.

Sometimes I'd pretend to be a famous archaeologist myself. When the men returned to work after breaks, I surveyed where they'd been sitting for evidence. Traces they'd left behind: three empty coffee cups, four cigarette butts, two balled-up tissues, an empty pack of chewing gum, a book in French about the dating of antique ceramic vases, one rubber glove. I lined it all up and pondered what the objects might reveal to future scientists about those brief gatherings. There's no denying that the museum excited my imagination.

During another shift, I had some free time so I compiled a list of possible places Jafar's lost eye might be found:

Seeing the world, currently in the Andes
Blindsided while circumnavigating the globe
In cahoots with silkworm smugglers—turning a blind eye
    to corruption
At Copacabana, feasting its eye on Brazilian beauties
Floating in a jar of formaldehyde in a mad scientist's lab
Playing chess in Helsinki, keeping an eye on the prize
Still in the operating room at St. George Hospital

"Very funny. Doesn't seem this job is doing you much good," he said when I showed him my list the next day.

I never tired of those evenings at the museum, in part because Jafar had less time on his hands; after the nasty look our teacher had given him while handing out report cards, Jafar was now expected home earlier. And there's no question my enthusiasm for the job was stoked by the three dead bodies discovered in one of the vaults, an event I was lucky enough to witness just two days in. Six men carried them into the main hall on stretchers. The entire crew gathered around and removed their helmets out of respect. I copied the gesture. For a minute I thought they were casualties of the civil war, until someone announced they were mummified bodies from the thirteenth century that had been stored downstairs in a specially air-conditioned chamber. Actually, the same man explained to me later on, mummification had never been practiced in Lebanon. These individuals had been found in Ouadi Qadisha, the Holy Valley, where the arid climate had preserved them. They had been clothed in those very garments, the fabric a blend of cotton and silk. A woman and two children. The mummies were carried off and the crew got back to work, while I assumed every evening would have a discovery like that in store.

When I got home after that second shift, around 10 p.m., I wanted to tell Grandmother what I had seen, down to the last detail, but she wasn't there and didn't return till after I was asleep. The dirty drinking glasses in the kitchen, though, told me there had been guests.

I still thought of the girl a lot, usually as I lay in bed after work, exhausted but too riled up to sleep. Some nights, I imagined telling her about the museum. About the crew or my experiences in the library. Although I often returned to the memory of standing near her, I realized I could barely picture her face. I knew I was losing details as time passed. I would think of the skin of her neck, the archipelago of beauty marks, and her eyes. When I recalled the way she had looked at me, it actually felt like I missed her. There was a tugging sensation around my stomach somewhere that triggered an unfamiliar restlessness in me. I took an aspirin, just to be safe, because it felt a little like I was coming down with something.

It was easiest to reawaken my memory of the day we met by taking the drawing of the circus tent out from under my bed and poring over it. The accuracy with which the young man had rendered it was astounding. The picture was so vivid, despite being in black and white. It was teeming with fascinating figures involved with one another in various scenes. To my surprise, I kept discovering new details where I least expected them. The coins the dwarves held pinched between their fingers, for instance, bore the emblem of a castle with twin turrets and falcons circling overhead. The same insignia could be found on the breast pocket of the fire-breather's vest, and then I spotted it again, this time appearing as a tattoo on a merchant's bicep. The drawing was a source of endless wonder and secrecy, full of codes and ciphers just waiting to be solved, like the symbols found on vases and mosaics at the museum. I often took it to bed with me and imagined it was a portal that could transport me back to the market, merely by looking at it. To that very spot on that very day. In these heroic fantasies, I seized the girl by the hand the instant our eyes met, and off we dashed, leaving a cloud of dust in our wake.

*

"Did you bring it?" Jafar asked.

"Yeah," I said.

"Okay, then let's see."

We were sitting on the top floor of a ruin, looking out over the neighborhood. I had gotten us three bags of chips, some pretzels, and four cans of 7UP at Hamit Malik's shop, and the bags rustled in the wind. In a display of absurd recklessness, we dangled our legs over the edge. It was early evening and already getting dark.

"What do you need it for?" I asked, handing Jafar the atlas. I had bought the book a few months earlier at a local junk shop, along with a discolored globe that lit up when you plugged it in.

Jafar took the atlas and flipped through it.

"Coordinates," he murmured. Then louder, he said, "It could be coordinates, don't you think?"

"Maybe, but what for? And how would the people at the exhibition know that?"

"That's what we're going to find out."

The area far below our feet had been a yard once. Now it was mostly filled with trash: busted sofas, broken shelving, and stained mattresses. Apple trees gave off a rotten, sweet smell.

Jafar and I had gone back to the café a few days earlier on some pretext or other. We'd stolen glances at the walls as we sipped our tea and Jafar jotted down the names of the paintings. That list now rested in his lap.

"Ever heard of someone named Dalida?" I asked as he continued to scour the pages of the atlas.

"Everyone's heard of her."

"Not me."

"Famous singer," he mumbled. "Once real pretty, now real old."

"She bought one of my teta's pictures."

"Really? One of these?" He held up the list of country names and waved it in my face.

"No," I said. "A long time ago."

"Good for her," Jafar said, but he had turned his attention back to whatever was on his mind. "L84/91," he finally muttered, trailing his finger down the atlas register. The tome contained colorful topographic maps, renderings of physical and political continents, ocean maps with depth readings, social statistics for certain big cities, and landscape zones in different continents and subcontinents.

"So what do you think the country names could mean?" I asked after a while.

"Hm?"

"The names she gave the pictures."

"Maybe places she's been on vacation?"

"My teta has never been to Nepal. Or Guatemala."

"You sure?"

I shook my head. The streetlights had turned on below, a dull orange gleam in the alleys. Cars rumbled over potholes in the street. Someone opened a window and a trash bag soared onto the sidewalk.

"No."

"Could it be places she wants to visit?"

"I doubt it," I said.

"Maybe it's honeymoon destinations for her and the silkworm farmer."

"Shut your trap."

"Or maybe it's where her 'business contacts' live," he said, forming air quotes around the words.

"What is up with these paintings?" I spat.

"Calling them 'paintings' is generous," Jafar said. "No offense, but I'd say either your grandma can't paint, or Dalida has terrible taste. Why not just ask her what it all means?"

"I already tried." And I had. The night of the opening, late, after all the guests had gone.

"And what'd she say?"

"She said, 'An artist doesn't discuss her work. It behooves the viewer to reach his own conclusions.'"

"People who say stuff like 'behooves' give me the creeps," Jafar said, leaning his good eye toward the open atlas.

The circus had left town a few days earlier. Where the tent once stood was now an empty square in the distance. Posters announcing its arrival were still plastered on traffic lights and bridges.

"I've got it." Jafar had opened to the spread in the middle of the atlas. Depicted there was the entire world, bound in lines of latitude and longitude. The tangle of lines confounded me. Jafar, though, ran along them with a pencil, like he was looking for something. He was concentrating so hard, the tip of his tongue peeked out between his lips.

"I think we've got a code on our hands," he concluded confidently. "L84/91. If we assume the L stands for *latitude* or *longitude*, then the numbers could be coordinates."

I looked at him in confusion, but he was already counting lines from left to right in the northern hemisphere. He marked a spot, then did the same thing on the eastern side with the lines that ran from top to bottom. "Eighty-four degrees north by ninety-one degrees east," he finally said.

The lines crossed at a point in the Arctic Ocean.

"Maybe a shipwreck?" Jafar asked with a shrug.

"Or an unmarked island?"

"Or a secret underwater lab for breeding aquatic drug-smuggling silkworms."

"Where'd you learn how to do that?"

"What, maritime espionage?"

"No, that," I said, gesturing toward the atlas.

He looked at the dot in the middle of the ocean. It took him a minute to respond. He spoke softly and didn't look up.

"During bombings my mom would sit and look through the atlas with us. With my sister and me. Sometimes we had to be quick, and there wasn't time to grab games or warm blankets for the basement, but the atlas was always right there by the door. 'The world's our oyster,' we'd say as we opened it. When we were down there, each of us would choose a number between 0 and 180, along with a cardinal direction. It was like a random generator for destinations we'd imagine visiting. We came up with so much stuff: The names of people who lived there. The names of our new schools and teachers. Or we memorized the rivers that flowed through these places: Usamacinta, Orinoco, Irrawaddy, Zambezi, Ganges, Kenai—I still remember them all. 'I'm building a zoo on the Zambezi,' my sister Soraya might say. 'I'm building a zoo on the Zambezi and feeding zucchini, zwieback, and ziti to my pet zebra, Zora.' That was the game, and we'd play it for hours. When the worst was over, the atlas would go back upstairs with us and next to the door."

Lights in the windows of new high-rises twinkled in the distance, presumably a sign of the many dinner parties being held there at vertiginous heights, with a gentle breeze and view of the sea. I suddenly felt cold, though it was still summer.

"I have to leave soon for work," I said.

Jafar cleared his throat.

"Hang on a sec. We have one more try." He looked at the world map and twirled the pencil between his fingers. "Eighty-four degrees south by ninety-one degrees west." He applied the same technique, counting off again, only swapping the values this time. Where he landed was a gray spot in the southern hemisphere that rose from a white background. White like the picture at the center of Grandmother's exhibit.

I leaned over and studied the marking and location. A snowy wasteland in the heart of Antarctica. Not a city or settlement for miles. Not a trace of human life.

I was sitting in my room late at night when Grandmother got home. She usually came in to see me first thing, but I heard her bustle around awhile before she knocked on my door. She told me there had been an incident at the café.

"Have you eaten?"

"Yeah."

"Are you sure?" She arched an eyebrow. "The fridge was bare."

"Bought something on my way home."

She stood in the doorway and looked around. Pens and open books lay scattered on the floor. Then she nodded, as if she'd forgotten I received my meager pay at the end of the week. I waited, giving her time to ask how things were going at the museum, but she appeared lost in thought.

"So, what was the incident?" I eventually asked.

"What? Oh, nothing major. You know Mara, of course, the girl who helps out. She cut her finger."

"Really? Was it bad?"

"Quite. Are you okay, Amin? You look tired."

"I'm fine," I answered, though perhaps too quickly, too defiantly, because she eyed me warily.

"With a knife?" I tried to sound as casual as possible, but Grandmother arched both eyebrows in apparent amusement.

"Why so curious?"

"You said the cut was pretty deep, so—was it a big knife?"

"You're being awfully weird today," she said.

"Did you have to call the doctor?"

"No, we have a first-aid kit at the café. You know that."

"So she didn't need stitches."

"No ... I mean ... maybe." She waved her hand as if shooing a fly. "I drove Mara to the doctor, but she didn't want me to wait. What's gotten into you?"

Did she sense my desire to check her story for inconsistencies, like a false alibi? To detect an error that proved her guilt—whatever that error may be? Could she sense my mistrust? I was certain she could and felt annoyed at my own transparency.

She stood there a little while longer, as though considering whether to enter the room. Then she knocked on the doorjamb, turned to leave, and said, "I'll make us something to eat."

The next day I went to the café and peered in the big front window. Only a few people were there. The silkworm farmer sat at the counter with another man. They sipped their drinks. Grandmother was nowhere to be seen, but Mara was waiting on some customers, and there on her ring finger was a bandage.

The weeks passed, and despite the stories Grandmother occasionally shared with me, granting me insight into her daily routine and mood, I couldn't shake the feeling that we were coexisting rather than actually living together. The more Grandmother settled into her new life, the less of her I saw. This level of activity was another unknown side of her. She had rarely left the apartment in Germany; I would often take my sweet time walking home from the bus stop after school—kicking pebbles or chestnuts down the street, stopping to chat with the neighbors—because I feared opening the door to our apartment and finding it cold and quiet, with Grandmother still in her pajamas with messy hair starting at the sight of me. I suddenly found myself of two minds: though I certainly didn't want the old version back, I was leery of this New Her. It seemed she was hurrying toward a life in which my presence was more of a burden to her than a joy.

When I came home from the museum at night, I'd often find dirty dishes on the kitchen counter, far more than a single person could have used. Or the dishes were clean, but the air was thick with the smell of recently extinguished hookah, which she certainly hadn't smoked on her own. Sometimes there would be a note on the table—*Food in the fridge*—and I'd open the refrigerator to find dozens of little bowls filled with the leftovers of whatever Grandmother's guests had brought. I tried to play down my displeasure. Told myself I was doing important work and earning my own money, that I was independent, and so on. But I felt excluded.

Our everyday life together had always allowed for more freedom, with fewer structures in place than in families with parents, but after I became convinced she was hiding something, using codes, it seemed as if our last remaining ties were loosening. In response, my behavior became contradictory: I was defiant and surly on some days, questioning everything she said, then clingy on others, seeking a lost closeness.

Today I believe that working at the museum also taught me to examine things more carefully and in some cases search for answers before a question even formed. I still couldn't say, though, whether she got me that job to get me out of the house at night, or if she was trying—in her own way—to point me more or less gently in a certain direction, to ensure that I learned firsthand what it meant to dig up the past.

*

Myth is the greatest of all truths.

One of the many maxims Saber Mounir passed on to me. Not long after the first evening I saw him stooped over the ashes, I began to seek out his presence. I wanted to find out what he was doing there—why he would show up at the museum two, three times a week, stride across the bustling main hall, and disappear behind the heavy double doors. As soon as I saw him coming, I would grab the broom and dustpan from the wall and begin sweeping at a snail's pace while peering over at him. Time and again, I saw him scoop up the ash and let it sift through his fingers. An odd ritual. Then he'd stare at his palms for minutes on end, as if there were a message to be found there. He never looked at me, but kept huddled in the shadows. Sometimes his murmuring was all I could discern. It went on like that for a while. I didn't dare approach him; it was as if we each had our designated turf, as if the room contained boundary lines only we could sense. We inched closer over time, till we stood face to face one evening in the middle of the library. The moonlight was like an arrow in the darkness. There was something silvery about Saber Mounir. Silvery hair, silvery skin, and a silvery gaze. As if the hours he'd spent in this room made him glow. I finally mustered the courage to address him.

"What do you do here?"

"I read."

"You read? But almost everything was burned up."

"Those were the shells. The stories are still being told."

"I don't see any stories around here. It's all ash."

"You have to look carefully." He smiled. "I see wondrous things."

It turned out stories and memories really did come to life through Saber Mounir. In a way, the man himself was a trove of secrets. The past became the present when he spoke, images rising like a mirage. His stories transformed the library back into a bright, undamaged room and shaped pages out of the ashes, books out of those pages. He spoke of this place as if it were a living thing, and suddenly every sensory experience came alive too: the peppery smell of paper and leather, the industrious hush accompanied by the turning of pages; polite whispering and someone clearing their throat.

"There used to be a clock hanging on the wall there," he said, pointing at a jagged hole below the vaulted ceiling, where the grenade had detonated. A gaping wound. Saber Mounir told me to get on my knees and run my hands through the ashes. He then instructed me to look at what was left on my palms. A handful of words. Recorded countless years ago on papyrus or animal hides.

... woven ...
... vision ...
in all its zones
mortal
... untold time ...

Some silenced grievance.

"It's an old language made even more beautiful, in a way, by the fire," Saber Mounir said.

"I see more empty spaces than words."

"Precisely."

"But if there are words missing, what's beautiful about it?"

He fell silent and looked at the scraps in my hand. The light that came in through the hole in the wall was advancing steadily across the floor.

"Before they were damaged, these poems were far less accessible to us," he said. "They may have been dazzling works at one point, but today they'd have less impact on us. They were special because they were old. Those who say the fire damaged these texts can't see past the surface. To be sure, as intact objects they are lost to us forever, but here's the thing: the space between the surviving words is an open invitation to fill it with imagination."

I loved the evenings with Saber Mounir. I had never heard anyone tell such vivid stories before. I soon realized he wasn't searching for anything in particular, but that these ruins provided him a space for reflection. If there was one thing I'd learned since our return to Lebanon, it was that the war had created a chasm for most people. There was their life before and their life after. Saber Mounir, though, seemed to view the library as a link connecting these two lives.

He told me he was born in Damascus and came to Lebanon as a teenager. From childhood, Saber Mounir recalled the smell of the shoes his parents would burn in winter to heat their apartment on the outskirts of Damascus because they could afford neither wood nor coal. They crowded around the fire with him and his five siblings. He also remembered the air after summer storms. Swarms of insects and white pollen hovered over the gardens; it drifted about like snowflakes that he followed here and there, at four or five years old. He would later enter the golden universe of cafés, where the aroma of cardamom mixed with the many odors of the many people who had squeezed in to escape a storm. There he sat quietly in a corner, listening to the storytellers on their platforms.

Hakawati.

It sounded like another magic spell the first time Saber Mounir uttered the word. He recalled that as a child, he'd wanted to learn all he could about these men. Who they were. Where they came from. Where they went after they finished telling a story and where on earth they discovered these tales. He told me how much he had loved those evenings and how much he'd hated it when his parents found him and dragged him home, just as the stories were reaching their climax.

Heyaka—story.

Wati—mastery of a form of street art.

Hakawati—a street artist who tells stories.

"The hakawati tradition is very old," he told me one evening. He had locked the door to the library behind us, as if there were a secret in there that needed protecting. "A long, long time ago, a hakawati was a prominent figure in his country, second only to the king or president. From Beirut to Damascus, Cairo to Isfahan, people would flock to cafés, marketplaces, and public squares to hear a hakawati share tales of adventure. In the olden days, people would even consult a hakawati about their problems. He'd then tell them a story, as a kind of parable."

We sat facing each other in the dark, our backs leaned against what was left of the bookshelves. I absorbed every last word with heightened senses.

"Hakawatis are masters of seduction. They assume the role of various figures, play with accents and dialects, bring their characters to life. And when the suspense is at its breaking point, they stop for the day and go home."

"Just like that?"

"Just like that. It's a trick. Listeners become addicted. According to legend, Ahmad al-Saidawi, one of the eighteenth century's most famous hakawatis, told one story in a café in Aleppo that lasted 372 nights and was so suspenseful that the governor himself begged al-Saidawi to cut it short, because he was desperate to hear how it ended."

"Three hundred seventy-two," I marveled.

What I also loved about the hours spent with Saber Mounir was how much older he made me feel. His memories were gateways to vast empires that were mine to discover. I don't know if he actually intended all his stories for me, or if he was simply reminiscing about his younger self in my presence. It may not have made any difference to him. Either way, he allowed me to venture for the first time into the unknown world of grown-ups. Saber Mounir had come to Beirut at age eighteen with no belongings and barely any money.

He had wanted to become a hakawati, and this city—with its cafés and dance halls, jazz clubs and neon signs, intrigue, rumors, and intersecting stories—had seemed the place to do it, caught as it was in a state of flux, even back then. His memories were so vivid! The smell of jasmine that infused his first liaison in the hushed garden of an old house. The girl's pale skin in the moonlight, her excited breath in his ear, her hand on his back, and the way she smoothed out her dress later and vanished between the hedges. He wandered the streets. The dance of colors on building facades along the harbor. The sound of piano coming from hotel bars. Couples kissing in corners of nightclubs, half-illuminated. He saw his reflection in café windows. He ran his finger along the job ads in the newspaper, got hired, then fired, because he'd lose track of time reading during breaks. He reenacted his employers' tirades as they kicked him to the curb, his exaggerated gestures and funny accents making me laugh.

Saber Mounir made a name for himself. He became a storyteller. First in small cafés, all very traditional, but eventually even top hotels would book him as an Oriental attraction for weddings and birthdays. He had finally made it. The coins lining the bottom of his hat by the end of the day were enough for him to get by.

"The job at the museum library," he said, winking at me, "was an added bonus."

"What happened to the girl?" My cheeks were glowing, and I hoped he wouldn't notice in the moth-gray gloom.

"There was something about her I couldn't fully grasp."

"Like an arrangement of beauty marks that can't be described?"

"She had a small scar above her collarbone. She was very aware of it there, felt it threw off the symmetry of her naked body, so she always wore a scarf, even in summer."

I was dumbstruck by the image that emerged before my eyes.

"What happened to her?"

"We lost sight of each other."

"Us too."

Alone in the stacks once, I scooped up a handful of paper shreds from the floor and put the words in order. It seemed to me the best method for remembering the girl. Blank spaces. Unredeemed promises. I didn't even know her name.

not a
ghost light
... in sight.
... remembering
our ... till
I ...
... you
or ... drifted away
...
find
still life.

Then I got back to work. I scrubbed and mopped the back area of the library, soap flakes sudsing and spreading across the floor. I was going to show Saber Mounir the fragment, but when I saw him enter the double doors a little later, I quickly destroyed the composition.

Today it seems odd not to have realized how much I

was learning till much later. Like kids figuring out how to cross the street by observing and imitating adults. I felt comfortable around Saber Mounir, even cared for, but intimidated too, which meant I absorbed a lot of what he said with some reservation. I can remember times when—despite long talks the night before—we maintained a certain distance the next day, as if we were strangers, and I wouldn't be surprised if he occasionally misinterpreted my coolness. My silence was not born of a wish to be alone, though; it reflected my insecurity and feeling of insignificance in the face of his words.

"What did you do during the war?"

I had mustered all my courage to ask Saber Mounir this question.

"When they closed the museum after all the attacks, I returned to Damascus," he said.

"I heard lots of people went to Syria."

"Yes, to Syria and around the world. Anywhere was safer than here."

I remembered the letter Jafar had found in one of the buildings. *Songbirds and bitter orange trees.*

"So why did you come back? To Beirut, I mean."

"I wanted to see it with my own eyes."

"The library?"

"All of it. Whatever remained."

He pulled an apple from his pocket and sliced it into small, red-rimmed crescent moons that he shared with me. We sat there and eyed each other.

"Beirut was no place for us traditional storytellers, and hadn't been for a long time." He shook his head as if trying to dispel a thought. "The war wrote its own stories. The new hakawatis wore balaclavas and carried guns. Theirs were tales of invasion, mighty weapons, martyrs, and the power of wrong information delivered at the right time. Besides, there weren't any public spaces left suited to the old storytelling. Life retreated into the home. It wasn't just the war, though. The true art of the hakawatis had been in decline for some time."

The word *decline* called to mind the slow disappearance of an entire civilization.

"With the advent of radio, followed by film and later TV, our tradition slowly began to die out. By the time I started, it had already changed from what it once was. New media introduced new options. Stories could be told in countless different ways and spread more quickly, now they were easier to access. Few remembered us. We sort of fell out of fashion."

He looked around. Little piles of ash in the corners. A broom leaned against the wall. The remains of shelves. The moonlight. As though everything in this room had meaning.

"People hardly ever tell me about the war," I said.

"Because this city is a ship, Amin. The old ship of Beirut. The principle keeping it afloat is repression."

"All the destroyed buildings are being torn down, though. Soon there won't be anything left to remind people of the war."

"There will be stories."

"There already are." I turned an apple slice between my fingers. "But which ones are true?"

"None of them," he said. "And all of them."

The skin on his face was rough and wrinkly like crumpled paper. The sounds that reached us in here were muted: cars that could once again move freely between East Beirut and West, invisible to us outside these towering walls. Muffled voices and the clamor of tools from the main hall. Saber Mounir had closed his eyes.

"She was the daughter of a lute maker," he whispered.

"Excuse me?"

"The girl. You asked about her. After losing her, for years I would find her everywhere I looked. Her face reflected in puddles and shop windows. Her shadow in photos of other women. I heard her on every street corner and radio station. And in couples' murmured exchanges on park benches. Always and everywhere.

"She would sometimes bring along a lute when we met up. Then she would sing. Quietly, so no one would detect us. Her father had forbidden her from playing his lutes. I pictured her sneaking into his workshop after our meetings and secretly returning the instrument to its display case. We always met in secluded spots. A barn, a sweeping meadow, the banks of a river. I don't recall the melodies, but I remember how they soothed me and how her dress slipped off her shoulder as she positioned the lute. She held the instrument backwards, strumming with her left hand, as if she were determined to play it differently than her father ever would. I wanted to touch her, but wasn't allowed— not when she was playing.

"The scar on her shoulder looked like a border, the way they appear on maps. She was sometimes shy with me, sometimes unrestrained. Sometimes open, sometimes withdrawn. She never asked to hear a story. As if my storytelling might invite deception. She seemed afraid of that. Clandestine kisses and moonlit conversations. We waded into the river once and she talked about running away together. I said I had only just gotten here. Later on, we lay on the shore and I remember how her foot twitched in that narrow no-man's-land between sleepiness and sleep. She would always fall asleep on me, and when I awoke, she was gone. I lay in bed later with the window open, trying to recall her smell, which was as ephemeral as her songs, and wondering if she'd turn up at the next meeting spot we'd arranged. She kept coming until one day she stopped."

He opened his eyes and blinked rapidly, as though surprised to discover me beside him. For a while we didn't speak. Just looked at each other.

"Do you understand why I'm telling you this, Amin?" he finally asked.

"I don't know ..."

"Stories," he said, "cannot recover that which has been lost. But they can allow others to experience it."

*

In the waters near the port city of Sasebo, a Japanese torpedo boat capsizes during target practice in stormy weather. At the summit of Mount Washington, New Hampshire, the fastest-ever wind gust on the surface of the earth is recorded: 231 miles per hour. At the same time, elsewhere in the United States, an unusual disruption to wind patterns in the Midwest occurs: a high over the Great Plains is blocking the yearly low-level jet stream in its regular northward course. Instead, dust storms approach, the worst of the century. The storms displace farmers, kill their livestock, carry millions of tons of virgin soil into the ocean, and transform vast expanses of cropland into wasteland. 1934. The year my grandmother is born the daughter of a dyer in Tripoli, northern Lebanon. Three brothers, one sister, and a house in the old city sheltered from the wind.

There are no wind reports remaining from 1948 when

she, as a fourteen-year-old, secretly painted her first picture from the corniche. Unsettled as the world was, then as now, the archives make no mention of catastrophic storms that year. As I imagine it, the sea off the coast of Tripoli couldn't make up its mind that day. Somewhere beyond the ships the girl was painting, there must have been rough wind on the water. Wind no one saw and no one noted.

And your father never found out?

No, no, he did. Eventually. But that's another story.

In 1950, when she's sixteen, her father discovers she's been painting. A smudge of paint on her apron that she missed doing laundry. She invents an excuse, says she was in the dyeworks looking for him—*I must have bumped into one of the furs,* she says, but he knows she's lying. He's a respected man in Tripoli, but he's not the only dyer, nor is he the best. He's reliable, though, and delivers on time. Everything hinges on his untainted reputation. He beats and kicks the girl, breaking a rib. Her body sinks against the wall, then he locks the door to her room and won't even let her mother in to see her. *She wants to be an artist!* she hears him rage, crashing about the house, while she can barely breathe. *An artist!*

Grandmother told me his name once: Soufjen, which means *like the wind.* In researching a story many years later, I discovered that 1950 was the first year they started naming hurricanes.

She told me all of this one afternoon in August. A rain shower had just passed, and we were walking down a street lined with dripping linden trees. I remember it so well because I hadn't even asked her about it. She just started sharing, unsolicited. She barreled through the years. Half a life in just a few sentences. The tumult of her youth. After checking to ensure no one was watching, she even lifted the hem of her sweater to show me a bump on her torso where the rib hadn't healed right. *His name was Soufjen.*

To her father it was the worst catastrophe imaginable: the family honor, dragged through the dirt by his own daughter. She had dared to stand alone on the seashore, like a whore. He had already arranged a marriage for her, but now the man reneged, which magnified the shame. From then on, whenever company came, she was hidden away in her room, and she could only leave the house accompanied by one of her brothers.

After two years, despair gave her the courage she needed to run away. At daybreak, her mother slipped her a bundle of money and closed the door behind her. She went to Beirut, the same place Saber Mounir had gone to seek his fortune as a young man. She described the city to me in similar terms: sophisticated, elegant, wicked, pulsating. A river she let whisk her away. Conduct that, in the Tripoli of her childhood, had been reserved exclusively for Mandate Nights was the norm here in the capital city, which saw no difference between night and day. People from around the world flocked to the Paris of the Middle East. Whenever asked where she was from or where she lived, she would create a new version of herself, inventing names and personal experiences. She blocked out her past.

In this city of seekers, nothing could be simpler than working odd jobs and meeting people. She met the man who would become my grandfather as he handed her his overcoat. At the time, she'd been working for several weeks in the coat check at the Grand Théâtre, where moneyed patrons left good tips. She described Amin el-Maalouf as a generous giver of flowers, writer of impassioned letters, and gallant suitor. There was one show he attended six times, just to see her again. One evening, long after the performance had ended, she was headed home and discovered him sitting on the steps outside the theater.

After a few brief, shy conversations and dinner at one of the city's finest restaurants, he brought her over to his side. He bought her a coat, too, and together they watched a celebrated performance by the Comédie-Française from one of the boxes. Their seats were directly beneath the magnificent glass dome. The noble architecture. The clarity of the acoustics. Afterward he took her backstage. He showed her the fog machines, the metal sheets used for thunder, the backdrops and props—all instruments of illusion. He freed his Yara from the world of regular theatergoers, who would never see these things. He led her through the rigging into narrow subterranean passages that led to the greenrooms, where he introduced her to the actors milling about and smoking.

Amin el-Maalouf, my grandfather, the man I have to thank for my first name, was high up at Intra Bank—the largest financial institute in the region—but as conversant in the world of art as he was in that of numbers. He opened doors for her. And he loved the way she painted. He secured her a small show at the Joseph Matar Gallery and invited journalists and friends to attend. He impressed the young woman. And when he requested to meet her father, as he wished to ask for her hand, she told him he was dead. A few months after the wedding, he bought them a house in the mountains. A house with an overgrown garden.

"Will you show me the house at some point?"

"You'll see it eventually."

I've never forgotten that afternoon, and not just

because of what happened a few hours later. Her terse sentences. As if she weren't describing her own life, but that of a stranger. As if she were protecting herself. As if she feared emotions might weasel their way into the many pauses between words—emotions that might ambush her or reveal more than she intended. Why was she telling me all this? What compelled her after weeks of silence and riddles? Could she sense what lay in store for us? Could she feel the change in the weather?

Feathery cloud cover had moved in, and people passing us on the sidewalk squinted at the sky and suddenly appeared to be in a hurry. A busker cut his song short. A wedding party assembled outside a crumbling church for a group photo urged the photographer to finish up. Mothers looked around for their kids. The papers would later describe it as a freak occurrence. Since the advent of weather data recording, they wrote, there hadn't been a storm of this kind in the Levant.

Winds and inner turmoil. Perhaps—yes, perhaps Grandmother had a sense of these things.

"So, is that where you met the people who come over to visit? You know them from the Grand Théâtre?"

"A handful of them, yes."

"Who?"

"Nadja, for one. Abbas. A couple others."

"What about Umm Jamil?"

"No, we hadn't met yet."

"How about the women from West Beirut? The widows?"

"How do you know they're widows?"

"Well, aren't they?"

"Yes, they are. And no, they never went to the theater."

She quickened her pace. Her hair was speckled with

sunlight filtering through the treetops. I noticed that the sky had taken on a yellowish hue, like a sepia photograph.

"Why won't you tell me where we're going?" I asked.

"I want it to be a surprise."

She grabbed my arm and shepherded me through whizzing traffic across the street. There was a forlorn quality to the area up here. Old buildings leaned against each other like lopsided film sets with dark alleys between them. I was struck by how little construction there was. In the heart of the city below, cranes emerged from all angles, and gray clearings indicated lots soon to be developed. It seemed they'd forgotten about this neighborhood, though.

A few minutes later, we turned into an alleyway so tucked away, I'd have missed it on my own. At first glance, it looked like any other little side street: laundry flapped on clotheslines overhead, obscuring the sky, and small balconies jutted out so far they nearly touched. Upon closer inspection, though, I noticed carpets laid on the ground, and as we rounded a bend, I saw people sitting on these carpets, parents and children with food spread out in front of them. Lit candles provided cozy light in the semidarkness. There was a hum in the air—quiet conversations and a sense of anticipation.

"This is where the Hakawati Café used to be," Grandmother whispered as we pushed our way through the bodies and farther up the street. She pointed out a grimy window to the right. Peering into the room inside, I could make out the contours of a bar. The sign over the door was askew, the lettering faded.

"The café was forced to close during the war and never reopened," she said. "But they recently started doing storytelling events again, here on the street. Just like they used to. I thought you might like it."

She squeezed my hand almost casually. However skeptically I'd viewed her in recent weeks, and however profound the rift between us sometimes felt, whenever she touched me—as she did now—I was flooded with affection. Every time, the fleeting quality of these gestures reminded me that, given the choice, I would readily trade any explanation, however illuminating, for another brief display of affection, because this affection amounted to home.

There was something different about her that day. I had finally learned my grandfather's name, and an image of Grandmother's younger years had formed in my mind. In what had once been a blank space, a story had taken root. I was torn between wonder and joy, skepticism and warmth.

Grandmother let go of my hand. She gathered her skirt and lowered herself onto the ground. I sat down beside her. Above us the building's walls were knitted together. A little boy beamed at me over his father's shoulder. A few moments later, Saber Mounir stepped into view. He was wearing a beige cloak, and his silver hair blew in the rising wind. By that point, I wasn't even surprised to see him.

I talked to someone at the National Museum. They have a job for you that I'm sure you'll like. Grandmother's words just a few weeks ago.

The hakawati took his place in a clearing left by the audience. Parents shushed their children. Every head in the crowd turned to face the front. Conversations died.

"Yeki bood, yeki nabood."

As far as I know, Grandmother had little time for stories. I think she mistrusted them. She was wise to the tools of illusion, having discovered what went on backstage as a young woman. When I returned to her apartment a few weeks after her death, there wasn't a single novel on the shelves. She had owned nonfiction, books about painting, James Ballantine's *The Life of David Roberts*, a brown leather-bound tome from 1915 called *Lithography and Lithographers*, Van Gogh's letters to his brother, and a slim publication by a Japanese writer about the art of India ink drawings. She had a few volumes of photography as well. The first book that caught my eye, which I assumed had been very important to her, lay flat on the shelf: *Madres de Plaza de Mayo* was printed on the cover above the image of a group of women holding banners in Spanish toward the camera.

I like to believe it was a sign of love, her taking me to the event that day, though she didn't care much for fiction. By contrast, I have always found refuge in stories—in books. For as long as I can remember, I've lived with books and within them. I'm aware of the happiness I've so often felt when the hero's efforts pay off, lovers get together in the end, the poor escape their misery, and all challenges have been mastered, riddles solved, missing people found, and villains brought to justice. And I'm reminded of something Saber Mounir once muttered to me in the museum: the fact that real life is random and doesn't follow a plan, that it's a series of mostly unconnected coincidences, does not release the storyteller from his responsibility to develop a blueprint for his tale. The chaos of real life is no excuse for bad art. The order I found in books gave me a reliable sense of security. But today I'd guess that's the very thing Grandmother distrusted. Because in real life, some cases go unsolved. Murderers aren't convicted; they get away with it, become state ministers and presidents. It's only in stories that they face fair punishment.

His name was Soufjen, which means: like the wind.

Life: a series of mostly unconnected coincidences. Storms and strange occurrences.

It was like a ghost swept down the street, because all the candles went out at once. No one reacted at first; we were too spellbound by what we were hearing. Saber Mounir spoke in a resounding voice and gesticulated madly. Here in the alley, enlivened by the atmosphere of bygone times, he appeared to grow in stature. He told the story of Omar, a potter's child in the bedouin tribe of Banu Hilal—sons of the sickle moon—who becomes separated from his parents and must wander the desert alone. The starry skies. The solitude. The crunch of sand beneath aching soles. His words came alive as he described these things, looking straight into our eyes and drawing us into the old world he was resurrecting. Then came the storm.

Clouds sailed across the sky like sketches drawn by an invisible hand. We detected a rustling like billions of locusts. Wind swept over the rooftops, but we heard it before we felt it—a rushing and howling and eddying and whipping. It tore laundry from the lines, drew groans from buildings, lifted roof tiles, and then Saharan sand poured from the sky, battering windows, ricocheting off walls and into our faces. It seemed like a magic trick. Magic summoned by an old master. I saw Saber Mounir lift his arm to shield his eyes, his silver hair ablaze, then I saw the shadow of a young boy jumping to his feet. He pointed at the dark wall of sand looming over us and screamed, his voice cracking, "Khamsin. It's the khamsin!"

Chaos erupted all around. Strangers' arms hoisted me up. Grandmother was already on her feet. She grabbed my hand, and we joined the crush. I couldn't see an arm's length in front of me. Grains of sand bit the nape of my neck and my forehead like fleas, the wind whistled overhead, and we didn't know where we were going, until suddenly a door appeared and we found ourselves coughing in a gaslit entryway. Someone who lived there had pulled us inside.

"*Tfaddal*," he said, gesturing toward a staircase that led upstairs, and with an utterance of "*Ahlan wa sahlan*," welcomed us into his home. He had a friendly face and smiled patiently as we—about fifteen strangers in his front hallway—shook the sand from our jackets and looked sheepishly at the tiny dunes piled at our feet. The smell of fried onions drifted across the upper landing. Only then did I realize how hungry I was. I peeked into the kitchen, where I saw a woman stirring a pot on the stove. She nodded warmly at me, but I was shoved along, past other rooms.

Depending on where I stood, the sound of the wind changed; it came through clearly in some spots but was muffled in others. There were locked doors that shook on their hinges, which I knew meant that this building was part ruin. There were no longer rooms beyond those doors, just collapsed walls or big holes blown by grenades during the war that now let in the wind, which rattled at the doors like an unbidden guest.

We got settled in the living room. Our host soon joined us, carrying a metal tray crowded with cups of mint tea with sugar. He apologized for not having a generator on the roof, and lit some candles. It felt almost festive. Then his wife came in with little bowls of lentil soup. Flatbread was passed around, so we could all tear off a piece. When the man of the house declined, I realized there must not be enough for everyone. He seemed happy about our being there, though, smiling at each of us in turn, and for a while the only sound to be heard was that of slurping, satisfied guests, the highest of compliments. Grandmother eyed me over the rim of her bowl, but she seemed uneasy, studying the unfamiliar faces.

"What do you know about the khamsin?"

It was Saber Mounir who had spoken. He was sitting across the room, on the floor, and pointed at the boy who had leapt to his feet earlier to call the wind by its name.

The boy looked at his father, who encouraged him with a nod to answer the hakawati.

"It comes from Egypt," the boy said quietly. "It comes over the sea."

Saber Mounir nodded. He sat in the shadows beside our host, and from across the room, I could see a faint sparkle in his eye.

"Ancient Egyptians called it *resetyu*," he said. "The resetyu was the ninth plague. And to this day, it returns as the khamsin when low pressure moves across the Mediterranean with an area of high pressure over Mesopotamia. It grows into a towering dust plume in southern Egypt—as it has for millennia, we're told—hot and dry and violent, until the plume turns into wind that tears through the country, through the region, and if the wind is angry enough, it becomes unstoppable, traveling all the way to us."

The old man's voice filled every last corner of the room. Even the cat, perched on the sofa's armrest, wasn't asleep, but listening. Outside, the sand scratched at the windowpanes.

"Why is the khamsin angry? Is it angry at us?" the boy whispered, leaning on his father's shoulder. His father brought a finger to his lips. *Shhh.*

Saber Mounir had heard the question.

"The khamsin is an aged wind," he said. "And they're known to be vain. The khamsin you hear outside feels slighted because it isn't the main character of the story I started telling earlier. It was the eighth century when the dust plume arrived, and Omar, the potter's boy, was living in Ifriqiya, where the nomadic tribe of Banu Hilal, sons of the sickle moon, had stopped for the time being ..." And before we knew it, Saber Mounir picked up the story where he had left off, like it was the easiest thing on earth.

In the hush of the room, he described families in that desert settlement split asunder by the seething storm; told us about newly orphaned children and parents who lost their young ones without a trace. He wove another thread into the main story, in which a pious man offers Omar and other strangers protection from the raging wind; as they shelter in his room, they tell stories within the story until parting ways the next morning to search for the missing. As sand descended on Beirut, Saber Mounir described the houses of Ifriqiya, buried by the wind for so long that people forgot the city's name, and as he spoke, something must have snapped inside Grandmother. Inaudible, invisible. I have long tried to recall how she looked, but beyond the wrinkles on her face, illuminated by the flickering candles, there was no sign of the storm raging within. She had closed her eyes—that much I remember—but I don't think she was crying.

The wind continued for hours. The candles soon burned down, wax hanging from the candelabras like stalactites. Well past midnight our host fetched pillows, and those who wanted went to sleep, while the others lowered their voices. It must have been the dark. The shared waiting. It must have been the noise outside—the slam of shutters, the howling and raging—that couldn't be tuned out and that reminded the people in the room of those evenings they had all buried in their minds.

As the hours passed, they recounted those memories, speaking quietly—so as not to wake the children —about a chapter I had not experienced. *Les événements*. The Events. That's how they referred to the war, and nights spent like this one, on the floor or in hallways, ideally under load-bearing walls either way, or in neighbors' basements. Two boys, not much older than me, said they could tell whether a missile was approaching their area or leaving it, and what kind of weapon had launched it, all from the change in pitch. That kind of wartime schooling, they stated, was critical for survival. They described tactics they had developed to get past sandbag barricades and snipers—creeping, walking, or running in turn—and how they edged mannequins around the corners of buildings to see if anyone fired, and how the streets still smelled of gunpowder when they emerged from their basement hideouts in the morning. I looked at Grandmother. She was staring at her open palms, as if answers were written there.

I must have fallen asleep at some point, because when I awoke, sunlight filled the room. The storm had finally abated. The city lay there in a hot, dusty haze, and I remember thinking that some freak occurrence had transported us to an alien planet or the Beirut of a distant future. The city seemed sunken. The air was yellow. Cars, streets, front yards, and buildings were covered in a thick layer of sand, and the few people we encountered on our way home were nearly all wearing surgical masks and hurrying home themselves. Cars inched their way along almost unrecognizable streets, headlights glowing. Public buildings and facilities were closed for two days. Weeks later, officials still warned against traveling into the highlands; the storm had dislodged warning signs indicating mined areas.

What sticks out most in my memory, though, is this: the hug between my grandmother and Saber Mounir as we left the home of our unknown host, and the way Saber Mounir looked at me over her shoulder, as he held her tight.

An Overgrown Garden

My memory of the autumn of 1994 is inconsistent, images and moods shifting the way bits of colored glass in a kaleidoscope create ever-changing shapes. The world kept turning, a banal realization it took me weeks to accept. I remember the natural transition between seasons and that certain days in September made me doubt summer had ever existed. August had passed by in a blur, and whatever promises the month held—its temptations, its challenges—had skipped over me as I spent most evenings at the museum. It felt like I'd learned a lot in a short time, but I struggled to put that newfound knowledge into words. I had to reorient myself. I noticed the rustle of leaves underfoot. Gardens bursting with color. People out strolling and chatting in midday sun that was finally bearable. Baskets loaded with overripe fruits and vegetables stood outside every front door in the neighborhood. As always in September, long lines of cars headed out of the city and into the mountains for the harvest.

Up here in late August, early September, I can watch tractors crossing the hillside from my study window. They're gathering the last of the harvest and preparing the soil for new seed, trailed by swarms of black birds. On my walks I often encounter families in the orchards, who come up here to collect fruit, because city prices soar in winter. All their kids help. They pile apples high and study the dark dirt under their fingernails in fascination. Parents check the sun to gauge the time and press their hands into their backs. By the time I return to my desk around noon, they've usually vanished, well on their way back home to Beirut.

Kaleidoscopic scenes with Jafar also emerge from the motley fragments of my recollection. There were days that fall when the wind came in from the sea, and we took the steep path down to the water by Pigeon Rocks. We raced each other to the smaller outcrops, where we leapt from rock to rock. The wind tore at our T-shirts. We had to yell to make ourselves heard. When we stood facing the water, we had to turn our heads to the side to breathe, the gusts were so powerful. On the shore above, we saw adults gesturing for caution. Waves collided with the boulders and soaked us in shimmering spray. We weren't afraid the wind might hurtle us against the rocks or into the sea. Jafar usually went first. I followed him everywhere. When the wind was strong, I would grab his shoulders, relying on him as we clambered over the slick stones.

After those August nights shrouded in mystery, I had a hard time going back to school, back to our stuffy third-floor classroom. I couldn't cast off the atmosphere of the museum library. Something about it kept tugging at my thoughts. In English class, we were interpreting a Keats poem about autumn that I really liked. I got to read it out loud, and as I did, I tried to channel the way Saber Mounir would intensify images with deliberate pauses and breathe life into mundane scenes with a tremble in his voice. As I reached the final line of verse, my classmates stared at me as if I'd lost my mind. We were reading Edmond Rostand's *Cyrano de Bergerac* in French class, and sometimes Jafar and I would pretend-fence with sticks on the rocks down by the water. After I dealt the fatal blow, he would sink into my arms, gasping, "I might rightly assume, Madame, that I began to die the moment I began to love you," before bursting into laughter.

It was a weird time. Every so often, the door to our classroom would open a crack, and a woman with perfectly straight teeth would poke her head in. She called out a few names, and those kids got up, grabbed something to write with, and followed her into another room. Jafar's name came up a lot. I remember the effort he put into appearing casual in those moments, clamping his pencil case under one arm and winking at me before the door closed behind him. I never found out exactly what happened in that room, and Jafar remained tight-lipped about it, but schoolyard rumors spread that the woman was from Paris, worked for UNICEF, and was interviewing kids about things that had happened to them during The Events.

One day our teacher handed out a worksheet with a writing prompt: *There is a famous song by Serge Lama called "Memories ... Caution ... Danger!" What does this title make you think of?* A girl named Amira went to the front of the room with her sheet and cleared her throat. "When I was five, my dad was found in the trunk of his car on the road to Damour," she said. "I was there too. They didn't steal anything from him. They killed him because of his religion. My mom says I'm not allowed to think about this memory anymore, because it's dangerous."

Once, after my classmates had gone out for recess, I approached the teacher's desk and asked when we would start covering the civil war. He studied me for a long time, turning a chewed pencil between his fingers, and finally responded that we were still centuries away from that point.

A few weeks later that same teacher, who taught geography and history, told us it took 450 years to destroy the fabled Library of Alexandria. It was first damaged during the Siege of Alexandria, when Caesar's legions set fire to the Egyptian fleet and flames presumably leapt from the ships to the building. The destruction continued over the centuries, as war upon war was fought, and consequently not a single piece of papyrus survived that had once been housed there.

When I visit libraries or bookstores today, I always keep an eye out for Saber Mounir's name. As if he might have collected his stories in a book along the way, however absurd that notion. Still, I view it as a secret greeting. I wonder what became of him. Those evenings in the library never went anywhere. My work there was done once most artifacts had been recovered from the vaults and transferred to laboratories and other facilities around the city for further examination. The museum was now populated exclusively by handymen and painters, its doors closed to me. There's plenty more I could say about Saber Mounir, to be sure, but those are stories for another time. We had only one more brief encounter after the night the storm ushered us into a stranger's home. We were in the library together, standing in the afternoon gloom and looking around. The room was empty. Workers had removed the last of the ruined bookshelves; lighter squares on the sooty floor and a few forgotten wrenches were the only signs left. Dozens of buckets of white paint waited in a corner. The hole near the ceiling left by the grenade had been patched up temporarily with a plastic tarp. In the end Saber Mounir shook my hand, though neither of us said goodbye. I never heard from him again. Maybe, I told myself, he had found his girl again, after all those years.

In the days after witnessing his embrace with my grandmother, I tried to peek at her collarbone a few times, thinking I might very well discover a scar in the form of a border.

Even now, years later, I think about the times Jafar and I would gaze out at the agitated sea. There must be a reason we returned to such a dangerous spot so often. Perhaps, without knowing it, we were sounding out just how much support we could provide each other. Maybe we could sense the presence of something inside us, a new life we would grow into.

One evening I was a little late reaching Pigeon Rocks, and I spotted him down by the water with a girl. We had seen her before; she was vacationing with her parents in a nearby hotel. The last couple of days, while exploring the area, she had appeared at the crest of the hill a few times and looked over at us. All I could see now was their silhouettes, their hair blowing in the wind. They were facing each other. As I approached— without their noticing me—the girl let the strap of her dress slip off her shoulder, exposing a narrow strip of lighter skin. She glanced at her shoulder and so did Jafar.

When the two finally saw me, they waved me over. They weren't acting cagey; in fact, they seemed happy to see me, yet I called back that I was too tired and left. I don't remember why. I walked away through the wet grass slowly, so Jafar could catch up. When I reached the spot where the path met the unlit street, I turned around again, but they had disappeared behind the rocks.

The cliffs looked different after rough wind, something Jafar and I discovered when we went back the next day. The elements had loosed boulders and worn away thin layers of shale and washed it out to sea, leaving behind an unexpectedly smooth surface. We don't often perceive changes, even those that affect us directly, as they're happening. Especially at an age when we don't want to be treated like little kids anymore, but aren't yet adults. We cross paths with people who disappear, then in retrospect we recognize their influence as seminal. Connections dissolve or grow stronger. We continually try to make sure of ourselves. Maybe it's no different than the sea and the cliffs—you don't notice what's changed till the morning after the storm.

*

Grandmother and I walked down deserted streets. I had never experienced Beirut like this before. We crossed lonely intersections where traffic lights pointlessly turned red. We waited at a bus stop, but when it became clear the bus wasn't coming, we kept walking. Under a railway bridge, she asked for a tissue, and as I unfolded it, sand poured out.

She had barely said a thing since we left. Her silence was unsettling, because she appeared fragile, still badly shaken. Her hair was unkempt, and it reminded me of those times in Germany when she had withdrawn so far I could no longer reach her. Under the bridge that morning, she was just approaching her sixtieth birthday, but for the first time ever, I saw her as an old person. She studied me with the hint of a smile. I took her hand and squeezed her trembling fingers. She sighed. I took a step closer and leaned my head on her shoulder.

When we got home, everything seemed smaller, as if it had shrunk beneath the sulfur-yellow sky. We were greeted inside with stale air; the apartment smelled like yesterday's cooking, the leftovers still on the stove, as if to remind us that we hadn't intended to spend the night elsewhere. The kitchen window was open a crack. Sand had blown in, covering not only the sill, but the sink and contents of the saucepan, too. For days we would find it in every last nook and cranny.

Grandmother felt for my head in the dim light of the hallway.

"I need to lie down, Amin. I'm sorry."

"What's wrong?"

"I don't feel good. I'm tired."

A siren howled outside. I heard the bedspread rustle in her room. When I checked a little later, her back was turned to me. I stood in the doorway for a while, studying the ridgeline her body created under the blanket and debating whether I should lie down next to her or just close the door quietly. Ultimately, I did neither. I set about clearing the sand from the apartment.

I was overcome with extreme fatigue later, but I knew there was something I still had to do. I went to the bathroom and took off my pants and T-shirt. In the mirror I saw my face and shoulders covered in dust. An unknown boy from a desert tale was looking back at me with flickering eyes. I remember that moment well. It's the first image of my ensuing adolescence, preserved as if behind glass—a shy kid who hasn't yet found a foothold, gazing uncertainly at his own reflection.

After a long shower, I called Jafar. I tried four times

before I even got a dial tone. We agreed to meet at his place in half an hour, then go to the café. I told him I had to see if there was any damage.

When I met him outside his building, he was wearing an eye patch. He looked like a pirate. He must have known what I was thinking, because he swiftly bowed, bared his teeth, and growled at me in greeting. From a second-story window, his mother blew me a kiss and warned her son not to take off the patch, otherwise the sand in the air could get behind his glass eye. It seemed a little far-fetched to me. At the very next street corner, Jafar yanked the thing off and stuffed it in his pocket.

It was sweltering, the sky still a surreal yellow with a threatening, swirling horizon like in a Thomas Fearnley painting, and as we talked, our pace slowed. The streets were empty. Like during the war, I thought, when some neighborhoods had curfews, and fighters in jeeps were the only ones on the road. We passed a vacant lot in complete silence.

As we neared our destination, Jafar told me the girl from the rocks had left the day before.

"Did you go to the airport with her?"

"Go to the airport? You serious? Her parents were there."

"So, will you write to her?"

"I don't know. Only if she does first."

We speculated as to whether her flight had been caught in the storm or taken off in the nick of time, then puzzled over which islands the atlas included between here and Europe, where—if worst came to worst—the pilot could make an emergency landing, and how long it might take an sos message in a bottle to reach us. Ever since people weren't allowed to take bottles on board, Jafar said, being rescued from desert islands was a near impossibility. Then he said the girl's neck had smelled like gardenias. I was dubious. He closed his eyes and theatrically sniffed the air, as if the scent still lingered. I elbowed him in the side, half-jokingly, unsure how to respond, but I was curious. I cautiously tried to find out what they had done behind the rocks, but Jafar pretended to lock his mouth with an imaginary key he tossed in the gutter.

From the outside, the café appeared largely un-scathed. The sand must have scratched the glass, but it was only visible up close, and even then, only from a certain angle.

The heat inside was trapped under the high ceilings. It was an active heat that drew sweat to our brows. To my relief, everything was still immaculate, save for the bit of sand we had tracked in. The chairs were neatly upturned on the tabletops, as always at the end of the day, so we could mop. Fresh-looking paper flowers were arranged in porcelain vases on the shelves, and tealights in glass holders adorned each table. At first glance, the place seemed ready to open for customers, but that's when I noticed something *had* changed. Shadows and shapes that didn't belong there were crowding my peripheral vision. I turned to look and was astounded by what I saw.

"Those weren't here last time, were they?" I heard Jafar ask.

I was so confused I didn't know how to respond at first.

"No, they must be new."

Grandmother had clearly made some recent addi-tions to the exhibition. Frames now hung on the wall opposite as well. There were four new pictures, all the same size and style as those we had already seen.

"Why would she make more of those?" Jafar almost seemed to be talking to himself. "No way the show was *that* successful."

"I wish I could tell you."

Then something dawned on me: she must have done these paintings while I was busy working at the museum. On evenings she was no longer needed at the café, she must have dug her paints out of a drawer and returned to the easel.

"I still say it's not art," Jafar remarked. He rounded the bar and checked the cooler for something to drink. I heard bottles clink. "Your grandma says it behooves the viewer to judge the pictures? Well, as a viewer, I say that's a load of bull." A moment later, he popped up behind the wood-paneled counter holding a Pepsi and looked at me expectantly.

I shrugged, at which he cracked the bottle and drained the whole thing in one go.

I tried to keep an open mind as I studied the paintings. To discover something I hadn't noticed before. I mentally connected the random dots on the canvases, but nothing concrete took form. Instead, I got trapped in the emptiness between those splashes of color, which looked like people who had lost their bearings in a snowscape photographed from high above.

I was about to go grab myself a drink, too, when something stopped me.

"Wait a minute," I said. "There is something different about these."

Jafar set his empty bottle on the counter and came over. I pointed at the cards pinned to the wall below the canvases.

"The names," I said, my finger still extended. I began to read: "Karantina. Burj el-Murr. Port District. Corniche el-Mazraa. Those aren't countries, right?"

Jafar didn't say anything for a while. His expression had darkened. Finally he shook his head. "No," he said, sounding more frightened than perplexed. "Those are the names of buildings and places."

Several years ago, when I was in my mid-twenties, I came across a notice for a local theater production in the paper and felt compelled to attend. I drove down to Beirut, to a small basement theater where fighters had held hostages during the war, torturing and interrogating them. There were few people in the audience. They slouched in their seats, messing around on their phones, so I assumed they were friends and relatives of the actors who had come to fill the space. I, meanwhile, was just following some unnamed impulse and didn't know a thing about the play, so when I checked the program I'd been handed on my way in, I was amazed to learn that the entire cast had experienced the civil war as children; the mission of this multi-confessional group, I read, was to perform original pieces to reawaken memories in the public consciousness and counteract the continued lack of a public reckoning. I was further surprised to find that there was no talking in the play, except for a short opening. One of the women in the ensemble stepped into the light and delivered a poem:

Why this emptiness following joy?
Why this ending following fame?
Why this void where once a city stood?
Who knows the answer? Only the wind,

which steals the songs of priests
and extinguishes the soul, which once was whole.

Sidi Mahrez's "Lament for Carthage," recited in one of
Beirut's many concealed scars.

What followed was all facial expressions and gesticu-
lation. The crumbling walls of the bare room. The
blinding spotlight. The absence of urban noise. There
was a young man center stage. I got lost in his performance, which oscillated between eruptive movements
and stillness, his face alternately frozen or contorted. I
was moved by the way his eyes gave tangible expression to a pain for which there were no words, just asso-
ciations, as awakened by the other actors, who flanked
him in silence, anonymous, sometimes swarming,
then scattering, outnumbering, thus isolating him, as
he jerked mutely back and forth, standing up tall or
sneaking through the room, stooped like a prisoner,
his hands groping, as though, somewhere in front of
him, he might find language.

There was no denouement, no Q&A. At some point
the play ended, someone turned off the spotlight, and
the actors withdrew. In the car on the way home, I could
still feel the pounding silence, and though years had
passed, I recalled that moment during the exhibition
opening at the café, surrounded by strangers all silently regarding something invisible to me. I thought
of Nadia, Fida, Abu Amar, and the silkworm farmer
from Sidon. I had stood among them and gazed at the
pictures, respectfully still in the hush of the room,
though part of me wanted to howl in bewilderment.

I felt the same bewilderment then with Jafar. I don't
know if it was the paintings themselves or their names,

but I could sense his uneasiness. We didn't move, didn't look at each other, just kept reading and rereading the names of those places. The low afternoon sun shone through the front window and transformed surfaces and mirrors with refracted light. Jafar was so close to me, our shoulders touched. His breathing was agitated.

We were standing there like that when suddenly the light changed, because Mara had appeared in the doorway.

"Amin, what on earth are you doing here?"

"Mara."

"Is everything all right?"

"Yeah. Grandmother's napping. We just wanted to check and make sure there wasn't too much damage."

"My thoughts exactly. What a storm."

She didn't immediately enter, though. She stood on the threshold and scanned the room. She edged her foot forward and back, as if testing the surface of a frozen lake. I had noticed that when she first saw us—two shadows inside the café, the door half-open—she had quickly clamped her arm down on her purse. Once she made sure it was just the three of us here, she lowered the bag and came in.

After looking around and conducting Jafar's empty Pepsi bottle to the trash, she walked over and the three of us stood by the paintings.

"Amin, *habibi*," she said after a while, her gaze fixed straight ahead. "Could you tell Yara I need to go see my grandparents in Jezzine for a few weeks? Please have her ask Kamila to cover for me."

I nodded. I glanced at Mara's hand. The dressing was gone, but she still had an adhesive bandage on her ring finger.

"Mara, how's your finger? Has the wound healed?"

"The wound?"

"Grandmother told me what happened."

"It's as good as new—almost. It was my mistake."

"What was?"

"Cutting myself. The knife slipped. The noise made me jump."

"What noise?"

"Didn't Yara tell you?"

"I forget."

"She really has to stop," Mara said. "The pictures. She should realize when enough is enough."

"Please tell me what happened."

She put her purse on the table now and turned to face me. "They said they'd be back, Amin. Three men. They were nice at first, but then they started yelling. They said something might happen if she didn't take the pictures down. An accident, they said. There might be an accident."

*

I headed home in the early evening. As I walked through the city, I prepared my script for confronting Grandmother. That moment of closeness and insight into her earlier life was just yesterday, followed today by the feeling that her orbit was a mystery to me. I was determined to put her on the spot, only I was met with the sharp smell of medication when I got home; the living room blinds were drawn, and her bedroom door was closed. My rage turned immediately to concern. I regretted having left her alone, and what Mara had said now echoed shrilly in my mind: *They said they'd be back, Amin. There might be an accident.*

Had they been here, too? I spun around in fear to inspect the front door, but there was no sign of tampering. My key was still in the lock.

I slowed my breathing, prepared for the worst, opened her bedroom door, and peered in. Then I heard her rattling breath.

"Amin?" Her voice in the darkened room.

"I'm home."

"Will you come sit with me?"

Shadows came in through the blinds and darted across the floor. There was the faint hum of traffic. The city was waking up. Sitting on the edge her bed, close to the dip in the mattress created by her body, felt like being caught in the moment of waking, when the lines between dreaming and daytime become blurred: my settling pulse, Grandmother's fingers on my hand, her touch unexpected and her skin chapped.

It later felt like, in the magnitude of the moment that followed, I was everywhere at once: beside her in a darkened room, in knee-high grass on a mountainside, or in a different age altogether, years before my birth. Something happened to us in her room that night.

I couldn't see her face. She was whispering.

"Would you like to join me for the fruit harvest?"

"Fruit harvest?"

"In the mountains. Once I feel better. It is autumn, after all."

The dim outline of her body in the darkness. Her breath streamed across my arm. There was a pause, and I could feel her shifting her weight and pressing her head deep into the pillow.

"The house in the mountains," she said. "It had an overgrown garden."

I didn't move. She felt around for my fingers and

brushed them distractedly, as if trailing her hand through river water, lost in thought.

"Your mother," she murmured, "loved the fruit harvest as a little girl." I wanted to pull back my hand, but she held it tight and sighed, "Please." There was another stifled pause. "She loved standing beneath the apple tree in our garden, gathering the fruit, and waving at me. I would watch from the kitchen window. Sometimes she appeared on the threshold out of nowhere, laughing, her arms full of apples. She loaded them into a basket, waved again, and said 'farewell.' She learned to say 'farewell' much earlier than 'hello.'"

Her words—so unsolicited, so warm—threw me off-balance. Skin touching skin. Grandmother's hand brushed back and forth across my forearm, as if she were imitating her daughter's waving from the garden.

I wanted to respond, but my lips were quivering. Stop, I wanted to say, but also: Don't stop.

"When she was older I gave her a bicycle. She attached a bell to the handlebars so I could keep track of her coming and going while I rested in the bedroom. That area up there. It has a boundless quality to it, especially in autumn."

Her memories sloshed in like waves, then surged back out, taking me with them. Images of notes my mother would leave as a young girl, even for the briefest of absences—*Back in five minutes!* Images of long hugs before she left for school, then her turning at the front gate and waving one last time.

Whatever prompted her during that time, Grandmother pierced through the cocoon of her reticence and seized upon speech. It was like this new idea she'd latched onto allowed her to latch onto me: the notion that, even as a little girl, my mother may have been trying to say goodbye.

I felt her body shift under the blanket. She pulled my hand to her cheek, and I felt her tears on my wrist.

"We're two sides of the same soul, Amin."

Excerpt from My Notebook

Entry from September 16, 1994, following a morning walk:

- *Joseph Tawil, 26; February 12, 1976 | Around 9 a.m.*
  while on a smoke break
- *Jamal Sweid, 20; March 18, 1980 | Around 2 p.m. on the*
  road to the airport
- *Arifa Shamandar, 15; July 5, 1985 | Around 5 p.m. while*
  taking a walk with friends
- *Youssef Ghandour, 52; April 13, 1977 | Around 8:30 a.m.*
  near Ali Sherkawi's auto-repair shop
- *Khaled Merhi, 44; August 11, 1979 | Between 12 and*
  2 p.m. at the Corniche el-Mazraa checkpoint
- *Fatima Tayyar, 24; November 21, 1987 | Around 4 p.m.*
  on the way to the pharmacy
- *Ali Fahmi, 30; January 12, 1989 | Around 11 a.m. near*
  Burj el-Murr
- *Laila Darwish, 17; November 21, 1983 | Around 6:30*
  p.m., taken from a friend's car
- *Hanna Najjar, 15; June 6, 1985 | Around 9:30 p.m. on the*
  road from Beirut to Damour
- *George Ghawi, 19; October 21, 1981 | Around 12:30 a.m.,*
  taken from his home

Lines I'd copied from slips of paper plastering a wall on Rue Merleau. Wind and the changing seasons had reduced the portraits accompanying these notices to shreds. During the war, strangers' hands must have hung the photos there, and beside them: name, age, date, time, and circumstances of their disappearance.

Zahrat al-Wala'a

These faded photos can still be found on certain city streets. But you need to look for them, images of the missing buried under inch-thick layers of job and personal ads, campaign posters, or fliers for restaurants and parties. So the missing go missing a second time. You can tell which streets by the mute processions of women sometimes passing along. They stream out of churches and mosques on leaden mornings, taking small steps across the asphalt in flat shoes, a twice-folded handkerchief always in hand, as if carrying around their own misfortune. They touch the slips of paper briefly and discreetly, as if by accident.

In 2005, I rediscovered the list I had copied into my notebook on Rue Merleau in '94. In an attempt to sort some mementos I'd hung onto, I was rifling through cardboard boxes and folders and happened upon these notes. My fingers lingered on the page. That walk eleven years earlier had been just one of many, yet I had a clear image of it in my mind: as was so often the case, I was simply wandering around that day in September, hopping walls and gates, scampering through rose gardens and back courtyards, not looking for anything in particular. The tattered sheets of paper on the wall stirred in the wind, a movement I noticed out of the corner of my eye. I stopped. I read *The Missing* on the topmost line and the list below:

... while taking a walk with friends
... on the way to the pharmacy
... on the road from Beirut to Damour

What jarred me was not so much the abstract loss of these people as it was the stories of losing that emerged from these lines.

At every turn, it seemed, I encountered the same phrase. Since returning to Beirut I'd heard it often, murmured behind shielding hands. Years later, I could still hear these voices, as if they were perched on windowsills or suspended from tree branches: "They lost someone." From the first time I heard it, the wording sounded strange to me, as if you could lose a person like a key or wallet. As if fathers, brothers, mothers, and sisters had stopped in their tracks one summer's day, but their loved ones hadn't noticed and kept walking.

The notion that someone could disappear without a trace, without any indication of their whereabouts, simply did not compute for me. In an effort, no doubt, to make sense of it, I envisioned a second world that existed behind things, beyond what was so deceptively familiar to us. A sort of half-space where the missing lived, no longer here, yet not entirely gone. Some afternoons, while sitting on people's stoops around the neighborhood, looking past the thicket of antennas and wires on flat rooftops, toward the sea, I would imagine that the fleeting things surrounding me—smoke curling out of a chimney, certain shapes in the clouds, falling cherry blossoms, or a book on a park bench blown open by the wind—were secret messages sent from one world to the other, signs the missing intended for those waiting for them back home.

My parents died in a car crash in 1981, before I could meet them. This was a certainty I grew up with, its underlying finality painless and thus incomparable with losing someone or having them go missing, which had evidently happened to thousands of people here. If nothing else, the countless movies I watched with Jafar taught me that when someone went missing, police, neighbors, and friends helped in the search. Black-and-yellow tape cordoned off the areas in question, police cruisers crept along back roads, tires crunching the gravel, and blue lights flashed over bushes and branches while a human chain poked through meadows and fields at dusk—but whatever turn the story took, there was always certainty in the end. In ways I've only recently come to comprehend, the assurance I had in my parents' death must have contributed to my long-held sense that I didn't belong and would always be an outsider in this city of missing people and those looking for them. Even in the form my loss took, I was a foreigner.

*

In 2005 I was living in the Old City of Tripoli, in a dingy apartment where the tap shot out brown water in the morning. At night I fell asleep on a mattress on the floor, the sounds of the building gathering in my room like an echo chamber: kids screaming in the hall, angry husbands cursing right next door, the clatter of plates and broadcast news themes. By then, months had passed since Grandmother and I had broken off contact, and I was adrift and withdrawn.

It didn't take much for this rift to form: just a knock on the door, a woman with a clipboard, two names, and one question. Although part of me had sensed this day coming for some time, I was slow to recover from what it unleashed inside me. I left Beirut abruptly, without telling Grandmother or anyone else where I was moving. I stepped off the bus in Tripoli with three tied-up cardboard boxes and a painting wrapped in paper, rented the first apartment I could find, and kept telling myself it was only temporary.

At first I was sleeping past noon every day, until a loud noise or my rumbling stomach drove me out of bed. I spent my time sitting in cafés and fast-food places. Or wandering around the Old City market, my mind fogged by the smell of incense and rosewood shavings, and whenever a merchant, craftsman, or carpet maker waved me over, offering tea and asking my name, I'd invent versions of myself, fabricated life experiences and anecdotes to hide behind.

"You're new here, aren't you?" the old bookseller, Khalil, asked the first time I visited his store.

"Yeah, that's right."

"And you're a cartographer?"

I nodded. I was standing by a shelf, my body half-turned, pretending to look for something specific. "These city maps are all outdated. Did you know that? The borders have changed, and different scales are now in use."

Khalil laughed. "Progress has always given Tripoli a wide berth. Overshadowed by Beirut, without an identity of our own, we are condemned to decline."

"A proper map would be a step in the right direction."

"A small one, yes. You're right. It would provide orientation."

"Yes," I said, turning to leave. "It would provide orientation."

Sometimes I walked for hours around the outskirts, where barking dogs lunged at corrugated tin fences and kids in tattered clothes eyed me apprehensively from where they sat under orange trees or outside apartment buildings. Other times I found myself standing outside the building Grandmother had shown me many years earlier. Our first trip together. She was born and raised behind these walls. It was here she discovered her passion for painting, and it was here she decided to flee for Beirut. Back when there were still night watchmen, it was here my great-grandfather had a leather dyeworks. Every morning the men who worked for him would unload cartloads of wet hides and lug them inside. The renovated building was now a Starbucks, with students on laptops on the other side of big windows.

I'd sought refuge in a second-story apartment above a laundromat, where up to thirteen washers and dryers would spin at once, which made the floors vibrate nonstop and the walls sweat. I hadn't been there two weeks when I developed a terrible fever with vivid dreams that haunted my sleep. A heavy rain fell in those dreams. It softened the ground in the mountains and hillsides, loosening boulders and rocks. Two children were playing marbles, the earth released in a landslide, and everything came undone.

I couldn't tell the difference between day and night. I tossed and turned, drenched in sweat. On the fourth day, a hand ran through my hair, and I shrieked and swatted at it in fear. It was my landlady's hand. I had been screaming in my sleep—*zahrat al-wala'a*, forget-me-not blue. The kids in the hallway, she said, had heard me and called for her. For the next two weeks, she came almost daily around lunchtime, a cloud of soup smells surrounding her.

By the time I finally regained the strength to leave the house, Lebanon was a different country. More than a ton of TNT had obliterated the prime minister's motorcade outside the Saint George Hotel in Beirut, and with it, the hopes of an entire region. In the days that followed, more than a million outraged Lebanese citizens flooded the street once known as the Green Line to demonstrate against the Syrian occupying force, which was believed to be responsible for the assassination. Every channel ran images of the sea of protest signs and banners that stretched from the harbor to the National Museum. The world was watching the city in anticipation. I soon found myself in a crowd of people on a hilltop overlooking Tripoli, watching incredulously as tanks rolled down the main thoroughfare and out of the city in the evening light. After thirty years of military presence, the Syrians were leaving Lebanon.

It's hard to describe the mood during that time. Words like *independence, future,* and *unity* floated through the streets like a warm breeze, settling over marketplaces, shops and their wares, church towers and the toll of their bells, mosques and their minarets. Although my very being balked at returning to the capital, I couldn't resist. I caught the bus from Tripoli to Beirut one afternoon, which dumped me out at Charles Helou Station. I was immediately carried off by the tide of waving flags. If I could travel back in time, of all the historical events of the past, that day, that very moment is when I would choose. I would choose to walk through that damp April air filled with voices and song. To walk through the city like it belonged to us, like its light, its dust, its scars belonged to us; the city we walked through as if it were a lit-up house without locks or doors. Photographers positioned under fluttering awnings alongside the route captured embraces and tears of joy on their memory cards, uncoupling these moments from time. And that's exactly how it felt: as if this street, this moment, this corner of the city were its own world, uncoupled from time and space, as if there were no more unbridgeable distances, no more yesterdays, no more tomorrows, no more missed connections, nothing more to be lost and never found again. Nothing yet hinted at what that year held in store—its destructive summer, its fury and Israeli bombs. The day Umm Jamil would hunt me down was still unimaginable. Grandmother was alive and would be for another year—time enough. Everything was possible. And there was something joyful, celebratory in the way we walked up the big street under a big sky, singing and dancing in the eyes of the world, as if we had just escaped something horrible and weren't, in fact, running straight into its arms.

I paused as we passed the National Museum. A familiar figure in a suit had muscled his way past and now walked ahead of me on the sidewalk. I had only caught a glimpse: the heavy gait, broad build, and thinning hair on the back of his head ... I recoiled, took cover behind a group of students, and when I checked, the silkworm farmer from Sidon had vanished in the surge.

*

"Get up, Amin. I want to show you something."
"What time is it?"

"It's still dark. The streets are empty, so it won't take us long to reach the mountains."

"The mountains. Are you going to show me the house today?"

"The house and everything else."

Bits of conversation from the past began surfacing with greater frequency. Alone in Tripoli, I was often filled with talk that required no one else. The memories of certain exchanges came and went like uninvited guests. Moonlight poured in the open window. I stood in the northeast corner of the room and repeated things said years earlier, as if rehearsing a play.

Sometimes I wrote letters to Grandmother that I tore up or burned as soon as the ink dried.

Dear Teta,

The ceaseless whir of cicadas mixes with night owls' voices: the address of the nearest bar, the revolution changing the country, or the name of an unrequited love. Talking, fighting, whispering beneath my window.

It would seem the city can't fall asleep. Sometimes I hear the crunch of gravel. Stifled laughter, quick footsteps. Shadowy caravans on the walls—it's kids sneaking out. No more night watchman these days.

The hours telescope uneventfully for me. And when the light fades for the day, the same dream always returns, like an old debt: the two kids playing marbles in the rain. They overshoot. Zahrat al-wala'a. Do you remember? When I woke up, I searched for words in the morning light. Trembling, I tried to write about the dream. My handwriting became illegible, resembled an unsteady heart-rate monitor. The words quietly drowned, and drop by drop, my letter absorbed the tears.

I'm often woken by a sudden flash of light. It steals into my room like a thief just looking to pilfer sleep. I got up once and, in the building across the street, saw an old man standing in his kitchen past midnight. He stood by the wall and tore off a sheet of the calendar. Then he sat down at the table—alone, with his legs tucked up—and reminded me of you.

Dear Teta,
    So many furious, inflamed hearts. How quickly everything can change. What are people saying about the revolution in Beirut? Now that the initial waves of joy have ebbed, Tripoli is keeling over. I'm sure you heard about the bomb. It wasn't far from where I live. They parked the car outside a convenience store and newspaper headquarters. Neighbors have gone back to calling each other traitors. The kids stay in at night now.
    I stood by the window late last night. Thought I might see the old man in his kitchen, but he never came. The fighting kept me up. Distant shots in the Jabal Mohsen neighborhood. He must have fallen asleep. Now, of all times. Maybe the sounds reminded him of the past, before he started counting the days.
    Do you often think about our fight? Before I slammed the door you said you always wanted to protect me. From what? I asked. And you responded: From the life I have had to endure. That just came back to me, and it made me think of your show. The first and last exhibit of yours I ever saw. I think I learned something from you without immediately realizing it. Thirteen is too young for that kind of message. I'd always thought of the splattered paint as abstract. The mess of color gave me the sense that something was happening on the edges or just beyond the periphery of my perception, and as a result, your paintings felt inaccessible to me. They scared me. I think I know now what you wanted to tell me. Art gives us a place to hide—isn't that right? It's similar with writing.

We can speak in the third person, slip into a different body, or construct a hideout where we find refuge or encounter loved ones. Like Yoknapatawpha County, the fictionalized Mississippi backdrop Faulkner created for his characters to move around in search of salvation.

Dear Teta,
Do you remember the first time we went to the house in the mountains? The ruddy gold of September clung to the tree branches. It was after the storm. Those were happy days. Earlier today, I really studied the painting you gave me when I left. My mother's painting. I've always felt it was part of you. I imagine your living room without it—empty. Less colorful. I know how much it meant to you. Maybe you'll take comfort in knowing that it's hanging right in front of me as I write to you.

*

The songs had barely faded before the first bombs detonated. The schism in our society had always been there, but it wasn't till the Syrians left that it finally became visible. Cities and towns became divided between those who'd supported their withdrawal, and those who'd have preferred they stay. Just a few weeks after my little trip to Beirut, assassinations began across the country.

It was no different in Tripoli. I walked around an empty city, past shuttered newsstands and greengrocers. The street outside the former newspaper headquarters, where a car bomb had exploded, was a moonscape. The hole in the facade reminded me of the hole in the wall of the museum library. Moments later, I had to press up against the building as an army truck thundered down the narrow street. From the bed of the truck, three young soldiers surveyed the balconies overhead. At the end of the street, the vehicle turned toward Jabal Mohsen, an Alawite enclave in Tripoli, where portraits of Bashar al-Assad plastered lampposts and there had been days of unrest. From their posts in Jabal Mohsen, men were shooting toward the Bab al-Tabbaneh neighborhood, home to primarily Sunni Muslims, who hadn't forgotten that people had vanished into torture chambers run by the Syrian secret service during the occupation. They shot back.

Books were a haven during that tumultuous period, once again providing me with a sense of stability. I entered the hush of Khalil's bookshop almost daily, bought a new novel—which the bookseller pressed into my hands with an encouraging nod—and withdrew to my apartment. The stories pushed Tripoli into the background. I sailed in a ship with Joseph Conrad *among dark islands on a blue reef-scarred sea* and sat beside Dickens in a carriage on the road to Dover, where the fog had *roamed in its forlornness up the hill, like an evil spirit, seeking rest and finding none.* All these stories about love and betrayal, loss and recovery, crime and punishment followed a comforting formula that was deteriorating out in the streets. There was a searing desolation to the sunlight that blazed in my bedroom window those afternoons in May, but retreating into these stories gave me a feeling of warmth and security and prompted me to recall brighter days when, in addition to reading, writing had also helped me escape. Eleven years had passed. My life had changed completely. I came to realize that I had skated past a childhood I'd never fully grasped. Immersing myself in these stories not only helped me flee—however briefly

—a world that had grown dangerously unstable, it also catapulted me with surprising force back to a state of being I had thought irretrievably lost. It was a feeling I wanted to track down. A quiet promise. A return to language. I hadn't planned it, hadn't summoned it. It came back on its own—the need to plunge into that chapter I'd locked away and write about it.

When I moved into the apartment in Tripoli, I'd hung my mother's painting above the desk and thrown the boxes in the broom closet to hide them from myself. I now brought them into the living room and dumped their contents out on the carpet. I flipped through yellowed photo albums, wiped dust off of postcards, and opened my notebooks. In an instant, I was thirteen again, it was summer, and Jafar was showing me his Beirut. *Made $27 on an ironing board*, I read on one page. Scribbled on another was the inscription: *Amin and Jafar of the Flea Market Hakawati Tribe*, next to which Jafar had drawn stick figures of us standing atop a mountain of cash, brandishing pen and paper like weapons. On one of the following pages, I discovered a list of names: *Aaliyah, Samira, Jamila, Layla, Rana.* Names I'd given the girl from the flea market, before I learned her actual name when we met again in the ghost train at Luna Park. And of course, the good old lists Jafar and I would write in school, furtively pushing the notebook back and forth:

> *List of persons who could help us solve the (L84/91) riddle:*
> *A code cracker with the secret service!*
> *Umm Jamil?*
> *An expert in abnormally ugly art!*
> *The silkworm farmer?*

Your grandma! (A sprinkle of pulverized truth serum in
her coffee should do the trick!)
The cartoonist from the flea market? (good idea!)

The streetlight was like fine, luminous gauze in my room when late one night I came across the list of the missing. I stared at it for a long time, read and reread the names aloud, then finally straightened up and went to the desk by the window. My mother's painting took up a ludicrous amount of wall space, but I hadn't had the heart to put it in the broom closet with the boxes.

Grandmother had insisted I take it with me. I had returned to our apartment one last time for my things. She stood in the hallway in her nightgown, her hair tousled. "Please, Amin, take it. It's the very least." She held out the painting with both arms and lowered her eyes.

The colors had always been brilliant, and the scene radiated an astonishing warmth. There was the suggestion of a wall the viewer seemed to be standing behind; beyond it, the meadow led to a tree, where a woman sat leaning against the trunk. I could rarely look away.

Sounds of conflict on nearby streets made their way faintly into the room. A gentle breeze came in the window, and as I peered at the painting, I heard Grandmother's voice getting louder, as from a great distance:

"Get up, Amin. I want to show you something."

"What time is it?"

"It's still dark. The streets are empty, so it won't take us long to reach the mountains."

*

We didn't make it there in time for sunrise. But the way the house sat at the base of the hill, surrounded by wild beauty, still made it seem like a fairy-tale setting. Grandmother stood beside me, holding my hand. We both gazed over the valley. I hadn't heard such silence in a long time; it seemed to rise from the valley and spread over the landscape dotted with cottages and whitewashed houses.

"Do you like it?"

I nodded.

"Why don't we live here, if the house belongs to you?"

"Because I sold it, Amin. We needed the money for the café, for your school, and for our new start in the city."

We didn't say anything else for a while. There was something about the area that I wanted to explore—that I wanted to grow into. "Boundless," Grandmother had said a few nights earlier. "That area up there. It has a boundless quality to it."

"So, when did you live here?"

"We bought the house in 1953. Two months after the wedding."

"Why? I mean, why did you want to leave?"

She laughed, released my hand, and brushed a hair out of her face. "Beirut had turned into the Elizabeth Taylor of cities."

"Who?"

"A famous diva. Just like her, the city was crazy, a slave to kitsch and in the grips of decline. A site of eternal drama. We liked it there, but it was nice to get away every now and then. It was clear when we moved that we'd keep going back to the city. Your grandfather was a sponsor of the Grand Théâtre, so he had lots of meetings in Beirut, and it's where all my friends were. But I also craved peace and quiet, you know? I wanted to paint up here. I was planning a show, and—careful, there's a tree stump "—we were walking down the hill through the tall grass, approaching the garden—"and I wanted to have children, Amin. I had dreamed of a place like this since I was little."

"Was my mom born up here?"

She nodded.

"Come with me. I want to show you something."

The terrain flattened. The house disappeared behind a row of trees. We walked up the gravel driveway. There was no car in sight, and the confidence with which Grandmother opened the front gate led me to suspect no one was home. Sure enough, we had stepped into a fairy-tale garden. It smelled of pitch and wild herbs. The air flickered the tops of the tall stalks. There weren't any flagstones marking a path to the house, just trampled grass, and here and there moss-covered sculptures peeked out from behind bushes and branches. It was like they'd sneaked out of the National Museum to hide away up here. I gaped in amazement. Then there was the house. It had looked bigger from a distance. Ivy adorned the walls and hydrangeas blossomed on the windowsills. A round table and weathered chairs stood in the garden. There was a jumble of dirt-flecked rubber boots outside the front door—three pairs, one of them very small.

"Don't worry," Grandmother said. "No one's home. And if they were, they'd welcome us."

From the front door the garden appeared endless, though an invisible property line was out there somewhere, the transition to open land beyond the apple tree and toolshed, out by the straggly bushes. No walls or fences, nothing to impede the eye.

It was a warm day, but Grandmother had a slight chill. She gathered her blouse around her belly and knotted the hems. Then she stood in the tangle of violets, wild clover, and puffy white dandelions and smiled at me.

"Well, what do you think?"

"It's so pretty. Is that the apple tree you told me about the night after the storm?"

"That's the one."

We ducked under the clothesline and crossed the meadow to the colossus below. The tree was leaning, but prodigious, its limbs casting long shadows over the grass.

"When your mother was seven, she fell from up there," Grandmother said. "Have I told you that story?"

I shook my head.

She placed a hand on the trunk and looked up. "Maya had climbed the tree to shake the branches. She was trying to show off. She and your grandfather had a running competition to see who could gather the most apples by the end of the season. He wasn't home that day, had something to do in the city. I was busy in the kitchen when the limb broke." She squinted at the house and seemed to be reliving the moment she'd burst through the door and sprinted to the tree. She shook her head, as if trying to banish the image, as if the memory were part of a bad dream. "A metal plate and two screws in her forearm—that was the outcome." She laughed out loud, but I noticed how quickly she fell silent, blinking hard and turning away.

The sound of a distant church bell floated over the meadow.

"Are you okay?" I asked.

"Yes," she replied softly. "I'd like to rest a while under

the tree. *Habibi ya eini*, why don't you poke around a little?"

There's plenty more she could have recounted about the place my mother was born, of course, but that was the only story she told me that day in the garden. Had it not been that particular memory she first recalled, there's a chance she might have shared others. For a time I often wondered why, of all memories, that was the one that came to her so abruptly. Obviously it could have been the location, the tree, the light, standing beneath the branches; and isn't it always the case that moments of horror lodge more deeply in our memory than those of joy? Considering what happened years later, though, it's a pretty strange coincidence, and I can still see her laugh, then blink quickly and turn away, shrinking as if she had revealed too much.

I roamed around the garden for a while. I snapped off a branch of rosemary behind the toolshed and rubbed it between my fingers. A tricycle lay in the grass. Gloves caked in dirt and a torn seed packet had been left in a garden bed. It seemed whoever had been there last had only just left. I stood on tiptoes at the kitchen window and pressed my forehead against the glass. There were dishes next to the sink, and I could make out the living room beyond—there was a teddy bear on the floor and a rumpled blanket on the couch. I had actually wanted to check if there was a back entrance, maybe a door someone had left ajar. I was tempted to sneak in and risk a look around, but some unnamable feeling made me reconsider.

That was the first experience of déjà vu I can remember having: I'm standing by the house, looking back over the meadow, where I see Grandmother leaning against the apple tree. The afternoon sun is like a spotlight shining through the leaves.

*

I jumped a little at the rumbling sound that swept over Tripoli. From the ledge above my window, a pair of pigeons flew into the night. Then it was quiet.

In the silence of my room, I stepped up to the painting. My mother hadn't left anything to chance. She had known what would attract the eye. Looking at it, you became more voyeur than viewer. The house wall positioned at the edge of the frame was like a hiding spot. From there you peered into a private space, across the sunbaked meadow to the tree, where the woman reclined against the trunk. I had never looked at the picture very closely as a kid. It was just decoration—that is, until the day I realized the significance of the scene. The moment my déjà vu occurred was the moment I realized that the painting in our living room depicted the house in the mountains, the garden, the tree, the autumn light. Everything my mother had loved as a child.

The delightful deception inherent to great novels is their ability to convince us that everything happened exactly as described. The painting must have had the same delightfully deceptive power over Grandmother all those years. It allowed her to believe that, by studying the scene, she could return to that distant place, where at some point, long before my time, she'd been happy.

I sank into a chair and held my head in my hands, remembering it all. I pulled out one of the notebooks. It was still half-empty. I searched a long time for the right words. It felt as if the past were suddenly more solid, and all I needed to do was capture it on paper to see it through new eyes.

By the time I emerged from the writing frenzy that followed, it was nearly morning. The night sky had turned blue, and the first glimmer of daylight stole into my room. I flipped back and reread the first line I'd written: *The khamsin had ushered in cooler nights, and once the air cleared of sand and we could see again, our days were marked by bright, boundless skies above, and it soon seemed nothing had ever happened ...*

Song for the Missing

The khamsin had ushered in cooler nights, and once the air cleared of sand and we could see again, our days were marked by bright, boundless skies above, and it soon seemed nothing had ever happened, like this was all perfectly normal, little more than a footnote one acknowledged with a shrug. For days after the storm, though, you had to be careful passing under balconies or open windows, as industrious residents tended to dump the sand they'd cleaned out from under sofas, inside cupboards, or between mattresses straight into the street. We only had electricity for a few hours a day, too, because the storm had wreaked as much havoc with Beirut's ailing power grid as it had with thousands of rooftop generators around the city. And yet no one said a thing about the khamsin. It was only during recess, where silence was a sin, that we traded stories about where we were when the storm hit; as soon as the bell rang, it was back to French vocabulary and geography of the Middle East.

Jafar didn't come to school that day. While our teacher located the mouth of the Jordan River in Lebanon's eastern mountain range on a map, I stared out the window over the schoolyard, all the way to the slight rise where our neighborhood was located.

After school I took a detour to stop by Jafar's house. His sister Soraya was sitting on the windowsill with a book propped on her knees.

I looked up from where I stood in the street.

"Hey, is Jafar home?"

She didn't take her eyes off her book, but she stopped reading. "Wasn't he at school?"

"No."

"Mama, Jafar didn't go to school!" she shrieked, and as my finger shot to my lips, she finally did look down and gave a diabolical grin.

Jafar's mother appeared in the window behind Soraya. "Is that true?"

"No, actually, Jafar just left early 'cause he had a headache." I pretended the sun was blinding me, lowered my arm, and gazed at my feet. "Can you please tell him I'll come back later?"

As I walked away, I heard Soraya say, "I bet he's up to something again."

Grandmother and I never talked about the night I had sat on the edge of her bed, but something had changed. Something had come over her and the things around her—something I couldn't name. For days after the storm, time seemed cast in a uniformity we'd never known in our life together. There was a deliberate slowness to the way Grandmother cut up fruit for breakfast and put it on our plates, the way she made coffee and watched the boiling black liquid rise, or the way she squished marinated balls of feta onto flatbread with a knife and topped it with thin slices of cucumber. As if the hour we had together in the morning, before she slipped on her coat and headed for the café, were a special occasion worth savoring. After she'd had her fill, but I was still eating, she wouldn't get up to wash the dishes or go get ready in the bathroom; instead, she would stay seated across the table, sip her coffee and make funny comments, or cock her head and murmur, "When did you get so big?" as if we hadn't spent every last year of my life together. She exuded a new warmth. I was happy during that time. I loved her sleepy affection, the jokes she played and the way she tousled my hair in the morning as she passed. It was like something inside her had finally moved over to make room for me. One morning, she leaned all the way across the breakfast table, right up to my face, intently studying a spot under my nose. She blinked a few times and smiled furtively. In the bathroom that night, I found my first razor, positioned beside the toothbrush cup. She looked at me when speaking or listening; she was fully present, and only rarely appeared to be whisked off by a sudden thought. She fell asleep next to me on the couch one night, her legs tucked up and head leaned to the side, and I realized how rarely I'd seen her sleep, as if even that were something she'd had to keep secret from me. She had nodded off once while watching TV back in Germany, and when she woke up several minutes later, she looked at me in concern, grabbed my wrist, and asked, "I didn't talk in my sleep, did I?"

Was this new side of her the result of that night spent at the stranger's house? Of stories whispered in candlelight, recalling The Events? Or was it all meant to be instructive, her transformation and physical affection, fleeting gestures, and little gifts intended to illustrate how she hoped to be remembered?

I often saw her walk down the street and disappear into rummage shops. She had done that a lot in the past, too, only the things she bought now—a floral lampshade, a porcelain tea set edged in gold, a doormat—weren't for the café, but for our apartment, as if our home had to change right along with us. She swapped out the vases on the dresser in the hall, the worn cutting board on the kitchen counter, and in the living room, she took down the yellowed curtains and replaced them with white ones woven in a pattern that cast a lattice of light on the opposite wall at noontime.

One morning, the silkworm farmer parked his pickup truck on the street outside our building. A trunk had been strapped down in the back. Grandmother climbed out the passenger side. She held the doors as Abbas and I hauled the trunk up the stairs and into my room. It was heavy and would have looked right at home buried in sand on some desert island in a pirate movie. This little gift amounted to a barely concealed wag of Grandmother's finger. My bedroom floor was littered with stuff, utter chaos, and she was clearly hoping I'd put this new storage space to good use. An old treasure chest. She couldn't have chosen a better surprise. They were both amazed at everything I had collected and now arranged in the chest as they watched. History books, a map of Beirut, or the volume I'd bought at the flea market that contained photographs of iconic sites now in need of restoration. Abbas flipped through my books, watching Grandmother and me over the top of the pages. He eventually leaned forward and carefully returned the last book to its place among the others. Then he stood beside me, his heavy hand on my shoulder.

I didn't forget about our unsolved riddles during that happy period, but their significance did wane. I lay awake at night thinking about Grandmother's exhibit. The men who'd supposedly threatened her. The weird place names she'd given the new paintings, which had even scared Jafar. Or I thought about the friendly strangers who used to come visit, and whom she still saw—outside the apartment. I was still dying to ask her about all these puzzles. Her behavior should have encouraged me to do so. I don't know why I didn't. Perhaps because some part of me sensed that this new Teta, in whose presence I suddenly felt seen, might be fragile and fall apart as soon as I touched her.

*

"Are you going to show me the house today?"

"The house and everything else."

Words whispered to me at dawn. That was a couple of weeks after the khamsin.

I threw back my blanket, got dressed, splashed water on my face, and slipped outside, where Grandmother was already waiting by the car.

We lingered on the property for some time after my déjà vu outside the house had passed. As that long day drew to a close, we finally left. Grandmother steered the car around steep switchbacks on the road back down to Beirut. I sat in the passenger seat, my hand out the open window and wind in my face.

Halfway down, she stopped the car. I knew what was coming when she reached for my hand.

The house and everything else.

She had, after all, promised to show me that, too.

We got out. There was a mud wall on the side of the road with weeds growing in the cracks.

"It was raining that night," she said quietly. "Your mom and dad were headed into the city. The asphalt was slick. The police said they were driving too fast."

I looked at the wall. It just about reached my hip and

separated the road from a sheer drop. "Was I in the car?"

"No. You were at home with me. They'd asked me to babysit for a few hours, till they got back."

I freed my hand from hers and crossed the street to see the wall up close, but once I got there, I didn't know how to act.

"So this is the place," I finally said.

And she nodded. "Here. Right here is where it happened."

I had a hard time falling asleep that night, and once I finally did, I was soon woken by an unsettling dream. My room was dark. The apartment was quiet. I felt for the switch on my reading lamp and turned it on. Then I tiptoed into the living room.

"It was this tree and this garden she painted, wasn't it?"

I had asked her that earlier in the afternoon. Grandmother, still sitting leaned against the trunk of the apple tree, had nodded silently and smiled, as if she were proud of me.

"Please," I'd said, "tell me more about it."

"Your mother painted the picture in France, but I've told you that before, haven't I?"

"A long time ago, yeah."

"She went to Paris in 1976, to study at the École nationale supérieure des beaux-arts. She was nineteen."

"So, four years before I was born?"

"Yes. Four years before she had you. There had been fighting in Beirut for a year by then, but none of us expected it would turn into a fifteen-year civil war. It was a constant back-and-forth, but we figured the Syrians would impose order soon enough. Your mother wanted to study art. Her father opposed the idea, but even he had to admit that Beirut wasn't the safest place to be. I hated imagining her so far away, but loved knowing that she would become the painter I hadn't been allowed to become myself, as a young woman. I wanted to make that possible for her. We visited her in Paris several times. She gave us that painting on one of our first trips. She had done it entirely from memory— isn't that amazing? You know, Amin, your mother and I were driven by the same passion, but she had a better eye for detail and a finer sense for color." Grandmother had paused and looked at me. "The pictures I painted in Tripoli as a girl were essentially one-to-one depictions of what I saw, while Maya had a special talent. Her paintings told stories."

The resemblance between the painting and what I'd seen that afternoon truly was astounding. My mother had loved that place. Grandmother had told me as much, but as I stood looking at the picture that night, I could feel it, and for the first time, I felt fully convinced. I had always "known" this painting, but I'd never studied it closely before, because I didn't associate it with any memories or specific feelings. Besides, it had always been part of Grandmother. Now, with the impressions of the day still fresh in my mind, I was conscious of the woman leaning against the trunk. It was clearly a younger person, but her face was in the shadows, and her expression was hard to discern. She sat there with her eyes closed and mouth half open. As if singing a song for her furtive observer.

"Maya," I said quietly, so as not to wake Grandmother. And then the looped writing at the bottom of the picture caught my eye, and I discovered the location, year, and title of the piece:

Paris, 1976: Song for the Missing.

Second Verse

You should protect and take
very good care of that painting.

Jafar's Eye

Why is it some people are driven to create characters and stories in their mind? Is it rebellion? I once read somewhere that the invention of interior worlds was an indirect critique and rejection of real life. It revealed the individual's desire to swap reality for a world tailored to their personal needs. I learned a lot from Saber Mounir. His storytelling showed me that we have the power to create beauty, even from the rubble of a broken world. In a pinch, words themselves would provide the foundation. The air following a summer storm. An exposed collarbone in a hushed nighttime garden. Two bodies in a meandering river. Those evenings in the library are so close at hand, I can effortlessly summon specific sessions and immerse myself in the memory. It's the reason I sometimes forget that—long before I met the hakawati—it was actually Jafar who opened the doors to a world in which stories played a central role.

When you're staring at something the moment light turns to shadow, Jafar said, the eye will sometimes remember what it was looking at, even after it's dark and the thing has disappeared. Its afterimage lingers in your mind's eye. It can be anything, but what's key is that the transition from light to dark occurs unexpectedly and instantaneously, like in a power outage or when people are struck blind.

Jafar had coined a term for it. He called it *larkness*.

When he first told me about larkness, we'd only known each other a few weeks. It wasn't easy to persuade Grandmother to let me run around with the kid hollering my name down in the street, but I told her I knew him from school, and she must have sensed how badly I needed friends.

It was almost night when Jafar dragged me into an abandoned apartment building, not far from Ras Beirut. As we slipped through the darkness, each holding a lighter, we groped along the walls for support. I didn't realize till later that the divots that kept catching my fingers were bullet holes. The pounding of the waves penetrated the porous walls and broken windows, and the light of the Ferris wheel at Luna Park intermittently raced across the dusty furniture.

As a young person, I'd say I had a keen sense of ugliness and danger; any awareness of beauty, meanwhile, was still buried away somewhere. In any case, I didn't appreciate how beautiful the city was from those heights. I could see the colors and lights below, of course, hear the roar of the sea beyond the coastal highway, and smell how much fresher the air was up here than at ground level. My primary concern, however, was not to fall.

"Come over here, next to me," Jafar said. He was standing at the far edge of the flat roof, pointing toward a few apartments with their lights on. With his arm extended, it looked like he was fishing for light. "Do you see those two buildings facing each other?"

I nodded.

"The street that runs between them is where the story takes place."

"The story? What story?"

"The story of the lost eye."

I didn't respond.

"Do you want to hear it?"

"Obviously."

Ever since our teacher had assigned me the seat beside Jafar on my first day, I had wondered what kind of accident was to blame for his glass eye. So many of my classmates had suffered trauma. I hadn't dared ask him about it directly, for fear he'd shut me out.

"It's a secret story," he continued. "One that's never been told before."

I tried to read his expression out of the corner of my eye, but he was looking straight ahead. I could make out every last detail on his neck—fine hairs standing on end in the night air, a tensed rope of muscle.

"I won't tell a soul."

"Promise?"

"Promise."

But he wouldn't start talking. I noticed a small bulge beneath his cheekbone as he clenched his jaw. Then, after I don't know how long, he raised his arm and traced lines in the air, dividing the scenery below into streets and neighborhoods.

"It was 1988," he finally said. "A night in August. Half the city was on fire. It was the era of car bombs. Buildings collapsing left and right. Missiles flying into surrounding neighborhoods. People would count the bursts of gunfire from their balconies, decks, and basements. The brief silence in between was torture, because it was nothing more than waiting—waiting for the next event. The violence took over every last inch of the city. At dawn they'd start tallying the dead.

"Fighters sneaked in from three sides that night. One of the groups came from the Commodore Hotel. Another unit moved north from the beach, and the third left from the Royal Garden Hotel. All at once, and all headed for al-Labban, where the enemy had a secret outpost. Someone had heard from someone else that somewhere in that neighborhood was a hidden stockpile of weapons and cash, guarded by just a handful of people. Their orders were clear: no long-range shooting. The enemy was installed on rooftops. Advance silently. Avoid skirmishes, and no roadblocks. It was meant to be a clean raid."

Jafar paused and pointed toward the left, where—beyond the skyscrapers—we both lived. He continued: "At the same time, the boy left his home and stepped onto the empty street. The radio was warning people not to go out. He knew what was coming. They all did. His mother and sister were on their way into the basement. They had the atlas but were out of candles. No light meant no way to distract yourself. 'I'll be right back.' That's what the boy told his sister before he left. 'I'll be right back. Pick a spot for us in the atlas, somewhere far away and exotic. Kiribati, Tuvalu, Antarctica.' The boy knew that Salman, who ran a shop at the end of the street, stocked candles. Prior to The Events, the old man had sold produce, but now he pushed a cart through the streets all day long, calling: 'Windowpanes! Candles, gas rings, batteries!'

"The ambush failed. Maybe the fighters made a wrong move and gave themselves away, or maybe it was a trap. The boy stood in Salman's store as the windows began to shake. Then the air began to burn. In sudden bursts of light, he saw the men approaching. They were everywhere. Signaling to each other, firing blindly toward the rooftops. Salman had taken cover behind the shop counter. He yelled something. The boy grabbed a pack of candles. Bolted out the door. Saw his sister standing halfway down the street in her pajamas with the atlas tucked under her arm. Their mother burst out of the house, chasing her, screaming at her to come inside. The girl raised her other arm at the sight of her brother and called, 'Jafar, hurry! I found candles!'

"The image of her standing there, her arm extended as if waving, was the last thing he saw before a bright light flashed near his eye, followed by total darkness."

"Larkness," I whispered.

I think I caught the first glimmer that night of the storyteller in Jafar, the same one who would soon show me—once we'd grown inseparable—how to make a small fortune with a pile of junk and a little imagination. We'd gotten along since day one, but to me, that was the night we became friends.

Back in my room, I tried to focus my gaze on individual objects before turning off my reading light, to see if they'd linger behind my eyelids.

Jafar told me these stories in installments. He was my gateway to that period no one else would talk about. I admired him. In my naivete, sometimes I even envied him all the things he knew, but he never made me feel inferior in that regard. He asked a lot of questions about my earlier life in Germany, and I told him everything I considered important, even if it meant touching up the truth here and there. Like when I turned the neighbor's cat, which had gotten treed and needed rescuing by the fire department, into a burning house. He asked about basic things or how certain experiences felt that I could rarely recall—the mood on the bus during field trips, secret notes from girls at school— but to keep him entertained, I made up a lot of stuff, inserting an extra dirty joke the class clown told in the back of the bus, or adding little hearts to all the notes I got from the prettiest girls in class, who were out of everyone else's league.

Although I wouldn't have known how to articulate it at the time, and he never breathed a word of it to me, I must have sensed that Jafar sometimes feared having grown up too quickly. At the time, I figured my stories depicted the kind of childhood he wished he could have had. It's how we struck a balance. There were also countless nights, though, when we just passed the time in the ruins, scratching our names onto walls, smoking cigarettes, or sitting in silence, shoulder to shoulder. I think that was the real adventure: never knowing how Jafar would behave, or what he'd divulge about himself.

His vulnerability usually revealed itself unexpectedly. Like the time the radio news music freaked him out so badly he couldn't breathe. Camera obscura. It was also impossible to predict when he might start talking about himself. As if he wanted to surprise me. He barely emphasized any words. There were no dramatic pauses, nor did he speed up when things got exciting. With him, it never seemed like he'd rehearsed his delivery to get the best response. Jafar shared personal accounts differently than Saber Mounir. He became more chronicler than storyteller, which I thought granted me a more objective view of an otherwise obscured period. Between the things he said and the slapdash scenes he constructed, that fractured world became tangible in a way it never had before. It never seemed the least bit strange to me that he referred to himself in the third person, as if the stories had nothing to do with him—as if he'd just been standing on a rooftop, watching.

Jafar trusted me, and that made me happy at a time when I still viewed our fresh start in Beirut as a massive tragedy. The other kids in our class were more reserved around me. They were nice enough, but more out of a sense of obligation. I spoke their language without a foreign accent, looked like them, with my black hair and dark eyes, and wore the same brown school uniform. Though I took great pains to conceal my time in Germany from them, the very knowledge that I hadn't been in Lebanon, hadn't shared in their experiences, seemed reason enough to treat me like the foreigner I would always remain in their eyes.

It was different with Jafar. We found each other without having to ask too many questions, and after sealing our bond with a handshake, we started spending more and more time together, whatever the weather, especially during that first summer, which he moved through so differently than anyone I'd ever met. At the time, I had no idea why he wanted to hang out with me. The life he had lived was incomprehensible to me. It never crossed my mind that I might exude the same mystery to him. Compared to his, I felt my background was bland and provincial. The truth of the matter was different, though, something I didn't discover until talking to his sister years later: "You represented a mirror to Jafar, one in which he recognized a different version of himself, one that wasn't damaged, and no sooner did you step into that classroom than he felt driven past the others and straight into your arms."

Yet another night in an abandoned building. We've opened all the dresser drawers and rummaged through their contents, searching in the darkness for traces of the family that once lived here. A shattered picture frame on the floor, but the photo's missing. Signs of a hasty departure at every turn. A gas ring and ashes in one corner. Either the former residents burned some private items before they fled, or there were squatters or looters here before us. No letters turn up, no new stories.

We sit in the bathroom later, on the edge of the tub, and stare outdoors through a hole in the wall. I say the outline of the hole reminds me of a shard of pottery, or maybe an antique spearhead, like I've seen at the museum. No, Jafar says, it reminds *him* of Madagascar, and when I don't respond, he insists: "Definitely Madagascar."

Is it this association that leads to further mental connections that then remind him of the atlas? Without my needling—or even asking—he suddenly continues the story where he left off a couple of weeks earlier:

"The boy's mother drove him to Saint George Hospital. The car screeched to a halt outside the main entrance. She jumped out, took him by the arm, and helped him from the vehicle. 'Hold that against your eye,' she said, pointing at her nightgown, which she had thrust into his hand earlier. She grabbed a passing nurse in the emergency room: 'Excuse me,' his mother said, 'my son ...' She couldn't even finish before the door burst open. A bearded militiaman in a blood-stained shirt stormed in, trailed by a group of armed fighters. 'Who's in charge here?' he barked. A doctor came running. The militiaman pointed at the fellow his unit had carried in on a stretcher: 'Take care of him!' he bellowed.

"The doctor checked the injured man's neck for a pulse, opened his eyes, placed the stethoscope on his chest, and said, 'There's nothing I can do for him.'

"'What d'you say?' the bearded man asked.

"'It's too late,' the doctor said.

"The militiaman took a step forward. He drew his pistol and held it to the doctor's head. 'You have ten minutes to save him,' he said.

"The doctor gave the nurses a sign. They moved the dead man to a gurney and wheeled him into the OR. The boy, his mother, and all the other injured people there waited alongside the fighters. Ten minutes later, the doctor returned and held up his gloved hands. 'We did everything we could,' he said.

"The young men immediately fell apart. Their leader clutched the doctor. Cried on his shoulder. Trembled like a child. The others were comforting each other. No one else moved. Sirens howled outside. The thunder of missiles. The boy and his mother held their breath. 'Don't look,' she whispered as the men shuffled by, their shoulders slumped. The boy pressed the nightgown more firmly against his eye. The hospital lobby stank of sweat and blood, disinfectant and formalin. The door kept swinging open; the injured kept coming.

"The nurse returned, her face pale and hair damp with sweat. 'What happened to your son?' she asked wearily."

*

The temperatures dropped noticeably as winter forced its way into the city. Afternoon rain gushed from gutters and drummed against windows. The light changed too, taking on a bluer quality. The heavens hung low, and the line between sea and sky above the choppy waters was lost in the hazy distance. When Jafar came to my house for the first time, the year was already well advanced.

We had barely seen or spoken to each other in recent weeks. He kept missing school; either that, or he wouldn't show up until third or fourth period. I now avoided walking by his house, because either his mother or Soraya was always at the window, and I had run out of excuses to cover for him. The few times we made plans, Jafar turned up late, if at all. I would sometimes wait on a street corner for an hour, or even two, before making my way home. Or he'd arrive on time, then take off fifteen minutes later, muttering something about a forgotten appointment. That had never happened in the past. On the surface, nothing had changed—he still had the same old mop of hair he never brushed, and his arms and legs were still covered in scratches that made it look like he'd tangled with a rosebush. There was a new restlessness in his movements, though, and his agitation was palpable. When I asked him once why he was late, he said he'd had to help his stepfather with something important. Another time, he claimed his mother had gotten stuck with an important client or demanding wedding party at Lieu de Lumière, the salon where she worked; she had called, he said, and asked him to watch Soraya. I still believed him at that point. It wasn't until these incidents started piling up that I confronted him and asked him to please tell me the truth. His response surprised me.

"I can't go into detail yet, but I'm working on something. Be patient. I think I can bring you on board soon."

"On board? For what?"

"Trust me, Amin."

I trusted him as a matter of course. Just as Jafar had never made me feel like the stories from my past were inferior to his, there was nothing now to suggest his unreliability might be a sign that he would soon ditch me. He apologized countless times. The fact that we saw each other less made my time with him—our excursions, roaming together in silence—all the more special, and I think I experienced those moments with heightened awareness. Sorting through memories is a complicated endeavor, to say the least, and a lot of what happened back then remains distant and indistinct, even when I consult my notebooks. When I revisit that strange phase on the cusp of winter, though, everything comes to life with astounding clarity, which makes me think that I was shaped by that time much more profoundly than I realized as it was happening. In a way, winter provided the colder, rougher continuation of those autumn days we'd spent on the shoreline boulders. I can still see us standing on rooftops, our clothes flapping, the days chilly and gray with fog, the nights black and windy and densely charged, and I remember the way Jafar moved through the darkness at those heights, silent as a creature without physical form. We were still very close. That said, there's a chance I missed certain clues that I might have caught had I missed him more.

I was still spending a lot of time with Grandmother, our days together cloaked in a new closeness. Some evenings, she brought me along to a different world, one she'd otherwise reserved for herself. Like an exhibit of Abu Amar's work we went to with Umm Jamil. He had collected and arranged dolls, tattered clothing, broken furniture, and the like in a warehouse, some of his materials covered in algae. I hovered by Grandmother's side in silence, and as we walked around, I imagined Abu Amar standing among the boulders, his pant legs rolled up, fishing all this junk out of the sea.

This other time, she took me to Luna Park. It was a late afternoon midweek, so we were virtually alone. There were some bored ticket takers sitting around, and the ice-cream sellers played chess outside their stands. First we had some cotton candy, then rode the old Ferris wheel. To my surprise, Grandmother told me about a trip she and my grandfather had taken to New York in the early sixties. New York! "By boat, which took three weeks." We sat suspended in the air, the sea behind us, the city below, all concrete blocks pitted by the sun, as she described the trip like a dream. Swarming taxis between massive buildings. The murky East River. The Gothic arches of the Brooklyn Bridge. And Coney Island, the amusement park at the southern tip of Brooklyn, where my grandfather had tried to win a rose for her at the shooting gallery.

"Do you know what 'Coney Island' means?" she asked. She had put her arm around my shoulders and closed her eyes. Her hair fluttered in the wind, and she smiled.

"No clue."

"'Island of bunnies,'" she said, and for some reason it made us both laugh out loud.

During this time, it often wouldn't occur to me until several days had passed that Jafar and I hadn't seen each other.

Then one day, he showed up at our house and clumsily hugged me hello the moment I opened the door. I felt something hard against my chest. When he stepped back, I saw a camera on a leather strap slung around his neck.

"So this is where you live," he said, stomping past me down the hall.

Soon we were sitting on the floor of my room with the door closed, surrounded by a jumble of opened books and notebooks. Jafar had proposed the meeting —he'd called it a *strategy session*. To my surprise, he'd brought along photos.

"Did you take these?" I asked. They were grainy black-and-white images of buildings, some of which I recognized, captured with a wide-angle lens from a low vantage point, as if the photographer had kneeled to fit everything into frame. "They're pretty good."

Jafar cradled the camera in his palm and nodded proudly. "In preparation for today's session. It's a small series. Three pictures of each building." He pulled out more prints from an envelope. These photos were different. They had been taken with a telephoto lens and zoomed in tightly on certain details. They drew the viewer inside the building, or at least much closer to it. Brick walls adorned with ivy. A chair in a windowless room. An iron chain on a hook.

"This is what you've been doing this whole time?"

"Sure is."

"But why?"

"Do you have a couple slips of paper? The time has come to bring you on board."

I grabbed a notebook, tore a few pages from the back, and handed them over.

"Pen?"

"Here."

Jafar carefully set aside the camera, tore the paper into smaller pieces, and started scribbling something.

"Buildings and places, remember?" he said as he wrote. "The new paintings at your café. We couldn't figure it out. I went to each and every one. Every last building, every last address, even if there's nothing there anymore, because it was torn down. Here," he said, handing back the slips of paper, now covered in writing, and arranging the photos on the floor, so they all faced me. "Move over." He navigated the chaos with some effort, then sat down beside me and tapped each picture. "Burj el-Murr, Karantina, Port District, Corniche el-Mazraa ..." As he provided the names, I placed the corresponding slip under the photos, until Jafar's own exhibit was laid out on my bedroom floor, each cluster of images depicting a location from a distance with two close-ups.

For a moment after all the photos were identified, we simply sat there.

Jafar smiled triumphantly.

I was impressed.

But also spooked. The pictures laid bare something I had covered up in the past months. Redirected my attention to something I had refused to examine more closely. Brought me back to that day Jafar and I had gone to check on the café after the storm: yellowish air that was hard to breathe. Trembling light on the tables and chairs. I myself had stood by the wall of pictures, adrift and swaying like a raft on water. Grandmother's glowing affection in recent weeks had outshone all that. I had loved closing my eyes and believing it was just a dream.

There was something oppressive about Jafar's photos. A sinister atmosphere.

"What can you tell me about these places?" I asked.

From my notebook:
Strategy Session with Jafar
Date: November 4, 1994
Re: Mystery of Grandmother's Exhibition

Karantina
Low-lying area of East Beirut, former shantytown home to Kurds, Syrians, Palestinian refugees, and poor Lebanese, most of them Muslim. Controlled by PLO troops. Early phase of the war, state structures collapsed. Easy pickings for right-wing Christian militias on 1/18/1976. Known today as the "Karantina massacre." Up to 20,000 residents flee into the mountains before fighters torch the slum. As the smoke clears, first come the men with machine guns, then the bulldozers. All night long, loaded trucks transport dead bodies from Karantina to the harbor. 1,500 people still missing today.

Burj el-Murr
A place that never really was. An unfinished tower. Fiercely fought over during The Events because of its height. Favored by snipers. Changed hands between occupying forces. There are so many stories about Burj el-Murr, it's become one in its own right. This tower preyed on people. They'd be led inside blindfolded and never come back out. Those who did make it out alive never talked about what had happened; they had spoken inside and lost all words.

Port District
December 6, 1975. The bodies of four members of a right-wing Christian militia are discovered in an abandoned vehicle outside a state-owned power plant, resulting in armed clashes in the city. Known as "Black Saturday." In revenge, the militia sets up roadblocks in the area around the harbor. Passing cars and pedestrians are forced to show identification. Palestinians

without papers (stateless status) and hundreds of Muslims are taken hostage or liquidated on the spot. The bodies are dumped in the Tahwita landfill. The next day, militia headquarters releases a statement claiming revenge was intended to have been limited to the taking of hostages, but escalated due to hysteria. Approximately 300 people still missing today.

Corniche el-Mazraa
Two streets meet here: Barbir and Mathaf. Not far from National Museum. The intersection is the primary crossing point from the western part of the city into the east, and the other way around. Site of frequent random arrests and kidnappings. Something unexpected happens on November 17, 1982: hundreds of women take to the streets, holding up pictures of relatives. They occupy the Green Line, and fighters don't touch them. It's the birth of a small movement. From this point on, the families of the missing gather every Friday and sit in the dusty street.

Jafar had visited all these places. He had taken buses and combed the streets, camera around his neck and pen in his pocket. He had talked to people, listened to them, taken notes. A shop owner in East Beirut, who stared out at the level terrain of Karantina. An old woman who lived on the eleventh floor of a building across from Burj el-Murr. A guy who worked at the Tahwita landfill. Two sisters looking for their brother.

I felt dizzy. A gust of wind carried the November hush into my room through the window. There was a fluttering in my chest, as if a small bird were trapped inside my ribcage.

Jafar took my notebook and read what I'd written while he was talking. Then he flipped back several pages. A few weeks earlier, we'd passed the pad back and forth during French class, mulling over who might be of help to us in solving the L84/91 riddle. At the bottom of a list of half-serious suggestions were the words:

The cartoonist from the flea market?

Jafar grabbed the pen and added something in parentheses after it:

(good idea!)

"He might be the only one who can help us," he said. "He knows all about art. You were there, you heard how much he knows! That knowledge saved our butts, remember? These pictures, the stories behind the locations, everything I've told you is useless until we find out what L84/91 means. That code is the key. It's what holds the whole exhibition together. We can't ask your grandma's friends, in case they tip her off. That's a risk we can't afford, Amin. She obviously doesn't want us to know what's going on."

He tried to look me in the eye, but I turned away. I saw myself riding the Ferris wheel with Grandmother. I saw us walking around the garden outside her old house, saw us sitting on the living room couch, silently gazing at my mother's painting. We'd come a long way since our reconciliation, a path that had been happy and bright. The notion of returning the way I'd come to start digging for something hidden beyond the bend not only seemed tedious, it scared me.

"Why?" I asked quietly.

What I actually meant was, *Why not just keep it that way?* The question must have come across differently to Jafar, though.

"Because we're friends," he responded. "We *are* friends, right?"

Later, after he'd left, the darkness made its way into my room, too. Long shadows, somber light, the pictures spread out before me. At the sound of Grandmother turning the key in the lock, I jumped, frantically scooping up everything on the floor and throwing it in the trunk under the window.

"Amin, habibi," she called. I heard her approaching, then she poked her head in. Her keen eyes. "I'm sorry I'm so late, there was so much going on at the café. Things are going great. The new tables were delivered, finally! It seems a little bigger inside now, even though we can actually accommodate more people, and there wasn't a single empty seat all day—not a single one! Are you hungry? I didn't buy any groceries, so if you want, we can go out."

"Sure," I said quietly. "I just have to go to the bathroom quick."

The flush of the toilet was so loud, I thought it would swallow me up. I leaned over the sink and ran cold water over my wrists. Looked at myself in the mirror. There was ink on my cheek, from the ballpoint pen. Then the power went out, and the room went dark.

Metamorphoses

Today it surprises me just how little I knew about what was going on in Jafar's world, despite all the time we spent together. Why didn't I ask why he insisted on personally hunting down the cartoonist, or why he never let me in on his plan to take those photos and talk to eyewitnesses? I couldn't see past my own happiness at the time. I clung to my notion of harmony. More than anything else, though, I wanted to maintain the illusion that nothing would change, that we were friends and there were no secrets between us.

I thought I knew my friend well, so I figured I could answer whatever questions I had myself. Jafar had gathered that Grandmother and I were getting along better, and he saw how happy it made me, so surely he hadn't wanted to make me go behind her back. Surely that was why he'd taken the pictures and interviewed witnesses on his own. Surely he'd meant no harm.

I would love nothing more than to study those winter days through someone else's eyes to figure out exactly what manner of loneliness drove me to be that way, think that way, and act that way. To close my eyes and not look. I was well on my way to becoming the young man I saw in the mirror the day after the storm, shy and erratic as heat lightning, most concerned with fitting in and being liked.

My notebooks reveal the questions I had about myself during that period. Do they explain why I was deaf and blind to what was going on around me? My body was obviously changing at that age, too, and I remember how much time I spent wondering which of my features and characteristics resembled those of my parents. Had my dad had the same thick eyebrows and prominent Adam's apple? Had I inherited my mother's thin lips? Her delicate hands? Or was she rooted in my personality? When I felt the urge to write stories or short poems, or got lost in the shapes of passing clouds, I'd wonder if these tendencies were a reflection of my mother's spirit in me.

I frequently compared these personal observations with my image of Jafar. I noticed his sinewy arm muscles and the way his biceps bulged whenever he lifted something or clasped his hands behind his head. He had grown significantly more in the past year than I had. I registered his self-confidence as he glided down the hallways at school, and I was acutely aware of the way girls huddled behind their locker doors as he passed. He'd recently started using hair gel. I can't count the number of times I revisited the scene of Jafar disappearing behind the rocks with the girl from Europe, surprised each time by the sting I felt. I clearly remember us lying in the grass under a tree once and him suddenly launching into push-ups and challenging me to follow suit, and me collapsing beside him, my face bright red and muscles on fire. He effortlessly kept going, then stood up, clapped his hands, and jumped up to grab a branch and start doing pull-ups. I resolved to work out in secret, before bed, to be better prepared next time. So much of what Jafar did was beyond my capacity.

I like to think of myself as a sensitive person. In difficult situations, I build walls to hide behind. This allows me to forgo intimacy without it breaking me. A woman I later spent a chapter of my life with told me, as we were splitting up, that she got the impression I had a hard time trusting people.

"Tell me. What could possibly have made you so guarded?"

"I don't know."

"You don't let anyone in. Who failed you so badly?"

"I really want to hug you right now."

"You want to hug me? That's not enough, Amin. You don't even trust your own words. It's why you hold back so much."

How different life appears in retrospect. How wistful we become, looking back on such chaotic chapters as adolescence, when personal misfortune and hope alike are boundless, experienced exclusively in the extreme. We do our utmost to escape our youth, because we're convinced there's a world beyond, just waiting to be discovered. Youth eventually passes, of course; only then do we turn around, and we're shocked by the banal realization that we can never go back to the magic of that period. The full force of some experiences takes years to unfold. That, too, is part of youth: we enrich and injure each other without even knowing it.

*

A few days after Jafar reasserted his desire to find the cartoonist, I was woken by the sound of screaming. I sat bolt upright in bed. It was coming from outside. I threw back my blanket and lunged toward the window. There was a black car with tinted windows outside. The engine was idling and both back doors were open. A broad-shouldered man was waiting on the driver's side with his arms crossed. Then the door to the apartment building opposite ours opened, and two men emerged, muscling our neighbor Tony out onto the street. He tripped over the front steps and fell headlong onto the ground. The men yanked him up. I saw blood on his undershirt. Tony's wife Nour appeared behind the men. She cried for help. The men stopped and turned around, as if they had all the time in the world, then one of them punched Tony in the gut. Nour's hand flew to her mouth, and she fell silent. Tony didn't fight the men as they dragged him to the car. Right before they shoved him into the back seat, Tony looked up and saw me standing by the window. One of the men followed his gaze. Terrified, I shrank back. Slamming doors and the sound of the engine as the car drove off were all I heard. When I peeked again, Nour had fallen to her knees outside the building and buried her face in her hands. The car tore down the street in a cloud of dust.

I felt a wave of nausea. I stumbled pulling on my pants and rushed downstairs. A cluster of concerned neighbors was gathering around the woman, who sat crying on the stoop. I raced past them. I ran so fast my throat hurt, all the way to the café. Mara's voice echoed in my mind: *They said they'd be back, Amin. There might be an accident.* I was certain I'd see a dark vehicle parked by the café. Or worse: that the men would be dragging Grandmother outside, too. But no one was there.

I burst in, sweating, red blotches covering my neck and chest. Grandmother stood at the counter with Kamila, who was filling in for Mara. They both looked at me in bewilderment.

That night, the lights were on in every window on our street. People in the neighborhood were saying Tony had been arrested. They said "arrested," although what I'd witnessed seemed more like an abduction. I called Jafar's house, but no one answered. I kept seeing people go into the building with bowls of food. Under the pretext of sympathy, they were hoping for details, but they soon reappeared outside, shrugging their shoulders.

Every so often, I saw Nour pacing back and forth behind the curtains.

Grandmother came home later. We sat across from each other in the kitchen, shifting in our seats, clattering our plates on the table. I tried to discern whether she seemed unsettled, but there was nothing unusual in her bearing. There was no further discussion of my sudden appearance at the café. All she said was: "It's none of our business, Amin. People say the craziest things. We shouldn't join in. It's not right. Poor Nour."

Overheard conversations, Beirut, Dec. 1994:
– "Your tomatoes aren't as good as they used to be, Bashar. Are you using a new distributor?"
– "They tore down this building, too? My goodness!"
– "Right, you're going to be rich and famous one day. Three boatloads of gold, sure, sure—but that won't begin to cover your medical bills, you lying ass! Someone should name a disease after you!"
– "You're at eighteen weeks, and you haven't told him yet?!"
– "... already the third arrest since Sunday. And that's just in this neighborhood. They're all being put on trial now."
– "I heard they're taking them to Yarzeh, to the Ministry of Defense."—"That's what I heard, too. Samir Geagea's locked up there."—"We'll never see them again ..."

*

How much did I ever know about the silkworm farmer from Sidon? How much did I think I knew? During our time in Germany, this plump man had been a constant presence, a source of structure in our everyday life. He provided a sense of order whenever he stopped by: he kept Grandmother company, and when he was around, she had real conversations, cooked more elaborately, and generally took better care of herself. I had also liked his visits because he was less careful in certain ways. He was more easily charmed, and I had fun drawing stories out of him about Grandmother's past. Like the rainy day he told me she'd been an artist once, while she stood at the stove in the dimly lit kitchen, obviously eavesdropping. Or the many memories of glorious performances at the Grand Théâtre de Beirut, which he was eager to share with me, his eyes sparkling. I was always happy to see his big belly appear in the doorway, and I liked the way he went into the kitchen, where Grandmother was preparing the mocha, to say hello and fan the smell of coffee toward his nose. Conversations with him were usually very interesting and on occasion downright unbelievable. Like the time he got up from the table after dinner, took his glass, and sat down noisily beside me on the couch. He asked if they still made us plant mulberry trees at school. I was surprised and amused, because I'd never heard of anything like that being required at school.

"Sounds like things have changed, then," he said with a shrug, before launching into one of his amazing tales from the world of silkworm breeding. He told me that in 1940, the Reich Minister of Science and Education had ordered elementary schools around the country to plant mulberry trees for silkworms to eat. I thought he was kidding at first.

"No, no, it's true," Abbas insisted, at my objections. "The Germans were convinced that breeding silkworms would help lead them to victory. A colossal error, as I'm sure you can imagine." He told me that students, under the supervision of official silk-farming instructors, were tasked with feeding the larvae mulberry leaves from the school grove, transferring them to mountages when the time came for spinning, and safely storing the cocoons after pupation, because the Wehrmacht was in desperate need of silk for parachutes. "Kids were even graded on it. Their service fell under 'war effort' on their report cards," he said. "They told students that 15,000 cocoons had to be harvested and processed for one parachute. That's about right. However, they soon discovered that the school silk was not of very high quality. Nazis tumbled from the sky by the dozen, so the Wehrmacht went back to manufacturing parachutes using Japanese silk, imported by submarine. No one told the schoolkids, though, because the Nazis wanted them believing they were saving the lives of German heroes. The school silk was sold on the black market after the war. What does this teach us, Amin?"

"That raising silkworms isn't for everyone?"

"Good one! Ha ha!"

Abbas had changed, though, since his unanticipated return to Beirut. Not that he was ever unfriendly or apathetic, but the questions he now asked me barely scratched the surface. They didn't reveal any great interest in how I'd been since the move, how I felt, or how I was adjusting to our new surroundings. I had reached the age where I would rather wander around outside than sit with him on the couch—an age he presumably found a tougher nut to crack. The Abbas I encountered in Beirut also seemed more nervous. He seemed less comfortable in our new apartment, and I wondered why he was never there in the evening, when all those strangers came knocking on our door. Was it the hectic pace of life in Beirut that set him on edge? Strangest of all was how often Abbas came over for no apparent reason, so I assumed he must be lonely and missing Germany as much as I was. I didn't know what his life had been like before, or what circumstances had driven him out of Sidon and into one of the neighboring buildings on our little street in a Munich suburb. He was both disheveled and seemingly concerned about his appearance—he wore button-down shirts, but they were usually wrinkled. As a teenager with an over-active imagination, I occasionally suspected him of shady machinations. Between the receding hairline and curved moustache, he bore more than a passing resemblance to Don Corleone from *The Godfather*, and the way he nervously touched things led me to cast him as some sort of master thief: shadowy villas, wall safes hidden behind paintings, the glint of a gold chain in the moonlight as he silently closed the door behind him. As far as I was concerned, Abbas was someone I'd liked a lot as a kid and later distanced myself from, for whatever reason. A friend of my grandmother's.

So it came as a surprise when, a few days after Tony's arrest, he knocked on my bedroom door and asked if I wanted to go for a drive. I nodded hesitantly.

We drove south. Abbas let me sit in the bed of his truck as we picked our way through traffic, the usual honking and cursing surrounding us. We passed construction sites and drove under swinging cranes. We arrived at one checkpoint after another, young Syrian soldiers waving us through. I'll never forget the force of the wind when, at certain points along the way, Abbas barked "Hold tight!" out the open window before accelerating. My hair and clothes flapped wildly, and I closed my eyes. Eventually I kept them closed and tried to guess where we were—which side streets we were taking, which neighborhood we were crossing—based on the sounds I heard. A hopeless endeavor. The truck slowed, then stopped. I felt a jolt, and suddenly we started reversing. I opened my eyes, looked back, and saw that the street was closed. A policeman was signaling for Abbas to turn around. Beyond the cordon: demonstrators, a roiling sea of signs, camera crews, and reporters. I could tell that there were two camps facing off, separated only by police. One side held aloft posters bearing Samir Geagea's likeness and waved his party flag. The others wielded cardboard signs with drawings—Lady Justice holding her sword and set of scales —or slogans, like *Justice!* or *Never forget!*

"No problem," I heard Abbas mutter. "We'll go around."

We were soon cruising down the coastal highway, past banana plantations and improvised food carts. After an hour of driving south, we reached Sidon. Abbas turned onto a dirt road, which led us to a big gate. Beyond it lay his silkworm farm.

Whenever I see a mulberry tree, I think of that day, but writing about it now, it occurs to me that this man, whom I never got a clear read on, played a role in my life similar to the one he played in Grandmother's. Abbas had been an old companion who stood as faithfully by her side in her new life in Germany as he had in her old life in Lebanon. The same applied to me, only in reverse. I recall that the silkworm farmer liked describing restagings of classic fairy tales at the Grand Théâtre, and that he was most intrigued by figures who operated from the shadows.

Several years ago, I tried to piece together what little information I could about all the folks I encountered in childhood, to complete a puzzle that might be of some use to me. In an old newspaper a distant niece of Abbas's had given me, I came across a photo of him taken in front of a synagogue. He's shaking hands with a man holding a check. I discovered that, before the war, the silkworm farmer had donated a sizable sum toward the upkeep of that synagogue, one of the oldest in the world. It seems he had been a respected man in Sidon. What I found most interesting about the article, however, which described Abbas as *generous* and *conscientious*, was an eight-line paragraph that further described him as *reclusive* and *something of a loner*. It created the image of a man who felt uncomfortable in the limelight and who'd rather remain in the background, which endowed him—whether rightfully or not—with an enigmatic aura.

That afternoon unfolded in a surprisingly wonderful, if strange, way. No sooner had the gate closed behind his pickup truck than the silkworm farmer showed a new side of himself, becoming approachable in a way I'd never seen. He led me through a field of mulberry bushes and showed me around the estate, where I learned he'd spent his childhood. Its past grandeur could be read in every crack in the mortar, every mortise, every crumbling building wall. The entire property was like one of his wrinkled shirts—nice, but neglected. Had Abbas ever told me about this place while we were still in Germany, I'd have thought it was the setting for another of his fairy tales.

He described his father, who had built all this, as an industrious but demanding man born on the outskirts of Sidon, who had earned his status as a respected businessman through hard work and doggedness alone. Who had taught his little boy everything he knew about silkworm breeding and the pearl-gray silkworm moth, a creature that subsisted on mulberry leaves and was known for the fine silk fibers it produced. His father specialized in selling and exporting that silk. These animals had fascinated Abbas as a child. He once took a small box to school and stowed it under his desk, so he could watch the larvae grow. Someone opened the box when Abbas wasn't paying attention, and it took days to find the escaped silkworms, which had spun their cocoons in the folds of the curtains. He was punished with extra homework.

After his father died, Abbas took over the business, but by then the golden age had already passed. It pained Abbas that he'd failed to maintain the company value and, as a result, assets had dwindled. The war took care of the rest. It became impossible to meet delivery deadlines. Sometimes the airport was open, other times it was closed; sometimes the harbor was available for commercial shipments, other times it wasn't. He soon had to dismiss most of his staff, as company assets were near exhausted. Israeli occupation of the area around Sidon began in 1982, and for a long time, farm operations ceased. That was the year he decided to follow Grandmother to Germany. That's when it all came full circle.

I liked listening to him. He ambled beside me with

his hands clasped behind his back, talking about his youth as he gazed into an invisible distance that extended far into the history of this place. I was astounded to hear him start listing the names of butterflies: the orange tip, the privet hawk moth and eyed hawk moth. These were names he'd learned as a child to identify the creatures he saw around the property. He was eight or nine when he started sketching them in his notebook, drawing their form or focusing on particular features: the dark edges of the painted lady's forewing, the lines arcing across the convolvulus hawk moth's hind wings. He hoped these notes would help him determine whether the animals he spotted in the bushes were the same ones he'd seen before and whether they might, in fact, be coming back to play with him.

"I've heard you keep a notebook too," he said at some point. We were walking toward a big white industrial tent that reflected the midday sun. I said yes and waited for him to ask what I wrote about, but all he said was: "Keep it up. It's a good habit."

A handful of workers bustled around inside the tent. They looked like astronauts in their white coveralls. It wasn't many people, considering the size of the tent. Abbas showed me the cocoons, which had been spread out on tall frames covered in branches and leaves. There were thousands of them.

"Will these all turn into butterflies?" I asked in amazement.

He shook his head. "No. It's the silk thread we want. When they hatch, butterflies soften and chew through their cocoon, destroying the silk. We can't let that happen, so after ten days, we steam the cocoons to kill the pupae inside and extract the thread."

"Brutal."

"It's unfortunately the only way to do it. But you're right. When I was your age, my dad told me that a single thunderstorm would knock millions of silkworms out of the trees, and then they starved because they couldn't find their way back to their food source. After hearing that, I ran outside after every storm and tore leaves off the bushes and spread them out on the ground, so the fallen silkworms wouldn't die. That's nature for you."

Later on we sat inside his house, where every path on the property led. It appeared grand from a distance, but as we approached, I detected signs of decay. It seemed unimaginable for Abbas to live all alone on this fading estate. His regular visits now appeared in a totally different light.

He carried a pitcher of chilled lemonade into the living room. We sat down at a table that was far too big for two people. Abbas brushed aside a few crumbs with his hand.

"What are you reading these days, Amin? Any books you could recommend? As you can see, there's not much going on here at the moment."

I listed off some titles.

"*Around the World in Eighty Days*," he murmured. "That's what I'd recommend to *you*. It's been a while, but Phileas Fogg and Passepartout—what a duo!"

"No way they're as good as Holmes and Watson."

"Or Han Solo and Chewbacca, right? Now, that's a real friendship!" Abbas beamed at my surprise. "I may be older than you, but it doesn't mean I can't have fun from time to time."

We chatted about movies a while longer and eventually started talking about the Grand Théâtre, where he'd first met Grandmother. He now went into greater detail about that night.

"It was opening night of *Orpheus and Eurydice*. Big event. Your grandfather was so proud to introduce his fiancée to us. As I've told you, Amin and I were both among the donors supporting the theater. Yara was wearing a long blue dress. The moment she took off her coat in the lobby, all eyes were on her. She, meanwhile, only had eyes for Amin—and the theater. She loved that building, and not just because it was where she had met her future husband. Once, after we'd gotten to know each other better, she told me the theater was like a portal that took her to strange worlds and bygone times, far, far away from Beirut."

"She told me something like that once, too."

"Is that so?" Abbas nodded pensively. He took the pitcher and refilled my glass. "Terrible, what's become of it."

"The theater?"

"Yes. It opened in 1929. Back then, it symbolized Beirut's status as a cultural hub. You have to understand that there was nothing comparable in all the Middle East. The Ballet des Champs-Élysées performed there, as did the renowned Egyptian Ramses Group, and beyond the stage productions, musicians like Dalida, Mohamed Abdel Wahab, and Umm Kulthum played there, too. The theater was as cosmopolitan as the city itself. It was decimated in the war. What little remained was occupied by militias, who turned it into a porno theater. Today it's in ruins. Its beauty, its brutalization, its deterioration—if you're ever trying to explain the history of Lebanon to someone, just tell them what happened to the Grand Théâtre." Abbas lifted his arm, coughed into his elbow, and looked down. "Or to this farm, for that matter," he added quietly.

In the silence that followed, I had the feeling it was hard for him to hold my gaze. "A while back," I nevertheless ventured, "Grandmother and I went to the house where she used to live. When we got home that night, she said our country was like a house with lots of rooms."

"She said that?"

"Yeah. People who didn't want to remember lived in some rooms, and people who couldn't forget were in the others. Upstairs was where the murderers lived. What did she mean by that?"

There was another pause, and Abbas reached for his glass without taking a drink. Instead, he slid it back and forth across the table, staring at me.

"I hear you witnessed your neighbor Tony's arrest," he finally said. "Yara told me."

"Yeah, it was horrible. Is that why we're here?"

"No, I just wanted to spend time with you. She also told me that you ran straight to the café after it happened. Were you scared?"

"Not for my own safety. I was worried about *her*."

"That shows how much you love your grandmother. Can you describe them to me?"

"Describe them? Who?"

"The men who took Tony."

I described the men and their car, then asked, "Is Grandmother in danger?"

Abbas studied me for a moment. "Yara has nothing to fear," he said. "She's done nothing wrong."

I considered how far to push my luck. Jafar was looking for the cartoonist. If he found him, we would solve this puzzle. I was afraid a careless comment might lead Abbas to divulge our plan to Grandmother. Jafar had cautioned against that very risk. I was curious, though. I couldn't help it.

"Mara, from the café? She told me some men threatened Grandmother."

"Those were different men, Amin."

"But why did they want her to take down her paintings? They said there might be an *accident*. What kind of accident?"

"Oh, it was just the landlord with a few people. The building the café is in belongs to him. There's no need for concern."

"The landlord? Come on."

"That building has been around since the French Mandate, just like this one here. The walls hold a lot of moisture. He thought Yara's paintings might be ruined, unless she took them down. That's what he meant by *accident*. Maybe he was afraid she'd sue him if her artwork was damaged."

"But Mara ..."

"A misunderstanding, Amin. It was a misunderstanding. It's wonderful that you're so concerned about her. Wonderful, but unnecessary."

I didn't believe a word he said. Abbas had flinched, but he sat up straight now and seemed more alert, so I tried a different approach.

"Who are the murderers she was talking about?"

"Ex-fighters. Do you know what a metaphor is? This country has always been controlled by a handful of powerful families. We might as well be stuck in the Middle Ages, as far as that's concerned. Today, the murderers who live upstairs are our politicians. During the war they led opposing militias. Now, the same men are writing our laws. They're standing in the way of reckoning and remembrance."

I could feel his eyes on me as I stared at my hands. "I've heard people talking about all the arrests," I said. "Everyone's talking about it. Are these arrests somehow connected to what *you're* talking about?"

More silence as I waited for him to answer. Abbas again slid his glass back and forth.

"Samir Geagea was one of those militia leaders. He did bad things during the war. Political murders. I'm sure you've heard about that on the news. In 1978, he led a commando into the mountains around Ehden to kill the former president's son and his family. That's just one of many examples. Although many of the men in power today represent different sects, they all share a similar past. Samir Geagea's militia was disbanded after the war and remade as a political party. Many of our parties today used to be militias. You know how much influence Syria has in our country. We're living in an age of upheaval, caught somewhere between war and peace. The Syrians offered Geagea's party a role in government. He refused, fought back against their influence, and accused them of pro-Muslim politics, saying it was his duty to protect Christian interests. Meanwhile, they accused him of undermining the peace process. And then came the explosion in that church. You know the one. Geagea was arrested and blamed for the attack. Did he do it? Who knows. So much of this process has been kept hidden. There are some who say Geagea is just a pawn whose time has come to be sacrificed."

"What about you? What do you say?"

"What I say is this: they should all stand trial. The things Geagea did are unforgivable, but everyone did them, on all sides. No one else will be tried, though. And now the secret service is running around in broad daylight, snatching his supporters from their homes …"

"Is that what happened to Tony? Is he one of them?"

Abbas nodded. "It's safe to assume. When the war ended, hundreds of thousands of young men returned to their old lives. They hadn't been fighters for long, but during that time, the rules didn't apply to them. They did things they'll never forget. Unforgivable things. And after the peace treaty was signed, they simply went home. Most of them are still trying to find their way back."

Why do I remember this conversation so well? We didn't raise our voices or argue, but I did get the feeling Abbas was being candid and cagey at once, like he was circling an empty space while sincerely trying to answer my questions. The way he paused while speaking gave him time to weigh his words. The bustle of Beirut had made him both more nervous and more careful. I obviously didn't believe what he'd said about the men in the café, but I thought better of probing any further. After all, Jafar and I would discover the truth soon enough, and it was better to let sleeping dogs lie. I'd pushed it too far as it was.

We talked about Tony and Nour for a while longer. I said I'd always thought he was a nice neighbor. He was a taxi driver and went out every day to earn money for his family. I chatted, filling the space with anecdotes about Tony: a passing joke on the sidewalk, a friendly *Good morning!* Or the time he drove me to school in his taxi, because it was so hot out. I think I did it to assure myself that he couldn't possibly be a bad person. That I wasn't living next door to liars and war criminals. What I recognize now is this: I had underestimated

Abbas. He was trickier than I'd thought. He got up at some point, cracked his knuckles, and stretched noisily.

"Batman and Robin," he said.

I blinked at him in utter confusion.

"We were talking about dynamic duos and best friends, weren't we? Batman and Robin. Another good example."

"Robinson Crusoe and Friday," I said, standing up as well.

"Don Quixote and Sancho Panza."

"Never heard of them."

"I'm sure you'll read about them someday. Now, how about Amin and Jafar?"

I hesitated.

"Yara tells me you've been staying out late with your buddy Jafar."

"So?"

He pushed in his chair and spread his arms. "I would imagine she worries, not knowing where you are and what you might be up to out in the city, late at night."

I looked at him. "But I—"

"I just want to make sure you're in good hands. Are you boys close?"

I nodded.

"You do realize, don't you, that the buildings you creep around in are unsafe? They're in danger of collapsing. They're criminal hideouts. Something could happen to you two."

"I've never told anyone about that."

Abbas merely smiled. "I was young once too." He rounded the table and came up to me, then said, "Promise me you won't take any stupid chances. You're quick to go along with things. If anything happened to you, it would break Yara."

I looked out the window. The living room was enormous, but at that moment it felt like the only way we'd both fit was if I looked outside.

"I can take care of myself," I said.

"Don't let people take advantage of you, Amin," the silkworm farmer said. "It's dangerous."

Butterflies are incredible animals, aren't they? A caterpillar pupates, seems good as dead, and a few days later, this magnificently colored creature emerges from its cocoon. A real miracle. The caterpillar dissolves into a fibrous goop and the organic matter reassembles, becoming a new form of existence.

I often picture the silkworm farmer from Sidon as a young boy, rushing out of the house after thunderstorms to save those little animals from starvation. He would grow up to become a man who knowingly disrupted the natural process of metamorphosis—evidence that he was capable of making decisions he didn't like, provided they served a higher purpose.

I still remember standing inside the big tent that day, a group of workers gathered round and thousands upon thousands of cocoons spread out in front of us.

"How long do you think one of these threads encasing the larvae is?" Abbas had asked.

"I don't know."

"Approximately ten thousand feet. Isn't that amazing? What a wonderful way to hide."

He placed a pupa in my hand. The cocoon was heavier than I'd expected. The tangle of thread was soft and glossy. Something occurred to me in that moment: Abbas had been in our apartment. He had carried the big trunk into my room and found a spot for it. The two of us then placed my books, photos, and notes inside.

Concealed them beneath the lid. Then we stood there in silence, his hand on my shoulder—a pose I haven't forgotten to this day.

*

It was getting dark by the time we got back to Beirut. We heard on the radio that there had been skirmishes that day. Parts of the demonstration outside the courthouse had turned violent and been broken up. There was no sign of it now on the streets.

Grandmother wasn't at home. I went into the kitchen, opened the fridge, and took a big swig of milk. Then I stood by the window in my room and looked at the building across the street. The lights were on in Tony's apartment. Nour was sitting alone at the dinner table. I started to turn away when I heard loud shouting. The sound terrified me—I thought those men might be back to abduct someone else on our street, but then I spotted a shadow dashing toward our building. A small figure.

"Amin, come quick. They're at Luna Park!"

Jafar stood outside our building, thoroughly winded. He leaned forward with his hands on his knees and struggled for breath.

"Come on, what are you waiting for?" he wheezed, as I was still planted in place. "We have to hurry!"

"*They*? At Luna Park?" I asked. "What? Did you find the cartoonist?"

Jafar shook his head. "Way better!" Then he straightened up, grinned, and formed a heart with his hands.

Ghost Train

It was drizzling, but we hardly noticed. We ran as fast as we could. There was a churning thrill inside me. We sprinted down the hill, through the jumble of narrow streets, not slowing until we reached the coastal highway, brightly lit in the twilight.

In the final few steps before the entrance, a dreamlike eddy of bodies and voices—I heard the shrieks of children, laughter, the faint echo of a merry-go-round melody. I kept trying to catch my breath, and with each exhale my heart pounded so hard I feared it might explode.

> *not a*
> *ghost light*
> *... in sight.*

How many times had I given this girl different names, said them out loud, and thought of her? How many times had I studied Younes Abboud's drawing in an effort to relive the sudden flame of familiarity in the girl's eyes when she looked at me and asked, "Are you hurt?"

> *... till*
> *I ...*
> *... you*
> *or ... drifted away*

...
find
still life.

It had taken me weeks to accept that I'd never see her again. Further weeks passed before the pain of this realization became more tolerable. Of course there were days when other joys or worries moved in, obscuring my thoughts of her, but I'd never forgotten.

Whenever Jafar trailed his fingers across a girl's shoulder as we passed, I told myself these girls existed far beyond my personal solar system—they were beauties reserved for others, girls who might at most glance at me absently, as if I were ruining a special moment for them. With her, though, it had been different.

In the confusion of voices and lights, our progress was slowed by strolling couples. They let go of each other's hands to let us through. Kids with ice cream all over their faces stumbled toward us; parents looked warily at the threatening rain clouds; and an old man dressed up like Spider-Man posed for pictures under some scaffolding. Amid the commotion, I felt certain we'd never find her, and something inside me almost felt a little relieved. Where did these doubts and nerves come from, anyway? Jafar always seemed so chill around girls. I saw him in front of me, clearing the way into the heart of Luna Park, and for a second I worried we'd find the girl and it would turn out the one she actually liked was Jafar.

He stopped so abruptly I almost rammed into him.

"They were over there by the raffle tickets," he said, turning and looking all around.

"Are you sure it was *her*? Maybe you confused her with someone else."

He gave me a meaningful look. "You think I could forget her brother's ugly mug? That little fat-ass was standing right there, with his dad, too, and your girl was holding his hand."

"She isn't *my girl*," I countered, but either Jafar didn't hear or he was ignoring me.

"They've got to be here somewhere. It wasn't even half an hour ago."

"Yeah, but what if they were about to leave?"

He didn't respond to that, either.

"Come on," he said.

We pushed past strangers. Raindrops fell. Shrieks from the Devil's Wheel were followed by cheers. The sound of cans clattering came from somewhere, and a father praised his son for his throw.

"In here," Jafar said.

Before I knew what was happening, I was looking at a metal grate and we lifted off, suddenly floating above the park, and everything big and imposing before now shrank rapidly to a manageable size.

Jafar sat facing me. He carefully used the hem of his sweater to dry his camera lens. Then he pulled the leather strap off over his head and handed me the camera. "It's got a 70–200 mm lens," he said, as if I should know what that meant. I must have made a face, because he added, "Not exactly a telescope, but pretty decent zoom."

The camera was heavier than I'd have thought. I held it up to my eye and squinted through the viewfinder.

"Just don't drop it, okay?"

The zoom was considerable. We were almost at the top of the Ferris wheel, but in the viewfinder, the bustle below appeared no farther than an arm's length. I was careful to avoid jerking motions as I panned from

the ice-cream and cotton-candy stands past other at-
tractions: the target shooting and ball toss games, the
merry-go-round, bumper cars, ghost ride. I zoomed in
on nearly every face I saw, but couldn't find her anywhere.

I sank back with a sigh.

Jafar looked at me in amusement. He seemed about
to say something, but then reconsidered and whistled
quietly through his teeth. "Someone's in love."

"Quit it."

"It's okay, Amin," he said, smiling broadly. "I've been
there before too."

"Fine, except I'm not in love."

He held up his hands to placate me. "Got it. Not in
love."

I couldn't tell if he was making fun of me. I glanced
nervously to the side.

After far too long a silence, I asked him, "Did you
really see her?"

He nodded. "Why would I make that up? They were
down there."

"But I don't see her."

"Yeah, well"—he rolled his eyes and heaved an exaggerated sigh—"that's the thing about love. You can't
always see it, but it's—"

I kicked him in the shin. He grimaced, then smiled.
"Sorry."

"What were you doing here, anyway?" I was nervous
and tired, and my voice sounded more impatient than
I'd intended. The gondola gave a small shudder. We were
on the other side of the Ferris wheel now, headed down.

"I was meeting someone." He gestured for me to give
back the camera.

"Anyone I know?"

He shook his head, turned away, and fiddled with the lens as he held the viewfinder up to his eye. The roar of the carnival was returning.

"A girl?" I asked.

"Nah," was all he said.

The carnival barker's tinny voice blared from the speakers: "One more round!"

I slid back and forth uneasily. "Why do I always have to coax everything out of you?"

"Why do I always have to tell you everything?"

I was annoyed by how calm he was and how little attention he was paying to me. "Where'd you get that thing, anyway?"

He was still scanning the scene below and didn't look at me. "What thing?"

"The camera."

"Oh. It was my uncle's. You know, the one in Canada."

"Wait, he actually exists?"

Jafar turned at this and blinked, uncomprehending. "Yeah, what do you think? He lives in Gatineau, Quebec. Has a big antique shop."

I gestured sheepishly. "I thought we made him up."

Cool waves of rain suddenly blew in from the side. Umbrellas opened in the crowd below, like drops of ink in a glass of water.

I was reminded of what the silkworm farmer had said to me earlier that afternoon: *We just want to make sure you're in good hands. Are you boys close?*

Jafar studied me. "You okay, man?"

"Yeah, man. Fine. Thanks."

I almost spilled everything at the sight of his watchful face, but I fought the impulse and kept the outing with Abbas to myself. Was that stubborn and childish of me? I didn't even cave when he leaned forward, put a hand on my knee, and said: "By the way, it's not like I didn't want you around. I rang your doorbell this afternoon, but no one was home."

The gondola suddenly felt claustrophobic.

"I went out for ice cream," I lied.

We all have that place inside us, unreachable by either light or language. In the years that followed, whenever I thought back to my work at the museum, I often felt it wasn't the sculptures themselves that were so fascinating, but rather their foreignness. They retained their allure as long as I didn't know anything about them. There was a narrow schism where the incontrovertible fact of their existence came up against the unknowable truths that neither scientific methods nor experts could demonstrate: What kind of life did the sculptor lead? Did his work make him rich? And what stories would his creations tell, if they could speak? As a kid I was convinced that the answers I sought were being withheld from me at every turn in this mute society. I told myself that I was doing everything humanly possible to learn as much as I could, but that there were too many roadblocks. I don't think that was entirely true, though. Take the silkworm farmer, for instance: he grew more disillusioned by the day, and there was something inherently tragic about him, but none of that came close to my speculations about him before we took that drive. Had I become integrated in this society more quickly than I realized? I'm sure there were plenty of instances when I feared the truth might be grayer, or simply more trivial, than the possible alternatives cloaking it, which was reason enough for me not to ask.

I eyed Jafar in silence as he looked at the carnival

through the camera's viewfinder. He'd always loved riddles. Maybe he loved riddles so much he became one himself some days, and maybe that was exactly what I loved so much about him. Maybe I didn't want to destroy that. Whomever he was meeting and whatever the reason, I told myself, must not be important. Jafar was focused entirely on what he was seeing. I heard the shutter release in the stillness. He would later give me this photo as a gift, along with a message.

There was a time when people believed all material or human bodies were comprised of a series of spectrums—overlapping layers beamed into space that landed on our irises as delicate membranes. This was how our sense of vision worked, they thought. For all his brains, even Honoré de Balzac was convinced that, to take a photograph, the camera had to remove a layer of the body and capture it on the plate or film; it stood to reason that if the subject were photographed enough times, he would eventually disintegrate and disappear.

I don't know if this was the effect Jafar was intending. His photo shows the carnival suspended in a state of flux—lights, people, everything flowing and blurred, captured just before the world began to disintegrate.

We ultimately spotted her waiting by the ghost train. The Ferris wheel came to a halt, and we hurried across the fairgrounds, ducking behind a claw machine at a safe distance. My racing heart. I kept sneaking peeks, but it took time to build up the courage to look at the girl properly. She was fourth or fifth in line and staring at the ground. Her father and brother were behind her. People were waiting for the gates to open for the next turn.

"Don't move a muscle," Jafar said and vanished into

the crowd. He handed me a ticket when he returned moments later, then gave me a look and a pat on the shoulder. His tone was friendly and warm as he said, "Don't you dare screw this up." He smiled.

I was so perplexed at first, I didn't know what to say. "You want me to go on that ride?"

He sighed. "No, I want you to crumple up the ticket and eat it. Tastes like licorice!" He stepped up and nudged me in the chest. "Yeah, man, you're going on that ride!"

"But," I stammered, "how'm I supposed to do that, cut in line? Did you *see* the line? There's no way!"

"Sure there is." He turned toward the ghost ride. "You trust me, don't you?"

I nodded.

"Good. Remember the magician in the circus last summer? He was blabbing away the entire time he was sawing that lady in half, remember?"

"I have no idea what your point is."

"Diversion," he said, bowing hammily. "Allow me to be your magician of love."

"You've lost your mind!"

"Maybe, maybe not." Jafar grinned. "Go on. I'll distract her bodyguards while you tend to the princess, Han Solo."

"You do realize her father is going to kill you, right? Whatever you're planning, he's going to catch you and both of us will be ..." But Jafar had already dashed off, and I had no choice but to follow.

What happened next was quite possibly the most spectacular pursuit in Luna Park history.

"May the Force be with you!" I heard Jafar yell before he slithered through the crowd. While I continued struggling to grasp what was going on, Jafar had sidled up to the girl's father, opened his coat pocket, and fished out his wallet. Jafar moved away a few yards, then waved the wallet in the air and cried out, "Excuse me, sir, don't I know you? Oh yeah—you still owe me thirty dollars for that comic book!"

The rest went something like this, as far as I can remember: The man and his son turned in unison, and as though their neural pathways were synchronized, their facial expressions changed in slow motion, from astonishment to recognition to incredulity to rage. In a comic, the speech bubble over their dopey faces would have read *What the ...?!* Then they both turned white and took off running. They clearly hadn't bargained for Jafar's agility. Even I was amazed, and I had seen him in action plenty of times, springing from narrow ledges to insane heights. The dad almost collared him, but Jafar sidestepped nimbly and shot to the left. He dove under a bundle of balloons a seller was leading across the fairground, then, pretending he'd hurt himself doing so, allowed his pursuer to gain several yards, before he sprinted to the right, toward the bumper cars.

After running just a few yards, the girl's brother was alarmingly winded. So was her dad, though in his case, it was out of blind rage. "Stop that thief!" he roared, but no one seemed terribly keen to end the spectacle prematurely. When they reached the merry-go-round, father and son split up, each going in a different direction, and for a minute, it looked like Jafar would fall into their trap. Maybe he just wanted them to think that, though, because he swerved again and trotted slowly past the boy—now completely out of breath—egging him on, while all the kid could do was halfheartedly extend his arm. Jafar didn't speed up again until the dad rounded the carousel, his bright red face emerging from behind a unicorn, and as Jafar ran, he dropped coins from the wallet like crumbs of bread for an abandoned child. The father tore through a group of young guys who didn't move aside quick enough. Their popcorn swirled in the air like snowflakes. The girl's brother crept on all fours by the merry-go-round, hurrying to gather all the coins, while her father chased Jafar clear across the fairground. They had almost reached the exit at this point, and people stopped and watched in amazement as the two ran a final victory lap before disappearing behind the lights. I was nudged forward. The line was moving. I turned around and saw that the entrance to the ride was open. Standing beside me was the girl. She looked surprised. The car hissed as it stopped on the tracks in front of us. The seats were sticky and patched with fabric tape. We sat down next to each other. My hands were soaked with sweat. The safety bar lowered and we slowly rolled into a dark blue light.

It later seemed to me I had fallen in love with her silence, because for most of the ride, we didn't speak, but the silence was happy and strange.

A sidelong glance. "Hello."

"Hello."

"My name is Amin."

"My name is Zahra."

She smiled and lowered her eyes.

She was smaller than I remembered.

Howling skeletons tumbled out of the walls.

"Are you from Beirut too?"

She shook her head. "I live near Jouaiya."

"I don't even know where that is."

"About an hour and a half."

"That's pretty far."

She smiled again. "I remember you."

The light overhead flickered and went out.

My knee was touching her knee—was she aware of that too?

We didn't say anything. The car clattered onward.

Her hand was resting in her lap, not far from mine. I slid my pinky finger a tiny bit to the side.

You have unleashed unspeakable evil! a giant cobra hissed. The snake's eyes glowed at us in the darkness.

"Do you like ghost trains?"

"They're okay. How about you?"

"They're okay."

We laughed nervously.

There was thunder and lightning.

"Can I call you sometime?"

"Call me?"

"Hang on a sec."

I rummaged for my notebook.

A one-eyed prisoner rattled the bars beside me. Fog rose all around us.

"Here, wanna write it down for me? Your number, I mean."

She shook her head. "I can't."

"Why not?"

"My dad ..."

"Oh. I understand ..."

"Sorry."

More silence.

We passed through a tangle of spiderwebs.

We looked at each other for the first time.

The entire alphabet separated the first letters of our

names, yet as I searched for words, the sentences collapsed inside my head. There was still so much to say.

I'd lost all sense of time.

"I want to send you something," I finally managed to say.

"Send me something? What, like a present?"

"Yeah, a present. A story. I'll write one for you. Do you like stories?"

The car suddenly went into a steep curve, and we both leaned to the side. I felt her weight against my body. The track straightened out again, and she slid over, farther away than before.

"I would love to get a story from you," she said, "but you can't send it to *me*."

"I'll send it wherever you want."

A troll emerged from the fog. *I will haunt your every move!* it growled.

She folded her hands. I could tell she was thinking it through.

"My cousin. Here in Beirut. Send it to her. She'll bring it to me. My cousin can keep a secret."

The shimmering lights of the park appeared at the end of the tunnel.

"Deal," I said hastily. "Write her address in here."

I darted past the line with my head down after the ride ended. The rain was coming down harder now. I hid behind a stall and watched as Zahra, holding her brother's hand, ambled toward the exit, where their father was waiting for them. Sweat had darkened the armpits and front of his shirt; he still looked furious. He had his wallet in hand, meaning Jafar had clearly dropped it when his lead was big enough.

I tucked the notebook into my waistband, pulled on

a sweater, and headed home. It was pitch dark by now. I kept turning around at first, but once Zahra was out of sight, I started running.

The One Safe Place

He died, so that Lebanon may live. These words were printed under the pictures of fighters plastered on buildings. Many of them looked younger than me. Martyr posters fashioned after images of saints. The colors saturated, the young men's faces in soft focus before a radiant background.

Every week now, newspapers reported on attacks that all followed a similar pattern. The bombs tended to explode at night, in Christian neighborhoods, and usually on Fridays. The perpetrators rarely claimed responsibility, but since the Syrian withdrawal, even someone like me—who could barely keep the underlying causes and web of entanglements straight—could see that this was about more than individual acts of revenge or pointed political messages; these bombings were symptomatic of a question that had gone unanswered for decades—the question of this country's identity.

At the time, it often felt like my entire world had shrunk to the size of that apartment. The May sunlight flickered at the window all day, but I kept the curtains closed most of the time and withdrew to the dim confines of the room. Dead flowers. Dirty dishes. Dusty shelves and piles of already-read novels by the bed. Sometimes, when gunfire sounded in the poor areas across town, I would blast the radio till the neighbors started pounding on the wall. Even at night, when it was quiet, I barely dared to approach the window; in my darkest moments, I became convinced a bullet might ricochet and find its way up to my floor and into my temple. I'd grown jumpy. The constant vigilance and startling at the sound of a car alarm or rattling windows. Sometimes I even thought I saw ghosts, though it may have been a lingering effect of my fever. One night, after taking two tranquilizers the souk pharmacist had sold me on the quiet, I did peer through the curtains. An emaciated dog was slinking down the sidewalk. He sniffed, lifted a leg, and peed on the lamppost. I was watching the dog when, just beyond the light, I detected a motionless figure looking up at me. I shrank back, went to the sink to fill my glass, and took a third pill. When I returned to the window, the figure was gone, leaving the sidewalk deserted.

Dear Teta,

There's the smell of incense and jasmine outside churches. People here feel drawn to prayer. By the wayside: the rubble of ruined reveries and kids lingering in doorways. Places to play have grown scarce. They stand there in dresses and overalls, wielding wooden weapons in their little hands with nowhere to go.

What you once told me about Tripoli now seems like a fairy tale. You and your father and nighttime in the New Town, all like figures and features you'd find in a ballad. Once upon a time, there was a girl who painted in secret on the seashore and was punished terribly for it. Once upon a time, there was a young woman named Yara who watched her own happiness unfold before her in the theater. Once upon a time, long, long ago, terrible things happened that a grandmother concealed behind a golden mask.

All these masks. There are days when it seems the revolution has done little more than wipe away makeup that the country has worn for years. Upheaval and unanswered questions: Who do we want to be? What do we stand for? Who are we, and how do we want to live? We grimace in response, finally showing our real face.

My world here is barely 300 square feet, yet I still grope my way around the rooms. Even the moths have grown disoriented. When the darkness fades, they fly smack into my window and tumble out, spinning, into daylight.

Khalil's bookshop remained one of my few constants.

"Ah, the cartographer!" he welcomed me warmly every time I stopped by. He then asked if I had enjoyed his last recommendation, and if there was anything I was looking for in particular this time. We chatted a while about books, his recall of stories he'd read years before astonishingly precise. He was no longer a young man, but he had a boyish face that registered surprise every time he heard the bell over the door, because few people strayed into his shop these days. If that saddened him, he showed no sign of it. To me, at least, he seemed the type of person who demonstrated the enviable ability to face the turbulence of the world with an air of romantic resignation; maybe that was why I sought out his company so often. Whenever I entered the store, he'd be sitting at an oak desk, his nose buried in receipt books and registers, a cup of coffee and a chewed pencil beside him, and at the sound of the bell, he would push his glasses up his nose, blink a few times, and greet me like an old friend.

It wasn't just Khalil I liked, it was the shop, too, although the shelves betrayed not the slightest effort at organization. It was welcome disorder that invited a bit of digging.

This is why I so clearly remember the day the bookshop stopped feeling like a safe place, because something strange happened.

I had just paid for my book and turned to leave when Khalil exclaimed, "Oh, good grief!"

I turned back around.

"Please wait just a second. How frustrating; where on earth did I put it?" He rifled through the countless piles of paper on his desk and even lifted the cash register, then opened a drawer and picked up books and shook them, setting them aside when nothing fell out. "This really is embarrassing, but I ... ha! There, I knew it!" He held out an envelope in triumph. "Message for you!"

I froze.

"There was a man here a few days ago, asking about you."

Rather than approach, I took two steps back. "Someone was asking about me? Could you describe him?"

He did, and my mouth went dry.

"Did he say what he wanted?"

"No, unfortunately. He said you had recently moved here and must have forgotten to give him your address. He said you hadn't seen each other for some time, but that he was an old friend. All I told him was that you come here every now and then; I don't know your address, either. I think he stopped by several stores to ask. Here." Khalil was still holding out the envelope to me. "He asked me to give you this."

I reluctantly took the envelope. It wasn't sealed. There was no letter inside, but a slip of paper. Four lines of chicken scratch, evidently written in haste:

Amin, please, we have to talk. I wasn't sent by Yara. She doesn't know a thing about this, I swear. It's about "Song for the Missing." I hope you still have it. Call me. Abbas

Art has a way of revealing unexpected truths about ourselves or the world. If you're curious about eighteenth-century Rome, they say you need look no further than Piranesi's *Vedute di Roma.* There have even been cases in which reality was modeled after artistic renderings. Following World War II, for instance, a Bernardo Bellotto painting was consulted in rebuilding Warsaw's destroyed old city. His *vedute* of Dresden were elevated to icons after that baroque city's bombing. My grandmother told me that when I was a kid. I later learned that Bellotto took certain liberties in his pictures, meaning they were also playful transgressions, adulterations of reality. He made corrections to spots where reality bored him or fell short of satisfying his aesthetic. In his representation of the Scuola Grande di San Marco in Venice, he crowned the gable of the building with three small towers that do not actually exist. He moved flagpoles, expanded city squares, and added visual metaphors for Venetian life, like arc lamps, reflections in water, laundry hung out to dry. Everyone knows Venice, even if they've never been, thanks in part to his paintings.

Which is truer: reality, or our representation of it? The answer to this question may contain a further truth valid beyond the realm of art. Because it's something human. What does Venice represent to most people, anyway? A moldering, putrid nest full of pigeon shit, or a floating vision, a dream, a romantic promise, suspended time—Casanova and Antonio Vivaldi, temptation and lament? What about Bellotto? Couldn't you argue that an image is truer than reality, because it's more human? Because it touches us?

I hurried home, note in hand.

It's about "Song for the Missing." I hope you still have it.

Of course I still had it. The more complicated the situation and the more pervasive my loneliness had grown in past weeks, the more I'd looked at it. It was like the act of viewing tapped into some wellspring of hope inside me. A great promise of happiness. I grew convinced, the longer I studied my mother's painting, that the house up there in the mountains, the one with the overgrown garden, was the only place I'd ever be safe.

On Concealment

As is the case in most utopias, concealed within my mother's dream was also a nightmare. She was nineteen in 1976 and all alone in Paris. She was sharing an apartment with a college friend in Montmartre, on Rue Lepic, just a stone's throw from Sacré-Coeur and about twenty minutes by metro—if she took the 12—from the École nationale supérieure des beaux-arts, where she was enrolled. My grandparents covered her costs. I learned this from a bundle of my mother's letters home, in which she thanked them for the support. I've never traced her footsteps, never been to Paris. A few years ago, though, I came across the '76 yearbook in a digital archive on her alma mater's website; there I found a black-and-white picture of her class assembled below a Gothic arch. She's standing off to one side, as if crowded out. She has her mother's sloping cheekbones and long, dark hair. It looks like she's shivering, her shoulders tensed. Her eyes screwed up. She seems isolated, nervous. Given how earnest and discomfited she appears in the image, it's obvious she mistrusted her good fortune. She seems cowed, almost, by the building's aura. Her mistrust is something I read about in the letters. Her descriptions of Paris and its beauty seem written out of a sense of obligation, rather than actual enthusiasm: the banks of the Seine, the aroma inside La Balle au Bond café, the grandeur of Notre-Dame. I get the impression that it was all meant to suggest a feeling of happiness and security to put her parents' minds at ease, back home.

But I already had a Paris.

Lines like that, rare moments in her letters, show me how much she missed her parents and home. The opulent world my grandparents had occupied up until, and even after, war broke out—a world of important Beirut families, businessmen, bankers, art collectors, a world in which you drank champagne to signify your social standing, evenings passed in hotels, upscale boutiques, and box seats at the theater—stood in stark contrast to the solitude she encountered in France. She doesn't mention any friends in her letters, nor a boyfriend, which comes as little surprise. Here and there she mentions the names of professors whose lectures really stuck with her. Her descriptions of things that moved her stand out because they're so infrequent. When she writes about art, it often seems she's talking about herself. She mentions Hélène de Beauvoir's triptych, *Les femmes souffrent, les hommes jugent,* in one of her later letters. She included a postcard-sized image of the work, depicting men in bloodred robes, pointing at the naked woman on the ground below, who are frozen in what looks like a block of ice.

It's little more than confessional painting ultimately, but the image moves me, she wrote to her mother.

What emerges from these letters is a portrait of a young woman who spent every free moment visiting museums and galleries or sitting in libraries and reading about artists and artworks, so as to avoid having to share her worries or reveal anything personal about her life in her correspondence. I think she was aware of her privilege, but also felt burdened by it.

I loved knowing that she would become the painter I hadn't been allowed to become myself, as a young woman.

Grandmother's words.

At that time, 1976, the conflict in Lebanon had not yet reached its horrific apogee. Other events dominated international news headlines: *Viking 1* landed on Mars. In China, Mao Zedong died. Vietnam was reunified. Lots was being written about Berlin, but very little about Beirut, the other divided city.

My mother had just turned eighteen when she watched from the mountains as the first plumes of smoke rose from the capital. She didn't suspect it at the time—no one did—but Lebanon was on its way to becoming the archetype for a new style of combat. Cold War–era postcolonial conflicts and proxy wars, which had played out on four continents over the past thirty years, from Angola to Indochina, were largely over. In 1975, two weeks after the first shots had been fired in Beirut, the last helicopter took off from the roof of the US embassy in Saigon, and the world witnessed the first signs of an age-old conflict stirring: sectarian warfare. The return of medieval ideologies. I know that leaving was hard for my mother, as she hugged her parents goodbye in the departures terminal before boarding the Middle East Airlines flight to Paris. Grandmother told me about that moment, and there's reference to it in her letters. She was looking forward to the new experiences that awaited, but the thought of leaving her parents here, amid burgeoning unrest, troubled her.

Even French news outlets covered the Karantina massacre. In retrospect, it almost seems the former peacekeeping power was turning a blind eye, loath to acknowledge its legacy and what had sprung from the foundation of the constitution it had left to Lebanon.

With every bloodbath, however, it became more difficult to abstain from reporting; my mother's distant home thus edged its way toward the front page and back into view as she sat at the table in her little apartment in Montmartre, reading the headlines. When she wrote to her parents, she asked about friends in Beirut and mentioned places she'd read had been razed. She also asked about the house and the overgrown garden. While she was away in Paris, the war dug in its heels. It extended past Beirut and soon made its way into the mountains.

I thought I sensed tension between you two during your last visit. I hope everything's okay.

She wrote that to her mother on July 8, 1976. Her parents had visited her in Paris a few weeks earlier. The letters don't reveal what prompted this feeling, if there had been an incident or if it was her intuition, but she must have started work on the painting soon after.

My sense is that *Song for the Missing* conceals her fear. Something had ruptured between her parents in her absence. It's why she painted herself into the scene, not as a girl, but as the young woman she had become, in the place that connected all three of them. The picture depicts her greatest wish—a perfect world. There's not a single wilted petal, irksome insect, bruised apple, or other sign of decay. Other paintings, especially those by the old masters, use such details to illustrate the inexorable march of time. These details remind us that nothing lasts forever. In the picture my mother painted for her parents, though, these elements don't exist. It's as though every element were intended for eternity.

*

As is the case in most utopias, concealed within my grandmother's dream was also a nightmare. Shortly after she died in 2006, I returned to her apartment one last time, wading through the silence she'd left behind. It was the day after the funeral. I opened the door, fully expecting to find evidence of her sudden death everywhere I looked: her nightgown on a hook in the bathroom, dirty dishes, an impression left in her favorite spot on the sofa. But of course Umm Jamil and other friends had come and cleaned the kitchen and bath, fluffed the pillows, and made her bed. There was a freshly made guest bed in my old room, as if she'd been awaiting my return. When we still lived together, the apartment was always decorated by season, but there were never any personal objects on the shelves or in drawers. No photo albums, no shoeboxes of souvenirs, no reminders of her marriage—it was like that had never happened, either. I wandered from room to room now, opening drawers and cabinets, but there was almost nothing of hers to be found. Her vaccination record. A calendar with only a few appointments noted. Objects utterly devoid of intimacy. Her habits clearly hadn't changed after our fight and my escape to Tripoli, and I was resigned to the fact that even now, after her death, I wouldn't gain any insight into her past, wouldn't glean any information to help me understand what had made her the woman she was—the woman who raised me. As I sat down on the couch, though, I did discover something: there was a box on the coffee table. Inside was a key on a keychain with an address. One of her friends must have left it there for me.

I drove to the address. It turned out Grandmother had rented a small garage in West Beirut, not far from the café. The owner told me that for twelve years, my teta had paid her sixty dollars a month to use it for storage. The owner was an old woman. When I showed her the key, a look of pity crossed her face. She invited me to sit down in her living room. The curtains were old and moth-eaten. Everywhere you looked were framed family pictures. The woman's hands trembled as she returned with a tray of coffee and cookies. I got up to offer help, but she didn't want any. Her name was Fatima; I knew her. She was one of the widows who had stood at the door to our apartment years earlier.

She later showed me to the garage beside her house. The space was empty, except for a cardboard box in the far corner.

"Your grandmother was a strong woman. A special woman," Fatima said. "I didn't want her money. She was familiar with my situation, though, from those visits of mine to your house, and she insisted." Fatima reached for my hand and squeezed it. She then excused herself and left me alone in the garage.

The box contained newspaper articles—a positive review of Grandmother's show at the Joseph Matar Gallery and a profile piece about my grandparents as patrons of the Grand Théâtre, which mentioned the names of other sponsors, including Abbas. The bundled letters from my mother lay beside the clippings. There were nearly forty. As I picked them up, a photo slipped out of the pile: Grandmother in a wedding dress next to Amin el-Maalouf, her husband. By her standards, she had told me a lot about how they met. About how he'd ensnared her at the theater, piloted their course through the frosty upper strata of Beirut's beau monde, and later bought them the house in the mountains. She'd never said a word about when he stopped being part of her life, though, or why. As a kid,

I figured she didn't keep personal stuff around the house because she suspected I'd snoop through her things while she was at work. I once told her as much, and she denied it so convincingly that I felt ashamed for having thought it. Having my suspicions confirmed now, so many years later, inspired neither disappointment nor anger in me. Just curiosity.

There were a few other things in the box, though they didn't reveal much to me. They communicated as little as their owner had. The one thing that did catch my eye also provided the missing piece to the puzzle regarding the end of their marriage. It was a religious court certificate dated May 1978. It was at the very bottom of the box. It confirmed that my grandparents had both converted to Sunni Islam. This came as a big surprise. Grandmother had never been remotely religious around me. She loved the modest church in our neighborhood and often relaxed in the shade of the church gardens, but I never once saw her pray, and certainly not according to Islam. It was only later that I learned it was essentially impossible for Maronite Christians like my grandparents to divorce. In the eyes of the church, even domestic abuse was deemed insufficient grounds for a woman to request a divorce. I don't think that's what was happening in my grandparents' marriage. The fact that *both* converted to Islam, in order to secure the divorce, leads me to believe it was amicable, as does the fact that Grandmother got to keep the house in the mountains. Had things been different, Amin el-Maalouf could have converted on his own and remarried, leaving his first wife without any claim to property or custody of their daughter—any man's privilege in a country of men. He would be divorced, whereas her marital status would remain unchanged according to her church, and she'd be shunned from society as a forsaken woman.

I locked the garage, returned the key to Fatima, and said goodbye. It had gotten late. All day long, Israeli aircraft had thundered overhead. There had been bombings in the southern suburbs, and I decided not to drive home to the mountains but to spend the night in Beirut. Back in Grandmother's apartment, I spread out the contents of the box on the floor. That's where I read my mother's letters. Her life in Paris, her concerns, and the joys she experienced in her studies unfolded in front of me. To this day, I believe they hold a clue regarding the reason for her parents' divorce. It's a short sentence I might have missed, had it not been in the same letter from July 8, 1976, in which she expressed her concern about the tension she thought she had witnessed between them. The line read:

How do you think he'll react if he finds out about him?

Something told me that these twelve words were the one and only reference to my father. For some reason, I was certain of it. I sensed that a connection had existed between mother and daughter that didn't require many words. They shared a secret. But my grandfather—did he sense it? This unassuming sentence hinted at a situation that remains problematic for many in Lebanon today, one that frequently leads to tragedy—a daughter's love affair. However worldly he may have been, Amin el-Maalouf belonged to a generation so deeply rooted in tradition that this would have shaken him to his foundations. Had he found out and blamed his wife for their daughter's lifestyle? After all, it had been her idea to send her to faraway France.

I sat cross-legged in the weak glow of the streetlight outside the window, and thought back to Saber Mounir and the charred remains in the library.

But if there are words missing, what's beautiful about it? I had asked the hakawati.

And he'd responded: *The space between the surviving words is an open invitation to fill it with imagination.*

I stared at the letter for a long time. I read and reread it, then I lay back on the parquet floor and gazed into the darkness, as I had done so often as a boy.

She met him while she was studying in Paris, didn't she? I asked into the silence.

Who? I heard Grandmother's voice ask back.

My father, I said. *He wasn't Lebanese. She had to hide that from her father. Keeping secrets from your fathers—you two had that in common. That really connected you, didn't it?*

*

As is the case in most utopias, concealed within Jafar's dream was also a nightmare. He dreamt of finding the cartoonist.

I realize today that our memories of that summer afternoon at the flea market were diametrically opposed. Mine were thoroughly informed by thoughts of Zahra. The way she'd spoken to me, the way she'd looked at me. Until I saw her again, those impressions outshone everything. It's why that day was never shrouded in distress for me, but rather yearning. It was different for Jafar, though. A sense of humiliation permeated his memories. He had lain in the dirt. People had kicked and spat at him. Whereas I simply viewed Younes Abboud as a young man who behaved calmly in a moment of great tension and displayed civil courage, to Jafar he had the aura of a savior who appeared out of nowhere and saved him from a graver fate, using just his words.

In a way, I think Jafar was falling for his own trick. Storytellers, we knew, were not necessarily confessors —they just had to be good liars. When you invent a drunken film star autographing a comic book in a dimly lit hotel bar, the extent to which you believe in your characters and their actions is limited, at best. You do, however, need to describe them in such a way that your reader or listener believes in them, at least in that moment. From his feeling of debasement, I think Jafar expected too much of the cartoonist. The young man became another one of our characters, and Jafar made the mistake of truly believing in him. He would always tell me: *The cartoonist is our only hope*. It seemed logical to him that this young man, who seemed to know so much about the world of art, would be able to decipher a code exhibited in a café in West Beirut. There was never any doubt about that to him. This demonstrates to me that Jafar, though he outpaced me in many regards, continued to exist in a childhood world himself. One might also say that his search for the cartoonist shows how desperate he was.

Several months ago, in early 2011—five years after Grandmother's death and half a lifetime since the events of 1994—I was taking a late afternoon walk in Hamra when I chanced upon a photo of Younes Abboud in a glass display case at the university. I wouldn't have recognized him, had his name not been printed below. He had shoulder-length hair and three-day stubble, and in the picture he was leaning casually against a stone wall with his arms crossed. It was advertising an exhibition of his drawings; the poster said he was coming from Paris for the occasion. The show was in two days. According to the brief biography under the event details, a graphic novel of his had been published in France and garnered a lot of attention. It was called *The Green Line* and told the story of his childhood and adolescence spent living with his family on that infamous street. The bio concluded with a review that described Younes Abboud as a talented artist whose story *employs humor to great effect to balance out the chaos and suffering, the human tragedies.* My eyes wandered back a few lines and I read the year he had evidently left Lebanon to study in France: 1994.

Much time had passed since I'd last thought of Jafar. In a way, we were still connected by this man, who looked at me with the rakish expression of an artist. Dusk was falling, and I could see my face reflected in the illuminated glass case.

Two days later I went back. The exhibition was in the foyer outside a lecture hall, where they'd be holding the Q&A. I got there way too early. The drawings, framed in black, were hung on the walls. There were thirty in all, a cross section of his work. Most were unpublished, I read on a placard. They were scenes of Beirut. The depictions were grotesque and alienating, but I recognized the city immediately. The pieces were arranged chronologically, so viewing them was like moving through Younes Abboud's life. The drawings at the beginning resonated most with me. He'd done them in a notebook as a child. In these early attempts, Beirut was still Beirut, but a nightmarish version of it. He had christened the series *Labyrinth City.* Mole people and mutant sewer creatures lived in subterranean barracks, while armed rats the size of dogs patrolled the streets above and knocked at the doors to the underworld, looking to recruit their young. The drawings moved me.

I've described how inscrutable Jafar was at times.

Why do I always have to tell you everything? he had asked me that afternoon on the Ferris wheel. It sometimes felt like he was withdrawing from me and the rest of the world, and at those times he seemed distant and inaccessible. Whenever he paid a little attention to me or did something nice, though, it felt like a grand gesture. The same thing was happening now with Younes Abboud's sketches. They took me back to dark, nameless buildings seen through the eyes of a boy, spooky and fascinating at the same time. It was interesting to see how his style had evolved. The drawings from 1994 reminded me of the picture he'd given us that now hung framed in my office. They were crawling with peculiar figures and details. By contrast, the images he had drawn after leaving Lebanon for Paris were remarkably pared down. They were still vibrant, showing the living environment in Beirut, but it was like the perspective from abroad had heightened his sense of the essential.

The lecture hall filled gradually. I was so immersed in his drawings, I didn't notice the crush, and I snagged the last remaining seat in the back row just as the talk was starting.

It was an entertaining evening, over the course of which Younes Abboud spoke candidly and patiently about his work and answered the students' questions. He was charming and approachable and joked around a lot. When a young woman asked why he had left Lebanon, he took a sip of water to give himself a moment to think, then responded: "It was no longer the Beirut I knew. The city was at peace but everyone kept silent, and in order to tell the stories I wanted to tell, I had to leave."

I just listened. Following the talk, the department

chair led his guest past the crowd to a table near the exit, where he signed books. They were only available in French, a language I hadn't used since high school. Nevertheless, I got in line. It took a while to reach the front. He looked at me expectantly, but nothing in his expression suggested he might recognize me.

"For Jafar," I said.

He signed the book and handed it over. I turned and left the foyer. I was greeted by a cool January night. I paused briefly on my way to the car and considered going back, but then I got in and drove off. What could I possibly have said to him?

*

I'd still like to recount the day Jafar came and got me to go looking for the cartoonist. It was early December, a few weeks after my encounter with Zahra on the ghost train.

Jafar was standing on the street under the leafless cherry tree. His face was split into thousands of little squares as I looked through the screen. He was waving a slip of paper at me. I hesitated. Should I really go down, despite how frustrating his recent behavior? He waved again, and finally I set aside my pen and notebook.

Written on the torn piece of paper was the cartoonist's address. It was printed in black ink and looked official.

"Where'd you get that?"

"From a friend."

"Who?"

"Who cares? Let's go."

The place he supposedly lived was tucked away on a

narrow street, not far from where the circus had been the summer before. We rang the bell. A woman opened the door, and we asked for Younes Abboud. We said we were cousins. She eyed us warily. Still, she led us up a steep staircase and opened the door to an apartment. It was empty.

"You can move in tomorrow," the woman said, laughing. "Your cousin seemed pretty certain he'd never be back."

Without a word, Jafar turned and bolted down the stairs. The front door slammed shut. I stammered an apology and followed him. He was nowhere to be seen. It took me several minutes to find him. He was on a side street, leaning his back against a wall. He was pounding the wall with his fist, over and over. I said his name as I approached. *Jafar.* He didn't respond. He closed his eyes. *Camera obscura,* I thought. I could hear the faraway sound of traffic and music, dampened as if underwater. He pressed his hands to his temples, and I took a step back. His knuckles were bleeding.

Notebook, December 7, 1994

I saw a storm in my dream.
A flash of lightning, and when I got up, Jafar stood
on the other side of the screen
and had a thousand faces.

The Final Days of Winter

What part of Jafar was revealed to me that afternoon? It was like witnessing something inside him derail. I didn't know what to say. The December twilight settled over the street, the reflection of light vanishing from windows, and as we stood there I was overcome with the hope that by tomorrow, whatever had just happened would have passed. A naive hope, of course. In a way, the alley represented a crossroads that would lead us in different directions, though we didn't know it at the time. How could we? After all, barely a month had passed since we'd ridden the Ferris wheel together, suspended up above the city lights, and Jafar had enabled my encounter with Zahra in the ghost train, thanks to his audacious performance.

*

The lights of Luna Park soon lay behind me. It was still drizzling and cars raced by in veils of mist, but I barely noticed. I felt alive and free. I bought a Pepsi at the supermarket and stumbled out, numb with happiness, without waiting for my change. I took a deep breath and experienced the intoxicating sensation of having grown at least two feet taller in the past hour.

She wanted me to write her a story, Zahra had said. The first images and scenes and sentences took shape before I even got home. I had to stop myself from dashing to my room and getting down to work. Jafar must have been waiting ages for me to call. It took a while for him to pick up. He was in a great mood, elated at having settled the score with Zahra's father. He told me he'd dropped the wallet at some point and slipped away from his pursuer, who had stopped running, totally beat, and cursed Jafar's family back to their earliest ancestors.

"Man, there were some swears in there I've got to be sure to remember," Jafar said. Then he asked how things had gone on my end.

"Pretty good," I said, which felt like a massive understatement. I described the ghost ride, told him her name, and maybe even invented a goodbye kiss.

"Good, then it was worth it to get the worst side stitch of all time, just for you."

There was a pause, and I felt a bit embarrassed.

"Thanks, man," I said.

After we hung up, I brushed my teeth quickly, took off my wet clothes, jumped into bed, and started writing. Something was still vibrating inside me; I felt inspired by what I was writing, the ideas, the vivid scenes in my head. There was something magical about creating a world just for her. The words flowed onto the page of their own accord. I had decided to write Zahra a story about what she had unleashed in me that day at the flea market: Once upon a time, there was a boy who moved to a big city. He didn't understand why it was impossible to make friends until he realized he was invisible. There was just one person who could see him, a girl named Sahar. Their first encounter—the first time their eyes met—was at the flea market. Their first dance was on the rocks along the coast, twirling shadows with hair blowing in the wind. I left it blank when the two disappeared behind the rocks ...

At some point later on, I heard Grandmother get up and go to the bathroom. If she noticed the sliver of light beneath my door, it didn't prompt her to check on me. I was up all night writing.

The days had grown colder and rainier, and cafés across the city were bursting. Grandmother had her hands full that November. She borrowed Abbas's car to vet wholesalers and distributors outside Beirut. She visited coffee roasters in Tyros, wading into the aroma and taste-testing on site, and one afternoon she drove over the mountains, all the way to Château Ksara in Zahlé, where she sampled the fabled wines she would later add to her menu. She put in orders with local bakeries for walnut-and-date-filled *maamoul* and other treats, because Christmas was approaching. She combed discount stores for Christmas lights and garden centers for pine boughs, which she arranged with candles and dried orange slices on the tables. One day Abbas's truck was parked outside the café, and together the two of them heaved a massive Christmas tree—which he'd felled for her in the woods—into a corner of the room and decorated it with straw angels and glass baubles. She seemed fulfilled, which made me feel good. Seeing her like that made it easier for me not to think of the photos Jafar had taken, now buried at the bottom of the trunk in my room. I hadn't dug them out since the day he came over, camera slung around his neck, to give them to me. The paintings from Grandmother's show still hung on the café walls like an admonition. They'd become one with the furnishings and decorations at Café Yara, as familiar as the sight of Grandmother bustling from table to table in her apron, asking how everyone was doing or how the cake tasted and giving the impression that everything was fine.

Wasn't it, though? There's no question that I was unsettled by the connections Jafar had discovered between the images. Though I may have feared change and willfully ignored certain things, I wasn't naive. I was rattled by the stories behind those buildings and locations so badly damaged in the war. Why Grandmother's artwork would address these crime scenes remained a mystery to me, though not one I couldn't explain away. The sites were representative of a war that, nearly fourteen years earlier, had compelled her to leave the country with me. Part of the magic of storytelling, Saber Mounir had said, was enabling others to experience that which has been lost. Wouldn't the same go for painting? She may not have had any reason beyond a desire to protect the memory of that time. All over the country, the old was being torn down to make way for new construction. Maybe her paintings were a silent protest against that. Such lines of reasoning served the primary purpose of making me feel better. Nevertheless, I can't deny that a subtle internal shift had occurred. I wouldn't go so far as to say I mistrusted her; Grandmother still had too strong a pull on me for that. She was allowing me to share in her life more than ever, to the point where I sometimes hoped Jafar would never find the cartoonist's address, so we could ditch our effort to find out what on earth L84/91 meant—if anything at all. Every now and then, though, I would feel uneasy, as if something had gotten caught in the roof tiles and was just waiting for the right moment to crash down onto me. I oscillated between feelings of trust and moments of irritation sparked by seemingly everyday occurrences. Tiny seismic waves in anticipation of greater quakes.

Around that time, for instance, there was a noticeable uptick in the frequency of power outages. It came as some surprise, given that we paid the butcher at the end of our street sixty dollars a month to divert power from his generator whenever the need arose. Soon after we moved in, Grandmother had reached an agreement with the man, who strung a cable from his rooftop to our apartment; that way, whenever we lost power, all we had to do was flip a switch to tap into his generator. Our system worked so well that I was surprised by the extent of electricity shortages others still faced after the war. The power cut out at least once a day, and when it returned, sometimes hours later, cries of "Power's back on!" could be heard from open windows across the neighborhood. Within moments, radios began playing, washing machines were hastily filled and turned on, dinner was cooked early, and every last kid was sent to take a shower, which often resulted in the grid collapsing again under the strain.

We were in the same boat that winter, though, because the switch wasn't working. It was usually by chance I'd notice the power was out during the day, spotting puddles under the fridge or other signs. But as I sat doing homework on my bedroom floor in the evening, the electricity on our street would go out so abruptly that the vocab words and equations danced before my eyes for a moment or two before I was completely enveloped in darkness.

During one such outage, I went over to the butcher shop. To my surprise, the cooler was humming in the corner, as if nothing were amiss. The fan was on, too. The butcher informed me his generator was running fine, only Grandmother had suspended payments for the shared usage, and until she decided to reinvest those sixty dollars, he was keeping the connection cut.

When I brought it up later, she responded, "Sorry, I thought we'd talked about it. There's so much going on right now with the holidays approaching. I'm trying to save us a little money, Amin. Half the country has learned to live with the outages, and we will too."

Another time, I came home in the evening to find our apartment filled with music. A woman was singing a mournful song. There was a record spinning on the turntable, but the living room was empty. I found Grandmother in the bathroom, standing at the mirror in the light of a bare bulb. Without looking at me, she asked, "Do you think I've changed a lot?"

"What do you mean?"

"My appearance. If we hadn't seen each other for many years and you passed me on the street, would you recognize me?"

"Yeah, of course."

A few days later, I found her in the bathroom again. This time she was wearing rubber gloves and applying hair dye. She had never done that before.

"I actually liked your natural hair color," I said when she appeared in the living room, her hair blow-dried, not a single silver strand in sight.

"It's unfortunately an unwritten law," she replied, regarding me with a smile, "that will not, however, apply to you later in life. While gray-haired men are seen as handsome, gray-haired women are seen as old."

Why did such scenes irritate me? I suspect it was the gestures that accompanied them: the way she studied herself in the mirror when she didn't know I was watching, or the way she raised her hand to touch her skin, as if seeing herself up close for the first time in a long time, surprised by the many fine lines that crossed her cheeks like tributaries on a map. Or the way she said *Sorry* in her toneless voice—*Sorry, I thought we'd talked about it*. In retrospect, the many moments form a mosaic. Sometimes Grandmother stood at the window, looking out, as if waiting for a sign of spring; waiting for the days to grow longer. She didn't like winter. Gray times, ceaseless rain pelting the windows. The storms that descended upon city and land, whipping up the sea, sweeping through streets, and rattling the shutters. It's another reason I think she spent so much time at the café, in the golden glow of the lamps and the affection of her guests, whose compliments warmed her. Occasionally, however, it seemed she was rebelling against those somber days. On such occasions she refused to wear a coat and marched into the drizzle in just a blouse. She bought a bag of potting soil, filled the terra-cotta flowerpots on the windowsill and planted lemons out of season. To anyone who didn't know her, this could be construed as stubbornness. I had lived through so many German winters with her, though—had seen her huddled in a chair for hours, legs tucked up, unable to form a single sentence—that I largely viewed her behavior now as a sign of strength. She seemed convinced she could influence the change of seasons through sheer resistance.

What a strange winter. Whenever I try to view what happened in a new light, I can't avoid considering the impact of the political situation—general upheaval that seemed so far removed from our lives but proved impossible to escape. The trial of Samir Geagea still held the city in suspense, even by November. His opponents made daily appeals for harsh sentencing in newspaper columns, on the radio, and on TV talk shows. At the same time, his supporters took to the streets to call for his release; several vanished from their homes, swallowed unnoticed by unlicensed limousines with tinted windows, only to be hauled to court in handcuffs, if they reappeared at all. Tony still hadn't returned. The neighborhood was awash in patchy facts and rumors. They said he'd been charged with membership in a former militia that was now trying—in the form of a political party—to undermine the sovereignty of the state. Whenever I stood by the window and saw Nour disappear, her head bowed, into the building across the street or pace behind the curtains in her apartment, I recalled the day I had witnessed Tony's arrest. I still didn't buy what Abbas had told me about the men who'd appeared at Café Yara. *The landlord with a few people.* It just didn't seem plausible. But four months later, the pictures from her show were still hanging and nothing had happened—no more threats, no "accident"—so I figured there really was a chance that Mara had misunderstood things. That it was all one big misunderstanding. It happens.

I would have been more than happy to embrace this notion, had the following not occurred: It was the first week of November, three days after the ghost ride, and I was sitting at a corner table in the café, drinking hot chocolate and working on my story for Zahra, when I noticed two men walking up and down the sidewalk outside the front window. One of them scribbled away on a clipboard while the other pointed at things on the facade and suddenly produced a yardstick. I looked over at Grandmother, who was drying dishes behind the counter. She had noticed the men too. For a while she kept fishing glasses out of the sink, but at some point she put down her towel and went outside. I

"No, pay the authorities."

"But no one's sitting outside in weather like this, anyway."

She nodded pensively. "The rules must have changed."

I looked out the window. The men had vanished, and the street glistened.

"Are we in debt now?" I asked quietly. When I looked back I saw that she had averted her eyes too. There was subtle tension in her face. I had seen her like this at home before, her features mirrored in the window. In the same way she would open the window at home, despite the cold, despite the wind and rain, she then knocked resolutely on the table, twisted her mouth into a smile, and said, "Don't worry, Amin. It must have been a misunderstanding."

She got up and crossed the room. She stopped halfway, crumpled up the official form, and threw it into the trash can by the counter.

November 30, 1994
List of criminal offenses of which my teta Yara el-Maalouf has been guilty in recent days:
Failing to register a floral-print awning with authorities
Outfitting public walkways with unauthorized sitting accommodations
Enabling various customers' addiction by serving exceptionally good coffee
Accepting my death by starvation by neglecting to stock domestic pantry with cookies
Increasing risk of my freezing to death by refusing monthly payment to Hamit M., butcher, for use of said butcher's generator
Endangering health & safety of customers by serving Legionella-contaminated tap water

Today the ironic tone in this and other entries makes me uneasy, no word to be found about the pain Grandmother must have felt. No hint at my own sense of uncertainty, though I remember feeling *extremely* uncertain. I remember sitting on the couch later that evening, watching her over the top of my book. She was pacing from room to room, cardigan tied around her waist. She kept running her hands through her dyed hair. It was like she'd woken with a start in the middle of the night and hadn't managed to lie back down yet. She tore a sheet from the notepad next to the phone, wrote something down, then crumpled it up and threw it away. I later saw that she'd been adding up numbers, but whatever the total represented did not seem to have calmed her nerves—quite the opposite.

Though there's no mention of it in my notebook, I remember being glued to her side at the time. I see us walking down the street in silence, carrying bags of groceries home, and as if trying to make doubly certain of her nearness, I would touch her in passing—her pastel-green sweater as we entered the apartment, her forearm as she handed me the olive oil to put in the kitchen cupboard, or the hem of her blouse one raw afternoon as we stood on the sidewalk and she hailed a cab. Whatever had happened, it was drawing her away from me again.

Jafar was skipping school more. He was even hard to pin down in the afternoon. His sister usually answered the phone and reminded me—her tone one of perfect indifference—that I was more than welcome to reduce the frequency of my calls, as her brother would get back to me when he got back to me. As a result, whenever I wasn't with Grandmother or revising Zahra's story, I wandered around to clear my mind. I can still see the scenes of dereliction on the outskirts, the stray dogs, wrecked cars, battered canisters. In central Beirut, meanwhile, the exuberant push to forget was as pervasive as signs of its failure—rain-sodden posters of grotesquely done-up brides, typos in the big promises made on construction banners hung from buildings, extinguished letters in the neon signs of shopping malls. I managed to forget myself and my worries while hunting down these fragments, and when things were going well it felt like I was disintegrating, becoming invisible like the boy in my story.

Interesting how time has allowed me to recognize my behavior as an instinctive attempt at self-preservation. Some call this trait of mine cowardice; I call it a peaceable inclination. The list in my notebook demonstrates the way I skated around conflict. I flat-out refused to endanger my notion of happiness. Instead I escaped by means of irony and ludicrous images I invented to cover up actual events. Even so, I can't believe I would make light of the tap water issue—a very real and very frightening episode—in that list.

It was late November. The café was filled with the scent of freshly baked treats and comforting sounds of clattering dishes. Why comforting? Because there was no sign of anything having changed since the day those men had shown up. Everything suggested everyday goings-on. Grandmother was animated, clearing, wiping down, and setting newly vacated tables, greeting regulars with kisses on the cheek, and switching out the tape in the player every now and again to ensure a nice mix of background music. I had just finished Zahra's story. The pages lay before me on the table, and I ran my pencil along the lines in concentration. I was so engrossed in my review that I didn't notice when three men came in and looked around. I jumped when one of them loudly demanded to see the owner. Christmas music was the only sound as the room fell silent. Faces turned toward the door. The men had returned, only this time they'd brought along another guy with rough skin and dirty hair. He appeared ill at ease, looking around, unsure what to do with his hands. Then something seemed to occur to him: "Mm-hmm, this is the place. Definitely, one hundred percent. That's the woman who served me," he said, pointing at Grandmother.

No one else uttered a word. On the tables, the candle flames twitched.

The man who'd held the clipboard during their last visit took a step forward. There was a yellowish tinge to his appearance in the lamplight. It was the first time I'd seen him up close. His gaze was alert, and despite his haggard frame, his presence was unusually powerful. He seemed to relish the silence like an actor taking the stage to deliver a monologue. He cleared his throat: "Ms. el-Maalouf, please pardon our coming unannounced, but it's urgent. This man has Pontiac fever. We are happy to provide documentation of the doctor's findings, if you like. He informs us that he drank a cup of coffee here a few days ago, along with a glass of tap water." The sentence seemed incomplete, but the man did not continue. In the silence that followed, the words *tap water* echoed ominously.

Chairs creaked as customers turned to look at Grandmother. She stood behind the counter and took her time in responding. She probably didn't want to appear intimidated, but I could see it was taking its toll. Her hands were folded as if in prayer, white knuckles all that betrayed how tightly she was squeezing.

"This man is mistaken," she finally said, and I was surprised at the steadiness in her voice. "A few days ago, you said? There must be some confusion. He has never been here before. I never forget a face. Besides, we serve our guests bottled water, not tap."

"Even alongside a cup of coffee?" the same man asked. The polite curiosity in his voice was especially vexing, given the space he commanded in the room.

"Yes, of course," she said decisively.

The man nodded as if acknowledging his error and turned to the alleged customer, who stood by the door with clasped hands.

He shook his head and repeated, "No, it was here. One hundred percent."

"You see," the speaker said, facing Grandmother again and spreading his arms in a gesture of uneasiness, "the situation is complicated. It's your word against his, but the fact remains that Pontiac fever is caused by *Legionella* bacteria, which were indisputably detected in this man's system." Raising his hands as if to mollify her, he continued: "Even if you *are* telling the truth—and I assure you that is not being called into doubt—surely you wash the dishes in tap water? Or do you use *bottled water* for that too?"

My throat was parched and I felt a wave of nausea. The other customers stared at the floor in embarrassment, pushed away their plates, or studied Grandmother with interest.

She shook her head. "Tap water," she said.

"Could you repeat that?"

"We wash our dishes in tap water." She forced out the words.

"Aha," the man tacked on with a look of concern. He

reached back and his colleague handed him a document. He crossed the floor and placed it on the counter, an arm's length from Grandmother. "This establishment will remain closed until further notice," he said. "We unfortunately have reason to suspect that the tap water is contaminated with *Legionella* bacteria. We'll have to test the water, and until the results are in, operations will be suspended. All of you," he now addressed the customers, "had better go home. Should you detect any flu-like symptoms in the coming days, please seek medical attention. And thank *you*," he said to Grandmother, "for understanding that the café must remain closed for the next two or three days, until we've conducted a full analysis. After all ..." He paused and, to my surprise, looked straight at me. "We wouldn't want anything worse to happen, would we?"

We made eye contact. I was stunned.

"No," I heard Grandmother say. "We wouldn't want that."

I walked around later, mulling over what had happened that afternoon. I couldn't let it go, so I thought maybe I'd catch an early-evening movie somewhere nearby. By the time I found a theater, though, the film—a popular Egyptian comedy—had already started, and the alternatives were a thriller I was too young for and a family drama I didn't feel like watching, so I ambled toward the city center. Pigeons flew into the air. The streets were clogged with rush-hour traffic and people hurrying home, and I sought refuge in imagining Zahra by my side as I wandered. As if giving me silent consent, she rested her hand in mine as we passed candy-colored shop windows and packed cafés, and then I led her to the rooftop of an abandoned building on a nameless side street and ... I took a quick step back—the light had changed and I'd almost stepped into oncoming traffic.

"Sorry," I muttered at the driver who swerved around me, honking furiously. In a panic, I patted down the breast pocket of my jacket. The story was still there; I could feel the weight of the pages against my heart.

I decided to go home. I passed by a bar on the way. There was a fight going on outside, and I hastened my steps. Then I heard a familiar voice. I turned around and saw three figures standing in the murky neon light outside the entrance, homeless men tussling over a bottle. I could have sworn, as I strained for a closer look, that one of them was the man who had turned up at Café Yara, pale and rumpled, and recited his lines just a few hours earlier.

*

Where was Jafar during that time? Sometimes I went to the boulders on the coast and watched the rough sea. I didn't dare tread on the slick terrain without him, except this one time I ditched my shoes in the grass and ventured up to where the waves hit the rocks. The moment my toes got wet, though, I quickly drew back. I was used to Jafar going first. Whenever we roved the streets, I never felt responsible for choosing our route. I had always relied on him. He radiated confidence that nothing, nobody could throw him off; being part of his world meant loving—or at least accepting—everything about him, whether his childlike curiosity or scampish pranks, his sometimes disastrous impulsivity or the fact that there were things he kept to himself.

This realization about my friend was hard to bear in

the days following the café's closure. I sensed that I needed Jafar, but ever since he'd started searching for the cartoonist, I barely saw him. Whenever we did meet up, he seemed different. In the boys' room at school, he'd recently shown off the fact that he was shaving now. He used his stepdad's razor and sandalwood soap. He left the peach fuzz on his upper lip, which made him look unbelievably grown up. He'd also started wearing a silver chain. He kept it tucked under his collar, but I spotted a cross dangling from it as he leaned forward once to tie his shoe. When he noticed, he stuffed it back into his T-shirt without a word. There were lots of new things like that. When he sat next to me in class, taking notes, I saw scratches on his inner wrists, as if he'd hoisted himself up onto a wall or jagged ledge. Most of the time, though, Jafar just stared out the window at the bare oak tree in the schoolyard and our teacher had to call his name repeatedly to get through to him.

Was he hoping I'd ask him about it? Did he want some indication that his transformation wasn't lost on me? If so, my response was off. I thought it best to act as if nothing had changed.

It wasn't unusual for classmates to disappear from one day to the next. Sometimes families emigrated, other times it was decided the kid should lend a hand in his father's store, rather than wasting time with foreign languages and math. There was a pattern to Jafar's truancy, though, that I began to detect that November. He tended to skip school on the days the UNICEF lady from Paris came to the classroom and read out the names of certain kids, who then got up and left the room with her. When she called Jafar's name, she and our teacher would look first at his empty seat, then at me, and when I shrugged, the lady would write something down, smile at the rest of us, and leave the room.

"The Lost Generation"—that's the title of an article I recently read to gain a better understanding of what was happening back then. As with all armed conflicts, the Lebanese tragedy left its deepest mark on the nation's children. Before the war, approximately one in five hundred kids required psychological intervention; following the conflict, it was one in twenty. From their earliest days, life and death were inextricably bound— a crash course in growing up. I remember a young woman from the Red Cross visiting our class one afternoon. She arranged a number of futuristic prostheses on the teacher's desk and explained that researchers in faraway Geneva had succeeded in manufacturing affordable artificial limbs using a material called polypropylene. Thanks to generous donations, they were being made available to those impacted by limb loss, which we should tell our families. At the start of her presentation, she asked how old we were. Before anyone could respond, a girl behind me whispered, "We're all a hundred years old."

The memory of Jafar scampering just out of reach of Zahra's father in the rain seemed like a hallucination to me now. When he came to school he was often overtired, and on multiple occasions I had to nudge him during class because he'd fallen asleep with his head down on his arms. Sometimes I hoped we'd walk home together after school, maybe taking a detour to explore an abandoned building and dangle our legs from the top floor like we used to, talking about all sorts of stuff. He would usually start muttering excuses as we packed up our books, though, before rushing out of the classroom with a look at the clock.

Our silent estrangement grew, and I certainly had a hand in it. In my skewed logic I assumed that if I acted aloof, Jafar would notice and eventually ask me what was up; he never did, so I told myself that was just the way he was.

I was stalking about the neighborhood one afternoon and passed by the café. Nine days had passed, yet it was still closed. No one had come to test the water. "These things take longer here than in Germany," Grandmother had told me. She had stuck a note to the glass door: *We'll be back soon!*

I had left the apartment with the intention of delivering Zahra's story to her cousin, but a litany of excuses suddenly occurred to me as to why the timing wasn't quite right. Instead I went for ice cream at a shop not far from the café. I was on the doorstep, about to leave, when I saw Jafar. He emerged from a building across the street and sauntered up to a black Volvo idling at the curb. He looked ridiculous to me. There were four young guys in the car. One of them moved over when Jafar opened the door. A rosary dangled from the rearview mirror. I heard the rumble of bass and peered at the boys, none of whom I recognized. It was hard to tell, but they must have been seventeen or eighteen—a lifetime of difference when you're fourteen.

Then in early December Jafar grabbed my arm at recess and pulled me aside. We left the bluish haze of the schoolyard and withdrew into the dark entrance to the school basement, where the custodian stored his tools.

"The café is closed?" he asked.

"Yeah, for a few days now."

"Why didn't you tell me?"

I bit back a nasty comment and told him what had happened.

"Sounds shady."

"Feels shady."

Silence.

"Then I'd better make sure we find the cartoonist soon."

*

What was I feeling as Jafar and I climbed the stairs, step by step, to Younes Abboud's apartment? I seem to recall a vague sense of unease. I was neither upset by the sight of the empty rooms nor relieved.

Jafar, on the other hand, seemed broken when I found him leaning against the wall, in harsh contrast to his demeanor climbing into the car just a few days earlier with an air of expectation that things should yield to him, and not the other way around.

"Have you ever been someplace you feel like you don't belong?" he asked a little later as we turned off the side street.

"Yeah, of course. For me that place was Beirut before I met you."

He didn't respond.

"Where do you feel that way?" I asked.

"I don't know," he shrugged, lowering his head. "Beirut, I guess, but just lately. The city feels unfamiliar."

"What do you mean?"

"Like it's losing its soul. It's weird. I don't know how to explain it. Everything's changing."

"When I first got here, I was scared of the destroyed buildings."

"I remember. You told me about your nightmares."

"Everything was unfamiliar to me."

There was a pause. Three, four steps in silence, then he said: "Those buildings are all I've ever known."

The wind shook the linden trees and drops of rain fell from the branches into our faces.

"Ever get the feeling everything around you might collapse?" he asked quietly.

"No," I lied.

"I do, all the time, and I don't mean that as a parable..."

"I think the word is *metaphor*."

"Whatever. I feel like these new buildings could just fall over like a film set, they seem so fake to me."

"What do you mean, fake?"

"Like they're ... I don't know ... tricking us into believing this is what ... or this is who we are as a city, but we *aren't*."

"I think lots of people like the change. They don't want to see all this stuff anymore."

"What stuff?"

"The ruined buildings."

"Maybe you're right. Maybe they think it'll help them forget."

"Don't you?"

Jafar shook his head forcefully. "I don't think it's possible."

"Why not?"

"You wouldn't understand."

"You mean because I didn't experience it myself?"

"Yeah, because to you it would just be another story. Your world ... and mine."

"Don't say that ..."

Beside us a bus door opened with a hiss. Jafar stopped walking and looked at me. Amid the stream of people elbowing past, he looked like a snagged piece of drift-wood.

"Do you remember that American poet we read in English class?" he asked.

"Whitman?"

"Yeah, Whitman. Mr. Labaki told us Whitman's message was that you appreciate the warmth of the sun more after you've experienced cold. The more you've suffered, the more you learn to love life."

"Yeah, so?"

He studied his injured hands. "Maybe in America that's the case."

We kept walking. The sky was the color of granite. Atoll islands of clouds drifted by.

"The way you feel about the city ..." I began. "Is that why you haven't been coming to school much?"

"I don't know," he said. Either he felt he'd been found out, or it was the truth, plain and simple. In any case, he didn't elaborate, and I didn't prod.

Where were we going? I didn't really know the area. I looked around, curious about what I was seeing and amazed at how little I shared Jafar's estimation. I had come to view Beirut—with its different neighborhoods, its hectic pace and noise—as a raw, unpolished beauty. Even in December. Christmas lights were strung across the streets and reflected in shop windows, stores in Christian areas blasted holiday music, and despite all the stressed-out people, to me the bustle had an appealing anonymity.

"If this isn't who we are as a city," I said, pointing at a building clad in scaffolding, where workers handed tools back and forth, "then what are we?"

Jafar answered immediately: "We're the city I showed you at night."

I glanced at him. Whenever he had talked about his feelings in the past, he'd spun a story around himself like a cocoon. Jafar had never granted me access to his internal self before, never shown me the depths hidden there. And I was thankful he was doing so now.

"So, what's the deal with the café?"

"It'll reopen after they test the water. Just a few more days," I responded, trying to sound convinced myself.

"What about the paintings? Think they have anything to do with it?"

"I don't think so," I said. "We may have been obsessing a little too much about those."

"You never wanted to find him, did you?" he asked quietly.

"Who? The cartoonist? That's not true."

"It's fine, you can admit it."

"But it's not true!" I yelled, shocked at how loud my voice was.

"You swear?"

"I swear."

Silence.

"Where'd you get his address, anyway?"

Jafar made a dismissive gesture. "Doesn't matter at this point."

We dodged as a man dumped out a bucket of water onto the street.

"Maybe it's better this way," I said. "My teta seems more stable these days, like she's gotten a hold of herself. Ever since she showed me their old house and garden and the spot where my parents ... you know ..."

"Where they died?"

I nodded.

"You don't remember them, do you?"

"No, not at all."

"I wonder if that's good or bad."

"What are you trying to say?"

Jafar lowered his head. A rectangle of light had climbed up his front and now framed his chest and head like a portrait. How to explain that I wanted nothing more than to return to those summer days we spent thinking up stories in the branches of poplars? I tried to come up with a way to redirect the conversation toward something more lighthearted, but he spoke first.

"Sometimes I don't even think I'm here. Do you ever get that feeling?" He rubbed his arms and chest and pawed at his face as if it were numb. "Like, right here this very moment. Do you remember standing on the rocks last fall? Whenever it was really windy, you'd get scared the waves might grab you and pull you in. That's exactly what my memories of the past are like. They always pull me back in. I'll forget about the things I saw a thousand times a day, and a thousand times a day, they come right back—both parts are awful. I can barely deal. You stand there and a wave rolls up, only it doesn't leave. Instead, more and more waves pile on top of it, till you can't breathe ..."

I just nodded. There had always been so much I admired about Jafar, and now I even admired the way he found words for what was happening inside him. How was it possible to turn feelings into sentences, just like that? Why the hell was I always left speechless when I didn't happen to have a notebook or piece of paper handy?

He'd been waiting for a response, but when none came he kept walking. I tried to keep up. We hopped over puddles that reflected buildings and clouds. The sound of televisions issued from open windows, as did the occasional sound of kids crying or adults yelling.

"Any updates on your neighbor Tony?" Jafar asked.

"They say he's being interrogated, but no one knows where he is."

"What about his wife?"

"She's not talking to anyone and barely leaves the apartment."

"Who could blame her ... Does your teta know her well?"

"Nour? I don't know. They would sometimes say hi, but I don't think they're friends."

Jafar kicked a rock. It soared a few yards and clanged against the side of a metal barrel.

"Listen," he said, "I don't know if you've heard, but people are talking."

"Yeah, they're saying Tony was in a militia, and he—"

"No, no." He stopped and lowered his voice. "I mean they're talking about your teta."

I gulped. "What are they saying?"

"They wonder if there might be a connection between the two ..."

"What? Between her and Tony's disappearance?"

Jafar gave a dismissive wave. "You know what people are like. The city's crawling with security police; folks are disappearing. I'm sure it's just rumors!"

"Jafar, what are they saying?"

"They wonder if it's just a coincidence that, you know, your teta returns after all these years and paints pictures of battle sites—places where people disappeared—then men show up and threaten her because of the paintings, and then someone who just happens to live across the street from you, who people suspect was in a militia, disappears. They say someone must have squealed on him ..."

I laughed out loud, but Jafar's expression remained serious.

"They're crazy!" I cried, but then noticed someone on the balcony above us and lowered my voice too. "They can't be for real."

"I'm just telling you what I've heard."

"What about you? There's no way you believe this bullshit."

He turned away.

Without thinking, my hand shot forward and I grabbed his T-shirt. "You don't believe it, do you?" My voice sounded pathetic.

"Let go of me, Amin," he said quietly.

"Whoever these people are suck!" I was furious suddenly, and I hissed: "What they're saying doesn't make any sense!"

"Sure, man, whatever you say," Jafar replied. He felt around his neck, then held out his silver chain. I had accidentally broken it.

The light changed. Jafar lifted his head and gazed past me. His eyelid twitched. I thought he was pissed off and about to let me have it when I turned and noticed four teenage boys had appeared behind us, standing there with their arms crossed. They were blocking our way down the street.

Although I would later replay every aspect of that afternoon—Jafar bolting from the cartoonist's apartment, his breakdown by the wall, us walking around, every gesture, every word—what happened next remained too great for me to comprehend. *Strange*, I would think, even years later. Strange, the way a few hours can change everything, the way life can fall apart in the blink of an eye. It's possible that this tendency had already taken hold as a result of Grandmother's influence on me, but certainly from that day on—and for many, many years to come—it would seem someone had switched on an X-ray, casting all personal relationships as emotional negatives. When it came to any situation that demanded intimacy and trust, the first thing I saw was a source of betrayal.

The boys stood in a row, and behind them I spotted the black Volvo with the rosary hanging from the rearview mirror. They had parked the car in such a way that the only way out of the alleyway was past them. I took a step back to stand next to Jafar, but he took one forward. The boys kept their arms crossed. The one who looked oldest and thus in charge approached Jafar. His sneakers were spotless, though his track pants had holes in them. He wore an undershirt with a plunging neckline and sewn-on breast pocket. There was a pack of cigarettes in the pocket, and I noticed a cross tattooed on his neck. They were all two feet taller than us. Boys like them would chase us off the soccer field, pelting rocks at us with glee. They were the lords of side streets and back courtyards.

The leader gave Jafar a nod. Jafar nodded back. The boy was wiry and seemed agile as a boxer. He didn't take his eyes off me as he stepped closer.

"Is there a problem here?"

"Nope," Jafar said. "No problem."

"Sure looked like one."

Jafar remained calm. "Must be a mistake."

The young man studied him. His eyes lingered on Jafar's neck, then moved down to his fist.

"Open your hand!"

Jafar obeyed.

The boy took the broken silver chain and weighed it in his palm.

Why was the street suddenly so empty? I looked up at the balconies. There was no one in sight, as if residents had withdrawn into their apartments the minute the gang arrived.

The leader turned and held up the chain for his three buddies to see. They took silent note of it. Then he leaned down, brought his mouth up to Jafar's ear, and making sure I could still hear, said, "You'd tell us if there was a problem, right? You know we're here for you."

"Of course." Unlike me, Jafar didn't seem scared anymore. Instead, he did something shocking. He nimbly reached forward and plucked the pack of cigarettes from the older boy's breast pocket. He calmly opened it, pulled one out, and put it in his mouth. "Got a light?"

The boy grinned. Just as calmly, he dug a lighter out of his pocket, cupped the flame with his hand, and lit the cigarette.

"Aren't you going to introduce us to your friend?" the leader asked, sneering at me.

Jafar took a long drag, held in the smoke for a moment, then exhaled through his nose. He took his silver chain back from the boy, cleared his throat, and looked at me as if I were something unspeakably pathetic.

"He's not my friend," he said, spitting at my feet. "He's nobody."

A Familiar Yearning

A tale from brighter times: In the early days of our friendship, when we got together to watch a movie, Jafar and I would usually buy VHS bootlegs from hawkers on the Corniche. They were spread out on blankets and cost just a few cents. If dissatisfied with the selection, we'd take a bus into the city and hop the chainlink fence into the back courtyard of the old Cinema Montréal. It was one of the few places that showed American movies. The theater itself was in the basement, but there was a flight of stairs that led down to a rusty emergency exit that could only be opened from the inside.

"If we give each other a leg up," Jafar explained the first time he brought me there, "we can still watch the movie." He pointed at a small barred window in the door, about six feet off the ground.

The first movie we watched like this was *The Lion King*. Giving each other a leg up wasn't quite enough, but if I used the wall for support, Jafar could sit on my shoulders, and vice versa. We took turns. Three minutes each. Since we couldn't hear through the window, we described what was on screen.

"There are some storks, or maybe pelicans. Now there's a waterfall. Giraffes, ants, lots of animals. Nice light. There's a monkey and a lion, and they're hugging."

"This movie sucks," Jafar said.

"Just wait. There's something weird about the monkey. He just stole the lion cub."

"Aren't the parents there?"

"Yeah, but they don't seem to care."

"Disney doesn't make any sense. Your time's up. My turn!"

We traded positions.

"You won't believe it," he said.

"What?!"

"The monkey. He's about to throw the lion cub off the rock. The animals are going berserk."

"Are you serious?"

"Oh, nope. False alarm. He's just showing it to them. They're celebrating."

"Do you think the cub is his?"

"What, you mean the monkey being the cub's father? Even Disney isn't that messed up ..."

I stumbled through the days following Jafar's betrayal in a daze. The two of us sitting by the mud wall at the flea market or in the stands at the circus, exploring silent buildings at night. Jafar and me ... The memory of our shared experiences crowded my consciousness painfully. I tossed and turned till dawn, but as soon as sunlight entered my room, I pulled the blankets over my head, at a loss for what to do. Looking back now, those days are defined by a yearning for the summertime adventures we'd had, when my world was a place I simply accepted without the need to understand it. There were moments, though, when I couldn't stand it in my room anymore. I visited all our places—scaled the fence behind the movie theater, went to the vast lot where the circus had stopped off, and climbed one of the bare poplar trees, as if the extra height would help me gain perspective. Traffic rushed past on its way toward the airport, the skyline beyond in relief as it extended toward a dingy gray horizon. Mosque loudspeakers played the tinny call to prayer, alien and uninviting, and for the first time I understood the impulse, so common at the time, that led families to abandon their homes, dig out their passports, and leave Beirut forever. An old yearning returned, as overwhelming as a piercing scream—a longing to return to Germany with its predictable everyday life, timetables and trains, neatly arranged supermarket shelves and feeling of reliable order.

I took out Jafar's photos one day and arranged them on the floor, but the thought that we'd sat here together just a few weeks earlier was more than I could bear, so I gathered them into a pile and chucked them back in the trunk. I would dial his number some nights but always hang up before anyone could answer. I felt nervous approaching the school building in the days leading up to vacation, but as I scanned the crowd of students for Jafar each morning, I realized my fear of encountering him was unfounded. He didn't come to school anymore. That hurt too. Part of me was desperate to talk to him, while another part was so hurt that the very thought of hearing his voice or bumping into him made me nauseous.

I didn't tell Grandmother what had happened. She was busy ensuring her suppliers that the café would reopen soon. She walked up and down the hall, phone to her ear, insisting she'd be able to receive deliveries and remit outstanding payment in no time. Meanwhile no one had come to test the water yet. She was trying to inspire me with confidence too. One evening I found her in the living room. She had just written invitations to her friends, and as she stuffed the addressed enve-lopes, she said, in a tone of voice that struck me as forced, "We're going to have a wonderful Christmas. Pull out all the stops. Like one big family."

In mid-December I finally decided to deliver my story to Zahra. I'd been carrying it around for weeks, so the pages were creased and torn. I neatly rewrote the whole thing, blew lightly to dry the ink, and slid the story into an envelope. I also popped in a little card with my address.

Her cousin Asifa lived in Mala'ab al-Baladi, a neigh-borhood in the south of Beirut where I'd never been. It took more than an hour to get there, over the course of which the aspect of the city changed drastically. More or less organized chaos reigned supreme in the south-ern districts. Reconstruction hadn't begun here yet.

There were no streets signs, but luckily I had the old city map Grandmother had given me when we moved to Beirut. I used it now to find the street and building I was looking for.

I rang the bell beside the nameplate. Nothing hap-pened. The standard sounds of family life drifted out the open windows. "Zahid," a woman called, "this is the last time I'm going to ask you to put the broom away!" Below the address, Zahra had written some-thing else: *7th floor*. I looked up. Laundry flapped on clotheslines and satellite dishes were secured to bal-cony railings with zip ties. The door to the building was open, and the smell of cooking poured out. I tried the doorbell again. Still nothing, so I climbed the stairs through the thick air. On the seventh floor I walked down the hallway until I found the door with Asifa's last name. I stopped and listened carefully. There was no sound from inside the apartment. I knocked. No response. I stood there holding the envelope, uncertain what to do. Could I just leave it there? I decided against that. Though I knew it was pointless, I knocked again and again nothing happened, so I turned and left. My head was down and my eyes fixed on the top step when I nearly collided with her. For a second I thought it was Zahra herself, they looked so similar.

"Asifa?"

"Yes?"

"I'm Amin."

I waited to see if my name triggered a reaction. She looked at me quizzically. I heard steps approaching from below and a child giggling.

"I'm a friend of Zahra's," I hastily added. "She said I could give you something to give her."

She glanced behind her and nodded at me.

I handed her the envelope. She tucked it into the folds of her robe.

"When's the next time you'll see her?"

"Next week," she whispered. "You need to go now. Quick."

The voices on the stairs were getting closer.

"Alright," I said, squeezing past her. I took a few steps then turned around, but she had already disappeared down the hall.

I passed by a tall man on my way down. Dark eyes and equally dark beard flecked with gray. He was carrying a little boy on his shoulders and pretending to be an ogre to make him laugh. When he saw me, the man stepped aside to make room on the narrow staircase. I nodded at him. He murmured a greeting and smiled, then continued heading up, growling all the way.

*

It rained on Christmas Eve. The wind scattered leaves and plastic bags in the street. I stood by the window and watched Nour slink down the sidewalk, in and out of shadows cast by streetlights. She had a bag in one hand and used the other to unlock her front door before slipping inside. A couple minutes later I saw her on the second floor, putting groceries in the refrigerator. She prepared a piece of flatbread and brought it into the dining room, where she sat down at the table, alone.

I turned on the Christmas lights in my window and closed the curtains. Grandmother had been cooking all day and the scent of meze now filled the rooms, the big table in the living room loaded with small bowls I'd carried in as she finished preparing each dish.

She disappeared into the bathroom at some point and emerged wearing earrings and a blue dress I'd never seen before.

"You look pretty," I told her.

Over the course of the evening, our apartment filled with the same people who had visited so often in the past. Each time the doorbell rang or someone knocked, I opened the door to a familiar face. A hint of summer. The good old days. Nadia, the costume designer from the Grand Théâtre, was wearing a deep-cut red velvet dress and looked like a fashion plate come to life. She kissed the air beside my cheeks three times and swooped past to greet my teta effusively, gushing over her dress. Everyone had accepted the invitation. Abu Amar, the loquacious artist, shook out his umbrella on the landing, bowed ceremoniously, and tousled my hair as he came in. I felt like the butler at a masquerade ball. Umm Jamil, dressed all in black, flashed her invitation with a smile, said "*Eid milad saeid, ya habibi*," and gave me a big wet kiss on the forehead, which I wiped off the instant she turned away. Abbas arrived a little later. Standing outside the door—as always in a wrinkled shirt—he pulled out a present and handed it to me. It was clearly a book. He winked as he lifted a finger to his lips and pushed past me.

It was like a beehive in our apartment. The living room was filled with the clatter of plates, quiet music, and lively conversation. The mood was relaxed. There was lots of laughter, and everyone sang the praises of Grandmother's cooking. Anecdotes and memories made the rounds. It all fell back into place, as if those summer visits had never stopped. Some of the stories were so outrageous I could hardly believe them. A man in a plum-colored suit explained that he was responsible for cleaning the sewer system every Thursday. The last time he did his rounds, he continued, he was underneath Rue Waygand when he came across a small colony of giant tortoises that are only known to live in the Bahamas. "I think it's a good sign," he said earnestly. "First the turtles come here on vacation, then the Europeans. Things are looking up." He raised his glass and drank a toast to me.

There was other stuff too, like the passionate love song an older gentleman named Yasin sang after several glasses of arrack, which was so unexpectedly explicit that Grandmother leaned over and covered my ears.

When was the last time I'd seen her in such a good mood? Everything was aglow that evening, the colors somehow brighter. And how reassuring to discover that certain customs remained unchanged, in spite of the troubling times! Abu Amar still took great pleasure in sharing things in hushed tones, as if meant for my ears alone.

"Amin, I've started meditating. I can see djinnis now," he said conspiratorially.

"You mean ghosts?"

He nodded. "Most people think it's hocus-pocus, despite the fact that Surah Adh-Dhariyat in the Holy Quran states that God created man and djinnis to worship him. If you really concentrate, you can see them."

"What do they do?"

He lowered his voice. "They want to control our lives, which can be bad. When it comes to women, for instance"—he looked around to make sure no one was eavesdropping—"the djinnis start sleeping with them. Many women sense it and develop impure thoughts." He studied me and nodded emphatically. He must have known the effect this description had on me, so he added, half-apologetically, "I probably shouldn't be telling you all this."

"No, no, I want to hear more about it."

"Forget what I said about women, Amin. I'm sure you've heard that more and more people are reporting UFO and alien sightings around the world. There's reason to believe that such sightings are simply djinnis—djinnis in various forms."

"Does it say that in the Holy Quran, too?"

"Shhh, not so loud. No, not exactly. But before you say I'm crazy, just think about how many cultures believe in ghosts. In China and India, people call upon the ghosts of their ancestors. Jews, Muslims, and Christians all believe in angels ..."

"I don't think you're crazy, Abu Amar."

"You're a good boy, Amin."

Grandmother's friends had always seemed like a

bunch of stranded souls to me. At some point in the past they must have boarded the same ship and capsized in a storm on the high seas. After washing up on a desert island, they came to know and value each other. That's kind of how I imagined it. How else could people from such different universes ever have met? They brought life to the table with their anecdotes and idiosyncrasies. There wasn't a single lull in chatter over the course of the meal. Everyone had something to share from their life.

Nadia, for instance, was currently obsessed with the French author Annie Saumont and had decided to try her hand at writing a novel. "It's about a plastic surgeon who receives an unexpected phone call that changes everything. That's all I'll say." She had taken a test administered by a so-called "academy" in Paris to assess her creative aptitude. The longer the evening wore on, the more metaphors she tried to weave into her sentences: "In the glow of the bulb, specks of dust drifted over the dining room table like hovering atoms," she said randomly, taking a drag off her cigarette and feasting on the sound of her words.

"Marvelous comparison!" Abu Amar applauded her.

"Are you calling me a bad house cleaner?" Grandmother asked, and everyone laughed.

Like one big family, she had said. That was how we would celebrate Christmas. I hadn't believed her. Sitting in the candlelight, though, wine glasses capturing the flicker of flames, I actually did get a vague sense of familial connection between these people. It's not something you can see, so much as feel. The curtains were drawn. A pleasant part of the outside world had made its way into our apartment, while the rest was locked out. In this festive atmosphere, I suddenly realized how alienated Grandmother and I had been in recent weeks, both consumed by our own concerns, both unable to confide in each other. To this day I can see Grandmother's friends in my mind's eye, their arrival on the scene meant to save us: Nadia in her red dress, enveloped in a cloud of cigarette smoke. Abu Amar half smiling, as if he didn't understand something a friend had been trying to explain for an hour. Umm Jamil, who kept saying I was wasting away and handing me bowls of food. For two of the widows from West Beirut, it was the first Christmas invitation they'd received in more than fourteen years. "We always used to celebrate with our neighbors, but, you know, times have changed …" Or Abbas. Abbas, of course! His silence was conspicuous among this group. It occurred to me that he'd never been in attendance at those summertime gatherings. As far as I knew, this was the first time he'd ever met these people. He sat there with his hands folded across his belly for the most part, his head lowered, listening closely, as if he had no right to speak himself. Grandmother sat at the head of the table. She seemed as cheery and relaxed as her guests, all the while making sure no one was left wanting. The moment a bowl was empty, she got up to refill it. As if every last detail counted on a night like that.

The mood didn't shift until much later. Outside, the rain had stopped. Abbas noisily pushed away his plate, stood up, and pulled back the curtain to crack a window for fresh air. I could see Nour from where I sat. She was staring across the street at us. When I waved, she stepped back and drew her curtains. It all happened quite quickly. I don't think anyone at the table noticed. Even so, something was thrown off-kilter. In retrospect I feel less surprised by what happened. There had been signs: the breathless storytelling around the table, the shrill laughter, the array of bizarre stories. For a while I'd fallen for it, but what had initially appeared to me as their *connecting* now revealed itself for what it truly was: *conniving*. It was Christmas, damn it, a time for peace! Up to that point every difficult topic of conversation had been avoided. And up to that point it had worked: with our living room as their stage, everyone had stuck dutifully to their respective roles. In the brief stillness that accompanied the cool air coming in from outside, though, something changed.

It was Abu Amar who set down his wine glass and—rather rashly, it seemed—asked Grandmother if there was any news regarding the café.

Silence settled over the room. Silverware was set aside and someone cleared their throat. Everyone looked embarrassed.

Grandmother blinked, as if someone had delivered a line that wasn't in the script. She looked first at me, then at Abu Amar.

"No news," she responded coolly. "We're still closed."

He pushed away his glass with a look of contrition and avoided her gaze. He was clearly puzzling out his next move. Guide the topic to a quick and painless conclusion or change course altogether? Despite his esoteric inclinations, Abu Amar was an artist who planned his works with an exactitude that left nothing to chance. Improvising wasn't his strong suit.

"Did they say when—"

"No. No one has told me anything," Grandmother interrupted him. "They said two to three days. That was four weeks ago." She wiped her mouth with a napkin. "Would anyone care for some *bûche de Noël?*"

Right after opening the window, Abbas had gone to

the bathroom. He now returned, noted the change in atmosphere, and sat down mutely.

Everyone had wanted dessert but just poked at their plates. They behaved as if they'd woken from a dream and were trying to figure out how on earth they'd wound up at this table.

A few desperate attempts were made at saving the situation. Abu Amar told a joke, but no one laughed. Yasin struck up a song but trailed off quickly in response to the looks he got.

Nadia finally stirred. "It'll all work out, habibi," she said, stroking Grandmother's arm.

The others murmured in agreement, but Grandmother did not respond. She reached for her wine glass.

"There must be something that can be done," Abu Amar insisted, fully aware of having ruined the mood.

"I'm wide open to suggestions."

Various ideas were floated. Perhaps they could file a joint emergency motion with the authorities, said Waseem, the man in purple. Or reopen the café as if nothing had happened, the widow Fatima proposed. A few more half-baked suggestions were made.

"Ever consider bribery?" someone interjected.

It was Abbas. I gaped at him.

"Yes, that's always an option," Yasin joined in. "For instance, I don't have health insurance. Whenever I need to see the doctor quick, I leave him a little thank-you on the table as I'm leaving. A couple bills. He'll remember that the next time I call. I never have to wait more than a few days."

Eager nodding.

Others shared tales of their own bribery attempts. Apparently they were all familiar with it. Nadia's brother, who had emigrated to Dearborn, Michigan, during the war, had died there a year earlier. To ensure she got her visa in time to attend the funeral, she had slipped the man at the embassy an envelope containing nearly $800. The matter-of-fact way they described these dealings made it seem to me like bribery was a perfectly reasonable avenue for Grandmother to take.

"It's out of the question," was all she said.

"Terrible idea, you're right." Abu Amar immediately sided with her. "There must be a different solution."

No one had any other suggestions.

"But why?" I finally asked.

"I said it's out of the question, Amin," she repeated.

"But what if it's what those people want?"

"It's exactly what they want."

"So why don't we give them money? We probably can't afford the café being closed for much longer, can we?"

"Don't you worry about that," she replied.

Umm Jamil grabbed my hand under the table. I looked at her in confusion. She shook her head almost imperceptibly.

I wasn't willing to let it go. My gaze fell upon the stunted citrus plant on the windowsill. Grandmother was obviously stubborn at times, like she was obviously stupid to ignore this well-meaning advice.

"We should give it a try. This whole thing is foul play, anyway …"

"Amin," said Abbas, raising his eyebrows, "you heard your teta."

"Yeah, but remember the guy who said he drank the water? Did you know he was paid off? He's homeless—I saw him on Rue Clemenceau!" I pounded the table with my fist, a lame gesture to underscore what I thought was a grand reveal.

Grandmother and the others looked at me as if I'd solved a simple math problem and were a little too proud.

"That comes as no surprise, Amin." She was trying to keep her tone gentle. "Here's the problem: if we give these people money, they'll keep coming back. They might accept $1,000 the first time around, but by the next time the price will have increased to four or five thousand, and keep going from there. This country is still diseased. It has never fully recovered ..."

"But if the café stays closed, we'll never recover, either."

"It *won't* stay closed."

"How do you know? What if your landlord sent those men to scare you off?"

"My landlord?"

"Abbas told me your landlord asked you to take down the paintings, which you obviously haven't done."

She shot him a dirty look. "My landlord has nothing to do with those men, habibi," she said flatly.

"Then why don't we just give them what they want?"

"I've already explained that to you, Amin."

"But you're being unreasonable!" I persisted.

Umm Jamil's grip on my hand under the table was tightening.

I thought of the constellations of numbers Grandmother had jotted down on bits of paper, then crumpled up and thrown away. Whatever the calculation, the number after the equal sign was always negative. I had dug those slips out of the trash. I had seen the math. As was always the case, I just hadn't wanted to look more closely.

"Our money's all gone, isn't it?" I said, surprised at how easily the words came out.

"It's just a phase," said Grandmother. "These things happen."

"But you sold the house ..."

"The café ate up a lot of money, child. If we'd been allowed to open over Christmas, I'm sure things would look different ..."

"You mean there's nothing left?" I was dumbfounded.

"We'll help, Amin," I heard Nadia say.

"Definitely," Abu Amar echoed. "You can count on us!"

"You have nothing to worry about, Amin," Umm Jamil whispered to me.

"So why don't we sell that painting?" I asked, pointing at the frame on the opposite wall. Mother's painting. I hadn't meant to say it; it just slipped out, but now the sentence hung in the air.

My words were followed by a clenched fist of silence. Although I found the silence unnerving, I continued in a soft voice: "It's a beautiful painting. I'm sure there's someone out there who'd pay a lot of money for it. We could use that money to pay off those people and settle our debt. Once we're back on our feet we'll just buy it back."

"Amin," Abbas started, but Grandmother held up a hand to silence him.

"Go to your room!" she hissed.

"But ..."

"You heard me." Her lower lip trembled. "Get out of my sight, Amin."

Terra Incognita

Another memory of mine contains a map, this one held in Saber Mounir's hands and illuminated by moonlight coming through the hole in the wall left by a grenade. A summer evening at the National Museum. I'm thirteen years old. The entrance hall is empty; the other workers have long since left for the day. Behind the heavy doors to the library, there's just the hakawati and me. I found the map in the ashes. It's still in good shape. He carefully removes some of the dirt.

"What you see here is part of the old Islamic empire," he says. "This map originated in the tenth century, from the famous *Book of the Paths and Provinces*. Just look at how vivid the colors remain. Look closely."

At first glance, the drawings made zero sense to me. It only became recognizable as a map after I'd studied the rendering more carefully and the old man had explained parts of it to me: cities were represented as trapezoids, islands as circles, mountain ranges as zigzags, rivers as thick lines, and coastlines as compressed undulate forms circumscribing a radiant blue-green sea. I was spellbound. Saber Mounir told me to repeat after him as he named the sunken provinces depicted there—former metropolises in the alluvial plains along the Euphrates and Tigris. They sounded beautiful and enigmatic.

"The present has ousted the past," he said. "The name Kabul no longer evokes images of the gardens the city was once famous for. And when people hear the word Iran, they don't think of calligraphy or the art of Persian miniature painting once produced in Isfahan. No one associates high culture and civilization with the East anymore, although it was Arabic scholars who preserved the wisdom of the ancient Greeks and later returned that knowledge to the Europeans, who seized upon it as the cornerstone of the Renaissance, which ultimately gave way to the Enlightenment."

He went on about those forgotten epochs for some time, allowing them to emerge from the folds of the map as he spoke.

"So, where's Lebanon?" I asked once he'd finished.

With a bony finger, the old man pointed all the way to the left. There, on the outermost edge of the map, was a sketchily delineated landmass, dark and unexplored.

It was labeled *terra incognita*.

*

Tripoli, 2005

Lebanon had grown alien to me, more alien than ever before. The Syrians had been chased out, but the initial elation had given way to unimaginable horror. Daily reports of car bombs loaded with explosives and parked by Assad supporters outside the homes and workplaces of his enemies. On the other side: attacks on tents and other temporary housing used by Syrian day laborers, who served as scapegoats. Decades of pent-up rage discharged in the aftermath of political optimism.

Tripoli was a flash point. Army checkpoints were hastily erected and anyone heading up the steep street toward the Jabal Mohsen neighborhood was stopped for questioning. It was there that Alawite Muslims and Sunni Muslims, separated only by a broad avenue, served as representatives of the conflict. This was all happening within eye- and earshot of my apartment, and yet my attention kept turning back to Beirut. The formation of government had stalled. The revolution had turned into a movement of ditherers. A puppet show was being performed for all those who had taken to the streets just months earlier, after the prime minister's assassination, to demonstrate against the old guard of corrupt political dynasties and sectarian power structures and to advocate for nationwide measures to overhaul the government.

"Beirut," said Khalil, during one of my visits to his bookshop, "is a blue-blooded bastard, the child of Western fathers and Arab mothers, addicted to pleasure and prone to disaster."

Terra incognita. Unknown land.

Now more than ever, my apartment felt like a makeshift raft barely keeping me afloat. I rarely went out. I awoke from tangled dreams in the middle of the night, feeling profoundly disoriented. Memories appeared in the darkness and fluttered into the light like moths.

"All I ever wanted was to protect you."

"Protect me? From what?"

"From the life I have had to endure."

Grandmother and me. Those were our parting words. That was more than six months ago. Her in her nightgown, standing in the doorway to the apartment—my final image of her.

After rage came voluntary isolation. And with isolation came emptiness. I had become a stranger to myself, alone in this inflamed city in the weeks following the revolution. Fear and the feeling of losing my grip engulfed me. *Ana ashar hasenherzig alyom.*

*

Amin, please, we have to talk. I wasn't sent by Yara. She doesn't know a thing about this, I swear. It's about "Song for the Missing." I hope you still have it. Call me. Abbas

Five days had passed since Khalil had given me the message. I hadn't called Abbas. The mere fact that he'd tracked me down in Tripoli paralyzed me. At the time it was impossible for me to imagine anyone meaning well. Even as a kid I had underestimated Abbas. As I later learned, his sphere of influence extended far beyond the walls of his farm in Sidon and into shadowy realms like the unmarked expanses on the antique map from the *Book of the Paths and Provinces*. I didn't know what Abbas wanted from me or why the painting was involved. I was afraid he may have been enlisted by Grandmother to demand it back under some pretext or other. By then I wouldn't have sold *Song for the Missing* for all the money in the world.

I've described my use of novels to escape into other realities during that time. Distant lands, distant ages. The effect the painting had on me, though, surpassed that of any book I'd ever read. It had become a place of refuge. Whenever I looked at it, sooner or later I'd enter a trancelike state in which I yearned for nothing more fervently than to glide out of my dismal existence in that apartment and into the golden splendor of that painted autumn day.

When the yearning became too much to bear one of those days, I borrowed Khalil's car and drove out to the house in the mountains. I didn't want to drive by the property too close, so I parked near the path and climbed up the hill through tall grass. When I reached the top and looked down at the house with the overgrown garden, a smile appeared on my face for the first time in months.

I soon found myself sitting in that garden, cup of coffee in hand. Across from me sat a young woman named Rabia. She was fifteen years old, the daughter of the owners. She'd been returning from a walk when she noticed me gazing at the house from a distance. After I explained who I was, she invited me to join her and wait for her parents to come home.

"So, you used to live here? Am I getting that right?"

"No, I never lived here, but it's where my mother was born and raised. See that apple tree? She used to climb it when she was little."

"The house is really beautiful, but we're only here during the summer, when it gets too hot in the city. Is this your first time here? Did you want to see where your mother grew up?"

"I was here once with my grandmother, eleven years ago. Do you have any siblings? No? In that case, it was your rubber boots I remember seeing by the door, next to your parents'. My teta showed me around outside. She had recently sold the house to your family."

"Right. Yeah, I think my mom mentioned that once."

The afternoon sunshine filled the garden. As I looked around I was amazed at how clearly I had remembered the place. The toolshed was maybe a little smaller in real life, but it still seemed like the garden flowed seamlessly into the open fields beyond the bushes, while at the same time I got the feeling the outside world had ceased to exist.

Rabia's parents returned about half an hour later. If they were surprised by my visit, they didn't let on. I told them I'd been in the area for work, passing by on my way back from Zahlé. A spontaneous decision, I said—I hadn't planned the visit. Their names were Faris and Samira. They were very friendly and asked after Grandmother. I told them she was well.

"In spite of what's happening in Beirut?"

"Yes, in spite of everything."

"Such a mess, isn't it?"

When they invited me inside, I had to conceal my excitement. I had hoped for a tour but not dared to ask. Terra incognita here as well. How many times had I imagined the inside of this house? I was surprised by how cool it was, how well the stone walls blocked the heat. Faris and Samira led me from room to room: The kitchen with its stone sink and view of the garden. The living room with its acacia wood table. Small bath, separate toilet. Smooth tiled floors throughout. As a kid I would have roller-skated around in here. On the back side of the house was a sizable room with big windows and piles of cardboard boxes.

"At the closing all those years ago, your grandmother told us this had been a kind of workshop or studio. We've never used the space. Visual arts, right?"

"Painting," I said quietly. "She and my mother were painters."

I remembered pressing my nose against the window and peering in during that earlier visit. It now felt like I was coming ashore after years of being lost at sea.

"Did my grandmother happen to tell you which room was my mother's?" I asked.

"It must have been Rabia's. The only rooms upstairs are two bedrooms and a study."

They let me enter the room and I tried hard not to seem overly curious. The furnishings were spartan:

just a bed, desk, and oak wardrobe. I noticed bits of adhesive tape on the walls, as if the girl had only recently taken down her posters.

She learned to say farewell much earlier than hello. Grandmother's words to me the night after the storm.

My gaze wandered out to the garden and lingered on the apple tree. I could see the broken branch.

"We'll be headed back to the city in about two weeks' time," Faris said.

I turned to face him. "Rabia tells me this is just your summer home?"

"That's right, to escape the heat in Beirut. We used to drive out more often, but you know how old this place is."

"Actually I don't. My grandparents didn't build it. They bought it in 1953."

"Right," Faris said, smiling. "Well, things may have looked a bit different back then. These days, beyond a few shepherds and old folks, no one lives here full-time. The houses are all ancient. It's a great retreat in summer, but not terribly exciting for a teenager. We moved back to the city years ago. The closest supermarket is several miles away, and things like medicine and bigger items are delivered twice a week by a guy who drives up from Beirut."

"My mother was very happy here."

"Oh, as are we—please don't get the wrong impression. If we wanted to live here year-round, though, we'd have to spend a lot of money winterizing it. The wind whistles in the woodwork and the walls get damp in winter." He led me back down the hallway and pointed at the ceiling, its edges mottled with water stains. "The roof leaks," he said. "Nothing major, and we've patched it up okay, but it needs more work, and I have no idea what it'll look like come winter, when it snows. At first glance the house is still very beautiful, but its age is starting to show. Over the years we haven't always had the time or extra cash to invest in the place. We weren't always sure it'd be worth it. The situation in this country ... you never know."

I nodded pensively. "Don't I know it."

I drove back to Tripoli as night was falling. I heated up a can of beans and sat down at the table. As it was imperative to keep abreast of news events, I had bought a used TV a few weeks earlier at the souk. I flicked through the channels as I ate, but it was all standard early-evening programming. Nothing big in the news. There was a game show on al-Manar, the Hezbollah station. The host read aloud the question.

"What is the name of the building, constructed out of gray sandstone in 1792, that has since served as the center of all malicious decision-making targeting the Arab world?"

The contestant didn't have to think long: "The White House." Music played and the audience applauded.

The usual drivel, but I didn't change the channel. I even turned it up. As long as I was looking at the screen, I could ignore the picture hanging next to me on the wall. As long as I didn't look at the painting, I could avoid thinking about the house.

Or Abbas.

and managing multimillion-dollar projects. It was a great story to tell clients while dining at upscale seafood restaurants on the harbor. There were many influential figures entangled in his net: commerce secretaries, local politicians, real-estate moguls from Kuwait and Saudi Arabia, or French investors. Later on, in dimly lit nightclubs, they would talk investments —a shipyard in La Ciotat near the French naval base of Toulon or a massive lot near the Champs-Élysées, perfect for opening another branch. And as belly dancers gyrated around their table, he would sketch out his vision on a cocktail napkin for an office complex with movie theaters and swimming pools on the upper floors. He became a different person on those nights, pretending to be proud of his country's profligate side, as if it were a privilege to show it off to European clients who'd come with suitcases full of cash to be plundered and heads full of clichés to be confirmed. Up in the mountains, meanwhile, things hadn't changed for hundreds of years. Up here, all that stuff was distant and insignificant, warded off by the walls of the house. Amin el-Maalouf essentially had two lives: one in the glitz and glam of Beirut, the other up here with his wife and daughter, where everything was so familiar and simple it helped him maintain balance.

He could watch the two of them in the garden together for hours. The goodbyes before heading into the city or leaving on business trips were getting harder. He would regularly travel to Intra Bank branches in Paris, London, Geneva, Frankfurt, or Rome. Falling asleep in bedrooms that weren't his own had become a challenge. He would lie awake to the rattle of his own breath, staring out the window and listening to the foreign languages in the darkness. Maya was ten years old by then. Ten years that had slipped past in the blink of an eye. How many times had he opened his briefcase upon reaching the office or hotel room and found a picture his daughter had drawn tucked inside with a message—*Come home soon!*—dictated by Yara but written in Maya's hand. The prospect of returning home was the only thing that made the loneliness of those trips bearable. The endless airport hallways, rolling suitcases, pushing and shoving at baggage claim, plastic tray tables, requests to please return tray tables to their full upright and locked position, takeoffs and landings ... but her drawings, too, small gestures that truly touched him. Promises for the future. He often imagined the way Yara—after the little one had been put down for a nap—became immersed in the landscape while she painted. And how she would keep the picture concealed until she was truly happy with it, then show him. This desire for perfection was something he loved about her. Just as he loved her confidence and the way she showed it at theater performances by laughing so unreservedly at funny moments that people seated in front of them would turn around to look and clear their throats. These were little moments of protest in which they snubbed the etiquette demanded by their new social standing, a tier they would never fully inhabit, both having ascended from lower classes and lives shaped by gruff and absent fathers.

You can't count on anyone but yourself. Your fate is in your own hands. This was one of his father's guiding beliefs, which he beat into his son in the most literal sense. Amin el-Maalouf rarely thought of the past; the future simply had more to offer him. He only looked back on the rare occasion he encountered an old friend from Hamra on the street or in foolish daydreams. He had started distancing himself from childhood friends by the late forties, once he started to wear suits. Every now and again he'd bump into them at a bar in Mar Mikhael, but their exchanges always ended in awkward silence, as his pals' behavior and visions struck him as childish and parochial. The men existed as little more than specters of his past now. They'd been replaced by the conviction that life would forever remain as it was now. Either that, or things would continue to go up—and up and up.

Amin el-Maalouf stood barefoot in the garden that October morning, and when the sunbeams finally reached his toes, he went inside and got dressed. After a quick bite he said bye to his family and drove down to the city. It seemed like any other day at Intra Bank. He greeted the porter, sent his briefcase through the scanner, passed through the metal detector, and took the elevator to the third floor from the top. Once in his office, which overlooked the entire harbor, he pulled out his chair and—though he couldn't have known it at the time—sat down at his desk for the last time.

Two things were happening concurrently that Amin el-Maalouf had no control over. Yousef Beidas, the president of Intra Bank, had fled to New York two nights earlier. He now sat in a hotel conference room near Wall Street, making a desperate and doomed attempt to avoid the bankruptcy he had caused by borrowing money from cooperative American banks. As he negotiated with various representatives, an unusual scene was unfolding at Beirut International Airport: bearded figures in white desert garb could be seen disembarking from Middle East Airlines flights. These men, each traveling with an empty suitcase, were oil sheikhs from around the Persian Gulf. They'd come to cut off the money supply to Intra Bank once and for all.

For weeks following the riots and in a state of deep depression, Amin el-Maalouf tugged every last thread in an attempt to unravel the hopeless tangle of failed speculation, business intrigue, and military power grabs, until finally he thought he understood what had happened.

Yousef Beidas—son of a Palestinian secondary school headmaster, president of Intra Bank, and mentor behind Amin el-Maalouf's professional success. In 1948, Beidas lost nearly his entire fortune and never got over the Israelis' forcing him from the financial center of Palestine and into exile in Lebanon. He was thus a long-time Fatah sympathizer; the group, stationed in Syria, was out to destroy Israel. Like Fatah, Beidas yearned for revenge. It was through Fatah that Beidas established contact with Egyptian president Gamal Abdel Nasser. Despite the economic crisis in his own country, Nasser waged war against Yemen's royalist leaders, who themselves had powerful friends, namely the oil barons of Kuwait and Saudi Arabia. Friends who just happened to be Intra Bank's most important clients. A closed loop. What Beidas found most appealing about Nasser, however, was that his primary adversaries weren't Yemenis but Israelis, whose sovereignty he refused to recognize. When Nasser approached the president of Intra Bank for a $320 million loan intended in part for developing rockets, Beidas readily agreed, provided the deal remain under wraps. Under no circumstances could his chief Kuwaiti and Saudi clients catch wind of the fact that the money they'd invested at Intra Bank was being used to this end, but who ever heard of a secret being kept in the Orient? In fact, there's a chance the planned transaction wouldn't have come to light, had said clients not been combing Lebanon for Nasser allies for weeks—and had their agents not discovered unexpected prey in Beidas. When Beidas learned he'd been found out, he tried to stop the wire transfer, but it was too late. Within a week the Saudi king and emirs of Kuwait withdrew their money in outrage. There was no stopping the catastrophe.

What Amin el-Maalouf witnessed that morning was the final outcome: incensed yelling and a swarm of people under his window. When everyday citizens realized their money was gone, they descended on the glass palace. Trucks rolled into position. Armed police jumped out and tried to contain the crowd. Amin el-Maalouf stood at his window for a full hour. He thought of his daughter and wife. His father, he now realized, had been wrong. Believe in yourself all you might, your fate would always be decided by others. He finally turned away from the scene, packed his bag, and left the office. He rode the elevator down one last time. From the sunny foyer, he could see the throng nearing. Policemen shot into the air.

*

About half an hour after my expulsion from Christmas dinner, Abbas came to my room and told me this story. My grandfather had approached the janitor—a Pakistani man standing frozen in fear on the polished tiles of the foyer, mop in hand—and paid him a hundred dollars to trade clothes. He'd then slipped out the back door in his new attire.

"This event really changed him," Abbas said.

We were sitting on my bedroom floor. Abbas leaned against my bed, hands folded in his lap. I sat across from him, my back to the trunk. He spoke slowly, as if thinking aloud. "A major economic crisis followed. Like your grandfather, the country never fully recovered. The collapse of Intra Bank was almost certainly part of the reason we later slid into civil war. Friends of your grandparents lost a lot of money because of what happened."

"But it wasn't his fault, was it?"

"No, Amin had nothing to do with it, but it was still humiliating. The bank's collapse clung to your grandfather like a shadow. He never found another job in the industry, which hit him hard. Your grandparents had saved, so they went on living as they always had, but Amin felt useless. He felt he had failed and let down his friends. People talked. He grew increasingly dissatisfied."

There was a pause. I noticed beads of sweat on Abbas's forehead, as if telling the story were physically taxing.

"Do you know where he is now?" I asked. "Grandmother never talks about him."

Abbas shook his head. "We aren't in touch. We used to be good friends. When things went south for my business, he lined up contracts for me. Really helped me out. He still knew a lot of people. After he and Yara divorced, though, our paths split. As far as I know, he left the country soon after."

"Why did they get divorced? If you know, please tell me. I won't tell her you told me."

He lowered his head. "Like I said: Amin was a damaged man. They stayed together for another twelve years but he was a different person. Then came the civil war. Your mother went to Paris for school, which was something Yara wanted and forced through against Amin's wishes. One humiliation after another must have become too much for him to bear."

On the other side of the door, the voices in the living room sounded farther away than they were. Occasionally someone would go to the bathroom or kitchen and return with heavy footsteps.

"She painted that picture in Paris. Did you know that?" I asked. "My mom, I mean."

"Yes." Abbas granted me the hint of a smile. "I remember the first time Amin and Yara showed it to me. They unrolled it on the table. I said Maya would be the next Mary Cassatt if she kept painting like that. They were incredibly proud."

"I didn't mean any harm when I suggested we sell the painting, Abbas."

He patted my head.

"I know," he said. "And deep down, Yara does too. Her love of that piece just makes her extremely sensitive. She wouldn't sell it for all the money in the world. Nor should you, Amin. You should keep it safe. Not only for your mother's sake, but because your grandfather is part of the painting too."

"My grandfather?"

"Yes. I told you about him to help you understand what kind of person he was. He was a complicated man, but he loved his family. It's important you not forget that."

"Then why did he leave them?"

Abbas compressed his lips. "Someday you'll understand. Just because you love someone doesn't mean you'll always do the right thing. It's only human."

I kept quiet and nodded. I remember his words exactly, and how urgently he spoke of my mother's painting that Christmas Eve.

"You said Grandfather's hidden in the painting too,"

I said. "What do you mean? Where?"

"Oh, in lots of little details," Abbas replied. He paused for a moment. "The title, for instance. Maya missed her dad while she was in Paris just as much as she missed her mother, which influenced her mood as she painted. Most importantly, though, he had a clear vision for the picture's presentation on the wall. He picked out the Empire-style frame himself."

"Are you serious?"

"Of course."

The frame really was striking, its beauty commensurate with that of the painting. It was incredibly heavy, richly ornamented in patinated old gold. Eleven years after that conversation, it took tremendous effort to lift and secure the painting on the wall of my Tripoli apartment.

"At the time you'd have been hard-pressed to find anyone in Lebanon capable of building the kind of frame Amin el-Maalouf would be satisfied with," Abbas continued. "Instead he commissioned it from a family of craftsmen in Florence who produce frames for the Uffizi Gallery. Only the best would do for his daughter's painting. That was during a trip he took with your teta, after visiting Paris."

"They went to Florence too?"

"Those two traveled so many different places. You see, this picture is the connective tissue for your grandmother. In some mysterious way it holds her family together—and thus yours, Amin. You might even say it holds a key to the past," Abbas said, looking straight at me.

*

There are times we feel compelled to make sure of our connection to past generations. In the same way we frame current events within their historical context, we assume that our family's past must contain clues about ourselves. My family history was closely interwoven with that of Lebanon, I learned from Abbas. As an adult I would spend months studying documents and reports housed in public archives and libraries to learn more about that period, which remained largely obscured.

Intra Bank's collapse had devastating consequences. At the time of its downfall it managed nearly 40 percent of all capital in Lebanese banks. From one day to the next, thousands of families had the rug pulled out from under them. Small and medium-sized businesses were robbed of their existence. As is so often the case, economic instability led directly to political volatility. Yousef Beidas was Palestinian. Among right-wing Christian factions he became emblematic of a Palestinian threat bound to destroy the country. Hundreds of thousands of Palestinian refugees were scapegoated and exploited by militant groups as a protective shield. Meanwhile, left-wing Muslim factions blamed the majority-Christian government for failing to engage the central bank to help prevent the crisis, thus grouping current leadership alongside past administrations, all of which had been so corrupt that the time had come for fundamental change. As I read, an image emerged of Lebanon as a mighty giant that had tumbled into the abyss. An age of upheaval. Student strikes, protests, miscarried attempts at reform, climbing gas, rent, and real-estate prices—the only people who enjoyed that period were political cartoonists. After years of violent flare-ups, war finally broke out in 1975. I learned that economic hardship—a direct consequence of the banking crisis—was the primary reason so many young men were susceptible to the recruiting efforts of militias, which promised monthly wages, and immortality, to boot.

I usually set out in the early morning and spent the whole day in the archives, which were tucked away in residential neighborhoods. Amid the whir of fans, a handful of mostly female employees sorted yellowed sheets of paper into folders like those I was digging through. It was tedious work, sifting through the glut of information to find details relevant to me, but I was convinced that if I spent enough time searching, I could figure out what was going on around me when I was thirteen. There weren't any official archives I could visit, a fact that hasn't changed to this day. Volunteers shoulder the responsibility for collecting and cataloging memories and evidence.

The war had been over for twenty years by then. An entire generation of those born after the conflict was looking for answers, yet not a single history book presented a neutral version of events, because an official version of events—one that could be taught in schools—simply didn't exist. Was that what Mr. Labaki had meant when I stood at his desk and he said we were still centuries away from discussing the civil war? I discovered that after the official end of the war, a new battle had started over the prerogative to interpret wartime events, a battle that was ongoing. There were only a few who broke their silence. In a windowless room at the archive in Haret Hreik, I read the anonymous testimonies of ex-fighters. They explained why, as young men, they had decided to don khaki-colored uniforms and shoot at former neighbors and friends. I copied the entries into my notebook:

My decision had nothing to do with an understanding of what war was and what it meant. It was primarily an act of rebellion against a certain financial and social reality. The attempt to change that reality through violence.

There was violence on all sides, but at the time we were convinced we weren't the ones hurting people.

Of course there was fear, but when you're young you don't feel it. You think: Others will die, but not me. Dead people turn into numbers and numbers don't hurt.

The social advantage we enjoyed over Muslims was based on a system that favored us Christians. I wanted to defend that system in order not to lose those advantages.

There was the "misery belt" on the outskirts of Beirut—a ring encircling the capital, comprised of poor families who'd moved from the country to the metro area in search of a better life. Those suburbs and refugee camps were ideal breeding grounds, the kids there receptive to all sorts of recruitment.

You know, everywhere I looked I saw social differences between us and the Christian population. It felt like we were losing out—that we didn't have the same opportunities.

I was thirteen when I got my first weapon. I felt invincible and important.

In the camps they showed us how to clean and quickly disassemble and reassemble our weapons. I was responsible for a group of about thirty people at age sixteen. Maybe it was because I had a beard and looked older.

*With every mortar round fired from the trench, the recoil
would stir up dust that I never wiped off. Today I think that
my willful neglect of personal hygiene was part of what
made me look like a fighter, further evidence, as it were, of
my involvement in the war and an unconscious expression of
my efforts to earn the others' approval. I was fourteen. They
were all older and treated me like a little kid.*

*When the weapons were too heavy for the kids, we'd shorten
the magazines, so the little ones could carry them.*

I don't remember what we dreamed about back then.

After spending an entire morning rooting through reports and other documentation, I invited one of the
volunteers to join me for lunch at the small restaurant
downstairs. For one, I didn't want to be alone after
spending hours immersed in these disturbing accounts, but I was also curious about what she did in the
archive. She informed me that most of their documents
came from private individuals—old newspapers, photos, and rolls of film, or diaries that had been saved and
donated.

"But aren't there any documents from former militia
headquarters or state institutions?" I asked. "Dossiers
that would tell us more about the chains of command
or about who interrogated whom or where they took all
the people who are still missing?"

The young woman put the straw in her mouth and
took a sip of coke before responding, "Do you really
think they'd tell us that?"

What was it Abbas had said to me at the silkworm
farm? *We're living in an age of upheaval.* During lunch I
learned that untold amounts of evidence were secretly

destroyed during the turbulent postwar years. While militia leaders made a public show of personal reform, relinquished their weapons and became politicians, for years their minions were busy in the background erasing all traces of wrongdoing. Signs of mass graves were obliterated, militia membership lists blacked out, fragments of the truth carefully eradicated. And every so often, a former hideout—an abandoned building, a hangar, an underground vault, whether on a residential street or in the middle of nowhere—might suddenly burst into flames. These fires burned across the country, the woman told me, from Beirut to midsize coastal cities to tiny mountain villages.

"I actually remember that," I said pensively. "I just didn't know the reason behind it at the time. It was Christmas Eve in 1994. There was a sudden commotion."

"What happened?"

"We had a bunch of people over. I was talking to a friend of my grandmother's in my room when someone shouted at us to get out, quick ..."

*

It was Umm Jamil. "Fire!" she yelled.

Abbas leapt to his feet and pulled me up. "Here in the building?"

"No." She shook her head and disappeared down the hall.

We ran downstairs and into the cold night air. The street was full of people. I saw Grandmother at the front of the crowd. All her guests and neighbors had come outside. Everyone was looking west, where the inky sky provided a backdrop for orange and yellow blazes.

"Must be the warehouses by the train tracks," Nadia commented. "Looks like the whole area is in flames."

I was standing between Umm Jamil and Abbas; each had a hand on my shoulder. I shook them off and pushed through the crowd. Grandmother was standing there in her blue party dress, squinting and pursing her lips. I reached for her hand. She squeezed mine without looking at me.

"What's going on?" I asked.

"Nothing," she said. "Just another fire."

From My Conversations with Saber Mounir

Recorded in the summer of 1994:

Lead the reader through your story, Amin. Say: Take my hand. Trust me. This will be a challenging and perhaps painful journey, but together we will reach the ruins at the end that hold all the answers.

Not a Ghost Light in Sight

We have thunderstorms up here some nights. They pass over my house and I'm woken by the sounds of shutters rattling and wind roaring in the trees. I lie awake and wait for the thunder to descend over the hills and valleys. Storms like these don't scare me. I go to the window and look across the meadows at the mountainside illuminated by lightning. Historians claim that the ancient convents in this area have provided shelter to the persecuted for centuries.

The region is bounded by two rivers: the Damour to the north and the Awali to the south. A branch of the Awali runs near my house, just a short walk through tall grass. The stream meanders unassumingly into the valley. Were I to follow the water, I would first pass through forestland and then end up on the shores of the Levantine Sea. Heading upstream—and uphill— the terrain grows rocky and rough. In some sections the river is little more than a trickle. At times it disappears and flows underground as if it were trying to say *Stop, nothing to see up here, turn around*. If you continue anyway, eventually you'll reach the outer walls of an old convent with a bolted gate.

Standing by the window during nighttime storms, in a blaze of lightning I'll sometimes spot a car on the mountainside. Like I imagined it. Time passes, and by the next flash it's gone. I now know what the car's appearance means. It means someone—a girl or a woman

—has been rescued after asking for help. The nuns receive a call hours earlier. One of the sisters gets in the car and navigates the many hairpin turns on the road down to Beirut. She makes her way to an agreed-upon public location—a café, a mall—and collects the girl, who in recent days has found refuge with a small group of allies dedicated to protecting women facing violence or even death at home, for supposedly having damaged the family honor. The nun is in civilian clothing so as to go undetected. She leads the girl by the arm to the car, and together they drive to the convent in the mountains, where the girl is hidden. When victims are over eighteen, it's easier to wrest them from their family and get them out of the country, should all mediation attempts fail. But if they're underage they sometimes spend years behind convent walls, because without the father's permission, they can't leave Lebanon. It's an elaborate network that has grown over many years and largely remains a secret. People rarely talk about the convents scattered throughout Lebanon, so as not to endanger the shelter they provide.

I seldom walk upstream. I much prefer turning toward the valley. Some days, I make a paper boat, place it in the water, and watch as it's whisked downstream.

not a
ghost light
... in sight,
I write on stern or prow. I imagine the boat reaching the distant coast the very same day.

Many years ago Saber Mounir compared Beirut to an old ship kept afloat by the principle of repression. I have been afraid of reaching this part of the story for a long time.

One January morning in 1995, I woke up knowing something was going to happen. I could feel it in my belly as I watched the rain out the window. It was one of those oppressive days we experienced more often than usual in Beirut that winter, when fog swallowed the mountains and a haze hung over the rooftops, obscuring any sense of distance.

I hadn't heard from Jafar since the day he betrayed me, and feeling both too proud and too hurt, I hadn't contacted him either.

A few days after Christmas, I had walked down to the train tracks. A couple of stray dogs roamed around the area, where buildings were still smoldering. Many months had passed since we'd last been here, Jafar and I. The windows in the main hall had burst. I thought of the empty offices with the impressions of filing cabinets in the carpeting. In the main hall, where we'd climbed into diesel tanks, the doors to other parts of the complex had been locked, blocking our access. I walked around the outside of the building because I didn't dare climb through a window. Behind the building I discovered what little remained of the adjacent structures. It wasn't just a fire that had destroyed the place; it seemed a series of explosions had caused these buildings to collapse.

I was still waiting for a response from Zahra. Nearly a month had passed since I tracked down her cousin in Mala'ab al-Baladi. Every day I swiped the mailbox key from the hook and ran downstairs, but there was never an envelope for me. I took the edge off my disappointment by inventing excuses for her: It was vacation, so maybe she was on a family trip. Or maybe she was writing her own story in response, which required way more time than a letter or card.

I showered longer than usual that January morning. I let the hot water drum against my head in the hopes that it would flush out the acidic feeling that had taken hold as I slept and not let go. I dried my body with a blow-dryer instead of a towel, brushed my teeth, and got dressed. I flopped back onto my bed and flipped through the book Abbas had rustled up and given me for Christmas—a small, German-language edition of Ovid's *Metamorphoses*. Around noon, the doorbell rang.

"Could you get that, please?" Grandmother called from the kitchen.

I careened down the hallway to the door, fumbled with the lock, then felt my stomach drop to bottomless depths. Standing on our doormat was a woman in a UNICEF jacket. It wasn't the woman I knew from school; I'd never seen this one before. She had a friendly face and warm eyes. There was nothing at all threatening about her, and yet I knew, as she said my name and held up the little card I'd included with Zahra's story, that I had made a terrible mistake.

It comes as little surprise that maps would be of interest to a kid who'd been searching for a sense of orientation all his life. I started collecting and studying maps the same summer I spent my evenings in the library with Saber Mounir. Views of the world at different points in time. I was even more fascinated by maps depicting made-up countries than those of real places, like the *Carte du pays de Tendre*. It's an old map of emotions set in an imaginary country that resembles France. The topography shows various aspects of love, as it was understood in the seventeenth century. There's the River of Appreciation and the village of Affection. At the top of the map, far to the north, lies the Dangerous Sea. All that's missing is sexual love. At a time when men defined public discourse, the *Carte du pays de Tendre* first appeared in a novel written by a woman—*Clélie*, by Madeleine de Scudéry. It was a plea for female autonomy. Of course there's a reason this particular map comes to mind. It's the little things that create connections to the past and usher them into the present. The River of Appreciation, the village of Affection, the Dangerous Sea ...

The three of us sat at the kitchen table, Grandmother and I both stone-faced.

"Do you understand everything I just told you?" the woman asked.

I felt unable to answer, until Grandmother's hand came to rest on mine.

"So, nothing happened to her, right?" I asked.

"Right. We removed her from the situation and she's safe, but I can't tell you where she is."

Given what she had just told us, the woman seemed amazingly calm. I wondered how many times she'd had similar conversations. I didn't understand entirely what had happened. Someone found my story—that much was clear. Maybe Asifa dropped it or maybe, after I encountered him on the stairs, her father suspected I had given his daughter something and hunted for it. Whatever the case, he found my note and turned it over to Zahra's father. My stupid little story about an invisible boy presumably wouldn't have caused any harm, either, had I not included that one ambiguous scene, in which the boy and girl dance on the coast and then disappear behind the rocks—the Dangerous Sea ...

There was a huge argument. Terrified of her father, Zahra approached the UNICEF woman at school and immediate steps were taken to ensure her safety. As the woman recounted what had happened, a flurry of images rushed past: Zahra wrapped in a blanket in a shed somewhere in the woods, Zahra on the floor of a barren room in a safe house right here in Beirut, maybe even nearby ... The good news was that she was safe. The bad news was that I was to blame for the situation.

"Can you pass on a message to her?" I asked quietly.

The woman looked at me. I sensed her hesitation. "I'm afraid I can't do that," she said. "Right now we're trying to dissuade the family from harming the girl. Her father is blind with rage and not just because of the story and insinuated transgression. He says you and a friend of yours humiliated him on two separate occasions. Zahra did not reveal your names, but he suspects you boys are behind it, which intensifies his sense of damaged honor. The spiritual leader in his community is currently trying to mediate."

Grandmother kept her hand on mine.

"Amin grew up in Germany," I heard her say. "He's unfamiliar with local customs. Many—" She faltered. "Many traditional practices are foreign to him. He knows he made a mistake ..."

"We see this a lot," the woman said. She was still wearing her official jacket, which I found intimidating. "Occasionally in Beirut, but mostly in rural areas. The power vacuum in those regions has allowed residents to create their own systems of justice, and this country ... let's just say there's a long road ahead to achieving a sense of order. Then there's pressure from relatives to reestablish family honor and good standing. The whole thing is extremely complex, and we're outsiders here too. We regularly encounter roadblocks. Many families have returned since the war ended, you know? Not because life's better here but because Lebanese fathers sense the power they have over their daughters slipping in those Western cultures. They don't know who the girl might be seeing at school or the youth center. From one day to the next they return to Lebanon with the family, and once they're here, it sometimes turns out the daughter had a boyfriend back in exile. Amin, in Lebanon daughters are like a precious vessel or fragile vase. A valuable object that holds the family honor and must be protected ..."

"But it was just a story," I stammered. "Nothing happened. It was just a story ..."

"I believe you," said the woman, "but all we can do is hope for successful mediation. There's no undoing what's been done."

I lay in bed later, still stunned. Upset stomach, worn nerves. I couldn't even bear the clock ticking as the hour wearily progressed from five to six.

"Are we in danger?" Grandmother asked the woman as she was leaving.

"No," was her response. "Zahra's cousin removed your address from the envelope before her father took the story. Asifa is a very sharp, very brave girl. She gave me the card when we spoke. She managed to convince her family that she didn't know Amin or what was in the envelope, so no one knows your name or where you live."

When searching for an example of something we've lost, suddenly it appears at every turn. There had been moments prior to that day when, despite my feelings of foreignness, the differences between everyday life in Beirut and Germany had an exotic appeal. I romanticized them. My perception remains forever altered by the experience. From then on, certain scenes and details took on a new quality, like a false bottom. Older women standing on their balconies all day, monitoring the action, is one such image. I had long thought this behavior simply suggested a slower pace of life or Oriental easygoingness. Even now, I can't walk down the street in Beirut without an uneasy look skyward. There they are, draped over the railings to see what's happening below. Who's going where, and when, and with whom? Young girls' honor attracts all the women's attention. Little goes unnoticed.

Just a few weeks ago I came across a newspaper article with the picture of a man posing for the camera with a rifle. He had used the weapon to shoot his wife and daughter. His wife had told him their daughter was no longer a virgin, potentially in an effort to protect the girl from being married off against her will. I read that the family had returned to Beirut from Germany. The man had found his daughter's diary, which contained mention of a boyfriend. The paper reported on the double murder without a hint of emotion. Neighbors justified the father's actions. Neither commentary nor outrage was presented.

That night, hours after the UNICEF lady had left, Grandmother gave me a few dropperfuls of the medicine she'd brought from Germany. She used to take it herself to avoid waking up in the middle of the night. As far as I knew, she hadn't needed it since our return, but now she produced the vial from the bathroom cabinet.

"This will help you fall asleep," she said. "Things will

make more sense in the morning. You'll see."

But it was like my body and spirit were at loggerheads. I couldn't keep my eyes open yet my mind was racing. I could hear Grandmother on the phone outside my door. She was talking to Abbas, her tone hushed. At some point—I'm not sure how late it was—a triangle of light spilled into the room and Grandmother came in. I lay there with my eyes closed and heard her approach the bed, then I felt her weight sink onto the mattress. She sat there for a while, running her hand over my blanket, something she hadn't done in years. To my amazement, she kicked off her slippers and lay down beside me. I felt her breath against my skin, her cheek against my neck.

I must have fallen asleep like that.

Evasive Maneuvers

Nothing had changed by morning, though, other than Grandmother no longer lying beside me when I woke with leaden limbs. I was home alone. She'd left breakfast for me in the kitchen, along with a note: *At the café.*

When I got there the awning had been lowered. A few tables and chairs were arranged on the sidewalk in the morning sun. A pile of limp foliage sat in a dustpan outside the open door. Soapy streaks of water ran down the inside of the front window; the suds were wiped away, revealing Grandmother's face. Abu Amar was on a ladder in the middle of the room, replacing a light bulb, while Nadia and Umm Jamil busily wiped down tables and the counter and placed bouquets of flowers around the room.

I was greeted with fanfare.

"Our water's fine," Grandmother proclaimed as we all sat down together. "We can get going again." She smiled and knocked three times on the wooden tabletop.

Nadia had stuck little cocktail umbrellas in our water glasses, which we raised in a toast.

All morning people stuck their heads in, offering their congratulations and promising to stop by: *You've reopened? Wonderful, we'll be back tomorrow with the whole family. We always knew it must be a misunderstanding.*

I could feel the aftereffects of the drops. Everything was distorted, but there was nowhere else I would rather be. Every so often Umm Jamil would drop what she was doing to hand me a cup of cocoa or glass of water. Nadia sat down beside me and folded a stack of napkins into little boats that she arranged on the tables. I caught Abu Amar's eye in the mirror behind the counter and he winked conspiratorially with a nod. There would always be something secretive about this group; that much I knew.

It's why I didn't bother asking about something I'd noticed as I entered the café. I simply accepted the change with relief: Grandmother's paintings had vanished from the walls.

*

Something else changed, too: the next morning our neighbor Tony returned from sixty-one days in custody. Wearing the same clothes as the day they came for him, Tony stepped off the bus on a busy corner and ran home in the drizzle. His left leg dragged slightly. He hunched his shoulders as if trying to hide his neck and ears, with his hands jammed in his pockets. People in the neighborhood avoided him as though he had a contagious disease. They averted their eyes as he walked past, but huddled up the moment his back was turned.

As soon as Tony's front door closed, folks headed for the kitchen to prepare a dish to bring over later, in the hopes that he and Nour would invite them in. That evening, though, I watched as every last neighbor issued from Tony's building, laden with the same heaped bowls they'd carried in.

Tony and Nour left the country that very night. I saw them outside their building in the glow of the streetlight. They loaded up the car. Nour tossed a set of keys into the mailbox. Then their car rolled away down the street.

There was more chatter than eating at neighborhood canteens for days after their departure. Some people said Tony must have cracked—how else could he have made it out alive? Others speculated that his arrest had been a mistake, and once it became clear how useless he was to the secret service, they'd let him go. Whatever the case, Tony and Nour no longer felt their home was a place they could sleep without fear of ambush or spend the day unmolested. And with that, they were gone.

*

After the café reopened Grandmother acted like everything was back on track. She took me to the mountains, higher than I'd ever been. We watched streams swollen with snowmelt surging into the valley and hiked along trails that had only recently become passable again. The area was still pretty lonely, despite yearslong efforts to get wartime exiles to return. Grandmother knew all sorts of secluded paths skirting the villages, and every so often a wooden bench would appear, inviting passersby to sit and rest. Had she come here to paint in the past?

We didn't talk much on these day trips. Despite our vast surroundings, we focused only on immediate concerns: *Is that a mosquito bite on your hand? Want me to carry the backpack for a while?* Or we imagined the near future, the same landscape in midsummer light: *We can bring along a tent—that's something we've never done.* We didn't talk about the café or the protests in the city, still fueled by the Samir Geagea trial. Nor did we talk about the horrific mistake I had made. I was, however, comforted by her care and clear effort to stand by me.

She had sensed my fear after we returned from Germany too. She'd taken me to Tripoli, back to her childhood, as a way of showing me that I was part of her life and belonged here.

A quality of silence I thought we had moved past returned on those outings, and while it's a hard truth, I know that the tight, warm embrace of silence created a closeness between us that remains my most profound experience of security.

*

Overheard conversations, January 1995:

– "I heard the weather's going to stay like this. About time, too."
– "Did you hear about the new law? It's illegal to hunt pelicans now."
– "You're approaching it all wrong, brother. It's more important to major in something you really like."
– "No, let's go somewhere else. This place was shut down recently for contaminated tap water."
– "Tony and Nour? Brazil. At least that's what I heard."
– "I'm telling you, it's true. The report was just made public. The project was called Stargate. The CIA had a secret department for paranormal activity and hired ghost hunters to track down missing people ..."

About a week had passed since the woman from UNICEF had rung our doorbell. I hadn't heard anyone talking about Zahra. People talked about all sorts of things at the bus stop, in line at the grocery store, or while having a snack or visiting outside their building, but I didn't catch wind of any rumors concerning a young girl from Jouaiya.

I considered confiding in Abbas. He had a real grab-the-bull-by-the-horns attitude that might come in handy. Besides, he lived farther south, closer to Jouaiya. Maybe he knew more.

I'd felt closer to Abbas ever since our day together at his silkworm farm. That impression was reinforced on Christmas Eve. I kept thinking of him as a young boy running outside after thunderstorms to save the caterpillars. I called his house, but the woman who answered said Abbas was away for the time being.

"Didn't he say when he was coming back?" I asked Grandmother that evening.

"No, Amin. I didn't even know he was planning a trip."

"Okay ... It's just that you were on the phone with him for a while. I thought he might have said something."

"Well, he didn't. Could you pass the flour?"

Grandmother's fingers sank into a ball of dough. She tossed it in the air, pulled it apart, then worked the pieces back together.

I set the flour down. "Have you heard of astral projection?"

"Astral projection? No."

"Apparently there are people who can leave their bodies and travel wherever they want. Some of them were hired by the CIA. They were blindfolded and then described buildings here in Beirut that looked exactly like the buildings where hostages were later released."

"Is that so?"

"It's what I heard. Do you think anyone like that is still working in Beirut?"

"I think it's nonsense, habibi." Grandmother turned back to the kitchen counter, fished the rolling pin from the drawer, and began vigorously flattening out the dough. "If that really worked, those astral projectionists would be the most sought-after people in the city."

I now recognize my readiness to consider all options, however outrageous, as nothing more than evasion. Meanwhile, the next step was obvious. I don't know why I hesitated to reach out to Jafar for so long. He was always on my mind, but approaching him would have meant admitting my own powerlessness to myself. By not contacting him, I could preserve what little dignity I thought I had, and I convinced myself that my obvious fear of further rejection was actually a sign of independence.

I hated how much I missed him. As usual I pushed everything away and blamed it all on him. I cursed the day at the flea market that triggered this whole avalanche and the fact that Jafar made me want to be like him. The image of him with the girl on the rocks haunted my dreams. By the time I felt ready to face him, though, it was too late.

"Want to know why you're unhappy all the time?"

The question, posed not too long ago, came from a woman who provided me something akin to refuge for a while.

"I've got to get going," I said. "The train ..."

"Because you always expect the worst, Amin, which lowers the height from which you might ultimately fall. You've settled into unhappiness to prevent falling as hard as you did back then."

"I turned up too late. My damn pride got in the way.

Had I just gotten over it sooner ..."

"You wouldn't have prevented anything."

"Actually I think I would have. That day we went looking for the cartoonist and failed ... Jafar was different somehow. He'd been distancing himself for weeks, but before he ditched me, Jafar revealed the scope of his insecurities. I think it was his way of asking for help."

"It wasn't your fault," said Soraya. "Jafar never asked anyone for help."

I have often wondered if there's an exact point at which we leave childhood behind. They say personality is built on memory. Every emotional experience we have leaves a trace in the matrix of our mind, bonds of friendship as much as moments of humiliation or desperation.

"Who was the girl?"

"Her name was Zahra. Jafar had helped me approach her."

"So you were hoping to work things out with him that day?"

"Yeah. I realized I needed him. I thought we might shake and move on. That was all I wanted."

"Makes sense. Tell me what happened next ..."

Larkness

I was two weeks too late.

The landlord showed me through the empty apartment. It was a small place, just three rooms, kitchen, bath. I hadn't believed the guy.

He leaned against the door, holding a bunch of keys. "They up and left, just like that," he said. "No call, no notice, nothing. The key appeared in my mailbox one day. As for the family?" He snapped his fingers. "It's like the ground swallowed them up."

I went into every room. I pressed my fingers into the textured wallpaper and touched light switches and door handles. I stopped in the doorway to one of the bigger rooms and ran my hand down the doorjamb. It was marked with lines charting the children's growth over the years. The markings on the left were labeled *Soraya*, those on the right *Jafar*.

"And they didn't say where they were going?"

"Nope. Not one word. I've never seen anything like it."

He told me he and his son had cleared out the furniture. Dressers, beds, cabinets—they'd left everything behind. I could tell by the imprints in the carpet where things had stood.

"And they didn't leave a note?"

The man looked me up and down. "Just that mess down the hallway," he said, pointing.

I entered the room and noticed a rectangle of light

from the window on the floor and opposite wall.

"It was the daughter's bedroom," I heard the man call as I moved in for a closer look.

A square had been drawn on the wallpaper in crayon, clearly by a child. The words SORAYA'S ATLAS were written above in all caps. Surrounding the square were boxy skyscrapers. They were on fire. Rockets flew overhead. Inside the square a well-ordered scene played out. It was the depiction of an imaginary place. Squiggly lines snaked through it, labeled *Usumacinta, Orinoco, Irrawaddy, Zambezi, Ganges, Kenai.*

It was like climbing out of a muddled dream and into the light. Suddenly it was summer. We were sitting on the top floor of a ruin, the city lights below.

"I'm building a zoo on the Zambezi," I whispered.

And Jafar said: "No light in the basement meant no way to distract yourself."

I turned. The landlord now stood in the doorway. "Could I please see the basement too?" I asked quietly.

I still remember the way he furrowed his brow, then said "Basement?" and burst out laughing.

Another thing I remember is stumbling onto the street a few minutes later. Building upon building as far as the eye could see.

"I'm looking for Salman's store," I said to a woman pushing a stroller. "Could you tell me where it is?"

She drew back in confusion. "There's no store by that name here," she said. "Sorry."

"Salman's store," I repeated. "I'm sure it was on this street. He sold candles and batteries during the war."

"No, I've lived here for twenty years," the woman said and walked away.

I've never forgotten the feeling of wind on my skin that night on the high-rise roof, when Jafar told me about losing his eye. I see myself standing on the brink, the shrimpy kid I was back then, and there he is beside me—Jafar, the storyteller from Achrafieh, Beirut—quietly speaking of himself in the third person.

I looked back at the building I'd just left. In his story Jafar was standing right about here when his sister ran outside on her way to a basement that didn't exist.

The image of her standing there, her arm extended as if waving, was the last thing he saw before a bright light flashed near his eye, followed by total darkness.

I pressed my temples to stop the street from spinning. Harsh sunlight glinted off the windows. I closed my eyes.

"What *really* happened to you?" I asked. "Where the hell did you go?"

And the afterimage of Jafar in my mind's eye closed the atlas in his lap and said: *We came up with so much stuff.*

The Boy in the Mirror

In the following weeks and months, or even years later, I thought of Zahra and Jafar as I fell asleep, in the hopes of dreaming about them. It never worked. Or rather, I dreamt about them constantly, but always in the context of their absence. These recurring dreams were filled with moments of everyday failure—missed phone calls, flat bike tires, a detour around a construction site—that delayed me in reaching our meeting spot, and they'd be gone ... Inherent to these images was a sense of anxiety that I couldn't shake in my waking hours either.

There are other scenes I could describe to illustrate what was happening inside me at that time, but suffice it to say I transformed entirely into the boy who appeared in the mirror the day after the sandstorm. Whoever I may have been before was lost to me.

*

Winter turned into spring and spring turned into summer. The world kept turning. People planted their gardens, played cards, went to Sunday school or church, and watched their soaps and talk shows; the power went out and came back on, wrecking balls demolished buildings, and cement mixers churned as the city of the future strove for greater heights.

In June Samir Geagea received a death sentence that

was immediately commuted to life in prison. The trial was over. Many ex-militiamen had left Lebanon during proceedings to avoid repression and arrest. Much remained uncertain following his sentencing. Observers classified both the process and outcome as politically motivated. Many witnesses later retracted their testimony, citing the use of torture to force confessions.

One day that June, gunfire could be heard for hours from the southern part of the city, though it was impossible to say whether shots were being fired in celebration or protest. Our living room curtains were drawn against the heat. The TV was on. I remember grainy images of enraged people behind police tape and Samir Geagea in handcuffs, surrounded by cameras. A newsperson stood outside the courthouse, reporting live:

"A spectacular criminal trial came to a close today, the verdict no less stunning than the proceedings leading up to it. Samir Geagea is the first and as yet only former militia leader to have been indicted and convicted. Nevertheless, outside observers predict further indictments are unlikely, as many onetime militiamen now hold high office and are thus shielded from prosecution by the General Amnesty Law of 1991, also known as Law No. 84/91. The law pardons any crimes such officials and other armed fighters committed during the civil war or before March 28, 1991. Exceptions are limited solely to attacks on religious and political leaders, as well as foreign and Arab diplomats. It is because of this exception that Samir Geagea was pronounced guilty in a trial observers described as fraught with disagreement. During the civil war, Geagea ..."

I looked at my hands. Grandmother sat beside me, staring at the screen. She had taken the news of the verdict silently, tucking up her legs and hugging them, as she had done so often in recent weeks.

Does it even exist outside of stories, the fissure that comes to light one day and determines the outcome of your life? There once was a time, and there once was no time. Someone was there, and someone wasn't there. The storyteller has the ability to lead the reader to the ruins that hold all the answers.

1981

She can tell it's going to be a good day the moment she wakes up. In the air there's a hint of the way things used to be. Yara opens her eyes and thinks of her studio downstairs and realizes she's in the mood to paint, which hasn't happened in a long time. It's a feeling she believed forgotten: to look forward to the day's work without becoming mired in it. This shard of time containing so many ways to start a picture, when everything is still just vision, trial and error.

She pulls on her robe and goes downstairs. After twenty-eight years in this house, she knows every last corner. She could navigate the space blindfolded. She's lived alone since her divorce from Amin, and since he's no longer here getting up before her, the house in the morning has a sleepy quality to it. She likes it that way, but she also likes that it currently isn't the case. It smells of coffee. Light pours through the kitchen window and the door to the garden is open. How late did she sleep? It must be early; the sun hasn't quite crested the hill. Maya's out by the apple tree, holding the baby.

She looks at her daughter, who's here for a visit and singing to her son. It never fails to amaze Yara that she gave birth to that girl, now a young woman of twenty-four who became a mother herself a few months earlier.

"Good morning," she says. "Sleep well?"

Yara nods. "Better than I have in ages."

"Gorgeous day," Maya says, looking up.

Scattered clouds edge the blue sky, and Yara decides not to tell her daughter that it will start raining by mid-afternoon. She's lived here for so long that she can gauge how fast the clouds are moving by the feel of the air or by watching birds' flight patterns. Moments like these are hard to come by and she doesn't want to spoil it. Yara feels overcome with love at the sight of Maya beaming with enthusiasm for the beauty of the morning and the child in her arms. She brushes aside the thought that it's a passing sight because it's a passing stay. Maya and her husband have come to introduce her to her grandson before the three of them return to France, where they live.

They have argued over this. Repeatedly. He and Maya have called her stubborn. She could easily move to France to be near her daughter and grandson, they reasoned. What on earth was keeping her here, now, of all times, in this situation, in this country? They asked these questions and she countered with evasion. A new life? This is where I belong—and the same goes for the child, you know. Truth be told, she's never ruled out the possibility. At times it seems likely that she'll soon sell the house and join them in France. Before that happens, though, just this once she had to see what she's seeing now from the doorway: the fragment of a decades-old dream, the continuation of a line. Her daughter and grandchild in this garden.

And so she smiles and leans her head against the

wood as Maya turns and walks barefoot through the grass.

She admires the way her daughter treats the child, the loving, effortless composure Maya demonstrates, as if mothering were in her blood. She seems to know instinctively what the baby needs, if he's hungry or simply wants to be held and rocked.

She cried the first time she saw the baby boy.

Amin.

Maya told her his name and looked at her, waiting for a reaction. Why did her daughter have to name the child after his grandfather? Yara hopes it's coming from a place of admiration and not as an act of rebellion against her, the mother who burdened her daughter with her own dreams and sent her to a foreign land. The absent father. Those two had always been close. As close as anyone can be to a man who withdrew so thoroughly over time. She knows she's too harsh. There's plenty to criticize about Amin but never that he was a bad father. He didn't blame Maya for marrying a non-Lebanese man; he held it against Yara. For many, many years. Years during which he changed. She never told Maya about their fights or the bitterness that beset him. Of course she noticed, though. *I thought I sensed tension between you two during your last visit. I hope everything's okay.* She wrote that once in a letter.

And so when Maya places the baby in her arms for the first time and says "His name is Amin," Yara cries, comfortable with the ambiguity of her tears.

The rain pelts the roof that afternoon. Wind whips around the house. She awakens from a trancelike state at the easel. She listens. The house is empty. A familiar hush. The little family went on a walk; the rain will have caught them by surprise. Now she's ashamed not to have said anything. She didn't want to seem patronizing.

The painting. She's happy with it, although she knows that by tomorrow she may find it hollow or histrionic. Whatever happens, at least she started painting again, and she hopes the mood will stick. She doffs her smock, cleans the brushes, shuts the box of paints, and leaves the studio. She feels a sudden uneasiness as she closes the door behind her. Should she let Maya know she was painting? She would love to share her happiness and tell her daughter that her sense of surprise and curiosity is finally back. At the same time, she fears how Maya might react. She's afraid her daughter might misinterpret her words to contain the timeworn, oblique accusation: Look, I'm painting. With talent like yours, why did you stop?

When the front door bursts open presently, she's at the stove. The two come crashing in, laughing and soaking wet. He shakes the water from his head and pulls Maya near, wiping the raindrops from her eyelashes and kissing her on the forehead. Though it's been years, Yara still doesn't know him well. He's quiet and gentle. Tall. Dark eyes, dark hair. He could easily be Lebanese, she thinks. It's rare to see him come out of his shell like this. He tends to retreat into the background when he's here. His face remains in the shadows. He knows he's foreign in this space, so he does all he can not to get in the way. He's polite, answers her questions and asks his own in return, but she can tell he's not approaching her—the mother-in-law—without reservation, and she wonders what Maya has told him. Or if he's the one who encouraged her to stop painting.

Maya opens her coat, revealing the baby inside.

"Hi."

"Hi. I'm sorry about the rain."

"No need to apologize; it was fun. What did you get up to?"

She hesitates. "I did some cooking."

She set the table. Three plates. Three glasses. Three sets of silverware. A ritual she has come to love these past few weeks, after all the years of living alone up here. Yes, she really could picture going to France with them.

Maya slips into the bath and reemerges a few minutes later with her wet hair twisted up in a towel. They stand facing each other under the low ceiling. At the sight of her daughter, she feels old, rough around the edges, pinched.

Maya hesitates. There's something on her mind, and Yara knows exactly what it is.

"I'm sorry," Maya says. "I thought we talked about this, but we were planning to eat out tonight." She stands there with a guilty expression, hands in her pockets, as she glances at the set table.

"Oh," says Yara. "I completely forgot."

A few days ago they agreed that if the situation there remained quiet, Maya and her husband would drive into Beirut. There's a restaurant where old friends of Maya's work as servers, not right in the city but a little farther south; a seaside restaurant that she, the visitor, has been talking about for days. Yara didn't actually forget, of course. She cooked, set the table, and lit candles because she hoped the two of them would stay: there was *fatayer bil lahme*, *dervish kibbeh*, *foul hammoud*, *coban kavurma*, more food than they'd ever manage to finish. She was hoping for a sign, a gesture of reconciliation or at least of readiness for reconciliation; she was hoping Maya would choose her mother, whom she so rarely sees, over her friends.

She knows it's pointless so she forces herself to smile and nod. Maya rounds the kitchen counter and kisses her on the cheek, a glancing kiss, a whisper of a kiss, and says "You're the best, *Maman!*" Then she's already running upstairs to get changed.

She stays in the kitchen and looks at the bowls of food. The flickering candles. The mountain of pans in the sink. She touches the spot where Maya kissed her.

You're the best, Maman!

She knows it should make her happy but there's no quieting the insecurity that so often takes hold in her solitude. Why *Maman?* Why French? Isn't it a sign of alienation and distance? Doesn't it indicate the loss of their common language? Or is she hinting at the elephant in the room that, like so many other things, has gone unmentioned for weeks: Pack your bags, Maman, sell the house, leave your memories here and come to Paris with us! The insecurity is always there, lying in wait. It takes its time in emerging, then assumes such concentrated power and defined contours, Yara could swear it was a living creature.

The two of them come downstairs. Maya's in jeans and a cognac-colored blouse. She considers offering her daughter one of the dresses hanging in the wardrobe upstairs. Maybe the blue one. She'd look stunning in that one, but Maya looks stunning no matter what she wears. At that age, she thinks, you can wear whatever you want.

Maya nursed the baby. He's asleep in the bassinet now. "He'll easily sleep for three or four hours," she says, setting a bottle on the table. "That's for later, but we won't stay out long."

She looks at the child. His hands twitch in his sleep. Can he sense that his mother is leaving? Will he wake up when they go? She refuses to let her anxiety gain purchase. Just a few hours, she thinks. She'll conceal her disappointment, wish them a pleasant evening, pour a glass of the wine she already opened, and then she'll eat and later hold and feed the baby.

The two of them are standing by the door, near the picture Maya painted just five years ago, though it seems like a different lifetime to her. They pay no attention to it; all they see is each other. He helps her with her coat and she slips it on with a smile. Suddenly she sees herself in her daughter's body, many years younger, only the front hallway is the foyer of a theater. She swallows. Forces herself to smile. The door opens, cold air pours in, and she hears the rain. Father and mother blow kisses to her and the sleeping child and head out.

They're halfway out the door, halfway into the rain when Maya turns back.

"Farewell!" she says, laughing.

This is the concession she's been yearning for, Yara realizes. Evidence of a connection they alone understand. A greeting addressed to the past and maybe even to a forgiving future.

"Farewell, farewell!"

Yara lifts her hand and waves back. She watches them cross the dark grass in the rain, open the front gate, and get in the car.

*

We're two sides of the same soul, Amin.

That's what Grandmother said to me the night after the storm, the first time she told me about the house and my mother's childhood. As we stared in silence at the TV a year later when Samir Geagea's sentence was announced, I started to sense what she'd meant. My whole life she had done everything in her power to save me from becoming like her. Now, after everything that had happened, she saw me slipping into profound darkness, saw all her failures mirrored in me. She was familiar with darkness. She reflexively returned to the bearing I knew so well from our time in Germany. More than anything, it was one of waiting.

I can picture her adopting the same bearing that night with me as an infant beside her. It's well past midnight. Sitting on a kitchen chair, she hugs her legs in close and lays her head on her knees. She can remain alert that way. She strains to hear in the rain and waits for the sound of tires in the driveway.

She will return to this bearing many times in the coming years. Whatever threatens to attack from below can't reach her this way. Waiting provides possibilities. The future remains a conceivable prospect. That night, between two and three o'clock, her notion of the future is limited to the next few minutes. In a bit she'll hear their laughter. The door will open and ...

As the minutes pass, *future* isn't a word meaning years or decades. It doesn't contain the image of this little boy, still asleep and dreaming by her side, standing in front of her at some point in a different country, in a different kitchen, and asking for breakfast as she sits there again, her legs tucked up as they have been since two in the morning. Or even further in the future, a future in which she dyes her hair and asks the boy: "If we hadn't seen each other for many years and you passed me on the street, would you recognize me?" because at some point she'll realize how old she's grown and that Maya, should she ever return, might not recognize her. All this remains inconceivable. It defies the laws of physics that a few hours could turn into twenty-four years.

Landslide

The one marble that missed its mark was forget-me-not blue, the kids—a boy and girl—recalled when the reporter interviewed them on TV. They traced the curve of its flight as if it had occurred in slow motion. They described the moment the marble landed in the wet grass with three points placed in quick succession at the end of the curve, to show that the marble hadn't stopped but instead bounced three times and rolled down the hill. There had been a lot of rain in the days prior. There had been a landslide.

It wasn't the kids' first time telling the story and it showed: they barely paused to think or breathe between words and the accompanying gestures were smooth, almost practiced. The drawn-out description of the marble's trajectory, however, and the way they kept mentioning its color—*zahrat al-wala'a*, forget-me-not blue—seemed to indicate how hard they were trying to delay reaching the end of their story, which they had been asked to share and which was the only reason they were seated in front of the camera. If you paid close enough attention, you could tell that the children's measured delivery concealed inner turmoil. They included minor details as if these were critical to how things played out: They recounted how they'd first wandered around the deserted orchard and climbed trees, the marbles rattling in their leather pouches with every movement. They said they'd played for hours without losing sight of a single marble. They placed particular importance on the shot in question, demonstrating the backswing and explaining that for fun they'd tried to gauge the strength and direction of the wind to ensure a successful shot. Even as the reporter began fidgeting in his chair, the kids were still in the meadow by the slope and in no hurry to finish. Almost as if storytelling had the power to freeze that critical moment in time—the moment at which the marble, still airborne, pauses at the apex of the arc because it's right before the kids realize they overshot the mark and the marble will disappear down the hill, compelling them to hunt for it in the dark new crevice that opened in the rock where the ground had slid away, and where they'll search for their lost toy deeper and deeper till they come upon the dead bodies.

Certainty

Canal+ newscast, January 9, 2005, 2:35 p.m.,
sound on tape:

*Over the weekend a mass grave containing the remains of
at least twenty-eight bodies was discovered in the eastern
Lebanese city of Anjar. Today's issue of the* Daily Star *newspaper in Beirut reports that authorities estimate more than
forty bodies were buried at the site.*

*"Some of the bones found in the grave have been there for
more than twenty years," forensic scientist Fouad Ayoub
states. Mr. Ayoub is overseeing the investigation into the site,
which was discovered last Friday by two children playing
nearby.*

*The mass grave is located half a mile away from former
Syrian secret-service headquarters in an area of Lebanon
controlled by Syrian troops from the early 1980s through the
end of the civil war. According to Ayoub,* DNA *samples collected from human remains discovered at the site will be
analyzed for potential matches with individuals reported
missing.*

*There has been no comment on the discovery by either Leb-
anese or Syrian officials. More than 17,000 people remain
missing from the time of the Lebanese Civil War, which
lasted from 1975 to 1990.*

Allegories of Loneliness

It was a drizzly Sunday, the world moving at a sluggish pace. The streets were quiet, as it was in the apartment. Grandmother was napping in the living room or had just woken from a nap as the news broke. I heard the blankets rustle and the couch creak. Then she turned up the TV.

Around four that very afternoon a woman knocked on our door. She wore a white Red Cross jacket and carried a clipboard.

Sitting at the kitchen table, she told us to consider ourselves lucky. She said this without phony compassion and certainly without irony. She said very few ever found out for certain.

An echo of the memory of a bright fall day: *See that apple tree? She used to climb it as a child ...*

That's what Grandmother said as we stood beneath its branches. Of all memories, I wondered at the time, why was this the one that occurred to her?

A metal plate and two screws in her forearm—that was the outcome.

She had laughed out loud then drawn back, as if she'd revealed too much.

*

One of the curses of youth is that we are sometimes as smart at fourteen as we are at forty, only we lack the life experience and circumspection to know how to put this knowledge to use. I'd always sensed that a deeper truth lay hidden behind Grandmother's detachment. We would ricochet off each other and occasionally get caught, but I never got through to her—as she never got through to me. People aren't born this way. They have to be formed.

All I ever wanted was to protect you.
Protect me? From what?
From the life I have had to endure.

Assuming silence will protect later generations is a colossal error. The very opposite is true. When a child's guardian is too wrapped up in her own concerns, the child is left without protection. The child views the adult's reactions as normal and not as aberrant behavior within an exceptional situation. The burden is passed on unwittingly and wordlessly.

And so I decided to track down my grandmother as I immersed myself in the hidden archives that had emerged following the war. Not in an effort to find myself but to discover what was happening during my childhood, a period I didn't understand. I drove to an apartment building in Beirut two or three times a week, where I took the elevator and passed through a nondescript door into a whispering community committed to collecting evidence.

I learned that in response to pressure from family members of the missing and various human rights organizations, in 1992 the government added the 17,415 missing persons to the total number of war casualties and thought its work done. The murderers lived upstairs. Men like Samir Geagea ran the country and were trying to close a book that hadn't yet been opened all the way. Further attempts to shed light on the fate of the missing were stymied or ensnared in red tape.

One day that spring, shortly after we moved into our small apartment in East Beirut, Grandmother must have set out to register my parents as missing. International aid groups were streaming into the country, as were countless families who'd been in exile for years and were now hoping for answers. The war was over. Amnesty laws had been signed. Excavators were steadily banishing the past from the cityscape. For the first time, though, there were official lists. External inquiries had just gotten started.

At the archive I retreated with stacks of folders to little nooks created by room dividers. Though I'd spent most of my life in this country, only now was I learning more about the atrocities and arbitrariness of an unprecedented period that Grandmother had shielded me from in fleeing to Germany.

- *Joseph Tawil, 26; February 12, 1976 | Around 9 a.m.
   while on a smoke break*
- *Jamal Sweid, 20; March 18, 1980 | Around 2 p.m. on
   the road to the airport*
- *Arifa Shamandar, 15; July 5, 1985 | Around 5 p.m.
   while taking a walk with friends*
- *Youssef Ghandour, 52; April 13, 1977 | Around 8:30 a.m.
   near Ali Sherkawi's auto repair shop*

It was difficult to grasp the scope of random aggression that dominated the streets and led to so many people's disappearance. Leafing through the folders, I came across hundreds of lists like the one I had discovered on a walk down Rue Merleau and copied into my notebook.

Among the stacks of binders, boxes of photos and microfiche, and shelves laden with files, I also found tape recordings. The cassettes were nondescript, labeled only by year. Perhaps it was their continuity—(1994–2010)—that made me pull them from the shelf, suspecting this was where I'd find a through line.

The woman with whom I occasionally ate lunch was working that day. She led me to a space that resembled an interrogation room: bare walls, a chair, and a table with a cassette player and headphones. For the first time I gained insight into the other side. I pressed play and heard a young female interviewer posing questions. Then the family members of the missing shared their stories:

My mother completely changed after my brother went missing. She always cooked far too much food, even years later, and set his place at the table, as if he might walk through the door at any minute.

I joined other mothers searching for their children back then. We knocked on every door. We approached militiamen and they said, "Forget you ever had those kids. Go home! Have new kids. If your husbands can't get the job done, just come back and we will."

I played the role of mother and father.

Whenever the phone rings, you think it must be him calling to say he's coming home. Whenever you see someone on the street who resembles him, you're tempted to subtract from this stranger's appearance all the years you waited ...

I was afraid for the kids, I said ... Let me issue passports for the kids, I couldn't, why? ... They said it had to be done by their guardian, meaning their father. I told them if their father were here I wouldn't think of applying for passports ... He asked me, "Where is their father?" I told him that their father was kidnapped; that's why I need to escape with my children. He said, "Bring their grandfather." He said that this is the law.

You know, the missing don't exist for authorities. There's no certificate or document that confirms your husband's been missing since the war. If you want to survive in this society, you're left with no option but to pronounce him dead, and I didn't want that. For a long time I didn't want that. I balked, refused, and battled myself, and I was ashamed, so ashamed, because I didn't want him to come home one day as a dead man ...

I have a right to know where my daughter is. I'm not seeking revenge; there's been enough revenge in this country. Just the truth. All I'm seeking is the truth.

Your husband's been missing for twelve years, but you don't even know your status. What are you? Not married? Not widowed? You don't know ... You bury the feminine side of you deep inside, by force ... I lost my life as a woman ... I worked hard to give my children a standard of living that was acceptable to us. But I did not live the life I should have lived.

We say inshallah he will return. We say inshallah but thirty years have passed.

After Grandmother's death in 2006 and long before I knew about the archive, I returned to her apartment one last time. It was a strange way to confront the life she'd left behind. With every drawer I opened, I felt like an intruder rummaging through someone else's secrets. All these objects that now, robbed of their function, stood around like museum pieces: An electric kettle. An apron. Her toothbrush on the sink. A washcloth with traces of soap. A hairbrush. A bottle of dye in the bathroom cabinet. Allegories of the loneliness that accompanied Grandmother as she made these mundane decisions: to make a cup of tea, brush her teeth, wash her face, or brush or dye her hair. I never would have dared go through her things as a little boy or teen, and though I felt like an intruder, I now studied the most unremarkable objects like relics that might tell a story or reveal a hidden truth if I just examined them carefully enough.

This is something I've already mentioned, but I was struck by the fact that she didn't own any novels. I figured she just didn't care for make-believe. As I pored over archival documents with a fascination bordering on obsession, though, I came to realize I probably hadn't paid enough attention to the handful of nonfiction titles on her shelf. Van Gogh's letters to his brother, for instance, or *Madres de Plaza de Mayo*, the book of photography. I discovered that the title referred to a group of Argentine women whose children and grandchildren had vanished under unknown circumstances during the military dictatorship. They gathered outside the presidential palace in Buenos Aires to protest the injustice and demand punishment for the perpetrators. The group came up repeatedly in my research, whenever authors highlighted strategies and structures that had led countries like Argentina to address the question of missing persons through official channels, however symbolic these government efforts may have been.

The discoveries I made were important to me. I had lost Grandmother but was finding her in the archive, and I sometimes got the strange feeling I was finally getting to know her. As details gradually coalesced into a unified picture, I started seeing clues to explain what had puzzled me for so long. Official reports by Amnesty International or the Red Cross published the names of countries that, unlike Lebanon, established truth commissions or similar initiatives following armed conflicts: Argentina. Cypress. Chad. Chile. Guatemala. El Salvador. Nepal.

*

In one of his last letters to his brother Theo, Vincent van Gogh writes about three canvases he plans to paint. He describes *vast stretches of wheat under troubled skies* that articulate his *sadness and extreme loneliness.* The paintings were meant to show what he couldn't express in words.

She reads this passage and underlines it. Certainly not for me, should I ever page through the book looking for clues—she doesn't do that sort of thing, not least because she gave up on the future years ago. She underlines the words because she sees herself in them.

It's 1994. Homesickness has finally turned into homecoming. Everything has moved in closer. Construction noise comes in the window. Beirut and all the sounds she missed for so long. The sounds of departure and change. New beginnings. Actually.

Yara sits on the couch and tries to concentrate on the

world out there. A few hours ago she was unexpectedly overcome by anxiety again, slight vertigo and the sense that just walking around the corner to the supermarket might end badly. She wishes the noise communicated something good to her; she tries to focus on the positive aspects of all these changes, but as she sees it, the world beyond the curtains is shabby and stale. Though it's barely noon, it's about time this day was over. Tomorrow: a new start, a new attempt. *It's all right,* she tells herself. *Pull yourself together.* She's been through this a thousand times before and knows that she just has to get through the next couple of hours, maybe the coming night and tomorrow morning, but sooner or later the turmoil will subside and be replaced just as suddenly by a sense of optimism in which nothing seems impossible. She sits up, sets the book aside, reties the bow of her blouse around her midsection, fixes her hair, and tries to summon that optimism by recalling everything she's accomplished since the move. The boy is enrolled in school and finally seems to be making friends. And she was there in the slums on the outskirts of town, where the Red Cross set up its tents. She got in line and added the names of her daughter and son-in-law to a list, along with the color of their car (navy-blue Volvo), time and date of their disappearance (between 7 and 10 p.m. on February 11, 1981), and any traits that might help to identify her daughter, should a misunderstanding at a barricade actually have led to her arrest and imprisonment in Syria or Israel, where she remains in detention like so many others. This has always been Yara's assumption.

She closes her eyes and takes a loud, deep breath, in and out. Sometimes that helps. Sometimes the dizziness abates for a moment, her thoughts clear, and the fog lifts. She'll be opening the café soon, she thinks. All the papers are signed. A routine will set in with distraction and company. She'll be patient. Keep going. She won't lose control. For her own sake and his.

She's amazed at how similar he is to her. Not in terms of appearance but in terms of the resolve he shows in withdrawing. Some days it seems impossible to break into his world or see things from his perspective; the most painful part is the feeling she gets of looking in the mirror. She can see he's unable to find the words for his questions. She's ashamed of the fact that it comes as a relief.

When a person is withdrawn, all you can do is watch. Someone might say: I'm cold. The same person might not say anything, but we notice goosebumps on his arms and see him shivering. What happens, though, when he not only keeps quiet but there's nothing to see? What if he's wearing long sleeves and refuses to disclose a single thing? She often watches Amin. And he watches her. Sometimes they even sit leaning against each other on this couch, yet remain trapped in some kind of limbo. Never fully here. And never fully there.

Wind blows in the window. As the curtain billows and more light enters the room, her gaze lands on the canvases she bought. They're propped against the wall. Her vertigo promptly intensifies. Treacherous. The mute white surfaces are like an accusation. Hours and hours of unused time. She senses that she'd like to paint—no, she *knows* it but is afraid of starting. She's also afraid of the outcome, the disappointment. What if whatever emerges appears vacuous to her? What if it doesn't do justice to the occasion? Will the vertigo ever go away? When was the last time she made a painting? She laughs quietly to herself, almost derisively, and shakes her head. No, no, those days are over. She'll get rid of the canvases today.

She gets up and opens the curtains. There's something metallic to the light. Even at a distance she can hear the traffic on the road toward Damascus. Such hustle and bustle. The flood of faces on the sidewalk. This city is transient. Everything and everyone seem to be moving, fleeing something. Quite possibly the feeling of guilt, which is ubiquitous. Beirut made the same impression on her when she arrived here as a young girl forty years ago. She saw through the sophisticated facade then willingly turned a blind eye, despite signs of impending catastrophe. People were always less likely to talk *with* than they were to talk *about* each other.

For her, though, it was a time to catch her breath. She felt grateful. She felt the pulse of expectation that accompanies a fresh start. Life was so unpredictable. One minute you're caught in a summer storm that whips you against the wall, breaking two ribs, and the next, because you found the courage to change things, you're sitting in box seats at the theater or crossing the Atlantic on a steamer, wedding ring on your finger, headed for New York, for the lights of Coney Island.

The air that afternoon is far from fresh—garbage that hasn't been collected is piling up in the cans under the window. Every move is encumbered by the mix of damp and dust. She sees trucks turn onto the street. A familiar image. They come from construction sites and thunder past, heading toward the sea. Reconstruction as repression. That is the city of the future. She's heard about the commissions in other countries. She's heard about the painful trials, the witness testimony, and the disappointments too—but at least some effort was made to understand. Unlike here. The injustice blinds her with rage but also touches her. She's well acquainted with the desire to forget. She knows what it's like to feel speechless, powerless. Strange, she thinks. You need language to explain the war, but you also need language in order to live with what you did and what you suffered. In Aeschylus's *The Persians*, the victims of the naval battle of Salamis admonish us to honor their memory by telling their story, because in silence the missing disappear anew—and maybe permanently. She was incredibly moved by the piece when she saw it in the late fifties at the Grand Théâtre, and all these years later she can't help but see something prophetic in that performance. But how can she, Yara el-Maalouf, possibly tell the victims' stories here, where no one wants to hear them? How can she possibly convey this message—one she can't even express in words to herself or her grandson—to the perpetrators or people who experienced it themselves or those who were uninvolved?

She knows how.

Ships on the horizon distancing themselves from the Tripoli coastline and the fourteen-year-old she once was, the image frozen in time and space like a dream. Her language has always been painting. So why is everything inside her resisting?

"Because I've changed," she says out loud in the silent room.

She has become a different woman, which means she has to work differently than before. Less representationally. Paintings as fragmented as she feels. Verbally expressive without using words. Accusatory without screaming. A riddle.

She recalls the lines she read in Van Gogh's letters:

Vast stretches of wheat under troubled skies. Extreme loneli-ness.

The canvas as a vessel that catches everything.

She listens for noise. The trucks are gone.

As is her vertigo, she notes with some vexation.

The Silkworm Farmer Emerges

They say we're the sum of our memories, that these fragments are woven into an elaborate fabric known as our identity. But how are we formed by things we've forgotten, suppressed, or never truly understood? How do we fill those voids?

With stories. That's one response.

The other is: by letting time pass.

In the same way ideas jotted in a notebook and peppered with question marks can seem laughably obvious years later, situations that initially confused us can suddenly take on remarkable clarity.

I experienced this myself during the period when I was at the archive in Beirut several times a week, working my way through audio recordings. One day I was surprised to hear a familiar voice on one of the cassettes.

I couldn't summon a clear memory of the speaker. It was an older woman. As in the other recordings, a younger woman was asking questions. The interview took place in 1996 and it seemed they were in a big room, maybe a restaurant or café. I could hear the clatter of plates, hushed conversations and quiet music in the background. The woman whose voice I thought I'd heard before was speaking softly too. The tape was repeatedly paused, whenever she asked to take a break, and sometimes the interviewer was slow to turn it back on, so I only caught snippets of her statement and had to infer the context. The recording was two or three hours long. It turned out the woman had been dealt a double blow. Her husband had been missing since the Karantina massacre, and at some point her brother had been abducted from his car in Port District. The way the woman spoke about searching for and missing them was similar to what I'd heard in other recordings. Occasionally, though—when her voice faltered or the memory seemed unspeakable—her descriptions returned to a group of people who provided her support for a time:

A small apartment in West Beirut ... No, we weren't activists. We were more like ... friends ... would sometimes just talk for hours and ... comforting to see I wasn't alone ... Never would have thought there were so many of us. We came from all different backgrounds ... Yes, exactly, like one big family.

Had someone come into the room then and seen me sitting there with headphones on, a smile on my face despite the heavy subject matter—what would they have thought?

"Like one big family ..." I repeated quietly.

I'd often wondered why Abbas never attended the gatherings at our apartment. It almost seemed he was trying to avoid Nadia, Abu Amar, or Umm Jamil. They didn't meet till Christmas.

Here was the overdue explanation. Or rather: here was confirmation of my suspicion. Abbas had kept his distance solely out of discretion. Grandmother's friends were a community of seekers, and the silkworm farmer from Sidon wasn't part of it.

On his farm that day, he said he was most fascinated by characters in fairy tales that operate from the shadows. Eleven years later I realized he was talking about himself. Grandmother and I had just had our big fight. I had withdrawn to my Tripoli apartment. And after I'd ignored his request to call him for more than two weeks, Abbas finally tracked me down in order to come clean.

*

1966

Amin el-Maalouf is still dressed as a janitor as he gets in his car two blocks away from Intra Bank. He passes barricades hastily installed to thwart angry crowds. But he doesn't drive east to his family in the mountains. He heads south toward Sidon.

All these years he's been moving up in the world, professionally and personally. Upon realizing his ascendancy may well have expired, however, Amin el-Maalouf remains quiet and composed. He hasn't panicked since he was a child and heard the sound of his father's footsteps approaching the barn door. He has maintained this iron self-control all his life; it's how he's made it this far. He already knew what needed to be done as he took the elevator down at the bank. The family fortune is well spread out. It's securely invested and can survive minor losses, no problem. Even if that weren't the case, they have the house. They have each other and their dreams. This existence is so fulfilling in its ordinariness that they'll still find a way to be happy, even if the luster of high society—a scene they sometimes join as if attending a masquerade ball—grows faded and forgotten.

Amin el-Maalouf smiles. This city. The constant commotion. He's certain it will be the same as always—people will fuss for a few weeks, then forget the whole thing ever happened. One door may have closed, but another will soon open. He'll clean out his office, take a trip with Yara and Maya for a month or two, and then find a new job. Maybe in the central bank. Besides, it's high time he emancipated himself from Youssef Beidas and went his own way.

He turns these thoughts over in his mind as he drives along the coastal highway with the car top down. Farmers stand by their carts in the banana fields. Sailboats rock on the water and in the rearview mirror, the high-rises are shrinking. A golden October day.

To Amin el-Maalouf, having money meant not having to consider what was going on in the world. His parents had never had money. He grew up in an age of heteronomy, an age in which the map of the Middle East was furnished with new borders drawn by Europeans. His childhood was defined by hardship and violence. To him, poverty meant being at the mercy of the world's moods. His father's moods. To him, the image of wealth was tantamount to that of protection. I know that now. This knowledge is critical to understanding why, on the day Intra Bank collapsed—and with it, life as he knew it—he did not drive straight home but instead went to Sidon.

He was going to ask his friend Abbas to make him a promise.

*

"Your grandfather reached my farm around noon. I had just stepped outside when his car pulled in the front gate. He wasn't wearing his usual suit. He looked like a cleaner, which is why I didn't recognize him at first."

Though it was tiny, Abbas appeared adrift in my

apartment. He'd lost weight. His skin was pale, like he hadn't left the house in weeks, and tufts of thinning hair stood up straight from his scalp.

Abbas had been waiting for me in a dark corner of the front hallway. "You didn't call."

"Why bother? I knew you'd find me."

I was now pouring two glasses of tap water. For days I had ignored the dirty dishes in the sink, but Abbas's presence made me acutely aware of the mess. I was ashamed by how obviously it betrayed my own desolation.

I didn't know why Abbas was revisiting that old story, which he launched into the moment we entered, but as long as he kept reminiscing, it meant no asking how I was doing or why I was here. I egged him on: "What did he want from you?"

"A favor," the silkworm farmer said. He glanced at the glass, then took a sip. "Amin had no way of anticipating the fallout from the Intra Bank collapse. As someone who'd planned every move he ever made, for the first time he sensed that unforeseen things might arise and affect him, too. As such, he wanted to make provisions."

"Provisions," I repeated, more scornfully than intended. "For whom, exactly? His family? Doesn't sound like the grandfather I've heard about, the guy who just split ..."

Abbas lowered his head. "Please," he said, "let me finish. I think he sought me out because I served as a cautionary example. The golden years of silkworm farming were long past. You know that his support was the only thing keeping the farm afloat. Thanks to him I was able to rehire part of my staff. Thanks to him things were starting to improve a little. Still, I can imagine him looking at me and my situation and catching a glimmer of what might be in store for him." Abbas turned his water glass back and forth. "Dependency and slow decline. Through no fault of one's own," he added. "We were friends. We trusted each other, so he beelined for me that day. He sat in my living room and said, *Abbas, should the time come that I'm not around, promise me you'll watch out for Yara and the little one.* He said it calmly, the way someone might say they're running to the grocery store for a few things, but I could sense how seriously he meant it. He was always a reticent man, even around friends. He didn't elaborate. News of the bank's collapse hadn't made it to Sidon yet. All I saw was my friend dressed like a janitor, asking a big favor. I gave him my word. Then he got back in his car and drove off."

I couldn't make sense of what he was telling me. Since receiving Abbas's note, I'd assumed Grandmother had sent him after me. I'd envisioned the argument we would have when he tried to persuade me to talk things out with her.

"I see you still have it," he said, jolting me out of my daydream. "That's good." Abbas pointed at my mother's painting on the wall. For the first time since he'd come in, I detected the hint of a smile on his face.

"It means a lot to me," I said quietly, "and I know how much it meant to *her*, but I don't want to give it back, if that's why you're here."

Abbas didn't respond. He just stood there and studied the picture.

An evening sunbeam pushed through the curtains like a blade, cutting a diagonal across the room and landing on the gilded frame.

"You came to my room on Christmas Eve eleven

years ago," I said. "You told me to make sure nothing ever happened to the picture."

"I remember."

"You said my whole family was contained within it. Now it sounds like you were getting me to make the same promise you had to make to him."

He bit his lip and nodded. "But unlike me, you kept your promise. I failed to prevent Maya's disappearance."

"No one could have."

"I wasn't in the city when it happened."

"I don't want to talk about it, Abbas."

"Well," he said, taking a deep breath and looking at the ceiling. "There's a reason I'm telling you all this. Your grandfather changed in the years that followed. The longer Amin went without finding work, the more useless he felt. I was equally good friends with them both and felt caught in the middle. He'd come and complain that she didn't give him any space. Other times Yara would tell me she couldn't stand it much longer, the way Amin withdrew into himself. It seemed they no longer had a common language. For a while they managed to stick together, but when Maya left for Paris against his will, things got worse. I think he felt he was losing the one person he still loved ..."

"My mother ..."

"Yes. Your grandparents visited her twice that year. They returned from the second trip with the painting Maya had given them. I'm sure they were on their best behavior in front of her, but their daughter was sensitive to the way things stood."

It was dark outside by now. The washing machines downstairs vibrated through the floor. There had been fighting in several neighborhoods that day, and we could hear soldiers patrolling the streets.

1976

Amin el-Maalouf drives past soldiers as he leaves the airport. There were skirmishes that afternoon, and army vehicles line the streets. It's a sunny day. Gulls circle overhead at Luna Park. Kids play by the side of the road. You wouldn't know it was wartime but for the details. Yara's voice, half swallowed by the wind, comes from the passenger seat. She mentions the shopping they need to do before returning to the mountains. They've invited Abbas for dinner that evening.

They're both exhausted. Less from the strain of travel than from the effort it cost to behave like two people who haven't run out of things to say to each other. There was no reviving their former closeness, even far from home.

Before they landed, Amin gazed out the window at the hazy landscape. The dull sea of buildings. The illusion of an unblemished existence. Business partners had often asked him to explain Lebanon to them—they'd all heard so much about the Switzerland of the Middle East. He would talk about possibilities. The beauty of contradictions. Ski resorts in the mountains and jet skis on the beach, filigree handicrafts and entrepreneurialism. He told them the Phoenicians had invented money here. It was the perfect segue. "We have everything here," he'd say, "and whatever we *don't* have is actually good for the country—like financial regulations." Laughter and appreciative knocking on the table. He was never able to articulate the country's fragmented society, though. The simmering beneath the surface. The faint tremors. He was never able to express how false that comparison to Switzerland was, because the population here had never been granted a single day of true democracy. So he'd always conclude by saying "This country is indescribable," raise his glass, and smile sheepishly.

He saw his reflection in the window as the airplane banked to the side. It looked like he was at once inside and out. His younger self peered in at the aging man he'd become. He shook his head mulishly. He once heard that a man knows where he comes from when he knows where he wants to be buried. He knows where he *doesn't* want to be buried—right here, in this abased country he no longer understands. All it takes is a glance out the window at this hub of prostitution, this gigantic construction zone, where asphalt is gradually devouring every last tree and patch of grass. Where could a man possibly be buried here with a shovel?

He did a lot of thinking during their trip, as he lay awake and Yara slept. In the past he spent every trip itching to come home. To this country. To their house. Now he wants nothing more than to leave.

That evening they drink a toast to their safe return and unroll the painting Maya gave them on the table for Abbas to see. They move a floor lamp in closer to view the piece in full light. They behold the canvas as if it were a treasure map.

"It's beautiful," Abbas says. "Maya will be the next Mary Cassatt, if she keeps it up."

Amin and Yara laugh a little too loudly.

Later, after their plates are cleared, Amin shows Abbas the frame he had made for the picture. He brings it into the light, holding it out proudly in front of himself. He looks like a framed portrait in that moment. Yara watches the men from behind the kitchen counter. It appears, Abbas muses, as if she were observing something alien from far above.

Amin tells him about Florence. He rhapsodizes about

the play of sunlight around the Ponte Vecchio, the bustle of the Mercato di San Lorenzo, and the hush of the Boboli Gardens. "Speaking of gardens," Amin says, taking his old friend by the arm. They step outside into the chill autumn night. The shadow of the apple tree is just a spot in the darkness. Amin looks over his shoulder for Yara, who is standing at the kitchen window with her glass of wine, so they take a few more steps.

Once they're no longer visible from the house, he pulls out a key and places it in Abbas's hand.

"'Ash can never be turned back into wood,' he said to me. Amin was referring to his marriage. That evening in the garden was the first time he voiced his intention to leave." Abbas stared blankly out the window at the brick building across the street. "I was surprised by how much he'd already planned," he continued. "He had decided to sign the house over to Yara, and he wanted to leave her with money, nearly half his fortune. He later wired a hefty sum to your mother in Paris, to afford her greater independence from Yara ..."

"So, he bought his way out," I said.

"It may seem that way to you from the outside, but I don't think he saw it like that."

"He was a coward."

"He was a broken man, Amin. Like I told you, money was equivalent to protection for him. He grew up believing that. He thought money could protect his family, even if he was no longer there himself."

"That's twisted and weak. Money won't bring back my parents. If he hadn't left ..."

"It was what he believed, and that conviction was ultimately the one thing that couldn't be taken from him. Melodramatic as it may sound, he was suffering.

That evening in the garden, he gave me the key and reminded me of the promise I'd made."

"What was the key for?"

"A safe-deposit box holding what he called emergency funds. He emphasized that repeatedly. 'Only in case of emergency, Abbas.'"

"What kind of emergency?"

"He didn't say."

"So, he left it up to you to decide."

He nodded.

"That doesn't make any sense," I said. "He did all that planning, yet overlooked the war going on? Something easily could have happened to you! There was fighting all around. You told me yourself that your farm was occupied."

"I made the same argument. All he said was I'd better be careful nothing happened to me. That was it."

"That's insane."

"I thought so too." Abbas hesitated. There was clearly more he wanted to say. As I kept quiet, he finally continued: "I couldn't tell if it was really him anymore, so I made a decision."

He who seeks to approach his own buried past must conduct himself like a man digging. These are the words Walter Benjamin uses to describe time, which forms layers, one on top of the other, rather than following a linear progression. It's like the hidden treasures sealed up and stored without any regard for chronology at the National Museum, before we brought them back to light; I can wander around my memories as if I were in a museum, contemplating each exhibit in turn.

I don't need to dig deep to unearth my first memory of Abbas standing outside the door to our apartment in Munich. I quickly got used to this man who gesticulated when he spoke and possessed the remarkable power to cheer up Grandmother. I remember the way he folded his hands across his belly as he sat in our easy chair, admiring the painting that meant nothing special to me at the time.

"What a wonderful way to hide," he would say five or six years later in the big industrial tent on his silkworm farm, pointing at the cocoons laid out in front of us, each a gleaming thatch of spun silk.

At the moment of metamorphosis, organic matter reconfigures itself into a new life-form. Abbas, the silkworm breeder from Sidon, turned into Abbas, executor of my grandfather's estate and keeper of his secrets, who in 2005 stood waiting for me in the dark entryway of my building with its broken lights. Not long after we sat in my room. "So I made a decision," he said, pulling out a pocketknife as he approached the painting. He drew it away from the wall with one hand and, with the other, slid the knife carefully between the canvas and frame on the back, creating a narrow opening.

Moments later, the key was in my hand. Silver and nondescript with a crumpled note listing the safe-deposit box number and address of the regional bank.

After my grandfather left, Abbas continued to visit Grandmother regularly at her house in the mountains. He sensed her loneliness. He also felt overwhelmed by the burden of responsibility. When Yara experienced the bouts of terror she told him about—was that the emergency? Could she use the money to follow her daughter to Paris without being forced to sell their cherished house? Abbas spent those years worrying he might miss the right moment, so he came up with a different solution: he knew how important *Song for the Missing* was to Grandmother. Wherever she might go, he knew it would go with her. Her love of the painting made it the most tightly guarded place he could ask for. What's more, he knew she couldn't stand the frame; it had always been too big, too imposing for her taste, and she felt it crowded the picture much like Amin el-Maalouf had crowded her. "It hung in the house entryway, and she talked constantly about replacing the frame," Abbas told me that evening.

"So that's where you hid the key?"

"Yes. It would have been foolish to keep it any longer, and I figured it was only a matter of time until she switched the frame. The key would fall into her hands like a kind of bequest. A hidden hello from Amin. Then she could decide for herself when to collect the money and how to use it."

"Why didn't you just give it to her?"

"I neither wanted to betray Amin nor continue going behind Yara's back," Abbas replied. "I felt beholden to both."

My mother disappeared in 1981. Upon her daughter's disappearance, Grandmother refused to make any change whatsoever to the painting, because the frame and picture had abruptly come to represent everything she once loved that was now lost. A few weeks later she climbed into the taxi that would take us over the mountains to the airport in Damascus, and nestled between us on the back seat was the painting, frame and all …

"Why now?" I asked, without looking up from the key. "And why me?"

Abbas sighed and squeezed his eyes shut, as if trying to marshal his thoughts. "The knowledge wouldn't have served Yara in Germany. When you two returned to Lebanon, I wanted to tell her about the key. While still in Germany, she had often talked about her dream of opening a café in Beirut. By the time I got back here, she had already sold the house. She hadn't wasted any time. After everything she'd experienced up there, she didn't want it anymore. She wanted to shield you from the past ..."

"You mean keep it secret from me."

"No. I'm talking about protection." He suddenly looked me straight in the eyes. "Anyway, I again came close to telling her when those men threatened to shut down the café for whatever bogus reason, when it was all because she had dared to make reference to the missing in her pictures. You remember that Christmas Eve. None of us knew what would happen next, money had gotten so tight. A few days later, though, she took down the pictures and business returned like nothing had happened." Abbas lowered his voice, as if he might rouse old ghosts if he spoke too loudly. "It was around the time that girl disappeared," he said. "Zahra, right? What a terrible thing. You were devastated."

"So she thought it best to carry on and pretend everything was fine?"

"She wanted to give you one less thing to worry about. To show you she was still there to take care of you ..."

"Funny, I always got the feeling she was turning away from me."

"Of course. She was scared. The wall you put up, your silence. She recognized it all too well from herself. Your guilty conscience was eating you up back then."

"Because it was my fault."

"You were new to the country, Amin."

"Because *she* brought me here."

He did not respond to that.

The wind blew the curtain to the side and cool air streamed in. I was cold. After a brief hesitation, I pulled up a chair and sat down.

It suddenly felt as though I'd spent all these years in a kind of waking dream: just barely managing to graduate high school, working a few odd jobs on the lousier end of the pay scale, diving almost constantly into the world of libraries and books, perhaps the only constants—that was a rough sketch of the landmarks I'd passed. Always starting from our apartment in Beirut, whose tense silence I returned to on a nightly basis.

Remarkable, I mused, how two people can share such tight quarters and talk without ever actually saying anything. And how draining it can be to ignore all the pressing questions, because you don't want to address them.

Abbas leaned back by the window, half turned toward me. The streetlight illuminated one side of his face. I was immediately reminded of having seen Jafar in a similar light many years ago, in one of the abandoned buildings. As he handed me the shimmering grenade, it had looked like his face was on fire, lit by a flickering glow.

What is the silkworm farmer's secret? I'd written in a notebook years earlier, after Abbas mentioned his *business contacts* to Grandmother and turned to look at me, as if the words weren't intended for my ears.

To this day I have a hard time writing about Abbas without either vilifying or glorifying him. I owe a lot to him in many ways. When it comes to depicting him, the temptation is greatest to embellish or simply re-invent his character because he still seems like a fairy-tale figure to me. He was never entirely transparent, even to those closest to him. Any traces he left led into darkness and were as impossible to follow as the reasons that occasionally prompted him to step out of the shadows. What I can say with certainty, though, is that he never played people. He was always loyal, despite his mistakes. And when I asked him about Jafar that evening, he appeared almost relieved.

It was the other reason he was there.

1994

"There's something strange about that boy Amin's been spending time with," says Yara.

"What do you mean?"

"I can't put my finger on it, but he bothers me."

"Amin's just trying to make friends."

"He has a troubled heart, Abbas."

They're standing in the kitchen. The door is closed. As long as Amin's in his room, they can speak freely.

Abbas knows what Yara will say next. He's known her so long. Twenty-eight years after making a promise to his old friend, the same scene is playing out in this new location.

He studies Yara, who still moves with uncertainty, even four weeks after their return. She hunts through cupboards for items clearly sitting on the counter, looks for silverware in the tool drawer, and lets small stuff get to her. He searches her features for the woman he first met more than thirty years ago at the Grand Théâtre. Though she's not yet sixty, any hint of the magic that once surrounded Yara disappeared years ago—drove off in a car and never returned. In moments like these, he sees his failure to keep his promise reflected in the person she's become.

"He sometimes leaves the house in the morning," Yara says, dribbling olive oil over a bowl of eggplant dip, "and doesn't come back till after dark. My heart can't take it, Abbas. What do I do, though, put my foot down? Lay down the law? Amin's had a hard enough time with this move as it is."

"He's just trying to fit in. It's perfectly understandable."

"I'm afraid the boy could get lost—in both the literal and figurative sense."

"I know. Why not take him to find his roots, then? The mountains, the house ..."

"That Jafar kid he's spending all his time with ..."

"What about him?"

"I want to know who he is."

"Come on, he's just a classmate. Show Amin *your* roots, Yara. Tripoli. The old streets ..."

She caps the olive oil and returns it to the counter. She takes a step closer, then places her hands on his shoulders and says, "Amin doesn't need field trips. He needs protection."

"It did feel like we were being watched at times," I said.

Abbas nodded. "There were lots of street children in those days. They lived near the ruins."

"We saw them all the time. Jafar and I. So, they followed us and reported back to you?"

"For a bit of pocket money, yes."

"We always wondered what you meant by *business contacts*. We thought it might even be drug related ..."

It was the one and only time Abbas laughed. It was so unexpected, so loud and frank, that I couldn't help but join in. We were both so surprised that an awkward silence followed.

After a while he cleared his throat and asked, "Have you heard from Jafar since?"

"No," I said, shaking my head. "I don't know what became of him."

"He was important to you, wasn't he?"

"You could say that."

"He left right after everything happened with Zahra, and you never understood why, did you?"

I shook my head.

Abbas slowly stepped away from the wall. He closed the window and crouched in front of my chair. We were suddenly very close. I looked at his hands. They trembled slightly. He clenched his fists, then released. Finally he folded them, as if in prayer.

"Did you have something to do with that?" I asked quietly.

He lowered his head.

"The day the woman from UNICEF came to tell you about Zahra," he said, his voice husky, "Yara called me later in the evening."

"I think I overheard some of that call."

"She was beside herself. She said the boy—Jafar—was to blame for what had happened. She told me he'd provoked Zahra's father, who wouldn't have been so angry otherwise ... and then she asked me to talk to Jafar, to tell him, in no uncertain terms, to stay away from you ..."

I swallowed. "The apartment was empty when I went looking for Jafar. His family had clearly left in a hurry. What on earth did you say to him?"

"Nothing," Abbas said.

"Nothing?"

"They were gone by the time I got there. I hope you believe me. I asked their landlord, but he was baffled by it too."

"I felt the same way. We'd had a big fight a few weeks earlier. Jafar told me I was a nobody ..."

"It definitely wasn't your fault. Unfortunately, I can't tell you why he did that or where he went. What I can tell you, though, is that you meant as much to him as he did to you. I must have missed them by only a few hours that day."

"What makes you think that?"

He hesitated. "Because this was in your mailbox when I came to see your grandmother later that evening."

Abbas had kept his jacket on the whole time, and he now reached into his inside pocket and produced a crumpled envelope.

My name was written on it.

Inside was a black-and-white photograph.

I had to look more closely to make out the scene. It was Luna Park, as viewed from the uppermost point of the Ferris wheel. Everything was frozen in motion— lights, people, all blurry, in a state of flux. Jafar had written a note on the back:

Dear Amin,

I'm really sorry I couldn't say bye. It had nothing to do with you.

And I'm sorry about what happened to Zahra. I'm going to try and find her for you.

Jafar

He'd included a PS under his name.

I think we'll have to learn to miss each other.

As Abbas steps into the fresh air outside Yara's apartment, the envelope is still in his jacket. The streets are deserted. He doesn't drive home. His farm feels too oppressive and bleak. He leaves his truck where it's parked and starts wandering the streets.

He checked on Amin just now. He was in his room, sitting on the bed with his legs tucked up. Sealed like a cocoon. It wasn't the right time to give him the letter. Eventually, Abbas tells himself, the currents will abate, and until then I'll try to be there for him, to keep him from getting dragged under and lost. In coming years, Abbas will often reach for the envelope. He'll put it in his back pocket while getting dressed, before leaving the house to shuttle Amin to one of the jobs he lined up for him. On countless occasions—while brushing his teeth or waiting in line or at a traffic light—he will rehearse his explanation for why he waited so long to give Amin the letter, and on just as many occasions, he'll remain silent, because both the courage and the words suddenly fail him.

"Look at the time," Abbas said.

"You have to be careful driving, especially at night. The city's crazy these days."

He smiled. Hesitated. Looked around again. "This isn't a place for healing, Amin."

"I know."

"I've told and given you the things I wanted to tell and give you. What you do with the key is up to you now. Just one more thing, Amin: she wasn't always like that, the Yara you knew. I know you sometimes blamed yourself, but it wasn't your fault she became so raw and desperate. Circumstance was to blame."

We both got up. He reached for my hand and gave it a quick squeeze. I opened the door for him, and he was halfway out when he turned one last time.

"Do you remember the piece playing at the Grand Théâtre the night Yara and I met the first time?"

"*Orpheus and Eurydice*. You told me that years ago."

"She loved that theater," Abbas said. "Not only was it where she met Amin, but it provided her an escape from her father. Neither of us really knew the others in our group yet, so we spent the evening talking to each other. She told me how implausible she found the plot. *Orpheus and Eurydice*: a man's wife dies, and his pleas inspire the gods to allow him to venture into the underworld to retrieve her. There's a catch, though: he's not allowed to turn around and look at her till they've returned to earth. Naturally he turns around while they're still in the underworld, and she dies again. He draws his sword in despair, ready to kill himself, when the god of love, appeased by this display of devotion, brings Eurydice back to life a second time."

Abbas smiled, as if reliving that moment: the jostle and hum in the foyer, the sparkle of chandeliers and champagne flutes, Grandmother in her blue gown, resting a hand on the slight swell of her midsection and speaking quietly to avoid the attention of those around them.

"It wasn't the details that bothered her," he continued. "Yara didn't mind the way the gods appeared out of nowhere and did as they pleased. She was a newlywed, though, and just a few months pregnant. She had finally found happiness, which was why she couldn't believe anyone with half a brain would turn to look at his lover, when he knew the consequences. It irritated her terribly." Abbas zipped up his jacket and shifted his weight from one leg to the other. "More than thirty years later, just after you returned from Germany, I was visiting Yara at your apartment one day and she took me aside. The night before, that group had gathered for the first time—those people who were missing a loved one, just like her. It seemed their conversations had awoken a memory in her. She was pensive. 'Abbas,' she said, 'do you remember the time we saw *Orpheus and Eurydice*? I've thought it over and understand it now. No one in their right mind would risk losing Eurydice so recklessly. Love and yearning for one you've lost can drive you out of your mind, though, can't they? You lose what matters most for the sake of a single glance ...'"

On Arriving

I stood on the hilltop and looked down at the house. Shutters once painted blue were now sun-bleached and weathered. The property appeared a little sickly and skewed, but the promise of something new hung above the stillness rising on all sides from the valleys.

A few weeks had passed since Abbas gave me the key to the safe-deposit box, and just a few days earlier I'd broached the topic of the house with Faris and Samira. The conversation didn't last long. I got the distinct impression, as we hung up the phone, that they'd been expecting my call for weeks.

The garden smelled of resin and fallen leaves. The meadow hadn't been mown in ages, the flower and vegetable patches had gone to seed, and moisture had gotten the better of the shed, its wooden planks now dark and rotted. Under the apple tree, insects buzzed and swarmed the dropped fruit. The afternoon sun shone through the branches and cloaked the garden in velvety light.

I walked over to the house, but paused on the threshold. There was a lizard sitting in the sunny, warm corner of the doorway.

"Don't worry," I said. "We're going to fix things up."

The air inside was stuffy and dead. I went from room to room, opening windows, then grouped my few belongings in the middle of the living room. *Song for the Missing* was securely bound in a blanket. I loosened the string and shifted the cloth to the side. I carefully lifted and hung it in the spot I'd chosen.

I stood there for a while with my arms crossed. From now on, sunlight would move through this space, reaching the walls at noon. Movement like someone waving in the distance.

Third Verse

… because maybe, just maybe
there's something you overlooked.

A Shadow to Start

In his *Naturalis historia*, Pliny the Elder portrays the advent of painting as the story of a young Corinthian woman who traces the shadow of her departing lover on the wall, that he may always be near. She outlines the dark shape cast by the oil lamp with a piece of coal, then colors it in black. It's her attempt to preserve something that cannot be preserved. The birth of art is thus tied to the fear of loss and the longing for that which has gone missing.

From one moment to the next, life comes to an end. In the restive days after Umm Jamil visited me in the mountains and delivered the news of Grandmother's death, I had neither the strength nor the courage to call back the Canadian number she had given me. By the time I finally managed to dial it, following the funeral, Jafar had been dead for ten days.

I was able to book a flight to Ottawa. After landing, I took a cab to a bed-and-breakfast across the river in Gatineau. Soraya had booked it for me. She'd also offered to pick me up from the airport, but I didn't want to inconvenience her. The plan was to meet for dinner at her mother's house later that evening. I'd been traveling for nearly thirty hours. I set my little suitcase down by the window and collapsed fully clothed on the bed, but I couldn't fall asleep, so I left the inn and went for a walk.

"You don't need to come," Soraya had said on the phone. She briefly shared the details of Jafar's death. Apparently he'd been hit by a car while crossing the street. I sensed Soraya's hesitation.

"He just moved to that house," she said. "He and his girlfriend of many years bought it together. Two stories, a porch, good neighborhood. The landline wasn't connected yet, which is why he went out—to use a payphone nearby."

It was strange to hear Soraya speak. The vague memory I had of a ten-year-old's face was difficult to align with the deep adult voice I was hearing.

"Rabea, Jafar's girlfriend, said they were watching the news that evening, when Jafar suddenly jumped up and ran out of the house. It was you he wanted to call, Amin."

I immediately said I was coming. There wasn't much insistence in Soraya's voice as she told me I didn't need to.

Jafar's shadow. I'd so often wondered where his family had disappeared to. I had thought maybe Canada, given the stories about the uncle who'd lived here so long, but I could never imagine Jafar in a place like this. Even now, I couldn't picture his movements on the tidy sidewalks I was now walking down, sleepless, to my right a wide river, a bridge, a park.

That evening Soraya picked me up at the inn. She was leaning against her car when I came out. Of course she had nothing in common with the girl who used to sit on the windowsill, reading. She was wearing jeans torn at the knees with a top and leather jacket. She had sounded calm on the phone, almost detached. She studied me closely too, as if searching my face for traces of someone she knew. I went to shake her hand, and she hugged me.

Jafar's mother stood on the front steps as we pulled into the driveway. She appeared small and bent, a careworn woman with silver hair and bags under her eyes. I'd never really met her. She had blown me a kiss from the window of their apartment once, as I waited in the street for Jafar to come out, but she was essentially a stranger, as was I. I'd never joined in the family's everyday life. I had been little more than a voice on the phone or just some kid outside, asking if her son was home. What part of me had the family held on to after leaving Lebanon so suddenly? Any particular story? Had Jafar ever talked about me, or was I another secret of his, my name a distant ripple in his family's memory that only resurfaced the moment Jafar called it out before rushing out of the house and onto a poorly lit street.

His mother hugged me in greeting too.

"*Ahlan wa sahlan, ya Amin*," she murmured, then gestured toward the open door.

In Jafar's mother's house I recognized the apartment Grandmother and I had shared in Germany, so sparsely decorated all those years. At the time I had seen it as a sign of humility or restraint. Today I recognize that such makeshift quarters actually reflect people's refusal to feel at home. Every first generation of exiles—those who have left behind their entire lives—is cursed by the impossibility of simply shedding the past. Here, too, the homeland cast its shadow over a paltry mix of furniture that spoke of fragmentation, Oriental pieces they'd brought with them alongside more recently acquired IKEA classics. A framed aerial shot of Beirut, of blue sea and Pigeon Rocks, hung over the couch. Even the TV was airing mute images from the old country: a man carried the dead body of a child past a bombed-out building as headlines in Arabic scrolled across the bottom of the screen.

While Soraya helped her mother set the table, I stood with my hands in my pockets and tried to picture Jafar living here as a teen, then coming and going as an adult. Canada. On the ride over: broad streets, drive-throughs, malls every half mile, a car wash, and an enormous parking lot, all orderly, all tailored to the flow of traffic. Presumptuous as it was, I simply couldn't see Jafar being happy here, restless and roving as he was. But what did I know of the man he'd become? There was a picture of him on a set of drawers. Older, darker. He was standing on a soccer field, clearly the coach, while a youth team behind him proudly held aloft a trophy. I studied the photo for a long time. If I had passed this Jafar on the street in Lebanon, I wouldn't have recognized him.

Someone touched my shoulder. A woman right beside me. She was about my age. Brown eyes, shy expression.

"Rabea?"

She nodded. "Amin. You're here."

I expressed my condolences. She took my hand in one of hers and touched my cheek with the other. Then she turned and vanished into the next room.

I hadn't felt anything concrete yet. There had been numbness, as if my soul were back in Beirut and only my body had traveled here to this setting, which might as well have been a dream. Maybe it was the sight of the young man in the picture that suddenly made Jafar real to me as a person with a life I knew nothing about. Maybe it was the grief that lurked on every shelf in the house and pounced on me, or the unexpected expression of familiarity when Rabea stroked my cheek, as if I were the one in need of consolation, not her. I was crying as Soraya emerged from the kitchen. She set the bowls on the table and crossed the room.

"Come with me, Amin," she said, and we went outside to the small yard.

Soraya lit a cigarette, took a drag, and exhaled smoke in the darkness. "It's the house," she said after a while. "It's oppressive."

I looked at her from the side—the way she held the cigarette or raised it to her lips, the way she shifted her weight or brushed a hair from her face—until I realized I was searching for traces of Jafar in her. I turned away in shame.

"I'm sorry," I said. I meant for having cried. It suddenly felt inappropriate. I hadn't seen Jafar in twelve years, hadn't heard from him once.

As Soraya silently reached for my hand and gave it a squeeze, though, I found myself fighting back tears again. This home, I now realized, was different from the one I'd grown up in. People touched each other in this home.

The lights were on inside, illuminating the yard in a muted glow. Through the window I could see Rabea and Jafar's mother standing together by the counter. They were talking.

I noticed they were both in black, whereas Soraya's clothing was different. Her grief wasn't on display. I could tell she and Jafar had been close, but they must have responded to this place in totally different ways. Beyond her complexion, it seemed there was nothing Lebanese about Soraya anymore. She'd been here twelve years now, which made her the one person in her family who had spent the majority of her life in this country, and had I asked where home was for her, there's no question she would have responded Canada. Rabea, on the other hand, held Lebanon close. She and her family were exiles, too, and as I got to know her I came to understand that this must have been another reason Jafar felt protected in her arms.

Soraya seemed to me like a peripheral figure that evening, which may explain why I felt so close to her. We never discussed that moment, and I don't think she realizes how much pain she relieved by grabbing my hand. Maybe it was just a gesture of kindness to her. In any case, I know now that Rabea and Jafar's mother had chosen words to process their grief, whereas the two of us—standing outside, looking in—were speechless.

I don't remember much of the meal, only that I oscillated between feeling like I was totally out of place and like I'd known these people well for a very long time. Soraya sat beside me, mostly with her head lowered as if she didn't feel comfortable with the seating arrangement, while her mother asked question after question about the situation in Lebanon, which I knew she was following closely on Arabic television. I told her about my house in the mountains and the Israeli aircraft I could hear from my garden. I was lucky not to be in Beirut, she said. Since they'd bombed the airport, too, my flight to Ottawa had left from Damascus. I boarded a bus at the French embassy with mostly women and children, and we rode north to the Syrian border on the one highway that hadn't been bombed yet. Traffic was abysmal. It was 2006, but as they had done during the civil war and so many times since, the Lebanese population was fleeing to the safe haven of Syria. People stood in the dust on the side of the road with babies and bags; border guards distributed bottled water and cookies. After waiting four hours at passport control, we were allowed to continue through the no-man's-land beyond the border. Then eventually: Damascus.

I gave such a detailed account so as to prevent any silence from settling. Dishes clattered as we reached our hands into bowls of Arabic food, some ingredients clearly missing, presumably impossible to come by here. Jafar's mother nodded while I described my journey.

"You won't remember this, Soraya, but that was the route nearly all our neighbors took when they left Beirut during The Events."

"No," said Soraya, "I remember."

Jafar's presence pervaded the gathering. He was in the things we said and didn't say. In the *Why?* I couldn't spit out, though it was on the tip of my tongue—*Why did you leave, anyway?*—or in Rabea's sudden pauses as she talked about the house they'd just moved into or Jafar's enthusiasm for learning new things and sharing them with her, like when he transformed their bathroom into a darkroom to develop photos, and I noticed the way Jafar's mother was touching Rabea's arm and the way Soraya was looking at me.

As she spoke, I kept glancing over Rabea's shoulder at the picture on the dresser. Jafar had made it to twenty-six, and his mother said he accomplished much of what he set out to do; marriage was the one thing he put off too long. It was the only hint of reproach I detected from her that evening, though it was more an expression of regret. She also said Jafar's stepfather *wasn't here anymore*, as if to confirm what I'd already observed, though the vague phrasing wasn't explained till days later, when Soraya told me that after five years in Canada, her stepfather had packed his bags one day and returned to his childhood village in Lebanon. He had never been happy in Gatineau. He complained constantly about the endless winters with frost that tore up the roads, and about spring, when rain and snowmelt caused the Ottawa River to crest its banks, flooding subway tunnels and leading to bridge closures.

"What about your brother? Was he happy here?"

"I think Jafar felt more or less safe here and was about as happy as he ever could be," Soraya said, fixing me with a long gaze.

I wondered if the weight of tradition was another thing that brought Rabea and Jafar together, the preservation of a Lebanese line in the bosom of a Lebanese community. It was obvious his mother loved this young woman like a daughter, whereas Soraya—who peppered her sentences with French when she couldn't think of the Arabic—seemed to do whatever she could not to be perceived as Lebanese, and told me once, as she lay in my arms, that she thought she was a bad daughter. Or, if not exactly bad, at least a disappointment, a source of sadness.

It was getting late, and a suburban stillness descended on the house and street, while we did whatever we could to keep conversation going. We moved cautiously during that first meal together, guarding against any careless misstep as if walking on thin ice with a dark lake below. Try as we might, though, it was impossible to ignore the lulls in conversation filled with silverware scraping on plates, napkins rustling, throats being cleared. Jafar was in our midst then, observing us closely. There was no wandering back to a life we had all shared. There was no talking our way down a path to examine the ways in which we were tied to Jafar. Before and after was all there was, with twelve years, 6,000 miles, an ocean, and a sea in between.

Rabea and Jafar's mother still spoke of him in the present tense. He'd pursued photography in his free time and worked helping juvenile offenders reintegrate into society after their release from detention. Both women kept dropping questions, the hopeful undertone belying the casual way in which they asked: "So, when was the last time you spoke?" "Did he ever ... confide in you?"

Uncertainty surrounding the circumstances of a person's death can destroy families—I know that all too well. The people I was sitting with had lost a vital link, and so unexpectedly it made your head spin. I came here looking for answers to questions I'd had for years, but I now realized they were hoping for answers from me. Jafar's final thoughts, which had moved him to leave his house that night, were not of them but of me—me, a stranger from the homeland, a childhood friend. But why?

We said good night around ten. It was a mild late-summer night, but I was shivering in the car next to Soraya. The dashboard lights illuminated our faces. She asked if I was tired, and though I was, I said no. She asked if I wanted to see Jafar's grave, and though I wasn't sure, I said yes.

We walked together down the cemetery path. When we reached the flowers laid out on the freshly piled soil, Soraya left my side and withdrew to a bench under the trees.

Grave candles burned in red holders. Inside a glass case, also adorned with flowers, was a small book of messages from funeral guests. Judging by the handwriting, many were notes from young people. A Lebanese poet was quoted on one page; on another, someone had simply written *Thanks for everything!*

Had the events of our childhood informed the person Jafar became? I didn't know. I would never know how much he had changed.

I rolled the pencil between my fingers, uncertain what to write. Various lines went through my head, but they all felt wrong, either too formal or inappropriately close. I ultimately drew two stick figures on one of the last pages. They were sitting on a mountain of cash and wielding pen and paper like weapons. I wrote *Amin and Jafar of the Flea Market Hakawati tribe* and put the book back.

More or Less Safe

"Are you awake?"

"Yeah, what time is it?"

"Still night. I dreamt I was standing in front of the atlas you drew on the bedroom wall as a child. It was in Beirut. And the rockets weren't drawings on the wallpaper; they were flying outside the window. I dreamt Jafar was somewhere outside, searching for a place to hide."

"It was just a dream, Amin. Go back to sleep," Soraya whispered.

A few nights earlier I couldn't fall asleep, so I left the inn and went across the street to a bar called The Coldroom. A guitarist sat on the small stage. As I ordered a drink, I noticed Soraya leaning against the wall on the other side of the dimly lit room. She was twirling a lock of hair around her finger, talking to a slightly older guy who stood in front of her, touching her elbow. When she saw me, she left him hanging mid-sentence and came over.

"Who's that?"

"Nobody. Let's go."

Was it crossing a line, what we did? We were both searching for something. A body, a song. The smell of a stranger's neck or arm the next morning. While it was happening, and for a long time after we finished, we didn't speak. As if by not speaking, even the physical might remain intangible.

As I drowsily reached for her later, she slipped away like an object in a riverbed caught by the current.

"*Yeki bood, yeki nabood.*"

"I beg your pardon?"

"It's a Persian expression an old friend taught me."

"It sounds beautiful. What does it mean?"

"That something's impalpable."

This was a different night.

Soraya stood by the corner of the window, looking out. She didn't respond.

"It's the opening line to fairy tales," I said.

"Jafar would have liked that," she said quietly, as if testing out the words for herself, and then, more loudly: "Jafar would have liked that."

We dove into childhood in our talks. We felt our way through the thicket of memory, handing each other fragments found in the underbrush, to piece together some sort of foundation.

Soraya was pained by the knowledge that Jafar never opened up to her completely. Something unspoken between them would endure. He was a loving, protective brother, but part of him would always remain in the dark.

"During our first few months in Gatineau there were nights I'd hear Jafar screaming in the next room," she told me once. "I couldn't tell what he was saying, but it was followed by the sound of his steps in the hallway. He'd quietly open the door to my room and sit down on the side of my bed. His pajamas were always soaked. Then he'd ask, 'Can I sleep here with you?'"

Soraya had transient tendencies. She never spent the night. At dawn she slipped into her clothes and out of the room. She seemed afraid of missing out on something, but I think what she really feared was stasis. We were bound by the thing we were both missing. Like planets we pulled each other in and pushed each other off. Without the other's orbit to hold us, we both knew we'd have drifted helplessly into the reaches of a dark universe, and we understood the laws governing this arrangement, which neither of us ever called a *relationship*.

Similar to her refusal to view Lebanon as part of her, Soraya refused to talk to me about herself and her grief —we were similar in that way. When Soraya was upset, though, her speech broke down into two languages. Sometimes she didn't notice until several sentences later. I found it fascinating, but she was exasperated by it, as Arabic was something she felt clung to her that she couldn't shake.

When two people are unable to speak, a rift will always divide them, however bare their bodies and tight their embrace. Whenever we used words to distract ourselves from desire, we ended up talking about Jafar.

At the National Museum they told me Lebanon had lost most of its collective memory when the library burned. Talking and thinking about Jafar was like piecing together what remained of the books I picked from the ashes that long-ago summer. For Soraya, on the other hand, her brother was the one door she could use—or wanted to—to be transported back to Lebanon, as though she'd never had any experience there without him. Then finally something overlapped, as she lay beside me one night and started telling a familiar story, only it was one I'd never heard.

It all began with a coin. Soraya was playing when she spotted it behind the shelf where she kept her piggy bank. It glittered like a secret among the dust bunnies. Later, as a grown woman, Soraya would always think of the way she reached for the coin as somehow fateful. I don't think she blamed herself for the turn things took; rather, it seemed the story of the coin served as a discrete incident she could point to and say: Things had started to change by then, at the very latest. It was the spring of 1990. Soraya was seven years old, and in some series of events she failed to detail, she accidentally swallowed the coin.

She told me her mother had initially explained that the metal would pass through her body the natural way. Soraya's stomach started to hurt later, though, so to be safe they drove to Saint George Hospital. Jafar sat with his sister in the back seat.

Soraya remembers the fighters. They storm into the lobby just as the nurse reaches for her hand to lead her to the doctor. Soraya has never known Beirut outside of wartime. In a city devoid of parks and greens, she and the other children spend their afternoons playing on hills of rubble and trash. They perch atop the heaps like kings, and she has often seen the young men drive by on the backs of mud-flecked jeeps—militiamen who look up as they pass but never wave. Now, as the door opens, they drag one of their comrades on a stretcher across the floor. Soraya lets go of the nurse's hand and shrinks back against the wall, where Jafar is standing. He reaches for her hand and squeezes it very hard. He doesn't let go the entire time the scene plays out. A little while later—after plenty of cursing and threats— the doctor returns from the operating room with his hands up and shakes his head, and the men collapse into each other's arms for everyone in the waiting room to see.

That's when Jafar lets go of his sister's hand.

Soraya and I lay in silence in the moonlight. *The Story of the Lost Eye.* That's what Jafar had called his report. I remembered us standing on the flat rooftop that night with Beirut below, shimmering like a fairy-tale city.

"I think it may have been the first time Jafar observed something akin to solidarity," Soraya said. "Solidarity within a group of boys, some of whom weren't much older than him. He must have been drawn to that."

"I never picked up on that fragility in him."

"Because you met him later. It was all behind him at that point."

I turned onto my side to look at Soraya.

"We were always warned about those boys," she said. "They were said to be dangerous and unpredictable, so we kept our distance. We ran away whenever we saw them on the street. What we witnessed that afternoon was a different side. Suddenly they were just regular boys in dirty shirts and boots, whose only comfort was crying on their buddies' shoulders."

I studied her profile in the darkness. With her wavy hair and fine contours down to her chin, Soraya's features were as delicate as her brother's had been pronounced.

I told her the story as I'd heard it from Jafar. The militia attack. The explosion. The drive to the hospital. Larkness: the image of his sister lingering on his retina.

Soraya was quiet. "There was a kingdom on the Orinoco he invented for me when we were young," she said after a while. "It was one of many. We would choose the settings for our stories from the atlas we had. Sometimes the characters' paths would cross, like it was one big, interconnected universe. For instance, the Zebra King of Zambezi once entered the kingdom on the Orinoco after a long voyage; he had left home in search of a way to save his people, who lived in darkness. All the bees had left the country, so there was no wax for candles ... Jafar's stories were often based in fantasy. There were hybrid creatures, fairies, djinnis, and magical horses, like in Arabic fairy tales, and the longer the story, the more everyday details he'd slip in. There was a pattern: the worse he'd been bullied that day about his glass eye, the more carefully he crafted his stories. He would retell old tales with slight variations, as if he'd overlooked something—a door or gate he could slip through to become one of the figures himself. At least, that's how I see it now."

"I didn't realize he was bullied. I never witnessed that."

Soraya patted me on the head, an irritating gesture that said: You don't get it, but that's okay.

"The kids on our street called him *Cyclops* when we played outside. *Frankenstein, one-eyed monster,* that kind of thing. You know how cruel children can be. Jafar would laugh with them, but when we got home he'd lock himself in his room and often stay in there for hours."

We could hear the rush of the Ottawa River through the window, which was open a crack. It was the only sound.

I tried to match the rhythm of Soraya's breathing, but couldn't.

"I never knew Jafar undamaged, as it were," she said. "The doctors removed his eye when he was two. He had a tumor, retinoblastoma. I don't know much about it. Wasn't hereditary. It's a sudden malignant growth that sometimes occurs in children. He was lucky."

"When we met, he was so different than you describe him. He was like a lighthouse to me."

"When did you meet?"

"1994."

"Okay, so four years had passed. By then he had learned to show you one side while hiding the other."

"I don't think I was a very good friend," I said. "Even at the time I wondered what he liked about me."

Soraya turned onto her side. Her face was close to mine, her breath in my eyelashes. Before getting up, putting her hair in a bun, and pulling on her coat, she said the following in such a peculiar tone of voice— one of quiet sadness—that I remember it to this day:

"You represented a mirror to Jafar, one in which he recognized a different version of himself, one that wasn't damaged, and no sooner did you step into that classroom than he felt driven past the others and straight into your arms."

*

Days, weeks, months passed. I visited the laundromat many times, waiting till my clothes were done, then returning to the inn and packing my suitcase, only to put off my departure yet again. When autumn came, I bought a warmer coat and wandered around Gatineau Park under ash trees that had turned yellow. The land-scape looked like it was just waiting for Monet to come paint it. Reflections of clouds in the water, the play of light and shadows on the fields, and any hint of shape in the distance disappearing, growing hazy beyond the multitude of colors.

During that time I walked the same paths Jafar had taken. The longer I stayed and the more conversations I had in busy cafés, in fenced-in yards, or under the trestle bridge by the soccer field, the more obvious it became that this was Jafar's world. He'd led a hopelessly normal life. He'd found an everyday groove and structure here. Security in the embrace of family. It was also a world of silence, though, a partially permeable membrane. The luster of the past was all that found its way into this cell. Thousands of miles from home, the members of this community now lived together on the far side of the river, opposite the Canadian capital, ever abiding by the golden rule that had trailed them from the homeland: It's not forgiveness that enables peaceful coexistence, but silence.

Whatever I learned about Jafar, any understanding gained was like a lenticular image that began to shift just as something solid came into view. The Jafar I knew had been lost in the folds of a map, on which the only visible city was Gatineau, Quebec, as if he'd never led a different life.

I followed the extended arms pointing me in the direction of spots that had been important to him, like al-Moulouk bakery on Rue de Duvernay, where he and Rabea went for breakfast some Saturday mornings, as one of the employees there told me. Or Paul Pelletier Aquatic Centre, where he often swam laps till closing, then jumped on his bike and pedaled home, duffel slung across his back. Or the community center on Rue Fabre, where Lebanese immigrants congregated and hosted block parties, small bazaars, or craft fairs. They had an Arabic-language library as well as a stage, where one October evening a school theater group performed a play. It was one of Rabea's classes, and I noticed audience members watching her with interest as she slipped into the front row.

Common to all these places was their public nature, as if the adult Jafar felt happiest being seen. As a boy he'd been drawn to the solitude of abandoned buildings. The universe he'd ushered me into encompassed the narrow alleys of Achrafieh that led down to the harbor, the gravel path to Pigeon Rocks, the depot by the train tracks—places I now suspected he'd sought out because they were so difficult to reach. It was strange. Although half a lifetime had passed, it felt like I had experienced the real Jafar.

But how well had we actually known each other?

The first time I visited the community center, Omar, who ran the library, led me across the sprawling foyer to a magazine rack. He licked a finger and rifled through the periodicals but didn't find what he was looking for, so he took me to a small storage closet he called *the archive*. He pulled a magazine from one of the shelves and handed it to me. It was a monthly publication in Arabic that included an events calendar and featured notable members of the Lebanese community in Gatineau. There were regular reports and interviews with people giving back to society, whether in Lebanon or abroad. The magazine was called *Al-Jisr*. The Bridge.

"This is the August issue. We printed an obituary for Jafar," Omar said.

Jafar didn't come through to me in the obituary, either. He died on Lailat al-Miraj, August 20, a Muslim holiday celebrating the Prophet Muhammad's ascent to heaven. Predictably, though in a fairly measured tone, a connection was made between Jafar's death and the holiday; I had a hard time believing Jafar would have liked the religious reference. Memories and anecdotes from his life were shared, which the author must have gleaned from Rabea and Jafar's mother and which were limited to his time in Canada. His work with local teens was praised at great length. He'd been a role model to them, the text read. Another part stated that his quiet but open and approachable presence would be missed.

Quiet. Evidently he'd been quiet. What did that word mean? Its connotation in the obituary was positive, of course. Someone who's *quiet* is pleasant and personable, ready to lend an ear, yet I clung to that short word as if it contained a deeper secret.

"What are you looking for, Amin?"

"Answers."

"After all these years? I don't believe you." Soraya was sitting up in bed, her body wrapped in a blanket, and she gazed straight ahead as she spoke. "I think you're looking for the kind of community closeness that reminds you of being a kid in Munich. Long before your grandmother went to buy you a suitcase."

"I can't leave yet. The conversations I've been having. They've given me so little to work with in forming a mental image of him. The Jafar I want to understand— really understand—is still a shadow."

"People mistrust you, Amin. They think you're hiding something. You've been knocking on doors, asking questions about Jafar. You're just prolonging our grief. Why?"

I reached for her. "Your hair smells good."

How could I explain—to her or anyone else—something I didn't understand myself? Jafar had been part of my first summer in Lebanon. My first friend and first riddle, and I'd never managed to bury the memory of him. I'd set it aside for a while but never forgot. I had always hoped to meet Jafar again when we were older.

It's presumptuous to put myself in his shoes. I'm aware of that. But Jafar would always be different—something I'd always sensed—and how else to find my way in?

When the weather's nice in the evening, he leaves his apartment on Rue Saint-Antoine and jogs along the river to visit his mother and help her in the garden or around the house. "In Beirut," she often says, as they kneel in the dirt weeding, a black bucket between them, "sons don't move out until they get married, and they don't move clear across town from their mother— they find an apartment on her street or build a roof addition to her house." She says it gently, without reproach, though she may actually mean it that way.

"But we're not in Beirut," Jafar responds as calmly, "and you know I'll always stay nearby."

When the work is done, they leave their shoes by the doormat and go inside. She boils water for tea, putting mint in the pot. In the living room she shares the neighborhood gossip her friends divulged that afternoon. "Arif's daughter Aylin," she says, "was seen sitting with a Canadian in his car in the Cineplex parking lot. The Canadian was dark-skinned." Jafar usually nods and sips his tea without really listening. He knows how important these moments are to her and that she isn't telling the stories for the sake of conversation, but for the sake of storytelling. She made this new life possible for him, and he's touched by her effort to keep memories alive and gather people round, all these years later. By her effort to carry on part of her old life here, or at least the illusion of it.

Twice a week he takes the early-morning train from Ottawa to Laval, where he transfers to a bus to the juvenile detention center. He holds office hours on Mondays and Wednesdays in a small office on the second floor of the workshop building, where the teens spend their day. Through the barred window he can see them in their work clothes in the courtyard below. Over the course of the morning, kids stop by and knock on his door. He talks to those whose release date is approaching about their options, asks what their interests are, their talents, their dreams, pulls his chair up and shares stories about himself as a teen. The boys, usually so distrustful and reticent, are captivated by his tales. He then catches one of the last trains home. As the landscape rolls past on the two-hour commute, he types up his meeting notes in a Word document and, if there's time left, he reads a book or thinks about Rabea, Abu Diab's daughter.

On Tuesdays and Thursdays he can be found in shorts and a T-shirt, standing on the sidelines of a floodlit soccer field to run practice. It's impossible to know what will become of these kids. There are still hundreds of ways they might grow up, and that fascinates him. He's sometimes reminded of the back courtyards of Beirut, of boundary lines drawn in chalk and the fact that two big rocks were all you needed for goalposts. Those memories are rare, though.

The boys he coaches are impressed by him. He never raises his voice. He gives them the feeling he's fully present, talking only to them, quietly but assertively. Whenever a blatant foul leads to smack talk and punches thrown on the field, he's able to get those involved to shake hands. He constantly reminds them of the importance of community and the shelter it provides.

Most of these kids are second-generation immigrants; they were born and raised gazing at Canadian scenery while the sumptuous Lebanese sunshine of their parents' stories filled their heads. Several of them used to frequent his office hours. The boys' backgrounds don't matter to him. They never feel judged by him. Everyone makes mistakes.

One fall evening, as they're still getting to know each other and sharing a glass of wine under the dining room light, Jafar shows Rabea his camera and tells her what he loves about photography is the ability to direct the viewer toward what's happening on the periphery. He's never much appreciated what other people deem essential.

He goes to Abu Diab's house the next day to pick up Rabea. He takes her to an exhibit of ten of his photos at the youth center café by the soccer fields. It's a way to tell her about himself without using words.

Jafar stole through the streets on countless evenings, silent as a thief, camera round his neck, and what he captured were things that no one would miss and that would soon vanish anyway: a raindrop on a maple leaf, photographed at such close proximity that the street and its lights were reflected in it. A homeless man's empty coin cup, his sleeping bag out of focus in the background. Footprints on the riverbank, sodden and half-gone.

He's been a valued member of this community for many years. He contributes. Only when it comes to his photographs is he an outsider.

One day Rabea asks Jafar to take a photo of them to frame and hang on the wall. She's moved in with him at this point, though the apartment really is too small. She only agreed to it so they can dream of a house together.

He positions a tabletop lamp to illuminate them from the back. What he captures is the shadow of their clasped hands on the living room wall.

When you look at the photo, you don't know which hand is Rabea's and which is Jafar's.

He'd become a different person, had evidently given up his past. During my time in Gatineau I was forced to acknowledge that—wherever I went in life, whatever impressions I made or were made on me, whosever paths I crossed or avoided—I had only ever convinced myself I was elsewhere. In reality I had never left the narrow alley in Beirut that winter day the sky was dark above the rooftops and the hint of a thunderstorm was in the air. The day Jafar said I was a nobody before getting in the car that had blocked our way. It was the last time I saw him.

A wound had existed from that point on, and I now realized just how deep it was. Instead of healing the wound, like I'd thought it would, my time in Canada had kept it wide open. There was nothing left for me here.

Jafar's mother kept her distance after realizing I had no answers for her. She hid behind her grief. Rabea still seemed to want me around at first. She sat facing me in a wool sweater, lost in thought as she listened to my stories about 1994, presumably trying to compare the Jafar I was describing to her partner of five years. Then one day a For Sale sign appeared in the yard outside her house, and she too began to steer clear of me.

The first snow fell in early November. The ash trees in the park had dropped their leaves. I woke one morning to the scratch of snow shovels on the sidewalk, and when I stepped into the cold air, the streets were mostly deserted.

I'd been in Gatineau nine weeks when I decided to make one final attempt at figuring out why Jafar's family had left Lebanon, so I went one wintry day to see his uncle Kalib, who had an antiques shop on the outskirts of town, and who I had long believed was a character we'd invented.

Many enterprising members of the Lebanese community in Gatineau had done very well for themselves. Old Kalib, meanwhile, seemed satisfied wandering around in his long housecoat and sandals, surrounded by antique picture frames, velvet armchairs, silver vases, and gilded dressers, welcoming neighbors who occasionally poked their head in for a chat on the way home without ever buying anything—as if the store weren't located on the main drag of a small Quebec city but on a serpentine side street in Beirut.

In fact, Kalib really did seem like he'd arisen from one of Jafar's stories: his gray hair was perpetually unkempt, as if he'd just gotten out of bed, and after four or five sentences, he would often pause for so long it was hard to tell if he was still talking or had unexpectedly gone mute. He could have been the older version of every last character we'd assigned him on those summer days spent outside the circus: the bartender at the Saint George who asked the great Peter O'Toole for an autograph, or the retired expert on lost paintings, who as a young man had been at home in the shadowy world of art trading and discovered the fabled picture frame that had once held *The Secret of the Juniper Tree* in a secondhand bookshop.

The first time I met Kalib, I told him about our stories and the role he'd played in them, and he joked that I owed him 10 percent of our flea-market earnings.

That's how he was around me: friendly, clever. Had

he stayed in Lebanon, I imagined how Jafar and I would have loved visiting his shop and asking about his wares to find inspiration for our stories.

Although Kalib put any old thing on display, provided it had the right patina, and everything about him seemed to imply an inability to let go of the past, this time was no different than the others: he wasn't willing to discuss his family history with me. He wasn't unfriendly; he didn't turn me away. Rather, I was met with the unruffled superiority of a significantly older man who had long since sorted through and sealed up the events of his life in the homeland. I still don't know whether he was hiding something from me or truly didn't know what had prompted his sister's family to move to where he was.

Kalib seemed surprised to see me when I knocked on the shop door. "You're still here?" he asked, stepping aside to let me in. "Are you staying forever?"

I shook my head, stomped the snow off my shoes, and entered. "No, not much longer."

Kalib shivered in the draft. He rubbed his hands together and walked into the store ahead of me.

"How's Soraya?" he asked innocently. "Haven't seen her in a long time."

I thought it might be a trick question, but it was pointless to play games. There are some secrets that can't be kept, even in the most secretive of communities. "She's been busy," I said.

"Mm-hmm," he replied. "Have a seat. Coffee?"

"No, thank you."

"So, what brings you here?"

I decided to cut to the chase. "There was a camera he had back then. I only recently remembered it. He said it was from you."

Kalib smiled as if by accident. "That's right. It was actually a gift to his mother, but she never used it. He was self-taught—aperture, shutter speed, everything you need to know. Amazing, isn't it? Have you seen his exhibit at the café? I think it's still up. He had a good eye."

"I know."

"But you didn't come all this way in the snow to tell me that."

"No." I hesitated, then pulled out the picture Jafar had taken at Luna Park.

Kalib studied it for a long time, as if searching for a familiar face in the motion blur. He turned it over and read the note Jafar had left me.

I'm really sorry I couldn't say bye. It had nothing to do with you.

"You were good friends," he said, his inflection neither stating a fact nor asking a question.

When I told him Jafar had wanted to give me the card as a parting gift before seemingly making a run for it, Kalib nodded ponderously, as if suddenly very tired. Without looking up from Jafar's handwriting, he said, "My sister called me in the middle of the night. She asked me to book flights for the family. I asked if they were coming here on vacation. She said no, they had to come for good. A few days later I picked her and the kids up at the airport."

"Had to?"

"Sorry?"

"She said they *had to* come here for good?"

He leaned back, suddenly wary. "I don't remember. It was a long time ago."

"Did she ever talk about the reasons?"

"You mean, the reasons she had for coming here?"

An End to Something

Over the centuries artists have depicted variations on Pliny's myth of the origins of painting. Joseph-Benoît Suvée renders the scene literally, whereas Giorgio Vasari eliminates the Corinthian maid: her lover is alone as he traces his own silhouette on the wall. Both paintings, however, convey the same message: art owes its existence to reality, even though it isn't real, just as a shadow emerges from the person, without ever being the person.

Spring 1990
Yeki bood, yeki nabood.
They name him Lion Cub. Ghost Shadow. Ibn Rambo—Son of Rambo. They call him Fogwalker, Cat-Eye, The Collector. They flatter him: "A great mission lies ahead," they say, "and we've got the power to keep going for many years." Their hands are clammy and arms twiggy as they hug him. They kiss his eyes. "You're one of us," they say. "You make us stronger."

The young men in khaki uniforms bearing the militia's insignia on the shoulder, with ammo belts and sawed-off shotguns, stand before Jafar and the other kids, ladling poison into receptive ears. They say: "You're our eyes in the dark. You make us proud—you're our seeker. We will speak of your feats."

Sunlight comes in the barred window. The city outside is loud. The children stand silently against the wall. Jafar watches the teens, takes note of their un-shaven faces. He recognizes the self-assurance he so admires in every move they make. Outside these walls none of these guys would even look at him, let alone speak to him, but it feels like he's changed in the last twenty minutes, as if simply by entering this building, he's become *more visible*.

He hears them give the other kids the same nick-names, court them with the same words. For him, though, what they're saying resonates differently: this is what appreciation sounds like. It's the sound of friendship.

He is ten. The civil war is five years older.

Like all children in this city, regardless of which side of the border they live on, he has been educated in the school of The Events. It's taught him what he needs to know, like going into the hallway during air raids, be-cause the *load-bearing walls* make it the safest spot in the apartment. He recognizes the sound of artillery fire as it approaches from the mountains and as it leaves the area, and what to do in either case. From the pam-phlet they handed out at school, he knows it's import-ant to put the greatest number of floors and ceilings possible between himself and the sky, because it's un-likely that a rocket will blast through more than three stories at a time. He also learned to set out whatever containers you can find—plates, bowls, pots, pans—when it rains, because for days on end sometimes, you'll turn on the faucet or flush the toilet and nothing happens. When bedsheets are hung in the alleys, it means a sniper is hidden on a rooftop and a certain choreography is required to cross the street: duck, run, wait.

He plans to recite what he knows, should anyone quiz him.

A few weeks have passed since Jafar saw these boys at the hospital. They seemed so strong, even in a moment of weakness. He's thought of them many times since. They entered his name into a ledger at party headquarters this morning. No one laughed when he walked in the door. No one said "Go home, you're too young, and what the hell are you doing here, missing an eye?" No one was looking to test him.

Now he's lined up with other kids in this room with no lights. The air is musty and stale. Chicken sandwiches and water are handed out. Kids with long hair get headbands. The older boys wear their filthy boots with pride and have nicknames lifted from comic books and Westerns. They're called John Wayne, Sniper, Doctor Doom, and Little Boy or Fat Man, like the atomic bombs. The folklore of revolution and display of nonchalance conceal their exhaustion.

They pace up and down the row of kids. They say: "We are the militia. We are in the right. Our names are proof of that. Our names are Ziad, Mounir, Jafar, and Samir. Our names will never be Muhammad, Ali, or Hassan. They're Muslims. We're fighting a war of liberation from Islam, from Palestinians and Syrians occupying our land and trying to take it away from us."

The children nod, though they don't understand. Silver cross necklaces are hung round their necks.

And with that, Jafar becomes a seeker.

He and the others are too young for urban warfare and not strong enough to dig trenches. Boys like him are engaged in other tasks, and only on certain days, meaning he doesn't sleep at headquarters—a destroyed theater they seized and now occupy—with the older kids. He goes home every night.

It feels like he has two lives. In the morning he goes

to school if it's open and sits at a rickety desk by broken windows, listening to the teacher blather on. He keeps to himself during recess, then beelines for party headquarters in the afternoon, where he and the others hang out on couches, waiting to be radioed. Sometimes nothing happens for days and they just sit around, legs spread wide, playing cards and smoking like the big kids they admire. No one admits to hoping the radio will remain silent, no one reveals that kind of weakness.

When the time comes and the little box does crackle and screech, when the alert comes through that somewhere in the city, a skirmish is over—a street captured, the kingdom expanded—they jump to their feet, crowd onto the bed of a big truck, and ride to the site.

The militia uses the children to crawl through the fumes into collapsed buildings and collect weapons and ammunition the enemy left behind. RPGs, crates of mines, Russian PKM rounds, M16s, G3s, FALs, B7 grenades. The smoke and soot is so thick sometimes Jafar can't see, but based on shape he identifies and labels the objects he finds, like he's been taught.

The more stuff he carries out, the louder the cheers. The higher he dares to venture in the ruins, the greater the recognition. He doesn't feel fear in those moments. When it does emerge, it's more incentive than hindrance. Not so long ago his fear was that of rejection, ostracism, and laughter at his expense. Now it's like a promise—what lies beyond fear is the embrace of others, the warmth of their words, their applause. All he has to do is overcome the fear.

His skill is lost on no one. Jafar's name makes the rounds, climbs the chain of command. No one's seen anything like it, the way he moves through smoldering ruins, clings to walls, and scrabbles through the darkness, a hundred feet above the ground.

On the ride back they sit on the crates they snagged and clap him on the shoulder, like a teammate who scored a big goal. It's something he's often seen others do while watching them play soccer in back courtyards. Now he's the one catching people's attention. It's a new feeling, being proud of himself.

Someone was there. And someone wasn't there.

To the other kids, Jafar is like a shadow that keeps moving past the spots where they themselves first hesitate, then turn around. Because the floor creaks. Because walls are no longer where they're supposed to be. Because holes that drop several stories suddenly open in front of them. And long after they've returned to the group on the street, their arms and faces covered in dirt, they spot him wandering on rooftops, unfazed by the gusts of wind.

He's soon invited into the Grand Théâtre, or what's left of it. He's heard stories. In a past he never knew, this was an important spot. Now it's a seedy movie theater with stained seats near the Green Line; it's the inner sanctum of the militia. In the once-resplendent hall, young men now sit in the dark with their flies open, staring at the screen, while in what used to be the foyer, boys show off their bloodstained shirts. They embellish their feats further with every retelling, until no more than fragments of truth remain in their memory. Jafar moves among them, wearing the necklace they gave him where everyone can see it, over his shirt.

No one says "Go home." No one chases him off.

"Lion Cub," they say, "c'mere. What's up with your eye?"

They circle round as he tells them the truth.

"No," they say, shaking their heads. "What you need is a better story, one that lives up to your reputation."

And so the summer passes. Rumors make the rounds. They say the Syrian army is preparing a final attack in Baabda, targeting the presidential palace, where General Michel Aoun is in hiding. If the palace falls, the war is over. If the palace falls, the Syrians will have won.

In September Jafar goes from being a seeker to a scout. It's a promotion, though you wouldn't know by looking at him. When he arrives at HQ one day, they tell him to take off his clothes. They give him rags to put on instead, then smear his arms, legs, face, and around his missing eye with soot. They rub oil from canned sardines into his hair and give him an address.

The city is practically deserted, the streets unlit. Jafar attracts no attention as he passes by Syrian soldiers loitering around their tanks. He wanders among them, dragging his left leg and bending his right arm at an unnatural angle.

"Do you have any food? Maybe a piece of chocolate?" he asks.

They shake their heads. "Go ask someone else," they say, shooing him away. "Goddamn street kids."

He's invisible in this disguise, but now invisibility feels like a strength. Back at headquarters later, they'll trot him out in front of the new recruits and say: "This is the boy everyone's talking about. He can slip into different characters." Pebbles dig into the soles of his feet. Smoke still curls from a pile of rubble to his right. Someone flicks a cigarette at his forehead and hisses "Get lost."

"Sorry," Jafar murmurs.

He makes mental notes of everything he sees: How

many men they have. Where the fortifications are, where their guards and snipers are posted. How many entrances the building has. Where the sleeping quarters and recreational areas are, and where they stash munitions.

"You smell like fish," Soraya says when he comes home at night.

"I went swimming," Jafar says. "If you dive between these two rocks by the old lighthouse on the boardwalk, then pass through a secret underwater gate, you can get to the source of the Usumacinta. I saw river crocodiles and disguised myself as a fish to escape."

"What else did you do on the Usumacinta?"

"Got you some chocolate," he says with a laugh, tossing her the candy bar.

"Tell me more," Soraya says.

"You're taking a shower first," his mother says.

Jafar arrives at the theater one day in October, only to find it deserted. He checks the rooms and calls out names, but his voice just echoes. The floor is littered with debris, crumpled-up uniforms, shards of glass and plaster. The basement corridors have been abandoned too, erstwhile greenrooms the militia had repurposed as offices cleared out, records destroyed. The performance hall is vacant. Jafar returns to the foyer, bewildered. He pushes the door open and goes outside.

He sees families blithely crossing Damascus Street. He tries to warn them. They laugh and yell something he doesn't understand. He understands the words but not the meaning.

The Green Line is open.

He watches, frozen in horror, as people cross the border into the western part of the city. He takes cover, flattens his body against a wall, and closes his eye—an ancient reflex—but no shots are fired. Nothing happens.

"The palace fell," he hears voices saying. "The general fled. In a tank! Slunk off like a beaten dog and is hiding out at the French embassy."

That night the streets are the fullest they've ever been. The air is alive with chatter. Children watch in amazement, holding their parents' hands as they walk. Jafar sits on the theater steps, resting his chin in his hands, waiting for someone to come back. Someone who can explain all this to him.

One minute, life is following an accustomed structure; and the next, peace is declared. Weeks pass, and he keeps returning to the Grand Théâtre in the hopes of seeing someone he knows. No one turns up. The building remains empty. Weeks pass, and he keeps combing the rooms, opening drawers and searching for clues or a note they might have left for him: *Had to move quick. You'll find us here*: with an address.

Then one day he opens the door to the foyer and dozens of journalists turn and stare. They've hauled in filing cabinets and desks and occupied his last remaining sanctuary, turning it into their own headquarters to report on the Green Line.

Jafar's confusion is boundless. He aches for a return to that collective, in which he felt appreciated. He doesn't get why people are so happy about the change. It's like phantom pain, as if he were missing a limb. Every step he takes around the neighborhood feels like an end to something. The city has suddenly doubled in size, and it scares him. Passageways emerge where brick walls once stood. It's as if these new, unknown paths swallowed up his friends. That, or they're avoiding him. He can't bear either thought. It's like the Beirut he knew has dissolved, like it's lost its contours and swollen unnaturally past every known border.

At home Soraya tells the family about her school day. A woman from Paris was there, she says, to play a few games with the kids. She let them draw pictures.

"Did she come to your class too?" she asks.

Jafar nods, though he hasn't been to school in several days. Because he can't stand how people are acting like everything's fine. Because his classmates are avoiding him.

In the morning he has breakfast with his family, takes the snack his mother hands him, stuffs it in his book bag, and leaves with his sister. He walks part of the way with Soraya, then invents an excuse and heads straight for the Green Line, without ever crossing into the other part of the city.

In place of barricades, journalists now line the street outside buildings whose walls teem with plant life. They stand there and say: "A reintegration is underway here." They wave down older residents, who say: "Once we rebuild, the city will look like it used to." But what does that mean? No one Jafar's age has ever known the city any other way.

He keeps walking. New checkpoints have cropped up all over the place. Soldiers wave cars through. Jafar lowers his head, shoves his hands in his pockets, and quickens his pace, the Syrian flag flapping above.

One night he doesn't go home. There's a building he remembers, located on a hill in his neighborhood. The wind collars him as he pushes open the door to the roof. He's never been up here. It's one of the highest points in Achrafieh. He's well acquainted with other rooftops in the area, but until recently, coming here would have been suicide—this spot is as exposed as an aerie in a tree with no leaves. He takes off his shoes to get a better feel for the surface underfoot, should it give way. His movements are practiced. He feels his way forward with his toes until he reaches the edge. He sits down. The view takes his breath away. The Green Line isn't visible from up here. The city looks like it was never divided. He's never been able to see this far. He can barely tell the difference—the forbidden zones look pretty much identical to here. A few minarets, sure, but otherwise the same boxy apartment buildings with rooftop water tanks, the same warm light in the windows, the same sea in the background, and there, in the distance, the shadow of a Ferris wheel.

As Jafar gazes out at the city, he reaches up to his neck. He pulls the silver chain over his head. He lets it slide from his palm to the tip of his index finger. He extends his hand. The necklace dangles over the precipice. It's up to the wind to decide.

There once was a time, and there once was no time.

*

"You storytellers," Soraya said. "You never let bygones be bygones. Nothing is sacred."

I didn't respond. I couldn't look at her.

"Did you know that history textbooks refer to us as *the lost generation?*"

"Yeah," I said, "I read that somewhere."

"However widely we scatter, looking for a fresh start, someone'll be there waiting for us. More Lebanese live abroad than at home. Isn't that crazy? There's no avoiding each other on the street and in bars across the globe, and to break the ice we ask where the person was

at the moment of this or that attack—attacks that occurred during our childhood and shaped us without
our realizing it. Try as we might, Amin, that country
will always be part of us."

Heavy snow was falling. My wheeled suitcase swerved.
I could see the lights of the train station ahead.

"You could come visit sometime," I said. "Whenever
you want."

"Sure, maybe."

"Yeah, of course. Whenever."

Soraya shook her head. "What you said about Jafar is
plausible."

I nodded. I knew not to expect more from her. Not
then.

The snow melted on our jackets inside the station. I
checked the departures board for the train to the airport. We had some time. We bought big cups of coffee
and warmed our hands on them. I asked Soraya what
her plans were. She wanted to go to night school and
get her GED, she said. Then maybe go to college.

She watched passersby as she spoke. Faces reddened
by the cold. She kept pausing, as if the announcements
over the loudspeaker called to mind things she could
talk about to kill time. We observed the arrivals and
departures at a remove, almost pretending we ourselves weren't part of it. We didn't touch each other.
Whatever consolation we'd provided each other was
exhausted, and we both knew it. Did we feel guilty?
Yes, in a way. I say that now, after having thought about
it for a long time. I had inserted myself into the life of
that family as if there'd always been a spot reserved for
me. Then I disappeared, taking all odds with me and
leaving nothing behind. We could sense that as we
stood there too.

"All these suitcases," Soraya said. That was all. As if she had just realized how many lives here were moving from A to B. As if she were imagining coming and going. As if she were exploring the possibility of departure.

"I've got to go," I said. "My train."

She stood at the top of the escalator as I took it down to the platform. There'd been a quick hug, as if this fleeting exchange were the only way to prevent any hint of ambiguity.

A Grain of Sand

2011

This story could have started in different ways—at different times, in different places—because that's how memory works, isn't it? We pick specific moments that have stayed with us, establish relationships between people and events, line everything up then look at it like a picture and say: That's what happened. As if it were all planned.

Saber Mounir always said that happenstance made life unpredictable and bewildering to the point that we sometimes felt caught in a whirlwind. *All the storyteller needs is a single grain of sand to set a great story in motion.* He said that the night we spent in the stranger's house as the storm outside battered the windows. How long ago that was.

A coat is handed over in a fabled old theater. An illustrator crosshatches shadows on a piece of paper one day without knowing what will become of it. Two boys keep each other from falling on wet shoreline rocks. One of them writes a girl a story. All signposts pointing in different directions. All beginnings of something. Even the end is a beginning, meaning I could just as easily have opened with this image: ashes falling on a street of burning buildings, only the street isn't a street anymore; it's a world.

A summer's day. Traffic is jammed. People get out of their cars, look up at a sky blackened by smoke billowing from broken windows. They whip out their cell phones and the photos go viral: *#lebanon #prayforbeirut #arabspring*.

The scene is a few weeks past but the smell of burning hasn't lifted. It hangs in the air like a rumor that can't be dispelled. The city keeps catching fire. Barricades are erected. Newspaper pages blow in the wind and get caught on debris-littered cars. Bold headlines speak of rage and revenge. Of decades of suppressed fury. Refugee camps are already in flames. The other side is already retaliating. It didn't take long.

Were the two bodies the reason? Probably. Or if not the reason, definitely the spark. Their remains were placed in simple wooden boxes, not coffins. A crowd of people watched as they were loaded into an ambulance that drove off without sirens.

Word spread quickly on the street and social media: the skeletons of two people had been found. In the heart of Beirut. During demolition of a collapsed building. The discovery itself wasn't unusual for a city with Beirut's history. These things happened as reconstruction progressed. Such remains often exhibited evidence of projectile impact or other bodily trauma. Like so many others, these two—a man and woman—had died about thirty years ago during the civil war. What *was* unusual about them was that they were found in an intimate embrace.

Within hours this detail made the rounds. An aura of romantic tragedy was ascribed to their deaths. The position in which they'd been found served as a media-friendly metaphor: two nameless innocents, whose devotion to each other had outlived the violence of war. Their embrace became a symbol of unity for a divided city and an entire country, in which tens of thousands of people were still missing.

They were called the Lovers of Beirut in tabloids and online. They could have been recovered and examined under the radar and maybe even identified, providing someone with closure at long last. Outside the public eye, the whole thing could have run its course, had the bodies not been found at that particular moment: the spring of 2011, a time of unrest.

The world was watching the Middle East. In Lebanon all eyes were on Syria. Just two hours away by car Bashar al-Assad ordered the military to open fire on demonstrators in Aleppo, Homs, and Damascus. The atmosphere in Beirut was tense. Tunisia, Egypt, Libya, Jordan, Syria. The revolts were getting closer. Al Jazeera was broadcasting around the world and around the clock. The images of protests turned violent flickered on TV screens in bars and restaurants in Beirut, and those of us in more remote pockets saw the same footage. Aerial shots of people streaming out of their embattled homeland in search of refuge. Refuge here in our homeland—in Lebanon. The tables had turned. This was a sea change: for the first time in history, people from Syria were fleeing en masse to our country.

I remember standing in the hills of Tripoli six years earlier, watching Syrian tanks roll down the main thoroughfare out of the city and ultimately out of the country. Now the Syrians were returning. Families, women, and children—not the military, yet many Lebanese still regarded them as oppressors.

In a place that knows only extremes, whether of euphoria or violence, all it took was a rumor spreading at the speed of a thousand online shares. Someone claimed the Lovers were discovered at the site of a building the Syrian army had used for interrogations during the war; people brought inside never came back out. The bodies were just two of many who had vanished without a trace and whose disappearance was blamed on the Syrians.

They cross the mountains by the hundreds every day. Tent cities pop up along the border and outside cities. Emergency shelters made of wood and tarps. For a few weeks now some have been burning.

The upheaval in recent months has shaken the world, yet it's merely history repeating itself. There was talk of an *Arab Revolution* among outside observers starting in the fifties and sixties. Old systems were crumbling then too. One after another, military men seen as reformers came into power: Egypt in 1952, Iraq in 1958, Yemen in 1962, Syria in 1963, Libya in 1969. No sooner had they supplanted their predecessors than they established military dictatorships, seizing upon state coffers for themselves and their clans, oppressing and deriding the public. These autocrats are now being stripped of power, chased from palaces by young people who have never known different rulers. The same mechanisms are at play; all that's changed are current circumstances.

Beirut remains a city on the move. It continues to defy definition, still a utopia that keeps being destroyed and reinventing itself. The past is disregarded with stoic composure. I returned from Canada to find large parts of Beirut had been destroyed during the thirty-three-day war with Israel. Any hint of optimism had been quashed, yet only three years later the *New York Times* named the metropolis City of the Year, describing it as a haven for artists and writers weary of censorship, the ideal getaway for gays, clubbers, and beach bums alike. The hotels were booked solid, and it seemed the city was finally coming full circle, living up to the Golden Age the old folks are so fond of evoking as they sit at their tables beneath the olive trees and reminisce about Elizabeth Taylor and Ava Gardner.

Now and then I look up from my desk at the apple tree and into the distant countryside. I see flocks of birds circling on my walks. We're approaching September; the harvest is underway.

Walid still motors up from the city every week, so I see my neighbors at the intersection as we emerge from all over with empty bags and wheelbarrows. Though he's graying at the temples, Walid is robust as ever. Neither his body nor his voice has lost strength. We gather round as he starts handing out people's orders from the bed of the truck, providing commentary on the radio newscast.

"The uprisings won't stop anytime soon."

It's these unchanging cycles that make me feel like everything, big or small, will eventually come back to where it started. It's a feeling I'm just starting to penetrate, and my wish to understand it better may be the main reason I've drawn this whole thing up.

In a way, this very text is a song for the missing—for those who will never read it, despite my having written it thinking they might someday. As if it were possible, however great the distance, to call out and tell them I'm here and I miss them. And yes, of course I realize how absurd it is to search for meaning in all this, and that certain patterns or clues may only appear to me because I've been staring at this stuff for too long, poring over my notebooks, for instance, in which I detailed everything in my life as a boy: the books I was reading, the quality of light on the street, how I felt, who had said what to me and in what tone of voice. Interspersed between entries were doodles, sketches, key words, lists.

This occasionally gives the impression of a coherent whole, but I know that's wishful thinking. My mother's painting at once reveals and conceals a great dream of hers. The same tiny brushstrokes exist here too, covering up that which cannot be depicted—the gap between truth and untruth hiding what Saber Mounir referred to as *what's been lost*, something even storytelling can't recover.

I don't know if Grandmother sent me to the museum back then in order to host her gatherings in peace or if she simply lacked the words to explain that I should view the past as something I could quarry with care to better understand the present. In any case I've never stopped digging. I transformed her studio into a kind of archive. A little museum of memory. I mounted squared timber on the walls and built shelves for piles of old notebooks, a cardboard box of letters from my mother to hers, and the many copies of documents and materials I've gathered from the archives of Beirut in recent years. Jafar's photo from the top of the Ferris wheel at Luna Park is there too. All these things that tell little stories. There's a story of my own too: the text I wrote for Zahra. Or rather, the wrinkled first draft I had carried around for weeks before rewriting a clean copy and making the handoff to her cousin in Mala'ab al-Baladi.

Every new beginning comes from some other beginning's end—one of those inspirational quotes superimposed over pictures of sunsets and shared on Facebook. We give it the thumbs-up because it allows us to believe that contained within our own destiny is opportunity.

We encounter these wonderfully simple aphorisms at every turn, and they all lead to the same conclusion, namely that he who listens to his heart will discover the path to joy. *Dance to the beat of your own drum. Practice random acts of kindness and senseless acts of beauty. Live your truth.* But what if yours is a heart that finds things to fear in moments of beauty—the mirror image of a boy, for instance, who puts up walls the instant he feels threatened? A restless heart that is drawn to fairytale characters who mistrust happiness; a heart that ceaselessly compels you to look back, because maybe, just maybe, there's something you overlooked.

Jafar's death was the end of our shared history. Something that felt so final it almost tore me apart. As I stood on the platform in Gatineau in 2006 and heaved my suitcase onto the train, I never could have dreamed that a new beginning could come from this other beginning's end.

I wrote a letter to Soraya several months after my return to Lebanon. I sent pictures of the house to show the progress I was making on renovations: the shutters, first stripped, then painted blue; the roof full of holes and later patched up. I even included a photo of my mother's painting, though I didn't tell her its name, to avoid sending the wrong message. In a way it was a sense of guilt that made me write to Soraya. I had dreamed up a lot based on the scant clues uncovered during our nights together, scenarios that formed a building with many rooms, though they offered little protection. An inquiring echo followed every step, and the biggest room was still empty and couldn't be closed: why had Jafar wanted to call me?

Soraya's response came a few weeks later. She teased

me, drawing my attention to a revolutionary techno-logical breakthrough known as *email*. She'd had my email address for ages, and yet she too wrote a letter. I recognized the same restlessness in her handwriting that characterized her movements, even in her sleep. She had started a GED prep class, she wrote. Rabea had sold the house and was living with her parents for now. She had tucked in a photo of Gatineau Park.

Over time the letters we exchanged dwindled, but we never fell out of touch entirely. We would write at least once a year, around the anniversary of Jafar's death, updating each other on our lives in the kind of forced casual tone you assume when you feel obligated to re-port on something while actively avoiding a different topic. There's no question she kept things from me. Now that she'd earned her GED she talked about poten-tial majors, or the latest thaw and bridges that were closed, or a trip to the museum; she never mentioned a boyfriend or partner and she never elaborated in re-sponse to my asking after her mother.

I meanwhile described Beirut in all its craziness, despite my familiarity with the city now, playing a bit into Soraya's suspicions. I did not, however, mention the winding drive down to the city during my long phases spent in the murk of library reading rooms or archives, where I discovered stories in the statements given by ex-fighters that corresponded to Jafar's past.

In one of her recent letters, Soraya asked me about the Lovers of Beirut. The news had spread worldwide. What started as a footnote in minor newspapers had developed into a viral sensation, with internet users on every continent sharing the piece and even changing their profile pictures. I would have expected Soraya to make fun of it—not with regard to those who died, but mocking the spectacle and how typically Lebanese it was to hype them in this way. Instead she seemed strangely moved by the story. She even wondered if there was a chance she knew the people. It seemed the story had opened something up inside her.

On Canadian TV they're saying the unrest in neighboring countries isn't affecting Lebanon. For one because the political system isn't autocratic, but also because memories of the civil war are still too fresh. They compare it to Algeria. What's your take?

These lines were written between the discovery of the bodies and the day the buildings burned. In her agitation, Soraya even mentioned that this year was the fifth anniversary of Jafar's death. The thought had already crossed my mind.

I read her letter out in the garden, then returned it to the envelope and sat there a while longer. I decided not to respond with a letter this time, but instead send something from my home archive that made more sense for her to have.

Soraya worked hard to stifle the Lebanese parts of herself. The strain was evident. Her restlessness was just one sign of it.

Did you know they refer to us as the lost generation?

She still felt like part of that community, saw her own experience of displacement now mirrored in tens of thousands of others. Her letter revealed a reawakened curiosity. She finally seemed ready to talk about it, so I got up and walked through the kitchen, past the stairs, and into my archive. There among all the other mementos was the book I had bought from the cartoonist after his reading earlier that year, which he'd inscribed with two words: *For Jafar.* Younes Abboud had looked back from the distance provided by exile. He had posed questions about his home country like Soraya was doing now. Unlike me, they had both lived through that unprecedented chapter. As I reached for the comic book, the copy of *Al-Jisr* I had brought back from Gatineau five years earlier fell off the shelf. I picked it up off the floor. The issue number was printed in the upper right-hand corner: 08/2006. I had never read the whole thing, but throwing it away was out of the question because it contained Jafar's obituary.

I took the comic book and magazine back outside. I left the latter on the table and slid the comic into an envelope I addressed to Soraya. I didn't leaf through *Al-Jisr* till the next morning.

The issue opened with a greeting from Hakim, the community leader; his signature was printed after the last line. In the events calendar, which covered three months, I came across an announcement for the play Rabea's class had put on. There were notices for an Arabic cooking class in the community center kitchen and a flea market in the foyer. Then came the obit with the picture of Jafar on the soccer field with his team cheering behind him.

For the first time I kept reading. Community member of the month Nawal Hamdan was profiled on the next page; she served as an interpreter to fellow Lebanese women in Gatineau and Ottawa who had not yet mastered the local language. Then came a two-page ad for a furniture store in the area. Finally I reached the interview. It didn't immediately register. All I sensed was a kind of perturbation, a tugging sensation in my stomach like I'd misplaced something important without knowing what or where. The interview was part of a regular column titled *Lebanese Abroad*. The intro read:

We Lebanese feel at home all around the world. In this interview series, we introduce readers to highly accomplished individuals making a difference far from the homeland. Today: women's rights advocate Sahar Sabia, who opened the first-ever women's shelter in Damascus six months ago. Female victims of violence and oppression find refuge there. Ms. Sabia became known to a wider public after a documentary showcasing her work was recently aired on Al Jazeera.

I slid around in my chair as my agitation grew. I took a sip of coffee and looked back at the page. The tug in my stomach was getting stronger. I took another sip and set down the mug. The tabletop was rutted. Weather had bleached it out. I would have to sand it and oil the wood. That's what happens when you leave furniture out in the sun for too long; the wood becomes brittle, so you have to treat it regularly. I forced myself to return to the article. It was the woman's picture at the end of the interview that made me so nervous. I reread the intro word for word, as if I'd missed something critical. Then, entranced by the sensation of occupying two dreams at once, I got up from the table.

Inside I pulled out the phone book and found the number for the Al Jazeera offices in Beirut. There wasn't much of a wait.

"We can easily issue a copy but there's a fee. When did you say the episode was first broadcast?" The voice at the other end of the line sounded indifferent.

"I'm not entirely sure. In 2006 sometime, during the summer."

I heard the click of a keyboard. "Mm-hmm. July?

August? Can you narrow it down at all?"

I hesitated. It sounded ludicrous even as I said the words: "It may have been on Lailat al-Miraj."

As my headlights illuminated the curves in the road, I tried to examine my suspicions in light of everything I knew, despite the glaring improbability. I drummed my fingers on the steering wheel. My pulse was elevated. I kept having to brake to stay in the lane. There was a small photo of the woman below the interview. Black and white and fuzzy. There was a name I knew all too well and a possible date of overlap. Nothing but drifting grains of sand.

It was close to midnight by the time I returned from Beirut. I parked my car in the driveway. On the passenger seat was a VHS cassette; on the back seat, a VCR.

*

Opening shot: close-up of a blue forget-me-not growing by a wall.

One or two seconds pass to the sound of children playing.

A narrator says: "An oasis located in the heart of Damascus."

The camera begins to glide along the wall. An iron door enters the frame. It slowly opens inward.

"Those for whom this door opens know that, for now, they have found safety."

Kids in the courtyard. The camera pans left. Women sit in small clusters in the shade of gnarled trees.

"In the face of great resistance, Sahar Sabia opened this safe house, and since then, not a night has passed with a single vacancy."

The camera pans right and the children stop playing to gather around a young woman standing under an awning with her hands folded.

The camera zooms in on her.

*

Sometimes the ground beneath our feet crumbles, but instead of dropping into an abyss, we land in a hidden passageway and follow it to the end, where we encounter something familiar.

Do you like ghost trains?

They're okay. How about you?

No one ever told me a thing. I never knew how much damage I had done. We're willful as adolescents, driven solely by self-preservation. I never looked for her. I always told myself it was better to cleave this part of the story from me; I convinced myself it was infected and had to be removed. In all honesty, though, it was because I feared what I might find out.

The TV screen glowed in the darkness. She looked at the camera with an expression of great curiosity, as if waiting for me to speak after all these years. I was frozen. It was her. And it wasn't her. I knew it was her by that look on her face, her pale skin, and the archipelago of beauty marks. At the same time, the improbability obliterated every last detail, and in that moment it felt like my house was a space in which time ceased to exist; or rather, one in which time moved in every direction so everything happened at once.

They say it takes the benefit of hindsight to realize just how much we loved our youth and those who populated it. I had looked back so often, yet mostly from behind a wall of my own creation. The abandoned child

I viewed myself as—he never actually existed. What did exist, though, was a responsibility I had never perceived.

Now was the first time I saw the connections. I realized I'd been returning doggedly to the wrong places and points in time. That humid day in the alleyway, when Jafar's old cohorts had cornered us, was far too late a starting point for my study. All these years I had felt sorry for myself and peevishly wondered why Jafar pretended not to know me that day and how it was I'd never noticed this cold side of him before. Not once did I dare wonder why he thought it necessary to renounce me and return to the confraternity of this group at a time when—it now occurred to me—he may very well have felt threatened by the many arrests being made around the city. By the trials.

Could it be that when he took me to the crumbling rooftops of the city, he wasn't trying to impress me but was instead searching for someone who'd grab him by the collar to stop him from going such dangerous places? Someone who cared about him?

Don't worry, man. It was just the camera obscura. That was his response whenever he felt ashamed about the fear or weakness he had shown.

It's okay. I feel that way all the time. You can tell me what you're afraid of, if you want ... I never said anything like that to him.

I've long clung to the belief that who I am today is the result of what happened back then, but maybe I'm the same today as I always have been, deep down. How disappointed was Jafar by my silence? Hadn't I missed countless opportunities to ask him, long before he turned away and got in the boys' car, how the hell he intended to find the cartoonist's address? Which old contacts he'd have to hit up for help? What he'd have to do in return?

I could see it all clearly now: The little fires. Accomplices destroying evidence in the years following the war. Orange flickering on the horizon the night the train depot burned. A hasty departure a few days later.

It can take years to realize the import of certain events. All that remained in this case were possibilities, though, and that's what made it so bad; it was far too late for any certainty.

I stared at the woman on TV. When she went into hiding, Zahra had evidently changed her name to that of the girl in my story. *Sahar.* It could serve as an accusation or sign of forgiveness. Either way, the new identity helped her fly under the radar. How easy would it have been to find Jafar, though? *He lives in Gatineau, Quebec. Has a big antique shop.*

You reach the end of a story. If you're lucky, it will make you pause long enough to ask yourself: what *other* mistakes have I made?

What did Jafar's life look like after he left? I knew about some of his duties, routines, friendships, but what did he feel? What scared him? Or made him happy? I suspect that in his final years in Gatineau he pretended that in his adopted homeland, he could easily shake things from the past; during that time, he disguised himself again, because he didn't trust anyone and never felt entirely safe.

We're two sides of the same soul, Jafar, I could say to him.

*

He feels Rabea's head on his shoulder. He sees the TV screen reflected in her eyes as she sits up and turns to him.

"Want something to drink?"

He nods.

She kicks off the blanket and goes to the kitchen. The house is practically empty. They're still waiting for most of the furniture to be delivered, and every step, every word echoes.

He hears Rabea turn on the faucet and open a cupboard. He turns back to the television.

The narrator says: "To understand how much this project means to her, one must know the story of her past. Sahar Sabia told us that story."

When Rabea returns to the living room with two glasses of water, Jafar is sitting on the floor, just an arm's length from the screen.

Amused, she asks what he's doing.

But he doesn't hear.

Now I know what he's thinking. I know what he sees as he jumps up and laughs: the blurry lines of a carnival on the print he kept and hung up in the living room. The back of the photo is blank, but as a boy he inscribed a promise on the back of the original:

I'm going to try and find her for you.

mamihlapinatapai

Sahar Sabia 05:43
i want to tell you about this one morning in july.
the memory just came to me when i woke up.
and with the memory came the need to tell you about
it.

Sahar Sabia 05:45
it says Active 4 hours ago in light gray under your name
in messenger.

you must not be up yet.

Sahar Sabia 05:49
i don't know why this old story came back to me. maybe
because you were telling me about your house with the
overgrown garden yesterday. maybe that's why i thought
of our house in jouaiya.

my parents had taken my brother to see a tailor in tyros
that day. he was getting fitted for a suit, a black one. i'd
been sick for a few days, had a cold in the middle of
summer, so they told me to stay in my room and wait
till they got back.
the silence in the house felt inviting, promising.
i was ten.

Sahar Sabia 05:53

i remember puddles of light on the tiles. i crossed the hallway to my brother's room, quietly, so as not to wake the housekeeper. she slept in a little room by the kitchen.

she was from sri lanka, her name was kumari.

i got undressed in front of my brother's wardrobe. i slipped on his shorts and t-shirt, it was all just lying on the floor.

then i stepped up to the mirror. it was the first time i ever saw myself in boys' clothing.

i thought i looked pretty. i felt special. none of the girls i knew dressed like that.

Sahar Sabia 06:04

when i was a girl, i was made to believe that i was in danger, along with others like me. we were endangered creatures. under no circumstances were we allowed to act of our own accord. those were the rules i followed back then. i didn't see how they curtailed my freedom till much later.

we were presented an image of the world that was violent, and the threats to us threatened our families. at an age when we should have spent our time playing, we were yoked with responsibility for something as abstract as honor. we were at once dangerous and in danger.

i was so captivated by what i saw in the mirror that i didn't hear the floorboards creak. when i turned around, i saw kumari standing in the doorway. i jumped. i was afraid she'd tell on me.

but she just smiled and put a finger to her lips.

Amin el-Maalouf 09:23
Are you there?

Amin el-Maalouf 09:49
I'll wait.

Sahar Sabia 09:52
the women are waiting for me in the dining room. i'll be away from my computer for a while.

Amin el-Maalouf 12:21
I was in the city last night. I've been going quite a lot lately. For the first time in a long time, there's something appealing to me about Beirut. The protests fascinate me somehow.

It all started when Syrian refugee camps went up in flames. Seemed like the same old story, but now the square outside the Blue Mosque is filled with people representing all different social classes and denominations. They're demonstrating for tolerance and against government corruption, calling for the old elites to step down. "Everyone means everyone," they chant.

Political goon squads roll up on mopeds to intimidate protesters, but the crowd doesn't budge.

Amin el-Maalouf 12:34
In my feed I posted a picture I took last night of the entrance to a bar. It came out kinda dark, but the neon red sign shows up pretty well. They set up a stage there recently with just a microphone and a chair.

Sahar Sabia 12:35
if you'd asked me a few months ago, amin, i'd have said: the arab world is infinitely large in size and infinitely small in scope. it exists, and it doesn't exist, at least not as a unified whole. whenever it *is* presented that way, it's either the brainchild of misguided nationalists or an image spread by western societies that can't be bothered to make any closer distinctions. all that connects us is a shared language and internal disarray. our world is shaped by individual clans, by ethnic and religious groups who know nothing beyond the sanctity of their laws, act on the authority of outdated structures, and in their midst are younger generations that want to bust out because they've discovered the entire world is just a mouse click away.

Amin el-Maalouf 12:39
Something's been set in motion, though.

Sahar Sabia 12:40
yes. there's movement in tunis, cairo, tripoli. there's movement here in damascus too.
millions have taken to the streets. the uprisings aren't ideological, there are no leaders, no bosses, there's not even a plan. just desperation. we stand side by side and say: kifaya! enough is enough!

our dignity is no longer negotiable.

Sahar Sabia 12:42

the bearded old guard, who -- courted by the west -- have exerted power and committed crimes for so long will have to admit that it was a mistake not to take the anger of the youth seriously.

Amin el-Maalouf 12:43

You were talking yesterday about your father's fear.

Sahar Sabia 15:24

i now see him as a tragic figure.

Sahar Sabia 21:08

everyone's questions are answered, everyone's doors are closed. quiet hours are in effect.
as i started to text back earlier, there were three dots moving up and down by your name. you were continuing something you'd started. what did you want to tell me about the bar?

Amin el-Maalouf 21:12

That it reveals a side of this change.

Amin el-Maalouf 21:16

It was packed again last night, full of young people. I got there really late—it took forever to find parking nearby. By the time I finally made it, they'd already stopped charging a cover. Standing room only, all the way in the back. I had to get on tiptoes to see the stage. Glasses clinked in the sink behind the bar, and here and there someone cleared their throat, but otherwise it was silent after each round of applause. A young woman stood at the mic. She kept making eye contact with the audience. She was holding a piece of paper, but it seemed to be only in case she got stuck—she barely glanced at it. She recited freely.

Sahar Sabia 21:18
you've told me about the old hakawati.

Amin el-Maalouf 21:22
Theirs was considered an extinct art form, but it's coming back—with new topics. Today it's young men and women. They get on stage and talk to audiences about life, about queer love, about politics, abuse, and the role of women in our society. They might be witty or enraged. They lob accusations.

Amin el-Maalouf 21:25
The young woman on stage reminded me of you.

Sahar Sabia 03:39
i can't sleep.

Amin el-Maalouf 03:43
I'm here.

The monitor casts bluish light onto the wall by my bed like a window. I was lying on my side when I noticed it moving. That's how I knew you had written.

Sahar Sabia 03:45
you know i was taken to a convent back then.

Sahar Sabia 03:46
a woman who worked for unicef first took me from jouaiya to an apartment in beirut, then two days later a nun came for me in the middle of the night.

Sahar Sabia 03:47
i lived in a shelter with 13 other women. six were young mothers who'd given birth against their families' wishes. there was a mentally disabled woman there too and four who'd been sexually assaulted and fled, because they would've been forced to marry their rapists to lessen the shame they had caused.

Sahar Sabia 03:49
the living area was small but comfortable. there was an open living room/kitchen area. christian and muslim women lived there together. only the nuns lived separately.

whenever we had trouble sleeping, the nuns would tell us stories.

Amin el-Maalouf 03:50
What kinds of stories?

Sahar Sabia 03:52
i'm sure you've heard of the river lethe.
one night the sisters told us the ancient greeks believed the lethe flowed through the underworld. the souls of the dead had to drink from it to wipe out any memory of the past. the sisters stressed that this was not the same as forgetting. when something is forgotten, they said, it can always be remembered, whereas the waters of the lethe ensured that every last memory was irretrievably obliterated.

i remember there was a woman beside me who got up from the rug after a while and asked, as she left the room, if that river flowed through lebanon too.

Amin el-Maalouf 04:01

There's a stream near my house. Part of it also flows underground. Years ago I made a paper boat with your name on the prow and set it afloat there.

Sahar Sabia 04:57

i just uploaded a video for you. it's on my wall, i changed the privacy settings so only you can see it.

Sahar Sabia 05:04

at first glance it'll look like just another one of countless videos from syria that go viral on facebook. the recording is shaky -- i had to hurry. you'll see the square outside the umayyad mosque. i'm sure you've heard of it, it's beautiful, it houses the remains of john the baptist. the video's kinda dark, but you can see the shadows of the pillars on people's faces. i took it during demonstrations there five days ago. i had turned on my phone right before the first shots were fired. you'll see. we all had to run. if it's too shaky for you, skip ahead to 3:13. i was on a side street and turned around to film the scattering crowd. that's not the reason i'm sending you this, though.

right before the video ends, you can see the roof of my building beyond the wall. the window in the middle is my room.

Amin el-Maalouf 05:11

I see it.

Amin el-Maalouf 06:14

Just saw some footage from Libya. Demonstrators stormed Abu Salim prison. The guards had long since fled. Insurgents made their way through the place without much resistance. Behind steel doors they found people who'd been missing for decades after vanishing from the streets.

Sahar Sabia 08:46
something like that could happen in syria too.

Amin el-Maalouf 08:49
I know.

Amin el-Maalouf 08:51
But it's already summer. The uprisings began nine months ago, yet they're still calling it the Arab Spring, as if this were a season of change that would be over in a few months.

Sahar Sabia 09:05
folks here say syria will be liberated by december at the latest.
i have to log off for now.

Sahar Sabia 20:49
the woman onstage you mentioned yesterday reminds me of scheherazade. the young woman from one thousand and one nights. we have a copy in our reading room. sometimes i'll see a mother who's sought refuge here paging through the book with her child in her lap.

Sahar Sabia 20:51
i've known scheherazade for a long time.

Sahar Sabia 20:53

when i was a girl, conversation sometimes turned to one thousand and one nights. whenever it came up, the men called scheherazade a cowardly woman who prostituted herself to the king to save her own skin. they said the women in the stories she told him were the root of all evil -- hideously ugly with gray hair, big noses, wrinkled faces and rotted teeth, yet so cunning that their actions tore lovers apart and even toppled kings.

the women at our table just nodded and murmured that the whore was confirming the king's worldview in doing so.

Sahar Sabia 21:04

when i read the book myself later on, i realized no one in my family had ever read to the end. they only knew the early stories. or maybe they actually had finished it and were deliberately keeping it from us. the image of women portrayed in scheherazade's later stories is a far cry from that of devious adulteresses and harem girls who throw themselves at men's feet. there are several tales of female warriors evenly matched with men in battle -- in the story of hassan of basra, the goldsmith, there are entire armies led by swordswomen. for the most part, though, women use words and cunning to revolt against tyrannical fathers, husbands, and kings, and i'm amazed no one ever mentions that.

Amin el-Maalouf 21:13

She uses her talents to save herself, her children, and the women of the city.

Sahar Sabia 21:14
yeah.

Sahar Sabia 21:18
have you ever been to syria?

Amin el-Maalouf 21:21
Once, at the airport in Damascus.

Sahar Sabia 21:26
you should visit this country.
it's beautiful.

Sahar Sabia 21:27
it's prettiest in may when everything's in bloom before
it gets really hot.

Sahar Sabia 21:39
i came here when i was 16. i lived with a family in the
old city at first, then we moved to a house on jabal
qasioun. if you come to damascus, amin, you have to
visit this lonesome mountain. it rises to the north of
the city, which has grown up the sides of it. the poorest
live at the very top -- they have the best view but little
else. it's where you'll find real friendliness, real warmth.
the wealthy live below, in homes surrounded by high
mud walls. from our house, i could see the way damascus changed when bashar al-assad succeeded his father;
when he promised to open up the country. at night the
city had been dotted with white lights in the past, but
now it glowed with signs for internet cafes, everything
neon.

during the daytime, though, things looked the same as they always had. once the sun rose, the problems came back into view -- poverty and scarce opportunities. our hopes and dreams grew skyward because there was no room for them in damascus or anywhere else, for that matter. i remember a girl in my class named sulaika. for a while we dreamed of forming a pop band and practiced our dance routines in her room. on the school bus we stuffed sulaika's white earbuds in our ears and listened to beyonce as the call to prayer rang out from the old city minarets. whenever the driver checked his rearview mirror, we lowered our heads and moved our lips so it looked like we were praying, when really we were singing along to the music. those were small acts of rebellion. we lost touch after school. i think i saw a photo of sulaika a few weeks ago, on a wall where missing person notices are hung.

even before the revolution we discussed injustice and our desire for freedom, but never in cafes or out in public, where the secret service has eyes and ears. only when we went out to the country and even then, never above a whisper.

Sahar Sabia 21:46
all that's changing now.

Amin el-Maalouf 21:48
All I know is the stories.

Sahar Sabia 21:49
they're all true.
i saw aleppo, amin. the historic citadel, the clock tower, the old city. you told me about the summer you spent at

the national museum, about the statues, the mosaics
-- wait till you see palmyra... after you pass under the
monumental arch and walk down the great colonnade,
through the temple of nabu to the immense stage in
the amphitheater, you'll forget all about baalbek, back
home in lebanon.
i'll send you a few links to it.

Amin el-Maalouf 04:13
I can't sleep.

Sahar Sabia 04:31
i'm here.

Amin el-Maalouf 04:38
I don't know what to say.

Sahar Sabia 04:58
mamihlapinatapai.

Sahar Sabia 05:06
four years ago i met a swedish exchange student while
shopping at the al-hamidiyah souk. she asked for directions to azm palace, we started chatting and have kept
in touch, even though she's back in malmo. she was
studying linguistics at the university of damascus. her
name is wilma, and she taught me that word.

Amin el-Maalouf 05:08
What does it mean?

Sahar Sabia 05:09
it's a yamana word, the language spoken by the yaghan,
the indigenous peoples of tierra del fuego. it means

someone not knowing what to do next. ihlapi is the root, which is bounded by a prefix and two suffixes that are all interrelated.

Amin el-Maalouf 05:12
I just said it out loud: mamihlapinatapai.

Sahar Sabia 05:14
that's right. mamihlapinatapai.

Sahar Sabia 05:15
a single term encapsulating an entire world: two people looking at each other, both wishing the other person would find the courage to speak.

Amin el-Maalouf 05:15
and neither can do it.

Afterword

This novel is a work of fiction, albeit one that revolves around historical facts and figures. To this day, the General Amnesty Law No. 84/91 grants immunity to those responsible for crimes committed during the Lebanese Civil War.

All efforts to ascertain the fate of the missing have been unsuccessful. Although a commission was formed in 2000 to address this concern, five of its members were also part of the administration's security apparatus. Within three months they produced a two-page report recommending that all missing persons be pronounced dead. Soon after, fifty-four of those individuals recently declared dead returned home from Syrian prisons. It was a public disgrace. The report also made brief mention of three mass graves located in Beirut, with the caveat that the sites could not be excavated because new buildings had been constructed on top. Beyond that, the report noted that many of the dead had been dumped into the sea following wartime battles.

A second commission, established in 2001, focused on those missing persons who might still be alive, but required loved ones to provide proof of life.

A third commission, started in 2005, did not publish a report at first. Missing persons' family and friends—or their proxies—were barred from proceedings.

In November of 2018, families and friends of the

missing celebrated a partial victory: a law was enacted granting missing persons legal recognition and calling for the establishment of an independent domestic commission. By the time this novel was completed, in November of 2019, the commission had not yet convened.

Samir Geagea was granted amnesty—in accordance with the law—and released from prison after eleven years, following the Syrian army's retreat in 2005. Today he's the head of the Lebanese Forces, a right-wing Christian political party. General Michel Aoun, who fought a bloody "war of liberation" against both Geagea and the Syrians before fleeing to France in 1990, has been the president of Lebanon since 2016.

The official count of missing persons totals 17,415. Decades after the end of the civil war, the unresolved question regarding the missing impedes the process of accounting for the past and achieving justice and lasting peace.

My Thanks

go to my wife Kathleen for her unwavering support, encouragement, and faith in moments of doubt. I thank my parents for seeing me down this path. I'm grateful to my agent Markus Michalek for his kind advice and for standing by me, come hell or high water, along with the whole team at AVA international. Big thanks to my editor Andreas Paschedag for putting up guardrails when I started to swerve and for providing endless advice, support, and assistance; the same goes for Felicitas von Lovenberg and the rest of the team at Berlin Verlag. I would also like to thank the Free State of Bavaria for its financial support.

The idea for this book changed significantly over the years, but the seed was planted in Genzano di Roma, where I enjoyed the hospitality of Andrea and Roman Hocke. Special thanks to Samh Youssef and Majd Al Ali, whose stories transported me to Damascus and Aleppo and gave me a real sense of everyday life during the Syrian Civil War; parts of what Zahra tells Amin in the epilogue, as well as details of Jafar's experience as a young boy in Beirut during the civil war, are drawn from their accounts. With regard to Zahra's story, I gained invaluable insight from my conversations with Friederike Weltzien, who—as a clergywoman at the German Evangelical Church in Beirut—provided pastoral care in similar cases and helped create a network to end violence against women.

I am indebted to all who helped answer my many questions, however big or small: the staff at UMAM Documentation & Research for granting me access to their archives in Beirut; Etrit Hasler, whose encyclopedic knowledge of comics could easily be deemed a superpower; Jorinde Bayer for providing a welcome retreat in Kattendijke; Olga and Babís for providing an equally welcome retreat in Athens; Hasune el-Choly for his poems; and Shida Bazyar, Senthuran Varatharajah, Sandra Hoffmann, Daniel Speck, Fabian Lay, Matthias Eisenschmid, and Dana Saba for their support.

*

In researching the topic of Lebanon's missing, I relied on a number of outstanding publications: "Fighting Amnesia: Ways to Uncover the Truth about Lebanon's Missing," by Iolanda Jaquemet (*International Journal of Transitional Justice*, New York, 2009); *Enforced Disappearances in Lebanon: A Nation's Unyielding Legacy*, by Lynn Maalouf (Act for the Disappeared, Beirut, 2009); "Space of Hope for Lebanon's Missing: Promoting Transitional Justice through a Digital Memorial," by Erik van Ommering and Reem el Soussi (*Conflict and Society*, New York, vol. 3, no. 1, June 2017); "The Power of Remembrance: Political Parties, Memory and Learning about the Past in Lebanon," by Mara Albrecht and Bassel Akar (Notre Dame University, April 2016); "Truth at Any Cost? Law's Power to Name Argentina's Disappeared Grandchildren," by Maria Rae (*Oñati Socio-Legal Series*, vol. 7, no. 2, 2017); and the essay "Liminality and Missing Persons: Encountering the Missing in Postwar Bosnia-Herzegovina," by Laura Huttunen (*Conflict and Society*, New York, vol. 2, no. 1, June 2016).

The taped interviews with family members of the missing that Amin discovers in the archives are drawn from original transcripts. Christalla Yakinthou spoke with these women and included their testimonies in her report, *Living with the Shadows of the Past: The Impact of Disappearance on Wives of the Missing in Lebanon* (International Center for Transitional Justice, New York, 2015). The statements made by ex-fighters that Amin copies into his notebook are also original quotations I translated into German. They can be found in the video series Testimonies of Change, in which former militia members discuss their reasons for joining the conflict (fightersforpeace.org). Furthermore, Yussef Bazzi's personal account, *Yasser Arafat Looked at Me and Smiled*, provided inspiration and direction in depicting the everyday lives and tasks of young fighters.

The following books provided useful information on the Arab Spring: *Fractured Lands: How the Arab World Came Apart*, by Scott Anderson (Anchor Books, New York, 2017); the essay *Das Ende des Nahen Ostens, wie wir ihn kennen* (Suhrkamp Verlag, Berlin, 2015) and *Der Aufstand: Die arabische Revolution und ihre Folgen* (Pantheon Verlag, Munich, 2011), both by Volker Perthes; *Wir wollen Freiheit! Der Aufstand der arabischen Jugend* (Verlag Herder, Freiburg im Breisgau, 2011), by Julia Gerlach; and Tahar Ben Jelloun's *Arabischer Frühling. Vom Wiedererlangen der arabischen Würde* (Berlin Verlag, Berlin, 2011).

The Schiller poem that Amin recites for his grandmother is titled "Expectation," translated here by Elisabeth Lauffer. The original German excerpt reads:

Des Tages Flammenauge selber bricht
In süßem Tod, und seine Farben blassen;
Kühn öffnen sich im holden Dämmerlicht
Die Kelche schon, die seine Gluten hassen.

Sidi Mahrez's "Lament for Carthage," words I put in the young actress's mouth, can be found in *Libya: The Lost Cities of the Roman Empire*, by Antonino Di Vitta, Ginette Die Vita-Evrard, et al. (Konemann, Cologne, 1999). The passage Amin mentions having read in the chapter "Jafar's Eye"—about writing as an act of rebellion—refers to Mario Vargas Llosa's *Letters to a Young Novelist*. The two novels Amin quotes in the chapter "Zahrat al-Wala'a" are Joseph Conrad's *The Shadow Line* and Charles Dickens's *A Tale of Two Cities*. I found inspiration for the story about Jafar's eye in Alexandre Najjar's memoir *The School of War*, which also provided me with the classroom exercise "Memories ... Caution ... Danger!"

The notion that storytelling can resurrect what's been lost is echoed in Judith Schalansky's *An Inventory of Losses*; her story about Sappho's love songs prompted Amin's piecing together burned words to form poems. Bookseller Khalil's description of Beirut as a "blue-blooded bastard" is attributed to journalist Erich Follath, who penned this epithet in his article "Herzlich, Ihre Hisbollah!" (*Spiegel Online*, July 25, 2013). I consulted two articles in researching the collapse of Intra Bank: "Geheimer Kredit," published on October 24, 1966 in *Der Spiegel* (4/1966) and "Am heißen Geld verbrannt," written by Kurt Wendt and published October 28, 1966 in ZEIT. The report on the discovery of a mass grave in Anjar was based on a news piece about an actual discovery of this kind, written by Christoph Sydow and published on December 12, 2005, in the online journal *dis:orient*. I found helpful information on Bellotto's adulterations of reality in Werner Busch's article "Die Wahrheit des Capriccio—die Lüge der Vedute" (in *Das Capriccio als Kunstprinzip*, Skira Editore, Milan, 1996). Abbas's anecdote about the staging of *Orpheus and Eurydice* was inspired by a passage in Julian Barnes's *Levels of Life*. In the chapter "Not a Ghost Light in Sight," the section that details the monitoring of young women in Lebanon as well as the later reference to a newspaper article about an honor killing are drawn from Friederike Weltzien's *Warum musstest du sterben, Fidaa?* (Verlag Herder, Freiburg im Breisgau, 2008) Etel Adnan's novel *Sitt Marie-Rose* provided further insight into the role of women in Lebanon.

ELISABETH LAUFFER is a German-English literary translator based in the US. In 2014, she won the Gutekunst Prize for Emerging Translators, which marked the beginning of her career in literary translation. In addition to her book publications, Liz's translations have appeared in *No Man's Land* and *Asymptote*. She has participated in the Frankfurt International Translators program (2019), the Artists-in-Residence program through KulturKontakt Austria (2019), and the Art Omi: Writers Translation Lab (2018).

On the Design

As book design is an integral part of the reading experience, we would like to acknowledge the work of those who shaped the form in which the story is housed.

Tessa van der Waals (Netherlands) is responsible for the cover design, cover typography, and art direction of all World Editions books. She works in the internationally renowned tradition of Dutch Design. Her bright and powerful visual aesthetic maintains a harmony between image and typography and captures the unique atmosphere of each book. She works closely with internationally celebrated photographers, artists, and letter designers. Her work has frequently been awarded prizes for Best Dutch Book Design.

The cover image is by Christopher Anderson, a Canadian photographer who grew up in West Texas and now lives in France. The image is of his son, Atlas, and was taken in Palamós, Spain. Anderson first gained recognition for his pictures in 1999 when he boarded a handmade wooden boat with Haitian refugees trying to sail to America. The boat, named *Believe In God*, sank in the Caribbean. Over the years, Anderson's work has moved from war reporting to something more personal, focusing on intensely intimate, emotionally charged portraiture, such as that of the cover.

The cover has been edited by lithographer Bert van der Horst of BFC Graphics (Netherlands).

Suzan Beijer (Netherlands) is responsible for the typography and careful interior book design of all World Editions titles.

The text on the inside covers and the press quotes are set in Circular, designed by Laurenz Brunner (Switzerland) and published by Swiss type foundry Lineto.

All World Editions books are set in the typeface Dolly, specifically designed for book typography. Dolly creates a warm page image perfect for an enjoyable reading experience. This typeface is designed by Underware, a European collective formed by Bas Jacobs (Netherlands), Akiem Helmling (Germany), and Sami Kortemäki (Finland). Underware are also the creators of the World Editions logo, which meets the design requirement that "a strong shape can always be drawn with a toe in the sand."